BADASS: ULTIMATE DEATHMATCH

Also by Ben Thompson

BADASS: THE BIRTH OF A LEGEND

BADASS

BAD

ULTIMATE DEATHMATCH

ASS

BEN THOMPSON

Skull-Crushing True Stories of
the Most Hardcore Duels, Showdowns,
Fistfights, Last Stands, Suicide Charges,
and Military Engagements of All Time

WILLIAM MORROW
An Imprint of HarperCollinsPublishers

HarperCollins books may be purchased for educational, business, or sales promotional use. For information please write: Special Markets Department, HarperCollins Publishers, 10 East 53rd Street, New York, NY 10022.

FIRST EDITION

Based on the design of Lorie Pagnozzi and Cassandra Pappas

Library of Congress Cataloging-in-Publication Data has been applied for.

ISBN 978-0-06-211234-7

13 14 15 16 17   OV/RRD   10 9 8 7 6 5 4 3 2 1

Far better is it to dare mighty things, to win glorious triumphs,
even though checkered by failure, than to rank with those
poor spirits who neither enjoy nor suffer much because they live
in a gray twilight that knows not victory nor defeat.

—TEDDY ROOSEVELT

CONTENTS

Before all else, be armed.

—MACHIAVELLI

AUTHOR'S NOTE

THE FIRST DRAFT OF THIS TEXT WAS WRITTEN BY FIRING A
MINIGUN INTO A LARGE BRICK WALL FOR SEVERAL HOURS AND
THEN TRANSCRIBING THE WORDS IT PRODUCED.

INTRODUCTION: THE FUNDAMENTALS OF A BADASS BATTLE

The way of revenge lies in simply forcing one's way into a place and being cut down. There is no shame in this. No matter if the enemy has thousands of men, there is fulfillment in simply standing them off and being determined to cut them all down, starting from one end.

—Yamamoto Tsunemoto, *Hagakure: The Book of the Samurai*

SINCE THE DAWN OF TIME, NEARLY EVERY MAN (AND I'D WAGER TO GUESS MOST WOMEN) HAS, AT HIS MOST VISCERAL LEVEL, SECRETLY DESIRED FOR ONE THING—TO BE STANDING TRI-UMPHANTLY ATOP A HEAPING PILE OF HIS SLAIN ENEMIES, HOLDING A GIGANTIC AXE ALOFT WHILE SOME UNBELIEVABLY ATTRACTIVE MEMBER OF WHATEVER GENDER HE'S ATTRACTED TO DESPERATELY CLUTCHES HIS LEG LIKE IT'S THE LAST LIFE RAFT ON THE HMS *TITANIC*. From the scrawniest D&D nerd (who would just as soon have the corpses be orcs and the naked babes be dark elves) to the most hardcore tatted-up Special Forces operatives (who actually have the equipment and training required to make a sce-nario like this happen in real life), we all dream of cleaving apart anyone who stands before us in a cavalcade of fiery blood-soaked destruction, plowing through endless hordes of screaming foes with only a trusty blade, a fashionable loincloth, and a Colt .45 with unlimited ammunition, and achieving the sort of hard-fought glory that gets you displayed prominently in history texts while less impressive people build gigantic bronze statues depicting your awesomeness. Some of us, of course, are more successful at living this dream than others, leaving the rest of us to read about Badass Battles of the Past and live vicariously through the ultraviolent heroes of times gone by.

The following pages are a collection of forty of my all-time favorite beatdowns from history—daring tales of glory, honor, vengeance, and dudes driving around in Jeeps with gigantic machine guns mounted on the back wasting everything in sight while psychotic barbarian warlords heave throwing axes at them. Now, for the purposes of this book, I am defining a "battle" as any physical conflict between at least two opposing individuals—everything from a no-holds-barred back-alley "Beat It" video–style knife fight to a continent-spanning military campaign with the fate of the free world hanging in the balance. While this fast and loose "Hell yeah, a spirited thumb-wrestling match counts as a battle" definition might probably give some West Point instructors a hernia, there are several key elements you will find across the board that make any confrontation badass.

1. HIGH STAKES

Nobody gives an anteater's scrotum about two drunk assholes oafishly beating the pants off of each other in a back alley behind an Irish pub at two in the morning, but if you take those same two guys, sober them up, and put them in the command center of a four-hundred-mile-long mining laser capable of overheating the Earth's core and destroying the planet, it suddenly becomes a hell of a lot more important who emerges victorious. Whether you're talking about an epic, earth-shattering campaign for ultimate control of Europe, a life-or-death sword fight to avenge one's honor, or a high-noon showdown with a lone lawman taking on a gang of murderous criminals, we need to know what's on the line, and what's on the line needs to be something we actually give a crap about.

2. IMPOSSIBLE ODDS

Whether it's two hundred grizzled Texans resolving to fight to the death against ten-to-one odds in a small San Antonio church or Rocky Balboa bumping gloves with Superhuman Russian Boxing Robot Ivan Drago, the most memorable fights in history are those that look utterly one-sided on paper. The reasoning behind this is simple: when you have a noticeable advantage, you're expected to win. When you're staring out at a seemingly-endless wall of battle flags and broadswords, Han Solo is reminding you never to tell him the odds, and your only other ally is currently engaged in hand-to-hand combat with a Great Wyrm Elder Dragon despite being armed only with a number-two pencil and a shield he made out of a stop sign, you've got the makings of an epic battle. Anyone can surrender, go home, and sustain basic life functions long enough to write a memoir about how they're totally misunderstood and anybody else would have done the same thing in their situation. It takes a real badass to measure what's on the line and decide, screw that, I'm going to kill as many of these bastards as possible before they take me down, and I'm going to keep fighting them as long as I have a single fingernail to claw at their eyes.

3. BLAZE OF GLORY

The difference between a heroic victory, a valiant last stand, and a crushing defeat is often measured by the badly outnumbered side's ability to launch a balls-out attack at exactly the right moment. Sure, turtling up behind fortifications and reinforcing them with heavy weapons will allow you to hold out much longer than those idiots running across the open field toward you, but until you suck it up and take the fight to the enemy you're always going to be stuck reacting to them rather than dictating the action. One thing you'll find about most impossible victories is that the beleaguered defenders will sit back, whittle down their numbers as best they can, wait for the enemy to do something stupid, and then launch one full-throttle offensive directly up their asses when they're least expecting it. Holding out is fine if you're expecting reinforcements, but if no help is coming, you might as well try something so crazy it might just work. One of two things will happen—you'll catch them off guard and smash them in the junk with a tack hammer of badassitude that will completely crush their spirits, or you'll go down, guns blazing, surrounded by the corpses of your enemies in a balls-out display of murderous bravery. I'd argue that both results are equally noteworthy.

I have applied the above criteria to choose forty battles so head-cleavingly awesome that just thinking about them makes me kind of want to spontaneously start vomiting blood out of my eyes and mouth (although I will refrain from doing so simply because I feel that the pages of this manuscript would feed on the blood and subsequently possibly become sentient and tear off my arms). Prepare yourself to feel like an inconsequential weakling as you behold the ultraviolent exploits of history's most brain-carving war heroes—men and women who went out every day, faced the sorts of life-threatening situations that would make most normal people curl up in the fetal position scream-crying the phrase "Game over, man, game over!" and dove straight on into combat, utterly undeterred by the copious amounts of violence, their minds singly determined to seek glory or death like true badasses.

BADASS: ULTIMATE DEATHMATCH

SECTION I

ANCIENT BATTLES

The Spartans do not ask how many, but where they are.

—Agis II, King of Sparta

1

FEAR THE CAMEL

The Battle of Thymbra
Sardis, Kingdom of Lydia
December, 547 BC

You know, I think, the prizes in this game. The victors pursue and smite and slay, and win wealth and fame and freedom and empire. The cowards lose them all. He who loves his own soul let him fight beside me—for I will have no disgrace.

—CYRUS THE GREAT, EMPEROR OF PERSIA

THE BATTLE OF THYMBRA IS THE TERRIBLE TRUE STORY OF HOW A DEVASTATING ONE-TWO DICKPUNCH OF FACE-EVISCERATING SCYTHED WAR CHARIOTS AND HILARIOUSLY PISSED-OFF CAMELS HELPED THE PERSIAN EMPEROR CYRUS THE GREAT FORGE THE BIGGEST AND MOST POWERFUL EMPIRE IN THE ANCIENT WORLD. If you're a fan of dudes getting shredded into bite-sized giblets by razor-sharp whirling blades while battle-raging pack animals threateningly stampede around the battlefield causing a ridiculous amount of chaos, then this double-stuffed combination platter of dromedary awesomeness and pointy destruction is exactly the sort of thing that's going to get you so friggin' pumped up out of your mind that your head might possibly burst into flames like the Ghost Rider after wolfing down a plate of thermonuclear hot wings.

The tale begins with a particularly brutal group of flesh-ripping bastards known as the Assyrians. The Assyrians were a fearsome, merciless menagerie of militaristic Middle Eastern mofos who beat the holy cake-eating whomp-ass out of every single tribe in the Fertile Crescent, built one of the world's first true multiethnic empires, and then celebrated their tremendous victories by hacking off the lips and ears of their vanquished foes, skinning their lipless bodies, and then using the flayed skin to cover giant stone obelisks proclaiming Ultimate Badass Assyrian Supremacy. For some mysterious reason the good people of the Middle East didn't really appreciate having their skin used as building material for some sick demented asshole's macabre architectural designs, and before long the Assyrians' conquered subjects rose up and overthrew their tyrannical masters. The Assyrian Empire split apart, and into the power vacuum arose three kingdoms: Media, Lydia, and Babylon. Naturally, these three kingdoms all came into being with one thought on their collective minds—kill the other two and rebuild the Assyrian Empire.

In the sixth century BC, the king of Media wasn't a hell of a lot better than the Assyrians, so one day a dirt-poor shepherd from the tiny, relatively obscure Median province of Persia decided he was sick and tired of obnoxious jackasses abusing their power all the time and decided to do something about it. This man, Cyrus (whose name comes from the Persian word *Kourash*, meaning either "Shepherd of His People," "One Who Is Like the Sun," or "One Who Verbally Humiliates His Enemies," because apparently ancient Persian translation is an inexact science), put together an army, rose up in revolt, overthrew the tyrant king of Media, renamed the kingdom Persia, and then brilliantly retconned his backstory to say that he was the king's true son, but that he'd been abandoned in the woods as a child like Snow White or Moses and was only just now getting around to assuming his rightful place on the throne. Since Cyrus was a hell of a lot more chill than the Assyrians and the Medians and he didn't really see the point in building towering creepy monuments out of the dried flesh of his slaughtered enemies, nobody really gave him a hard time about it.

Unfortunately for the new Persian ruler, one guy who wasn't really feeling the Cyrus-love was King Croesus of Lydia—a humorless asshat who, oh yeah, just so happened to be the half brother of the recently deposed tyrant king of Media. Croesus wasn't really as cunning as Cyrus, but he was really filthy stinking rich, so in 547 BC he simply went out New York Yankees style and assembled the best mercenary army money could buy. He brought spearmen from Egypt, hoplites from Sparta, and chariots from Babylon; outfitted his own Lydian cavalry with the best armor, horses, and weapons in the known world; and then marched his dream team army into Persia and tried to piss Cyrus off by burning down a bunch of cities in Syria and selling all their populations into slavery.

It worked.

When Cyrus heard what the Lydians were up to he immediately grabbed his sword, grew out his battle beard, and took the full might of the Persian Empire out there to teach Croesus what it felt like to shotgun a keg of whoop-ass out of a fire hose.

Cyrus charged across the Middle East toward Lydia (located in present-day Turkey), and immediately launched balls-out into combat against Croesus's men. Despite all of Cyrus's extensive military genius, however, the Lydian heavy cavalry had almost impenetrable armor, and it didn't help that they carried gigantic spears that were like three times the size of the Persian weapons. The Lydian cav easily broke through

Cyrus's lines, scattered his cavalry, and barreled straight down on his baggage train.

Then something weird happened. Out of nowhere, the Lydian horses suddenly started freaking the hell out, throwing their riders and running out of there like their shoes were on fire. Well, it turns out that Turkish horses don't really get the chance to see a lot of camels in their day-to-day lives, so when they got one glimpse of these weirdo-looking humped dromedary monstrosities standing around absently chewing the cud it completely weirded the Lydian horses the hell out, breaking their concentration and causing them to turn tail and run for it, because horses are stupid. When Cyrus saw this, he raised one eyebrow like Dwayne "The Rock" Johnson, looked off into the distance, and stroked his chin thoughtfully while a holographic lightbulb materialized over his head.

Shortly after this battle, winter started to settle in. Now, back in the ancient times, nobody fought in the winter, mostly because sword-fighting in the snow totally sucks ass when your military uniform consists of sandals and a knee-length tunic, so King Croesus returned to Lydia and spent the winter months chilling in his capital.

But not even the bitter, subzero temperatures of the miserable Lydian winter could match the bitterness Cyrus the Great felt from suffering disrespect at the hands of the Lydians, and instead of turning back into Persia, Cyrus instead force-marched his men a couple hundred miles through waist-deep snow into the mountains of Anatolia with only one thought on his mind—kicking Croesus's ass, squishing his corpse down to the size of a basketball, and then 360-degree tomahawk-jamming it into a compost bin. So you can imagine Croesus's surprise when one cool winter morning the Lydian king got up from his bed, walked to the window of his diamond-studded, gold-plated pimp palace, and saw 192,000 Persian warriors camped outside the walls of his capital. That's right—he immediately dropped a terror-deuce.

But Croesus wasn't about to back down either. You see, Cyrus's plan had been based on the assumption that Croesus would dismiss his mercenaries for the winter (because why the hell would he pay those freeloading scrubs to sit around doing nothing for four months), but this didn't happen (historians aren't sure why, but my guess is that it's because these guys laughed at his stupid jokes so he didn't mind paying to keep them around). And when the now-apoplectic King Croesus marched out to the battlefield at Thymbra with 420,000 warriors—a force over twice the size of Cyrus's army—it was the Persian emperor's turn to defecate a brick of his own.

On the battlefield at Thymbra, Croesus deployed his men in one gigantic line, with a beefy phalanx of badass Egyptian spearmen in the middle and his vaunted ultraheavy cavalry fanned out on either side. Cyrus responded by forming all of his infantry up into a giant hollow square of spearmen, then packed the center with about a dozen awesome-looking three-story wooden towers bristling with crack-shot archers packing deadly fire-arrows. Cyrus then put his scythed war chariots in the rear, outside the square, so they could maneuver around without screwing up the giant hollow Death Box he'd constructed.

King Croesus's plan was a simple, tried-and-true tactic for kicking ass in ancient warfare when you outnumber your enemy by such a ridiculous margin: he charged his spear phalanx straight into the middle of Cyrus's Death Box and then swung his heavy cavalry around the sides in a flanking maneuver that kind of resembled a giant pointy Man-Hug of Face-Stabbing. With Cyrus's men deployed in a tight box, it was supereasy for Croesus's expansive battle line to completely surround the Persians on three sides, closing in using a pincer move that should have by all accounts meant certain death for the Persians. The

Lydian cavalry, seeing victory in their grasp, lowered their oversized, "Hey, aren't you guys maybe overcompensating for something" lances, shouted some insulting things about the Persians' mothers, wives, sisters, and slutty first cousins, and prepared to charge full speed into Cyrus's lines.

It was at this moment that Cyrus unleashed his secret weapon—he was going to make sure those bastards choked on domesticated dromedaries until they barfed.

The Persian infantry lines suddenly parted, and out of either side of the square wobbled an unruly horde of lightly armored warriors riding on friggin' camels in a sight that could only have been ridiculous, awesome, and/or ridiculously awesome. The camel cavalry came charging dead on into the heart of the Lydian knights, squawking, honking, spitting, and/or making whatever the hell kind of obscene noise it is that camels make, while the men riding them tried to launch flaming arrows into the hard-charging Lydians.

Now, to you and me, camels are just these hilarious-looking humped desert creatures that spit brown stuff at people they don't like, but to the Lydians and their horses, this was like being suddenly sneak-attacked by a phalanx of Moon Raptor Cthulhus from Outer Space. The Lydian horses looked straight into the camel-lipped face of insanity, completely lost their fragile grip on reality, freaked the hell out, threw off their riders, and sprinted off into the sunset like small mammalian wildlife fleeing a crossbow-toting Ted Nugent through the Michigan wilderness. The Lydian cavalrymen, for their part, were nothing if not brave—even after these battle-hardened warriors were thrown from their horses, they continued to fight on foot, swinging those obscenely long, unwieldy lances around like dumbasses in a scene that unfavorably resembled a couple kids trying to beat each other up with foam pool noodles at a birthday party.

It was at this point that Cyrus personally led the counterattack—a coordinated charge of heavy scythed war chariots. These things were significantly less hilarious than the camels.

Scythed war chariots are probably some of the most badass and most underappreciated weapons in all of ancient warfare. Basically, you take a regular chariot—an open-topped wooden cart pulled by a team of horses—and then turn it into a gut-eviscerating Death Wagon from Hell by equipping it with a matched set of gigantic, ultrasharp blades protruding from the spokes of the wheels on either side. As the horses charge across the battlefield, the wheels spin, causing the gruesome-looking blades to whirl around like the business end of a blender. Put a hundred of these horrible murder tanks in a line and drive them straight on into a group of disorganized foot soldiers armed with use-less weapons, and the mental image isn't all that pretty. The Lydian heavy cavalry was obliterated like gingerbread men in a food processor, the war chariots flanked the Lydian positions, and the Egyptian pha-lanx at Croesus's center suddenly found itself completely surrounded by the Persian forces. The Egyptians, clearly defeated, continued to hold their ground, determined to fight to the last man in some mis-guided idiotic Ned Stark sense of honor to their mercenary contract, but Cyrus was so impressed with these guys' unbelievable bravery that he called a cease-fire and offered to buy the Egyptian mercs off at three times whatever Croesus was paying them. Seeing an opportunity to honorably escape a bloodbath and get paid extra for doing so, the Egyptians wisely agreed.

Croesus and his surviving men bitched out back to Sardis, where they were conquered almost immediately. The Lydian king was dragged out to the center of town and set on fire for a while, but once he was sufficiently crispy Cyrus let him go, and Croesus actually ended up serving as one of Cyrus's chief military advisors during future Persian conquests. The conquest of Lydia would be the last major stepping-stone in his transformation of Persia from a regional to a world power—Cyrus would not only go on to reunite the former Assyrian Empire, but expand it, and his successors would spend the next two hundred years ruling the most expansive realm the world had ever seen.

The camels, by the way, were sent back to the baggage train, because no Persian nobleman in his right mind actually wanted to fight his enemy while riding on a camel. It was too humiliating.

With Lydia thoroughly assimilated, Cyrus the Great moved on to attack the mighty fortress-city of Babylon—a towering stronghold with gigantic, impenetrable walls, a huge moat, and countless defensive towers so unassailable that it had never been successfully invaded by any army on Earth. That, of course, didn't stop Cyrus from trying—the Persian emperor knew that the mighty Euphrates River ran right through the middle of the city, so using some of his ancient engineering skills he somehow had his men *reroute the river*, drying up the Euphrates to the point where a child could walk through it without getting his knees wet. Once that was taken care of, Cyrus simply marched his entire army up the riverbed, walked right into the heart of the city, overthrew the king, assimilated Babylon into his empire, and then, just to show how chill he was, released the Jews from the Babylonian Captivity—a feat that earns him megamad props in the Bible.

As it expanded in later years, the Persian army also began to feature large contingents of Ethiopian troops. These tribal warriors carried awesome-looking spears tipped with antelope horns, and to prepare for battle each of them covered half of his body with white chalk and the other half with red war paint. They pretty much scared the pants off of everybody.

During the later years of the Chinese Han Dynasty, a provincial commander named Gongsun Zan was dispatched to battle barbarian rebels along the northern frontier. According to some stories, this resourceful warrior learned that the highly superstitious barbarians considered white horses to be sacred and refused to face them in battle. Naturally, Gongsun put together a cavalry force consisting entirely of guys on white horses and used them to repeatedly crush the barbarian forces into submission with their own stupid religious beliefs.

2

The Battle of Salamis

The Second Persian Invasion of Greece
The Straits of Salamis, Greece
September, 480 BC

Forward, sons of the Greeks! Liberate the fatherland, liberate your children,
your women, the altars of the gods of your fathers and the graves
of your forebears: Now is the fight for everything.

—Aeschylus, *Persians*

In the years following the Battle of Thymbra, the descendants of Cyrus the Great forged a ridiculously huge empire that covered a good portion of Central Asia, the Middle East, and East Africa, but despite the Persians' much-deserved street cred as no-nonsense face-wrecking hardasses, the stubborn Greek city-states of Sparta and Athens still refused to suck it up and submit to the will of their would-be future overlords. In 490 BC the great Persian emperor Darius I tried to pound some sense into their Hellenistic crotches with an obscene amount of club-wielding violence, but his incomprehensibly huge invasion armada of six hundred ships and a hundred thousand soldiers was miraculously defeated outside the city of Marathon when a heavily armored phalanx of ten thousand balls-out (literally—there wasn't much under those tunic skirts) Athenian warriors met an amphibious landing force ten times their size on the beaches, drove the invaders back to their boats on a crimson tide of severed limbs and mutilated corpses, and then torched the Persian transports for good measure.

A Greek warrior named Themistocles had been on the front lines at the Battle of Marathon, and as he watched the shattered remnants of the fleet limp back to Persia this grizzled warrior knew that the Persians weren't the sort of guys who were going let a defeat like that go unpunished—you don't build the largest empire in the world by going home and crying into a plate of hummus every time you lose a battle, and Themistocles knew that if the Greeks wanted to keep the Persian emperor from sailing right back into town and offloading another hundred-thousand-man invasion force 26.2 miles from the Acropolis, Athens needed to clog the Aegean Sea with enough ship-mounted battering rams and pitch-filled firebombs to nuke a small island off the map. Now, in addition to having a name that sort of looks like "Testicles," Themistocles also happened to be an archon of Athens, meaning that he was one of a small group of men responsible for the day-to-day governance of the city-state. Well, this guy was so single-mindedly hardcore about building warships that when one of the other dumbass archons defiantly announced that he thought blowing the entire treasury on boat construction projects wasn't really the most totally bitchin' idea ever conceived in the history of idiot politicians, Themistocles fabricated a political scandal that resulted in that asshole being disgraced, stripped of his office, and exiled out of town forever, because screw him for not appreciating the awesomeness of fire-breathing battle boats.

Say what you want about this guy's shady political muckraking, but it turned out that Themistocles was right. Ten years after Marathon, Darius's son, Xerxes, returned with an obscene amount of arrogance, some daddy issues, one of the coolest names in history, and a force three times the size of the army the Persians had fielded at Marathon— three hundred thousand warriors and twelve hundred ships all intent on spear-humping the face of every man, woman, and child in Greece. As Athens was evacuated, King Leonidas of Sparta headed out on a fateful journey to stuff the mountain pass at Thermopylae with the rock-hard abs of three hundred screaming Spartans, but as brave as this was, the stand at Thermopylae wouldn't have been all that useful if the Persians had been able to simply load their warriors into ships, sail around the pass, and stab the Greeks in their asses when they weren't looking. Xerxes thought about this, but unfortunately for him one thing stood in the way of the Persian fleet, blocking their path around Thermopylae and forcing the Persians to send thousands of their toughest warriors marching to their horrific deaths in a narrow pass against a heavily entrenched and almost-unkillable Spartan phalanx. That thing was the newly constructed Greek fleet, and the primary object blocking their passage was the gigantic nutsack of the Athenian naval commander Themistocles.

While Leonidas barricaded the only land entrance to Greece with heaping piles of dead bodies, dented breastplates, and empty bottles of baby oil, Themistocles covered the Spartans' flank by wedging his two hundred warships into a narrow strait just off the coast of Thermopylae at a place called Artemesium. Outnumbered almost four to one and facing off against an armada crewed by some of the world's best seamen—the Phoenicians and the Egyptians—Themistocles used the terrain to his advantage, forcing the Persians to attack in a single-file line, one squadron of ships at a time, ensuring that when the two fleets closed to ramming distance the Persians didn't have any room to maneuver. On three separate occasions Xerxes's admirals attempted to straight-up pimp-slap Themistocles with wild, unruly bum-rushes, but on all three occasions the Athenian hero shoved a battering ram so far up their poop decks that every Persian within fifty miles was coughing up splinters. The Persian admiral, seeing that charging straight on into the Greek fleet was producing roughly the same result as if he had just ordered his ships to set themselves on fire and blitz full speed into some rocks, dispatched one-third of his fleet to circle around the island Themistocles had been using to cover his flank and attack the Greeks from the rear. After a freak storm obliterated the entire expedition, Themistocles was careful to pour one out for Poseidon.

When word came down that Leonidas and the Spartans had finally ended up on the bad end of the ol' stabbity-stab and that their crucified corpses were now being used as delightfully macabre decorations outside the pass at Thermopylae, Themistocles was forced to pull the fleet back. The Persians immediately started sprinting their way across Greece, burning and plundering and kicking the crapballs out of everything in their path, but, thankfully, by this point most of the residents of those doomed towns had already evacuated to safety. The Persian war machine was still plowing along, however, and hard-hitting warmongers like Themistocles don't exactly take it all that well when foreign invader sons-of-bitches come in and start ravaging their countryside like frat boys on homecoming week. In the aftermath of Thermopylae, the Greek leaders ordered Themistocles to set up a blockade to try and slow down the Persian advance, but screw that— even though he was heavily outnumbered, he wasn't about to run from those bastards, and he sure as hell wasn't going to sit back and turtle up when he should be out there cracking the enemy in the jaw with a flaming two-by-four until they needed skin grafts and steel rebar to wire their mouths shut. Themistocles knew that if he could cripple the Persian navy with one decisive battle, they wouldn't be able to supply their land forces and the entire invasion would completely implode on itself.

And so, despite strict orders not to engage the enemy in a full-scale battle, and seemingly unaware that he had a mere 366 triremes staring down an armada of over a thousand Persian warships (they'd been reinforced since Artemesium), Themistocles resolved to make a stand. He decided that in a small, narrow inlet known as Salamis, just seven miles from his beloved Athens, he was going to put up a fight that would determine the fate of the war forever—a no-holds-barred ocean brawl that would be reminiscent of the battlestar *Galactica* taking on three Cylon basestars in orbit above New Caprica or Rocky Balboa knocking the piss out of Tommy "Machine" Gunn in that one *Rocky* movie everyone forgot about.

First, Themistocles positioned almost all of his ships inside the inlet of Salamis (which I now have it on good authority is *not* pronounced the same way you would refer to multiple slices of salami). He made damned sure that the Persians knew exactly where they could come to find him, and then he started spreading BS rumors about how Greek morale was in the toilet and how the Athenians had all lost the will to fight and were now considering abandoning war altogether and enrolling in quilt-making classes at the local fabric store. The Persian admirals knew that the destruction of Themistocles's fleet would spell the end of Greece once and for all, and so, when dawn arose one crisp September morning, the Greek crews looked to the horizon and saw the entire Persian navy plowing through the bottlenecked entrance to the inlet at full speed, anxious to crush Themistocles before he could get away and regroup. Emperor Xerxes himself, confident that the end of the war was at hand, had a golden throne positioned high on the rocks above the inlet so he could witness the final defeat of Greece personally, laugh his ass off the whole time, and then urinate down onto the ashes of Athens as it burned into charcoal.

The Greeks took one look at this armada, hesitated for a second, and then promptly ran for it like bitches.

The Persians, already tasting their sweet, delicious, cinnamon-infused victory, greedily broke ranks and pursued the fleeing Greek fleet as fast as they could, each ship's commander looking to seek glory for himself by destroying as many of the enemy as possible as they ran for it like cowards in the face of unstoppable Persian might.

But then something incredible happened. Almost in unison, the Greek ships suddenly stopped running. In one motion, Themistocles's triremes quickly wheeled around with chilling precision and formed up immediately into perfect battle lines. Just like that, the Athenian commander now found himself at the helm of a spearhead of wooden vengeance, staring down his ship's battering ram at a disorganized mass of Persian ships all crushed together inside a narrow, tiny inlet without any place to maneuver or escape.

If this were a movie, this is the part where we'd get the close-up shot of the Persian admiral looking surprised and shouting, "It's a trap!"

Naval battles in antiquity were totally sweet because they were little more than aquatic demolition derbies with arrows, battering rams, and gigantic shipboard flamethrowers smashing the crap out of each other in a semi-anarchistic explosion of destruction. Essentially, it worked like this: a fleet of insane wooden deathtraps masquerading as warships would load up with enough sword-swinging warriors to choke a Rancor, cram their holds full of volatile, unstable explosives, and then sail around at top speed with the single-minded goal of crashing head-on into an enemy ship, punching a hole in its hull, lighting it on fire, and then lowering a boarding plank so the marines could start carving their names on the skulls of the poor chumps on the opposing ship. It was like a homicidal fiery cross between a monster truck rally and a really spirited game of bumper boats, and in this no-holds-barred, *Beyond Thunderdome* arena of nautical face annihilation, Themistocles was like the Classical Age equivalent of Truckzilla—the twenty-story-tall, fire-breathing, dinosaur-shaped robot that lives only to devour hope and frighten children and that gets its nutrition from a steady diet of late-1980s model sedans and the unclean souls of wretched humans hurled forth into its unforgiving diabolical chomping steel jaws.

In the seasickness-inducing aquatic anarchy off the coast of Salamis that day, Themistocles was right in the middle of the action, punching Persian vessels into wreckage with his prow and ruining the ass of Xerxes's once-proud fleet in an epically spectacular fashion. Those Persian ships that weren't disintegrated by battering rams or set ablaze by flaming arrows either ran ashore on the rocks or had their decks swarmed by armored Greek warriors anxious to get their murder on. The Persian admiral's flagship was sunk in the early minutes of the fight (taking him down with it), further contributing to the hair-pulling WTF disorder among their ranks, and before long all Emperor Xerxes could do was scream maniacally from his golden throne and swear like a sailor as he helplessly watched the Greek formation drive a wedge of hull-obliterating ruination through his entire fleet. The Persian armada fell into disarray; their ships started accidentally crashing into each other, and the entire Persian fleet was bludgeoned into flotsam in a matter of hours, leaving nothing but a floating slick of blood and grease on the water's surface. Xerxes, afraid for his own safety and disgusted by his navy's poor showing, ran away and headed home, abandoning the entire invasion force to their fate. Victory was now impossible. The Persians, unable to bring supplies or reinforcements to the battlefront due to Themistocles's complete control of the seas, were overrun by a Greek counterattack, and it would take less than a year for the Greeks to recapture their homeland from the invaders.

Themistocles obviously became a huge celebrity in Athens overnight. He continued to serve as an archon, building the city-state into a naval power that would last for decades, but eventually the Spartans got all jealous and started going out of their way to spread mean rumors and politically undermine him at every possible turn. They were damn good at it, too—less than ten years after saving Greece's bacon from the Persians, the hero of Salamis was declared a traitor to Greece and banished from Athens forever. He escaped a Spartan assassination attempt while in exile, then fled to Asia Minor, where he was interestingly given asylum by Xerxes's son, Emperor Artaxerxes I of Persia. Artaxerxes was a totally chill guy who knew a good badass when he saw one: Themistocles was appointed governor of Magnesia, a region in southern Thessaly, and all of his female relatives and descendants were revered as priestesses of Artemis. He lived to the age of sixty-five.

Greek trireme ships were usually 125 to 135 feet long and were powered by 170 oars situated along three decks (hence the "tri" in "trireme"). It usually carried a crew of 200—170 rowers, 15 deck hands and officers, and 15 heavily armed marines.

The lone bright spot for the Persian navy at Salamis was the work performed by Artemisia, the fresh-to-death princess of Halicarnassus. This swashbuckling woman had originally suggested to Xerxes that a two-pronged pincer attack on land and sea would have been a better strategy than some cockbrained single-file death charge into the middle of the inlet of Salamis, but when Xerxes stupidly insisted on bum-rushing the Greek fleet she jumped right in and took part in the battle anyway. During the seaborne carnage at Salamis, Artemisia commanded a squadron of five ships and seems to have acquitted herself quite nicely amid the chaos—so much so that that the last thing Xerxes said before hightailing it out of there was "Today my men have fought like women, and my women have fought like men!"

3

THE SACRED BAND
OF THEBES

The Battle of Leuctra

Leuctra, Boetia

July, 371 BC

Abstaining from all dishonor, and emulating one another in honor;
and when fighting at each other's side, although a mere handful,
they would overcome the world.

—PLATO

AFTER TAKING DOWN THE PERSIANS WITH A RELENTLESS SE-
RIES OF SANDALED BOOTS TO THE JUNKBAGS, ATHENS AND
SPARTA EMERGED FROM THE GRECO-PERSIAN WARS AS THE
TWO MOST POWERFUL CITY-STATES IN GREECE. So, of course,
the only logical thing left was for the two armies to beat the crap out
of each other in a long and bloody war to determine whose cuisine
would reign supreme in Classical Europe. Sparta would emerge from
the Peloponnesian War victorious, and the Spartans would celebrate
their new domination over Greece by abolishing democracy in the city-

states and replacing majority-elected civic leaders with hand-selected groups of despotic Spartan overlords known as *tyrants* who spent most of their free time persecuting their rivals, executing freedom-loving citizens, and confiscating any property they thought was cool or shiny or potentially dangerous, and basically being such gigantic tools that the word *tyrant* is now synonymous with terrible leadership and political irresponsibility. This dictatorship thing of course was a sweet deal for the Spartans, but for everyone else not so much.

There's no debate, of course, that the Spartans were seriously tough hombres, but it probably shouldn't come as a tremendous surprise to hear that not everybody in Greece was really all that pumped about throwing their kids to rabid wolves to "toughen them up" or trading in their Socrates texts and nubile tunic-wearing mistresses for sixty pounds of bronze body armor and a daily regimen that involved sweating, being clubbed in the jaw with truncheons, and having their video games violently pried from their hands with a bloody crowbar and then smashed to pieces in front of them. One guy in particular who didn't see what the big deal was with these Spartan jerkweeds was a badass military officer named Epaminondas, a low-level commander living in the northern Greek city of Thebes. The senior ranking military official left alive during the initial purges of the Spartan tyrants (who considered him too much of an insignificant dickburger to threaten their rule), Epaminondas used his influence to free political prisoners from unjust incarceration, then organized a Theban resistance movement by secretly coordinating rebel forces, dissidents, and local military units in an armed insurrection that resulted in most of the Spartan tyrants being shanked to death in the Theban town center by a horde of megapissed Greeks. The people of Thebes were so excited about violently getting rid of the oligarchy that they crowned Epaminondas king almost immediately.

The Spartans, meanwhile, weren't quite as thrilled about this particular turn of events. When the king of Sparta heard that the tyrants had been relieved of their positions by an angry mob who attached pink slips to the ends of their daggers and then had horses kick those daggers into the crotches of Sparta's most trusted politicians, he immediately declared that Thebes was now "officially in the getting-humped-by-us business." As if this weren't enough, Epaminondas then went to a big political conference and publicly told the Spartan king to go stick his beanbag in an electric socket in front of delegates from every Greek city-state, so the Spartans responded to this insult by mobilizing their mooks for war and vowing to crush Epaminondas's balls into dust and then wear his scrotum around as a hat. Eleven thousand grizzled warriors—many of them Spartan citizens who had been training in the military arts since they were old enough to hoist the severed heads of their enemies—formed ranks, marched north, and converged on Thebes, preparing to burn it to the ground, bulldoze the rubble, build a parking lot on the ruins, and then bulldoze the parking lot.

Of course, unlike the Spartans, the Thebans weren't exactly a bunch of military lifers who spent their adolescence fistfighting bears and eating charcoal sprinkled with broken glass (nor were they reincarnated spirits of dead aliens banished to Earth by the alien overlord Xenu . . . sorry, John Travolta)—they were just regular Average Joe citizen-soldiers called up to fight when their city needed them, and for these guys the idea of facing the Spartans toe-to-toe in an all-out slugfest was about as appealing as giving themselves mohawks with a weed whacker. So you can probably imagine why the six thousand farmers of the Theban militia weren't exactly superpsyched about fighting eleven thousand hardcore, crap-your-pants-scary Spartan warriors in a battle to determine whether or not Sparta was going to burn Thebes to the ground and slaughter, enslave, and/or give purple nurples to every man, woman, and child inside the city walls. (The Spartans, meanwhile, had no such worries—they had a "Hey, it's gonna be awesome when we murder some Thebans" party in their camp, pregaming the battle by drinking a few casks of ouzo and telling dirty jokes about all the deliciously-horrible stuff they were going to do to the population once they plundered the city.)

But Epaminondas knew it was time to make a stand. Victory or death. Or some combination of the two. But preferably with more of the former than the latter.

While it's probably safe to say that the Vegas odds weren't exactly in his favor (I wasn't able to find any research to document this; I assume it was lost with the destruction of the Library of Alexandria), Epaminondas still had a couple of tricks up his sleeve. First and foremost was an elite infantry unit known as the Sacred Band of Thebes—a hulking cadre of the biggest, strongest, and toughest men that Thebes had to offer. Of course, while this was one of the only units of professional soldiers in the world at the time, perhaps the most noteworthy aspect of the Sacred Band is that it was composed entirely of 150 homosexual couples. Now, to some folks (most notably the contemporary Greek historian/soldier Xenophon), the idea of 300 gay men fighting alongside one another was pretty much the exact opposite of badass (nice ass? I suppose that still works . . .), but the theory behind the unit made perfect sense to Epaminondas (and Plato, who came up with the idea): the presence of your lover in combat would supposedly inspire you to fight harder (to impress him with your combat prowess), and you'd be less likely to desert your squad on the field if it meant you were going to look like a coward in front of your boyfriend. Say what you want, but it worked—the Sacred Band had already defeated a Spartan vanguard before taking the field at Leuctra, and they were eager to repeat the performance on a grander scale.

Now before I explain to you how inexplicably brilliant Epaminondas was, let me first talk for a second about how Classical Greek battles worked. Very generally speaking, if you were going to impale your enemies to death with a phalanx of long pointy evilness, you would just form one huge line of armored spearmen known as hoplites, stacked twelve ranks deep, with your toughest men on the right side of your formation, and everyone would charge forward at the same time, crashing into the enemy with a solid wall of spears and shields and chiseled six-pack abs. The strong right sides would battle the weaker left sides, and the first group of badass elite units to break the enemy's weak spot would usually end up rolling up the flank and winning the battle.

Aside from the Sacred Band, Epaminondas knew he was outnumbered and outclassed almost universally across the board, so he improvised. For him, it was a simple question of numbers—instead of a phalanx twelve men deep with the wussbags on the left and the heroes on the right, he formed his men up into one giant MEGAPHALANX fifty warriors deep and positioned it and the Sacred Band on his left, directly in front of the Spartan's toughest regiments (the ultraheavy hoplite units of full-blooded Spartan citizens rather than allied troops from neighboring regions). Before the Spartan king could figure out what in the damn hell was going on (nobody had ever really thought to overload one side of the line before, for some reason), Epaminondas charged—only he didn't charge straight on, in the traditional Greek style, but at a 45-degree angle, with the Sacred Band and the MEGAPHALANX positioned to hit the Spartans first and his weaker men hanging back at a diagonal, angled away from the action.

As the infantry moved across the field and the Spartans struggled to counter this bizarre attack, the Theban cavalry suddenly rushed in from nowhere and launched an assault straight at the Spartan flank. The Spartan cavalry rode out to counter them, but the Spartan cavalry pretty much always completely sucked ass (the Spartans figured cav was useless compared to heavy infantry and rarely wasted their time with it), so not only were they completely routed, but the Thebans ended up chasing the damned Spartan cavalry directly into their own infantry ranks, causing confusion and disorder in a flurry of hooves, dust, and slobbering horse faces.

Before the Spartan commanders could restore order in the ranks and get their guys back into a cohesive unified battle line, the Theban MEGAPHALANX crashed into them. Between the Sacred Band and the MEGAPHALANX, the Spartan citizens on the right side of the formation suddenly found themselves outnumbered, surrounded, flanked, and getting the crap kicked out of them by three hundred homos. The Spartan king tried to use his overwhelming numerical superiority to his advantage by charging his unengaged left toward the enemy, but as the Spartans moved their troops forward, Epaminondas just casually wheeled his weaker troops away, keeping them out of the battle while his heavy hitters did the hard work.

The Sacred Band penetrated through the gaps in the Spartan formation, and after fierce fighting the king of Sparta himself was impaled by unbelievably fabulous warriors of the Sacred Band. The Spartan king's bodyguard fought valorously to recover the body of their fallen king, but were beaten off, and it quickly became obvious that the battle was lost. When Sparta's allies saw their commander and its toughest warriors struck down by the Sacred Band's onslaught, they retreated immediately, many of them fleeing the field without even so much as raising their spears for combat. Epaminondas's oblique attack, charging the Spartan citizens with a massed group of hardened soldiers while wheeling away from a counterattack (a plan he dubbed "Crushing the Head of the Serpent," which I don't believe was intended to be a double-entendre), had been successful.

The number of Spartans killed in the battle was between fourteen hundred and four thousand, depending on who you ask, but the important thing here is that a large portion of those dead were full-blooded Spartan citizens—and Sparta was not a big enough city-state that they could afford to lose that many of its citizens. It was the first time the

Spartans had been defeated in a full-scale pitched infantry battle in over a century.

Epaminondas routed the enemy and chased the Spartans all the way back to the isthmus of Corinth, liberating Greece from Spartan domination along the way, establishing Thebes as the dominant power in the region, and even going so far as to invade Spartan territory on four separate occasions. Sparta would never again be considered the dominant military force in the world. Their power was broken forever.

When word reached Sparta of the defeat at Leuctra, every man, woman, and child took the news without crying. They collectively mourned in silence for one day, then took solace in the fact that their loved ones had died with honor. The only dejected faces in Sparta the day after were from those who had not been lucky enough to have a kinsman die in combat. Spartans were weird people.

At the Battle of Chaeronea in 338 BC, King Philip II of Macedon would deal the Sacred Band the only defeat it would ever suffer in its forty-year existence. Charged head-on by the ultraheavy Companion Cavalry of Philip's son, Alexander (the dude we know today as Alexander the Great), the Sacred Band valiantly stood its ground and fought to the end, with every man killed where he stood on the battle line, dying in a heap next to his fellow soldiers. When he heard the entire band had been slain by his Yoko Ono of a son, King Philip is said to have fallen to his knees and wept manly tears of sadness on the battlefield.

4

THE SECOND PUNIC WAR

Scipio Africanus vs. Hannibal Barca
Italy, Spain, and North Africa
218–201 BC

Prepare for war, since you have been unable to endure a peace.

—SCIPIO AFRICANUS, SPOKEN TO HANNIBAL BEFORE THE BATTLE OF ZAMA

THE SECOND PUNIC WAR IS THE STORY OF TWO OF THE GREAT-
EST AND MOST BADASS MILITARY COMMANDERS WHO EVER
LIVED—HANNIBAL BARCA AND SCIPIO AFRICANUS. As far as
ultimate mecha blood feud death rivalries go, these two warmongering hardasses were like the Manning–Brady, Kobe–LeBron, or Aunt
Jemima–Mrs. Butterworth of the third century BC, and their epic
struggle bashing each other repeatedly about the head and neck with
a vast assortment of increasingly deadly instruments ultimately altered
the course of ancient history forever.

The chest-cavity-eviscerating unpleasantness all started when the
insane-o megabrilliant military general Hannibal thought it would be
totally xtreme to the max to leave his homeland, the incredibly wealthy

North African city-state of Carthage (located in present-day Tunisia), march a tremendously huge mercenary army across Spain, invade Italy, and burn Rome to the ground as a way of showing them that they weren't nearly as badass as they thought they were. This crazy bastard assembled a multinational force of fifty thousand soldiers from across Gaul, Spain, and North Africa, equipped them with ten thousand horses and a couple hundred gigantic angry war elephants, and somehow crossed with this motley crew of battle-hungry warriors over the mighty Rhone River on homemade rafts so freakishly sweet that they'd give Bear Grylls a boner. Hannibal then led his mercenaries, warriors, and pachyderms up into the Alps, crossing one of the deadliest, tallest, and most dangerous mountain ranges on Earth in the middle of the frigid winter and attacking Rome from the direction they least expected an African invasion to come from.

I don't know how well versed you are in the sociopolitical makeup of ancient civilizations, but I probably don't need to point out that the Romans weren't the sort of folks that melodramatically blubbered like they'd lost *American Idol* just because some kooky jerk with a sword rode a couple of elephants into town and told everyone to suck his nards. No, when word went around that a new Carthaginian challenger had appeared and was currently rolling down the mountains toward them, the Romans responded the same way they responded to anything—with excessive, brutal, over-the-top violence. The Senate dispatched Rome's most senior military commander, a dude named Tiberius Sempronius Longus, with orders to take Rome's legions, batter this annoying invasion force into a miserable slurry of entrails and failure, feed Hannibal's battered corpse to his own elephants, and then have the elephants crucified.

Unfortunately for Rome, Tiberius Sempronius Longus was an almost comically incompetent dickweed, and this witless numbnuts decided that it would be a magnificent idea to display his encyclopedic ignorance by just riding out and attacking Hannibal straight on like a dumbass—a tactic that quite shockingly did not work out so hot for him. Hannibal, being the diabolical evil-genius-grade mastermind that he was, saw this insane frontal attack, laughed a single terrifying laugh, cracked his knuckles so loudly it generated a mushroom cloud, and then wiped out two-thirds of Tiberius's army in a single day at the Battle of the Trebia. When Rome dispatched two more legions and four thousand cavalry to reinforce Tiberius's shattered ranks, Hannibal ambushed the relief column at a place called Lake Trasimene, riding his cavalry downhill through a thick fog, crashing into the Roman flank, and utterly deballing them with an ice cream scoop in a battle that lasted less than three hours and left fifteen thousand Romans dead or dying on the field.

After making Rome's best and brightest military commanders look like ten pounds of crap stuffed into a five-pound bag, Hannibal marched on over to a gigantic food depot the Romans had conveniently left unguarded and threw a massive keg party to celebrate his awesomeness. The Romans, desperately seeking any way to put an end to Hannibal's serrated gonad-wrecking African rampage and save the largest source of grain in the republic, marched out their last hope—a massive force consisting of the last eighty thousand fighting men in Rome, personally commanded by both of its two consuls (the highest-ranking political officials in the republic—this is like the President and Vice-President picking up weapons and leading the troops on the front lines). Rome's last hope faced off against Hannibal's Carthaginians in an all-or-nothing deathmatch at a little place known as Cannae.

Hannibal was badly outnumbered and facing a disciplined Roman army twice his size, but he didn't even pretend like he gave a crap. In one of the all-time most horrific military depantsings ever recorded, the Carthaginian God of Face-Smashing Badassitude charged his battle line ahead, engaged the enemy, faked a withdrawal, lured the Roman army into a trap, completely encircled them with a move known as the double envelopment, and then gave them all atomic wedgies so hard that it ripped a hole in the universe. Nearly the entire Roman force was hemmed in so tightly the men could barely swing their swords (the centurions resorted to biting and punching, according to some sources), and while they were crammed in like sardines by a solid wall of enemy shields, Hannibal's cavalry came up from behind and hamstrung them until all that remained of them was "a giant pile of legless corpses with career-ending injuries." Hannibal lost eight thousand men. Rome lost fifty thousand, including both consuls.

Rome suddenly realized it was pretty much totally screwed. This Hannibal character was evidentally the real deal, and by single-handedly orchestrating three of the greatest one-sided tactical victories in human history he'd caused the death of something on the order of two hundred thousand veteran Roman legionaries in the course of a year and a half of nonstop unholy asswhompings and then ate their brains with a side of fava beans.

But this is where the story gets weird. You see, even though Hannibal had all but assured Carthaginian dominance of the Italian peninsula, from this point on the African warlord was kind of stuck in a bizarre limbo—two years of constant battle had taken its toll on Hannibal's forces, leaving him with a depleted army that was too small to lay siege to the Eternal City itself, yet for some utterly incomprehensible reason the douchebag brain trust in Carthage still stupidly refused to send their greatest hero any reinforcements. Frustratingly trapped in Tuscany with nothing to do and no one left to kill, Hannibal just spent the next ten years (!) wandering aimlessly around the Italian countryside beating up random people for their lunch money and dreaming of the day when he'd finally have enough men to assault Rome itself.

Well, with every other human being in Italy pissing their togas at the mere mention of Hannibal's name, there was only one Roman asskicker who decided he wasn't just going to sit around on his chaise longue being fed grapes by beautiful women while some bastard-coated bastard with bastard filling ran around dropping his countrymen crotch-first onto an electric fruit-juicing machine. Publius Cornelius Scipio had been there from the beginning of this ungodly carnage—as a sixteen-year-old cavalry officer he'd fought alongside his father at the Battle of Ticinus and had been cited for bravery for slicing his way through a Carthaginian horde to save his dad's life. Scipio had also been there on the battlefield when the Roman legions got their teeth kicked out through their urethras at Cannae, and as one of the few survivors of that humiliating debacle this Roman officer became more and more irate every miserable day that passed in which Hannibal wasn't getting a much-deserved boot to the hogchoker. Finally, one day Scipio snapped. He got up, stormed into the Senate, and told them it was time for vengeance—someone needed to stick it to Hannibal, and Scipio was the man who was going to bring the pain.

But Scipio's plan wasn't to take the fight directly to Hannibal. Forget that. Scipio was perfectly content to let that Carthaginian knucklehead wander around like a hobo playing grabass with his buddies in the Italian wilderness—while Hannibal was sitting around on his thumbs waiting for reinforcements, Scipio was going to drill the Carthaginians with an old-school reach-around rabbit punch to the kidneys when they least expected it. Scipio turned west, emptied his *2 Fast 2 Furious* Vin Diesel nitro tanks in a frothing-at-the-mouth charge toward Spain, and flying-sidekicked the Carthaginian-controlled province in the bozak with a daring amphibious sneak attack that caught the enemy completely off guard. Before anybody actually even realized what the sweet mother hell was going on, the Carthaginian forward base at Cartagena had already fallen to the Roman invasion, and the overconfident defenders were fleeing in disarray. Hannibal's two kid brothers (both of whom had been cavalry commanders at Cannae) rode out with armies to confront him, but Scipio kicked the snot out of Hannibal's bros by single-handedly bludgeoning them all into bone dust with a giant mallet he'd carved from the skeleton of a sea monster (or something like that) in two separate battles against vastly-superior forces that outnumbered him and had him almost completely surrounded in unfamiliar territory. When he was finished turning Hannibal's stooge brothers into chew toys for his rottweilers, Scipio crossed the Strait of Gibraltar into North Africa, marched toward Tunisia, deposed the ruler of Namibia, and then defeated yet another Carthaginian army that had been hastily thrown together in a half-assed attempt to slow down this Roman Republican Vengeance Machine. When the Carthaginian government finally got their heads unglued from their rectums and realized what the crapballs was going on they immediately got on the horn and ordered Hannibal to get his ass back home to save them from the unstoppable assbeating that Scipio was about to lay upon them.

Hannibal was a man of action, and if there was one thing this guy could do, it was move a lot of troops very quickly, through impossible terrain, and murder everyone he found on the other side. So when he heard the news of Scipio's raid, the Carthaginian tactician immediately facepalmed at the idiocy of his political leadership, built some ships, burned rubber back home, and in 202 BC he and Scipio finally met mano-a-mano in an epic battle just 105 miles from the gates of Carthage. Scipio, the best thing that happened to Rome in twenty years, found himself suddenly outnumbered and facing a brilliant general who had spent the better part of two decades standing triumphantly on top of heaping piles of Roman corpses rubbing his balls on their legionary eagles. But this guy had come to North Africa seeking this exact matchup, and now that the opportunity to achieve sweet delicious revenge had been fortuitously placed directly in front of him he wasn't about to waste the opportunity.

Hannibal started out the battle by positioning a few hundred super-cantankerous war elephants at the head of his army and then charging his organic T-34s trunk-first into the Roman legions like those wacky Elf-smashing oliphaunts running amok in *The Return of the King*. The Carthaginian commander understandably believed that this onslaught of tusked ferocity would probably cause most of Scipio's infantry to obey their natural self-preservation instincts and run screaming away from the rampaging two-ton armored pachyderms, but this time it was the great Hannibal who underestimated the will of the Romans—the grizzled veterans of Cannae were bitter as hell, and these tenacious buzz saws of fury were race cars in the red just itching for an opportunity to kick their ferocity into overdrive. These guys weren't going to back down just because some monstrous war elephants were getting ready to flatten them into giant bloody smears on the dirt with their gigantic creepy circular feet. Instead, the legionaries responded by screaming insults as loud as possible, clanging their swords and shields together, and blaring trumpet music at volumes that bordered on possibly being cranked up to eleven. The megaloud noise and hurtful profane insults completely freaked the elephants out, and instead of the Romans it was THE ELEPHANTS who turned and ran for it in terror, trampling the holy hell out of the Carthaginian ranks in their desperate attempt to escape the lividly pissed Romans. With the enemy lines shattered by the Classical Age equivalent of an own goal and Hannibal's warriors now being violently crushed by thirteen thousand pounds of irony and elephant meat, Scipio then charged forward, crashed into the enemy lines, turned Hannibal's flanks, and took his revenge. On the battle-field at Zama, Scipio lost three thousand men while inflicting twenty-five thousand casualties on the enemy. Hannibal's force was shattered, the path to the gates of Carthage now lay unguarded, and the Second Punic War was effectively over.

Despite all the pain Carthage had inflicted on his people, Scipio spared the city-state from the ultimate drunk-shaming humiliation that most Romans felt it deserved, refusing to burn the city or wipe out the populace no matter how bad the Senate wanted him to. He returned home in heroic triumph, received the honorific title of "Africanus" (which basically means "He who kicked ass in Africa"), was elected consul like a dozen times, and is still remembered today as one of Rome's greatest heroes and one of the most badass military commanders to ever live.

Of course, as a side note, Scipio's adoptive grandson wouldn't be as laid back toward the Carthaginians—a few years later the Carthaginians would get all uppity again, and Scipio's grandkid (also known as Scipio Africanus) would stomp their balls in the Third Punic War, sack Carthage, sell its entire population into slavery, burn everything to the ground, urinate on the ashes, and salt the earth so that no crops could ever grow there again. And that, as you can probably imagine, was the end of that.

During the period of the Roman Republic, one of the most popular political sayings was "Carthago delenda est," which translates to "Carthage must be destroyed." One Roman politician, Cato the Elder, was famous for ending all of his speeches with this phrase, even when he wasn't actually talking about anything even remotely related to Carthage.

———

Despite being a vengeance-seeking cruise missile of Roman fury, Scipio was also completely awesome and chill pretty much all of the time. Whereas Hannibal had a grand old time trashing the Roman countryside, Scipio was the exact opposite, ordering his men to treat the captured soldiers as Roman citizens instead of vanquished foes. For instance, after defeating the Carthaginian army in Spain and capturing their provincial capital, Scipio's men brought the hottest babe in the land for him to keep as a concubine or girlfriend or whatever. Scipio wasn't really down with keeping women as plunder, so he insisted that his men return the pillaged chickie to her family and to knock off all those wacky human-trafficking shenanigans. He was just good like that, and sometimes karma rewards people who aren't giant raging dickheads all the time.

———

After the war Hannibal went into politics and was eventually elected chief magistrate of Carthage. This pissed off the Romans (not to mention those douchebags in the Carthaginian government who were pissed he was stealing their influence), so, fearing for his life, he fled Africa, tried (usually unsuccessfully) to encourage the Syrians, Armenians, and Seleucids to fight Rome, and was eventually betrayed and had to chug the contents of a poison ring to avoid falling into Roman hands. He was in his mid-sixties.

———

5

THE TEUTOBURG FOREST

The Varian Disaster
Teutoburger Wald, Germania
September, AD 9

The scene lived up to its horrible expectations. Varus's extensive first camp,
with its broad extent and headquarters marked out, testified to the whole
army's labors. Then a half-ruined breastwork and shallow ditch where the
last pathetic remnant had gathered. On the open ground were whitening
bones, scattered where men had fled, heaped up where they had stood and
fought back. Fragments of spears and of horses' limbs lay there—also human
heads, fastened to tree trunks. In groves nearby were the outlandish altars at
which the Germans had massacred the Roman colonels and senior company
commanders.

—TACITUS, *Annals*

IT WAS A COLD, WET, WINDY AFTERNOON IN SEPTEMBER OF
AD 9 WHEN THE BATTLE-HARDENED WARRIORS OF THE
ROMAN SEVENTEENTH, EIGHTEENTH, AND NINETEENTH LE-
GIONS TRUDGED THROUGH THE ANKLE-DEEP MUD OF THE TEU-
TOBURGER WALD—A DARK, CREEPY-AS-HELL FOREST THAT
LOOKED LESS LIKE A BATTLEFIELD AND MORE LIKE THE SORT
OF PLACE YOU USED TO READ ABOUT IN FAIRY TALES WHERE

PSYCHOTIC EVIL WART-FACED WITCHES BUILD HOUSES OUT OF FOOD PRODUCTS, DISMEMBER WILDLIFE, AND SPEND THEIR SPARE TIME KICKING CHILDREN INTO OVENS JUST TO BE ASS-HOLES. The imperial column—roughly thirty thousand troops, aux-iliary soldiers, support personnel, and camp followers—marched through the uncharted wilderness of this miserable, impenetrable wood, following their aimless commander, a career politician and rag-ing dumbass known as Publius Quinctilius Varus, who had been dis-patched by Emperor Augustus to conquer Germania and plunder/tax/ enslave the loincloths off of everyone he found there despite the notable handicap that this guy had no damn idea how to go about doing any of those things. Far from being the imperial Roman version of Darth Vader wiping out Rebel forces by Force-hurling TIE fighters into their battle lines, Varus was a vain, brash, soft-handed cubicle jockey who was much more at home giving boring speeches, kissing babies, and organizing bitchy political smear campaigns than he was standing in knee-deep muck swinging a gladius at the enemies of Rome. By force-marching his exhausted men through the unknown, rain-swept wilder-ness of the German-infested Teutoburg Forest, this guy had just made a brain-explodingly boneheaded mistake so amazing in its incompe-tence that it makes the Roman consuls at Cannae look like a conjoined triplet made out of Napoleon Bonaparte, Alexander the Great, and that dude from *Total Recall* who had the baby coming out of his stomach. In terms of career moves, marching three legions into the Teutoberg was the Classical Age equivalent of coauthoring an academic paper with the Unabomber or asking Charles Manson to write you a letter of recom-mendation for law school.

Unsurprisingly, this came back to bite him in the ass.

We don't know exactly how many Germans were hiding in the woods, watching the column of imperial invaders trudge past. The Germans didn't bother to write anything down more detailed than "killed sum d00ds 2day lulz," and the only Romans who managed to run screaming out of this forest alive were the ones who knew better than to sit there and try to count how many GWAR fans were currently trying to brutally dismember them with axes. Let's just say it was probably a crapload, and that when these long-haired death metal freaks unleashed a bloodcurdling shout and started charging through the forest like a bunch of gigantic mutant Ewok-Wookies ambushing the Imperial Stormtroopers on the Forest Moon of Endor it wasn't exactly the sort of hilarious laugh riot you might see in an animated GIF involving unicorns, rainbows, and cartoon kitties with Pop-Tarts where their bodies are supposed to be. Bellowing like madmen, these balls-out, frothing-at-the-mouth, beer-swilling sausage fiends went Leeroy Jenkins toward the enemy, blitzkrieging out of the woods from every side seemingly at the same time, their ferociousness magnified not only by their savage blood rage, but by the fact that some of the dudes had taken to painting their entire bodies black with mud to help them hide in the dark forest like how Schwarzenegger hid from the Predator's infrared vision. It was so damned terrifying that it took every ounce of Roman discipline to not simply spontaneously combust into blood vapor on the spot.

The German horde was commanded by a hard-as-hell war hero known as Arminius—a Conan the Barbarian–style bladder-stabbing hellraiser who could allegedly cleave a man from head to groin with one swing of his massive axe (a detail of his life so awesome that when I typed my initial reaction to it in the notepad on my iPhone it autocorrected to "holy shot"). Arminius had spent the previous decade of his life commanding the auxiliary forces of Rome against the Gauls and the Britons, crushing Caesar's enemies so successfully that he'd actually been promoted to a member of the Roman nobility, and while being a Roman citizen was fun and everything, when the emperor directed his legions at Arminius's countrymen, this guy freaked the hell out, ragequit his job, organized the unruly tribes of Germany, and set up the perfect ambush geared specifically to combat the weaknesses of Roman military tactics. As a grizzled veteran he knew that the cramped quarters of the dense woods were terrible for the Roman style of formation-based warfare, but that it was pretty much perfect for a bunch of gigantic unruly Germans seeking the glory of one-on-one combat.

The exact blow-by-blow details of the massacre in the forest are sketchy at best. We know the initial charge of German berserkers smashed into the imperial ranks and dealt a crippling blow, cutting off parts of the Roman column, isolating and surrounding entire legions, and ruthlessly hacking through the Romans like Bruce Campbell plowing through an army of undead warriors with a chainsaw hand and a double-barreled shotgun. Over the course of the afternoon the disciplined Romans kept their cool, and some of their brave legionaries even managed to form up into ranks and fight their way out, cutting out a swath big enough for them to set up a camp complete with fortifications and defensive walls. From the security of the protected, fortified high ground, the Romans resolved to make their final stand, bracing themselves for an onslaught of enemy warriors, but the wily Arminius knew better than to screw with that—he ordered his eager men to patiently hang back and wait for the Romans to move, somehow chilling out a horde of bloodlusting berserkers and preventing them from hurling themselves into an unwise suicide charge. Knowing they didn't have enough men or supplies to maintain an extended siege in their makeshift camp, Romans attempted to sneak away after darkness fell (going so far as to stuff grass into the bells of their pack animals to keep them from making noise), but Arminius was ready for that as well. There would be no escape. As soon as the German commander saw the Romans moving through the darkness he ordered his men to light their torches, and the pagan horde unleashed another massive charge, screaming through the forest in a spiteful frenzy of wacky Teutonic mayhem led by Arminius himself. Those brave legionaries who drew their weapons and made a stand in the open were killed where they fought. Those who ran were cut down as they fled.

Three full legions were utterly annihilated in twenty-four hours of battle. Only a handful of lucky Romans managed to escape with their lives, and those guys were so shell-shocked that they spent their entire lives having flashbacks every time someone offered them a hefeweisen or responded to a sneeze by saying *gezhuntheit*. Varus himself was wounded in the initial melee, and that ill-fated asshat of a Roman commander wisely opted to fall on his sword rather than end up in the clutches of the murderous Germans. The triumphant Arminius built a podium, where he addressed the assembled warriors, praised their battle prowess, and held aloft the three captured legionary eagles—the battle standards of the Roman legions they'd just annihilated. During the victory celebration, the Germans honored their gods by offering live human sacrifices of captured Roman officers, disemboweling them on stone altars and then presumably making bratwurst out of their intestines. Captured enlisted men were thrown into spiked pits, which oddly seems more humane somehow.

Five years after the massacre, the Roman hero Germanicus fought his way back across the Rhine to bury the dead and recover the lost eagles (he found two of the three; the third one is still lost). When he reached the forest he found the skulls of twenty thousand dead Romans nailed to tree trunks throughout the Teutoberg Forest, a monument as to why crossing the Rhine was a really, really bad idea.

The Romans never made another serious effort to conquer Germany again. Incidentally, this is why Germanic, Anglo-Saxon, and (by extension) English culture and language survived intact while much of the rest of Europe was thoroughly latinized.

Shortly after his triumphant asskicking in the Teutoberg Forest, Arminius tried to rally the men to launch a cohesive raid against Rome, but was never able to get enough support for an attack. He was eventually betrayed by his wife's parents (the dashing hero's blushing bride had eloped without the expressed written consent of her parents and Major League Baseball, and her folks were still a little pissy about it) and was stabbed to death in his sleep, thus proving that the full might of the Roman Empire is nothing compared to terrible in-laws.

———

While Germans were excellent at killing anything that moved, they were also highly prized as bodyguards in the early days of the Roman Empire, mostly because no matter how flesh-rippingly vicious they were in combat, they also had an unflinching sense of honor that meant that first-degree murder was incredibly uncommon among the German tribes. This is of course exactly what you want in a bodyguard, which explains why emperors like Claudius and Nero spent a lot of their time singing Whitney Houston songs to big German dudes in Roman-style armor.

Kill them all. God will recognize His own.

—ARNAUD AMALRIC, ABBOT OF CITEAUX

THE BATTLE OF PANIPAT (1519)

Early in the sixteenth century, Central Asian warlord/xtreme sports aficionado Zahir-ud-din Muhammad Babur marched his forces through the Afghan mountains toward Delhi in an attempt to capture the wealthy Indian capital in the name of his newly formed (and rapidly expanding) Mughal Empire of Mughalness. The mighty sultan of India, one of the most powerful men in the world at the time, wasn't all that intimidated by Babur (it didn't help Babur's cause that his name literally translates to "beaver"), and the he certainly wasn't impressed by Babur's adorably quaint little ten-thousand-man force. So, looking for a good opportunity to send this would-be conqueror back to Kabul in a flaming body bag, the sultan rode out with fifty thousand warriors and decided to teach this uppity whippersnapper a lesson in pain tolerance. But, as it happens, Babur had a secret weapon his adversary had never seen before—a newfangled siege weapon known as the cannon. Babur lined up seven hundred wagons end-to-end, chained them all together, and positioned a few cannon batteries behind them, and when the sultan's men charged forward trying to force their way through the wall of wagons they were immediately blasted into the next zip code by large-caliber gunfire. Their five-to-one advantage nullified by Babur's ability to put a cannonball through their faces whenever he wanted, the sultan's entire force was annihilated, and Babur waltzed right into Delhi, where he installed a dynasty that would rule India with an iron fist for the next two and a half centuries.

THE BATTLE OF SAN JACINTO (1836)

Mexican *presidente-por-vida* Antonio López de Santa Anna had done a hell of a job massacring the valiant yet doomed defenders of the Alamo during the Texas War of Independence, but he soon learned the hard way why you're not really supposed to mess with Texas when General Sam

Houston rode into town looking for revenge. At first, Santa Anna acquitted himself fairly well—the self-proclaimed "Napoleon of the West" outmaneuvered Houston's Texans, cornering them up against the San Jacinto River with no place to escape, but then, just when it looked like all was lost, the ragtag band of Texans did the last thing Santa Anna expected—they charged full throttle toward the Mexican lines, guns blazing, in a Texas-style onslaught of six-cylindered mayhem. With a battle cry of "Remember the Alamo," the Texans opened fire with grapeshot from their two cannons (nicknamed the "Twin Sisters") at two hundred yards, ripping a hole in the Mexican lines, and then, despite being outnumbered two to one, the Texans rushed right into the breach, catastrophically laying into the enemy hand-to-hand with bayonets, Bowie knives, rifle butts, and ammunition boxes shaped like Dale Junior's No. 88 Chevy Impala. The Texans suffered 9 dead and 23 wounded, but in their fury (and the ensuing rout) they killed 603 of the enemy, wounded 208 more, and took 730 prisoners, utterly obliterating the enemy army and ensuring Texas's (temporary) independence. The only notable survivor of the Mexican force was Santa Anna himself, but that guy would get what was coming to him a few years later during the Mexican-American War.

The Fetterman Massacre (1866)

Notable jackass William Fetterman was a rampagingly stupid egomaniac who mistakenly thought he was a tomahawk-proof Indian-killing bastard machine. When the Sioux Indians started getting a little agitated about the American expansionist policy of "Screw the Sioux, let's do whatever the hell we want all the time, particularly if whatever the hell we want to do involves killing Sioux people" and began launching increasingly deadly raids on American forts, Captain Fetterman told his commanding officer, "Give me eighty men and I'll ride through the whole Sioux Nation!" Fetterman got his wish, took his eighty men out into the forest, ignored orders not to march out of sight of the American stockade, and promptly chased a small band of fleeing Sioux braves right into a two-thousand-man ambush led by none other than Crazy Horse himself. It took the Sioux about twenty minutes to slaughter Fetterman, wipe out his entire column, and scalp/teabag their dead bodies.

THE BATTLE OF TANNENBERG (1914)

In the early days of World War I, the German command staff, already fully-engaged one-to-one with what they believed to be the full might of the Russian Army, was suddenly surprised by intelligence reports suggesting that a previously unknown, second full-strength Russian Field Army had been mobilized to the south and was currently poised to start blitzing unopposed straight toward the heart of Germany. Now faced with almost a million Russkies attacking from two directions at once in a semicoordinated pincer move, and with only one army's worth of troops to defend the battlefront, über-hardcore German commanders Paul von Hindenburg and Erich Ludendorff had to improvise. What resulted was one of the most absurdly successful bluffs in modern military history.

Leaving behind just two semiuseless cavalry brigades (roughly two thousand dudes on horseback at a time when every military unit larger than a baseball team came equipped with a heavy machine gun section) to defend a one-hundred-mile-wide battlefront against six hundred thousand Russian soldiers in the north, Ludendorff somehow loaded the entire German Eighth Army—about five hundred thousand men—on trains and rerouted them south without the Russians knowing about it. The Russian southern army, thinking it was sneaking by undetected, suddenly found itself trapped in a dark forest, completely surrounded, and being bombarded by nonstop artillery fire from every side. The Germans lost a handful men in the battle and ended up killing or capturing hundreds of thousands of Russians, obliterating the southern army in a defeat so humiliating that when the Russian commander realized what was happening, he capped himself in the head right there on the battlefield to save the Germans the trouble. With the Russian southern group effectively liquidated in just five days, the Germans immediately rerouted the Eighth Army north, then promptly defeated the Russian northern army as well. The beatdown was so humiliating that some historians cite it as a cause of the Bolshevik Revolution, and you know you suck as a military commander when you get your ass kicked so hard that your native country decides to become Communist just to dissociate themselves from your crippling idiocy.

6

BOUDICCA'S REVOLT

Britain's Warrior Queen takes on Rome
Britannia Province, Roman Empire
AD 61

The Roman legion which dared to fight us is annihilated.
The others cower in their camps, or watch for a chance to escape.
They will never face even the din and roar of all our thousands, much less
the shock of our onslaught. Consider how many of you are fighting—and why.
Then you will win this battle or perish. That is what I, a woman,
plan to do—let the men live in slavery if they will.

—BOUDICCA, WARRIOR QUEEN OF THE ICENI TRIBE

BOUDICCA IS ONE OF THE FEW PEOPLE IN HISTORY TO HAVE A
STATUE OF THEMSELVES PROMINENTLY DISPLAYED IN A CITY
THEY'RE FAMOUS FOR BURNING TO THE GROUND.

The story of how the fiery slaughter and wanton ruination of the
city of London became so fondly remembered begins in the year AD
61, when some painfully uninteresting ruler of the Iceni tribe of northern Britannia had the audacity to die of old age and leave behind the

most tragically misunderstood will in the history of last wills and testaments. Without getting too much into the mind-numbing world of common-law litigation, when this old codger kicked it he left behind a poorly spelled handwritten note in crayon and food coloring that granted control of his tribe to his daughters, but also made the Roman emperor a co-ruler of the land as well. Because the Iceni were a client state of Rome, the now-dead king figured he didn't really have much say in the matter in the first place, but with this terrible will he unwittingly gave Rome more power than it already had over his people, and probably gave his attorney an aneurysm in the process.

Well, the Roman emperor at this time was a guy named Nero. For those of you who don't have alarm bells going off in your head when you read that name, Nero is famous for being a complete bastard who assassinated his own mother, executed anyone who disagreed with him, "accidentally" burned Rome to the ground, and was so despised by his own people that he eventually cried himself to death in a hysterical fit of emo self-loathing. Needless to say, this wasn't the sort of self-righteous prick who saw some barbarian random queens as his socio-political equal, and he certainly wasn't about to pass up an opportunity to seize a prime strip of the Britannia countryside from the hands of some uncivilized sheep sodomizers from BFE.

Within days of the chieftain's death, Nero's representative in Britannia, an even more obnoxious human colostomy bag named Decianus Catus, showed up in Iceni lands with a few hundred Roman troops, promptly took the Iceni crown for themselves', stripped the tribe's noblemen of their land, and held pretty much every single person in the realm upside down by their ankles and shook them until the change fell out of their pockets. Nobles and royal family members were enslaved, regular peasants were force-conscripted into the Roman army, the Iceni Queen Boudicca (the wife of the recently-dead king) was publicly whipped for "insolence," and her daughters—the rightful rulers of the tribe—were viciously raped by Roman soldiers.

This, of course, only succeeded in making Queen Boudicca angry. And, as it turns out, you wouldn't like Boudicca when she's angry.

You see, unbeknownst to the Romans, the queen of the Iceni was a hellraising, gore-fanatic, aferocious skull-crushing force of nature capable of unleashing an epic fury-driven murder-rage so unbelievably foul that, according to legend, within days of Decianus Catus's incursion, the people living in nearby Roman cities actually started having wild visions of their impending apocalyptic doom. All across Britannia, horror-movie-grade eyewitness reports started rolling in of some seriously heavy shiz: The ocean waters were turning red with blood. Corpses were washing up on the beach only to disappear when the authorities showed up. Torrents of blood were raining from the sky. Burning houses were allegedly flipped upside down like parked cars after an EPL soccer riot. Totally jacked-up Four Horsemen–Plagues of Egypt stuff going down.

Even if these visions weren't just mass-hysteria hallucinations brought on by reports of Boudicca's limitless desire to personally eat the faces off of every Roman in Britannia, they were pretty good descriptors of what happened next. Shaking with righteous anger, the warrior queen pulled herself together, painted half of her body blue, received the blessing of the badass creepy Stonehenge druids, called her countrymen together, and publicly told them, "Let us show them they are hares and foxes trying to rule over dogs and wolves . . . the gods will grant us the vengeance we deserve."

It was on. Big time.

Amped up on Red Bull and sporting raging killboners (and whatever the girl version of that is), the Iceni men, women, and adolescents went totally Beast Mode and started charging across the countryside taking torches, axes, and chainsaws to every item larger or more valu-

able than a matchbook. The flood of barbarian rage-flesh blitzed into the nearby city of Colchester, mercilessly wiped out the military garrison (the same legionaries who had perpetrated the aforementioned crimes against the Iceni), massacred the entire civilian population of the city without mercy, then waded through knee-deep rivers of gore to set fire to every structure they could find. A handful of quick-thinking Romans took refuge inside the one building in the city that wasn't capable of bursting into flames—the giant stone temple of the god-emperor Claudius—but after the Britons were done destroying the town they simply kicked in the front doors, decapitated everyone inside, pulled the structure apart brick by brick, and then broke the bricks into dust and stuffed them down their pants.

And Boudicca was just getting started. This human mushroom cloud of a woman stood on the charred ashes of Colchester, amid heaps of mutilated burning corpses, delivered a pump-up speech inspiring her bloodlusting warriors to continue execrating their cruel vengeance on the world, then sent her warriors off to put an end to the life functions of every sentient creature they could get their hands on.

According to contemporary sources, the mighty war queen cut an imposing figure—she was tall, strong, and fully committed to the cause, with a harsh, commanding voice that demanded respect and obedience from anyone who heard her (kind of like a sexy Saruman). A fierce-to-death warrior in her own right, Boudicca also personally rode into battle on a badass giant war chariot, carrying a large scrotum-piercing spear and shanking the nuts off of any roadkill that didn't get lodged in the axles of her juggernaut war wagon.

Rome eventually got their junk together, figured out that Boudicca wasn't just going to "get over" the whole public-flogging, daughter-raping thing, and marched a full legion of Rome's toughest warriors out to meet her on the field of battle. The veterans of Legio IX Hispania positioned themselves directly in the path of the Iceni warriors, formed battle lines, and prepared to meet the charge head-on.

The Ninth Legion was slaughtered almost to the last man, merely a speed bump for Boudicca's war chariots as they hauled ass across the ravaged countryside. There isn't even a great description of how the battle went down.

When the lightly armed, undermanned Roman garrisons in Britannia heard that a full-strength Roman legion had just had its face rearranged by a horde of screaming dudes who painted themselves blue and came sprinting out of the woods chucking severed human heads like ninety-mile-an-hour fastballs, they immediately tucked their balls away, dropped their pila, and made a mad dash for the nearest fall-out shelter, giving Boudicca free rein to have her ultraviolent way with the people of Britain. She headed south, to present-day London, which at the time was already a decent-sized city bustling with industry and lucrative trade. She put the entire population to death, finger-painted amateur artwork in their blood, and then immolated London with fires so obscenely hot that the entire city melted into a ten-inch-thick layer of scorched earth that can allegedly still be seen whenever London construction companies dig foundations for large buildings. After this they hit Verulamium, wiping that city off the map forever, then stabbed, burned, crucified, and/or otherwise killed the entire human population as sacrifices to the gods. In just a few months of total war, the warrior queen of the Iceni had annihilated three major cities, refusing to spare a single town, village, estate, farm, or doghouse in between. The death toll of her rampage is believed to be something like seventy thousand people, a number that doesn't even include the five thousand men of the Ninth Legion who were now high-fiving the war god Mars in the afterlife.

At this point everybody realized that things were getting totally out of hand. Unfortunately, there was only one Roman legion left in Britannia—a mere five thousand veteran warriors staring down a teeming, unruly horde of spine-snapping barbarians who had up to this point responded to all opposition by rolling decapitated heads like bowling balls into their formations and then face-kicking the survivors unconscious with fuzzy spiked boots. The legion commander, a grizzled-as-Eastwood hardass known as Gaius Suetonius Paulinus, knew he was the last hope for Roman Britain—if he couldn't stop Boudicca's death march, the Iceni hordes would easily overrun the remaining cities on the island, execute the entire population in even crueler and more un-usual ways, and throw the empire out on its ass. Failure would not be an option.

So, in true badass Roman fashion, Suetonius resolved to make a stand—to solve this way-out-of-control situation in an all-or-nothing deathmatch against impossible odds. And so, outnumbered ten to one by blue dudes with gigantic axes and spears, he drew up a bat-tle line right in front of the Briton horde, hoping to take advantage of their newfound overconfidence by forcing them to fight on a field of the Roman commander's choosing. Suetonius put his men at the top of a hill, flanked by supersteep inclines on either side with a dense for-est covering his back—there would only be one direction from which Boudicca could attack, and the field was small enough that he could block the entire hill while still cycling fresh troops in and out of the fray. Suetonius was certain she wouldn't pass up the opportunity if it presented itself.

Boudicca didn't disappoint. Eager to end the war in one final blood-soaked deathstroke, the utterly-fearless queen marched her entire tribe straight into the valley after Suetonius's tiny yet dedicated force. The Iceni were so confident of their victory that they brought their baggage trains with them to the battlefield, loaded up with the soldiers' families so they could all witness the final destruction of the Roman Empire in Britain firsthand. Eighty thousand beefy barbarians rushed straight on into a solid wall of five thousand Roman tower shields. When they got close enough, they threw human heads. The Romans threw javelins back.

The javelins were slightly more effective.

Disoriented by a whistling volley of polished javelins impaling their bravest warriors, the Iceni charge faltered somewhat, and, their tower shields raised and braced, the Roman lines somehow withstood the tremendous crush of Briton fury. Suetonius's disciplined veterans frantically stabbed out between their shields with their short swords in a shank-tastic frenzy of groin stabs, cutting down the Britons while they struggled to swing their oversized weapons in such tight quarters. The Briton charge stalled, then broke, and before long it was the Romans who were pushing their adversaries backward—straight into the baggage train they'd brought along with them. Suetonius ordered a full-on charge, unleashed his cavalry, and chomped through them like a fat kid obliterating an oversized handful of cotton candy at the county fair as the Iceni desperately struggled to flee the field. Boudicca herself managed to fight her way out through the carnage, but when the smoke cleared she was left with only about a quarter of her once-mighty force. Seeing her triumphant army now horribly mutilated, she chugged some poisonous Jell-O shots and died. For her efforts in boldly defying Rome to her last breath and leading her people to glorious (if only temporary) victories against their hated enemies, Boudicca's people gave their queen a hero's burial, entombing her with a hoard of royal gold that to this day has never been found. Nowadays there's an appropriately epic statue of her standing near the Parliament buildings in London (you know, the city she burned to the ground), and she's also got about a half-dozen British navy warships named after her.

Another famous warrior queen who led a successful rebellion against Rome was the Arab ruler Zenobia. In the third century, this steel-skinned warrior took command of the mighty Syrian Palmyrene Empire, and her armies promptly swept across the Middle East, captured a swath of land that stretched from Turkey to Egypt, and then defeated and beheaded the Roman governor when he tried to tell her to knock it off. After a valiant struggle against the Roman Empire she was eventually defeated, captured, and brought back to Rome in a fashionable-looking set of golden chains. There are two wildly different accounts of what happened to the deposed empress—she either starved herself to death in captivity or lived a life of luxury, married a Roman senator, and became a prominent philosopher and writer. Since nobody knows the truth, please feel free to believe whichever one makes you feel better about yourself.

After the war, Suetonius wasn't really ready to let this whole situation die down. This guy had witnessed the Iceni massacres firsthand, visiting many of the cities shortly after their demolition, and he was itching to go forth and do unto others as they had done unto him. But Nero, in a rare display of nondetestable behavior, decided that maybe massacring everybody all the time wasn't the best answer, so he replaced Suetonius with a pacifist who was a little more into negotiating and a little less into beheading everyone and then setting the severed heads on fire. The massacres in Britannia ended, peace was restored, and everybody involved in this whole thing ended up winning and losing at the same time.

THE TRUNG SISTERS

My wish is to ride the wind and tame the waves, slay the sharks of the open sea, drive out the oppressors, and save the people from drowning. Why should I imitate others, bow my head, stoop over and be a slave?

—TRIEU THI TRINH, THIRD-CENTURY VIETNAMESE WARRIOR QUEEN

Raised to hate their domineering Chinese overlords, the aristocratic Trung sisters of Vietnam were finally pushed too far in the year AD 39, when the pipe-smokin' local Chinese magistrate had one of the sisters' husbands arrested as a traitor, tortured excessively, and then subsequently beheaded. These two charismatic, confrontational-as-hell twin sisters immediately grabbed their swords, impaled the magistrate's head on a pike, and organized a coordinated Vietnam-wide rebellion against imperial China. Riding into battle on top of massive war elephants, the Trung sisters amassed an army of eighty thousand warriors so devoted to kicking the teeth out of the Chinese that there are even stories of vastly pregnant women charging into battle, perforating the faces of their enemies, taking a break to give birth on the battlefield, strapping their newborns to their backs, and running right back into combat with their children carrying adorable little baby weapons. All across Vietnam, nobles and peasants alike took arms against the emperor, and after a series of bloody battles, the victorious Vietnamese people surfed the corpses of their vanquished enemies all the way back to China on an ocean of blood (note: This was back when Charlie still surfed). The Chinese were ousted, and the sisters ruled a liberated Vietnam as joint queens for the next two years. They abolished oppressive Chinese laws, reinstated the old Viet ways, and set up a system of sixty-five defensive fortresses and outposts, and the land of Vietnam enjoyed total autonomy for the first time in over 150 years.

Of course, eventually the Chinese returned looking for vengeance, and this time they sent a pitiless general named Ma Yuan (one of the few generals in Chinese history not to be known for his chicken dishes) to crush this uprising once and for all. As if it wasn't enough that this experienced, barbarian-smiting war hero commanded a near-limitless army that had been forged in countless battles against Mongolian tribes, legend has it that Ma Yuan's soldiers also ran into battle obscenely butt naked, which understandably kind of freaked out the Vietnamese a little—apparently the ungodly sight of full frontal nudity flopping all over the place threw off their concentration a little. Despite the odds being stacked overwhelmingly against them, the Trung sisters fought valiantly but were ultimately unable to hold back the Chinese penile onslaught. They were defeated in AD 43 and, seeking to avoid capture, the twins killed themselves by jumping into the Red River. The stories of the Trungs' guerrilla tactics lived on for millennia after their deaths, to the point where their history and tactics were required reading for North Vietnamese army commanders fighting against French and American forces in the twentieth century. The anniversary of their deaths remains a national holiday in Vietnam to this day.

7

RED CLIFF

The Battle of Chi Bi
Hubei Province, China
Winter, AD 208

If your enemy is secure at all points, be prepared for him.
If he is in superior strength, evade him.
If your opponent is temperamental, seek to irritate him.
Pretend to be weak, that he may grow arrogant . . .
Attack him where he is unprepared, appear where you are not expected.

—SUN TZU, *THE ART OF WAR*

BY THE THIRD CENTURY AD, THE ONCE-GLORIOUS HAN EM-
PIRE OF CHINA WAS COLLAPSING—A HOLLOW, CANDY-COATED
SHELL OF ITS FORMER GREATNESS. Sure, the emperor was still
hanging around being all imperial, wearing fancy clothes and nailing
concubines and stuff, but for the most part the people's loyalty was now
divided between two powerful regional warlords—the laid-back Liu Bei
and his former frenemy, the moderately more intense Cao Cao. Liu Bei
was an easygoing nobleman who appreciated fine art, knew the value

of a good 'stache, and enjoyed twangy music, gardening, finely brewed tea, and other hipster garbage. Cao Cao was a man who was constantly frothing at the mouth with pure rabid military genius, and thought, Sure, art is cool and all, but I'd much rather be standing alone on a battlefield pulling my sword out of a gigantic pile of flaming corpses than sipping merlot while sitting on IKEA furniture in a crowded art gallery trying to figure out if this eight-and-a-half-by-eleven canvas counts as postmodern expressionism or if it has French impressionist tendencies. Liu Bei had the support of the peasants and a trace of imperial blood in his veins. Cao Cao had near-limitless military power.

Power won.

Using nothing more than the sheer force of his unstoppable will (and a few hundred thousand men armed with spears, swords, firebombs, and crossbows), Cao Cao crushed all who opposed him, sweeping China's most menacing warlords off the map with a no-nonsense combination of military genius, tactical acumen, and a strategy that involved pummeling his enemies to death by ballknocking entire enemy divisions into smoking craters with his giant evil platinum-plated testes. The Grand Warlord of China unified all the provinces north of the Yangtze River under the banner of imperial power, driving Liu Bei out of town in the process and setting up a series of megalomaniacal monuments to himself that would remind all future generations that Cao Cao was truly the baddest mofo low down 'round this town. Then, realizing that he was so awesome that not even the emperor could stand against him, Cao Cao moved on the imperial capital, seized the throne, and forced the captive emperor to declare him prime minister of China (Cao Cao was wise enough to realize he couldn't declare himself emperor without stirring up a metric crap-ton of trouble he didn't need). In his first act as prime minister, Cao Cao declared Liu Bei an outlaw and had the emperor rubber-stamp a document authorizing him to go kick Liu's molars out his rectum, decapitate all of his friends, and steal all of the kingdom's hottest women for himself.

Cao Cao marched south, burno-urinating on everything along the way in a mighty spectacle of imperial military might. When Liu Bei heard that Cao Cao was storming south, he evacuated over one hundred thousand peasants and civilians from his capital city, personally escorting them south to safety and refusing to abandon his people to Cao Cao's swords and torches just to save his own life. Unfortunately, Liu Bei was so caught up in the whole "Don't let Cao Cao flame-smash my entire civilization" thing that he stupidly fell into the whole "Whoops, I left my wife and son back in the capital" thing in the process (he was cool, but ditzy), but luckily for the absent-minded warlord a badass military asswhipper named Zhao Yun rode full-speed back to the capital, cut his way through Cao Cao's legions in an epic display of one-man spear-slinging Jet Li–style belligerence, rescued Liu's family, and then cleaved his way back through the enemy with the wife and kid riding shotgun on his horse.

Correctly realizing that by torching Liu Bei's capital he was only Kevorkian-ing out a small fraction of his hated rival's dinks, Cao Cao pressed onward. Liu Bei, homeless and marked for a violent torture-related death he almost certainly would not find enjoyable, crossed the Yangtze River and headed south. His rearguard action was carried out by a terrifying behemoth known as Zhang Fei, a dude so baller that in the movie about his life he shoulder-checks a horse to the ground, and nobody complained about historical inaccuracy. According to legend, Zhang Fei stood on the bridge alone, carrying a huge bladed halberd, and Cao Cao's men took one look at this guy and decided, Hell no, I don't want any part of anything this nutcase has to offer. Then, when it looked like nothing was actually going to happen, Zhang Fei stared out through the souls of the entire enemy army and abruptly yelled something like "WTF?!" and one of Cao Cao's guys got scared and died right there. The rest of the army fled, and, needless to say, the refugees had enough time to cross the river to safety. I'm not sure how true that story is, but I love it anyways.

While the north was now firmly in Cao Cao's iron kung fu grip, the region south of the Yangtze River was occupied by the peaceful, quiet, slightly effeminate kingdom of Wu. With no real options to speak of and nothing even remotely resembling a military force capable of standing against Cao Cao, Liu Bei dispatched his chief advisor, a brilliant military strategist named Zhuge Liang, to see if the Wu would be interested in joining a war against the most vindictive military badass in China—a dude who, oh yeah, just happened to be headed their way with a force of something like eight hundred thousand soldiers.

They weren't.

It wasn't until Cao Cao started building the largest fleet in Chinese history and preparing for a full crossing of the Yangtze River that the kingdom of Wu finally realized that an alliance with perpetual-loser sad sack Liu Bei was the only possible chance they had of not getting their skulls turned into bongo drums in Cao Cao's court. That, combined with Zhuge Liang successfully convincing the king of Wu that Cao Cao was going to pork his favorite wife and then take her back to the imperial capital with him, finally got the Wu off their asses to mobilize for war.

Of course, this was still only a small consolation—between the twenty thousand soldiers limping along with Liu Bei and the thirty thousand men Wu was capable of fielding, the newfound allies were still outnumbered approximately sixteen to one by a force that had just spent the previous decade dismantling the most invincible armies in China. But all was not lost. Cao Cao's men were from the desertlike lands of the north, unused to the tropical climate of southern China, and they'd sure as hell never fought on boats before. Within days of

pushing off on their immense naval expedition, Cao Cao's men started suffering from typhoid fever and extreme crippling seasickness, two things that can totally ruin your day no matter how many buffalo you can bench-press at a time or how many military victories you've managed to fight through. Meanwhile, the top Wu general was a dude who once used to be a notorious pirate leader, and in a daring attack his former pirate crew defeated the squadrons in Cao Cao's vanguard, forcing the prime minister to anchor his voluminously barfing troops across the Yangtze River from the allied base, at a place known as Chi Bi, or Red Cliff.

This was only a minor setback, though, and now Cao Cao was staring across the third largest river on Earth at a pathetically tiny allied fleet that was about as threatening to him as a taxidermied housecat carrying a chainsaw made out of pipe cleaners. His first order of business was to have all of his ships locked together with heavy chains: with all of his men barfing their faces off like idiots and his entire fleet looking like Sorority Row on New Year's Day, he couldn't coordinate a damn thing, and clamping the ships together went a long way to alleviate the seasickness. Then, with the wind blowing toward the enemy fleet, Cao Cao came up with a diabolical means of dispatching his hated enemy Liu Bei and his stupid newfound friends—he would burn the hell out of them with a fiery maelstrom so righteous that it would make Slayer want to write a song about it. He ordered his men to load their ships up with brimstone, oil, firebombs, hair spray, torches, and tons of matches and lighter fluid (or whatever they used for lighter fluid back then), and decreed that the next morning he would ram a fistful of fireballs up the allied tailpipes like a wizard until the entire allied fleet had been melted into a solid ball of congealed failure. Then he'd probably harness all of the Wu king's concubines to a chariot and have them pull him back to his capital.

Cao Cao's plan could not have backfired worse if it had been an overly-elaborate scene in some contrived Hollywood blockbuster. You see, it turned out our homeboy Zhuge Liang was an amateur meteorologist, and this hyperintense Chinese Jim Cantore knew that during the night the winds were going to shift and start blowing toward Cao Cao's fleet. So Zhuge Liang diabolically decided to use the invader's own trick against him. Staring down a fleet that stretched out to either horizon, the allies did the last thing Cao Cao expected.

They attacked.

Appropriately commanded by a dude named Huang Gai (which I

assume to be pronounced "Hung Guy"), an intrepid assault squadron of twenty ships charged straight into the enemy force in the middle of the night, blitzing through a storm of arrows in a desperate suicide attack. Seconds before plowing the Cao Cao's parked vessels at full-on ludicrous speed, the crewmen ignited hundreds of bales of hay and oil on the deck, turning their ships into giant mobile crew-served Molotov cocktails in one of the most balls-out naval fire attacks ever launched. The flaming allied ships crashed into the fleet, and, if that's not enough, some of the crazy bastards on board decided not to abandon their burning ships, but instead rushed onto the enemy ships and hurled homemade firebombs right into the faces of the first assholes they could find. Cao Cao's front lines caught fire, and the shifting winds kicked up and blew the inferno toward the rest of the fleet, whose crews, in their panic regarding the hurricane of fiery death rapidly coming their way, failed to unhook their boats fast enough.

It didn't take long for the fire spread to the brimstone stores that Cao Cao's ships had intended to use against Liu Bei. If this isn't the origin of the word "backfire," it epitomizes it nonetheless.

The entire thing went up like a Chinese New Year's celebration at Ted Kaczynski's house, and from that point on all hell broke loose. The main allied fleet charged and liquified the inexperienced, stabbing the crap out of the overly crispified sailors of Cao Cao's fleet as they just stood there burning to death like morons. Seeing his entire fleet literally going up in flames before his eyes, Cao Cao ordered a full retreat, but even this was a damn disaster as well. Rainstorms earlier in the week had turned the dirt roads into muddy sludge, and the only way to get the cavalry through the muck was to clear out the hospitals and have a bunch of sick, wounded, and exhausted footsoldiers carry grass and lay it down to cover the mud so the horses could run across. The hardworking, half-dead peasant soldiers were rewarded for their diligence by being trampled by the cavalry they were helping, and those that didn't die of tramplization or illness were simply abandoned to be disemboweled by the pursuing allied forces.

Cao Cao's army was melted into charcoal and gristle at almost the exact moment it had complete victory in its grasp. It would take the prime minister decades to rebuild. He'd had his chance to grab ultimate power once and for all, but thanks to the quick thinking of Zhuge Liang and a heaping dose of gasoline-fueled fire, from this point on power in China would be almost equally divided between Cao Cao, Liu Bei, and the kingdom of Wu. Their seventy-year war for supremacy—known as the Three Kingdoms era—is to this day one of the most popular and romanticized periods of Chinese history.

Even though he got his ass handed to him on a fire-drenched silver platter at Chi Bi, Cao Cao would eventually get the last laugh. Liu Bei unsurprisingly ended up battling his former allies in the Wu kingdom, giving Cao Cao time to regroup, and Cao's successors would end up uniting all of China and formally installing the Jin Dynasty in AD 280. The Jin would lead China into a glorious period of severe economic recession and internal turmoil and would rule for just ten years before the country splintered into civil war again.

The English faced a similar situation to that of the allied fleet at Chi Bi when they stared down the vaunted Spanish Armada in May of 1588—a massive fleet of 122 warships and nineteen thousand men attacking from the richest kingdom and the largest navy in the world, all rolling through the deep on a mission to fist-bump a knuckle sandwich of Catholicism down the throats of those uppity Protestant English bastards. Queen Elizabeth's hopelessly outdated coastal defenses couldn't possibly be expected to deal with an assault of that magnitude, so she dispatched her own Hung Guy—infamous privateer turned admiral Sir Francis Drake—to launch a preemptive strike. Drake sent a squadron of his own fire ships across the Channel, plowing into the Armada while it was in port off the coast of Calais, France, smashing it into firewood before their ill-fated attack even got started. The fireboats sunk or burned several Spanish ships and sent the rest of the Armada fleeing north in disarray, where they ran into a huge storm—those vessels that weren't sunk or blown off course into unfriendly waters filled with rocks and pirates and Irishmen immediately bolted and ran back home to Spain without so much as coming into visual contact with the English coast.

The *c* in "Cao Cao" (as in all Chinese pinyin) is pronounced *ts*. Sure, this is unnecessarily confusing and kind of annoying, but it's important when you want to talk about Cao Cao's son, the unfortunately named Cao Pi.

8

AD DECIMUM

The Vandal War
August–December, AD 533
Carthage, North Africa

Fellow soldiers, the decisive moment of the struggle is already at hand. Our hope of safety lies in the strength of our hands. There is not a friendly city, nor any other stronghold, in which we may put our trust. But if we know ourselves brave men, it is probable that we shall still overcome the enemy in the war. If we should weaken at all, it will remain for us to fall under the hand of the Vandals and be destroyed disgracefully. I pray that each one of you, calling to mind his own valor and those whom he has left at home, may so march with contempt against the enemy.

—BELISARIUS, BYZANTINE GENERAL

THE LATER YEARS OF THE ROMAN EMPIRE ARE CHARACTER-IZED BY THE ETERNAL CITY BEING CONQUERED PRETTY MUCH EVERY OTHER WEEKEND BY SOME RANDOM TRIBE OF MULLET-HEADED, WALLET-CHAIN-WEARING HEADBANGERS WHO LOOKED LIKE THEY'D JUST RODE OUT OF A MEGADETH CONCERT IN A TURBOCHARGED LATE-80S MODEL CAMARO Z28. Between the Vandals, Goths, Avars, Lombards, Visigoths, Ostrogoths, Megagoths, Ultragoths, and Super-Mechagoths Digitally Remastered Special Edition, this city was getting sacked more than David Carr if he had the munchkins from *The Wizard of Oz* as his starting offensive line, to the point where the citizens of Rome eventually found it more annoying than anything else.

In 455 it was the Vandals' turn to make their way through Rome, plundering the city so hard that to this day the word "vandalize" is synonymous with spray-painting giant ejaculating-penis graffiti all over the charred-out remains of a structure you've just trashed and burned into charcoal. The Vandals decided not to stick around after smashing the place into glitterdust, however, and a few years later they sailed their horde across the Mediterranean and settled in North Africa, making their new base in the now-rebuilt city of Carthage. Over the years the once-uncivilized Vandal nomads became somewhat more civilized in terms of not massacring everyone around them in a firestorm of blood and steel, and things were going fine right up until the year 530, when a Vandal dude named Gelimer bypassed the lawful succession rules for Vandal kings with some cunning, subtle political maneuvering that more or less amounted to imprisoning the rightful heir to the throne, executing him, then murdering his immediate family, his servants, his administrators, his closest advisors, and all of his pets.

It's bad enough that the recently massacred-beyond-recognition ex-king was Gelimer's cousin, but even worse than the awkward family reunions is that this move really chapped the ass of the Byzantine emperor Justinian—a guy who was not only a personal friend of the now-dismembered king, but a guy who also had a gigantic hard-on for reassembling the Roman Empire under Greek rule. Justinian knew Carthage was the perfect jumping-off point for coordinating a full-scale invasion of barbarian-controlled Italy, and he'd really just been looking for one good excuse to march his army in there and start busting faces in the first place, so when he heard what was going down in Vandal town, he immediately pledged his full support and deployed a guy named Belisarius to deal with the situation.

Born in Thrace (present-day Bulgaria) around AD 500, Belisarius was a humorless, barbarian-quelling face obliterator who undertook a meteoric career path that was unprecedented in the nepotism-happy culture of the Byzantine Empire, rising from nameless enlisted peasant jobber footsoldier to decorated officer in the Imperial Guard, then to overall commander of the Eastern Roman Army, then to the sort of over-the-top tactical genius who makes hardcore military historians pop a boner faster than Olivia Wilde sitting topless in the cupola of a Tiger tank. But despite the fact that this tack-eating skull masher was pretty much the only dude in the Byzantine army who knew what the hell was going on (except when it came to his wife, who was so out-of-control skanky that she apparently has an entire volume of ancient Greek literature devoted to her sexual adventures), his Justin Bieber–scale popularity among the adoring masses of Byzantium made the emperor a little uncomfortable, so Justinian usually went out of his way to screw with Belisarius whenever possible. Usually what this meant was that Justinian would give his general the toughest and most impossible missions available, but then make sure the dude never had enough soldiers under his command to raise a formal revolt against the emperor. If Belisarius succeeded and somehow pulled out an impossible victory, great. If he died, oh well.

So that's why, in 533, General Belisarius was recalled from the war he was in the middle of winning against Persia, given a crappy little fleet of transport ships and fifteen thousand highly unreliable mercenary muppets, and ordered to conquer the entire Vandal Empire with a group of men who were just as likely to stab him in the back as they were to follow orders. Sure thing, boss. I'll get right on that. Belisarius went ashore in August 533, landing his men 140 miles from Carthage, and began marching toward the Vandal capital.

When King Gelimer heard that the Byzantines had landed in North Africa, he immediately proceeded to urinate uncontrollably and with incredible volume. Then when he heard how idiotically small the invasion force was, he laughed his ass off, changed his armor, and prepared to launch an all-out attack determined to dismember Belisarius's nutsack and drop-kick his sorry butt into the ocean. He assembled fifty thousand warriors, divided them into three groups, and then positioned them so they could gangbang Belisarius's column from three sides at once.

For most people this would mean big-time trouble, but, as you will see, Belisarius wasn't most people. Look at it this way: this is a guy who once put down an out-of-control Constantinople sports riot by marching his troops into the Hippodrome (the Byzantine Empire's version of Yankee Stadium) and massacring thirty-five thousand drunk hooligans in a single afternoon. He's a guy who was always outnumbered, never had support or reinforcements, and didn't have a problem utilizing excessive force any time he felt the situation required it. He was a no-bullcrap asswhipper, and he just wasn't impressed just because he was outnumbered five to one and completely surrounded by a bioengineered horde of semiorganized Vandals rapidly closing in on him from every direction. Before the Battle of Ad Decimum, ten miles from the gates of Carthage, he simply called his men together, told them that he'd fought his way out of situations worse than this in his sleep, and said, "As for the host of Vandals, let no one of you consider them. For not by numbers of men, nor by measure of body, but by valor of soul is war wont to be decided."

Luckily for Belisarius, Gelimer cocked up the timing of his attacks. The first wave of his forces came early in the day, when the garrison of Carthage, commanded by Gelimer's brother Ammatas, rode south in a high-octane death charge straight into the front of the Byzantine column, completely unaware that the rest of Gelimer's army was still brushing their teeth and was nowhere near the battlefield. Ammatas's men charged sword-first into a vanguard of three hundred Byzantine horsemen under the command of a lights-out cataclysmic knight named John the Armenian—a double-edged serrated codpiece-kicker who wasn't in the mood to play around. Ammatas acquitted himself nicely in the initial charge, blasting straight into the heart of the Greek formation, sword at the ready, personally cutting down twelve of John's best warriors by himself, but when that dude finally got his throat cut out by a Byzantine blade, dying in a badass blaze of glory, his men immediately sucked their testicles up into their body cavities and bolted out of there. The entire Vandal assault force immediately turned and hightailed it for the safety of the Carthaginian walls, and John the Armenian Asskicker chased them all the way into the city, cutting them down by the dozens in a ten-mile cavalry death charge so over-the-top violent that when Belisarius came down the road later in the day he remarked that it looked like an army of ten thousand had ripped through there—not a mere three hundred pissed-off horseback-riding Orthodox Christians with an overhyped sense of personal vengeance and a finely tuned taste for human blood.

The second Vandal attack came from the west an hour or so later, when two thousand of the Vandal Empire's greatest horsemen came flying in, seemingly out of nowhere, riding hard in an effort to drive a blood-soaked wedge straight into the soft fleshy flank of the Byzantine army. This would have been trouble if Belisarius hadn't already expected something along these lines—instead of sneak-attacking the flank and making mincemeat of the Byzantine warriors, these hard-charging warriors instead ran into Belisarius's cavalry screen, which, oh yeah, just so happened to be made up of six hundred mercenary Huns and Iranians that the Byzantine general had wisely recruited just before he'd left Constantinople. And, quite honestly, the Huns were a group of people who *really* didn't like being sneak-attacked in the flank.

It's worth noting here that the Vandals didn't wear any armor, and that they fought with some bizarre misguided sense of honor that meant that all of their warriors carried only swords and didn't go into combat with anything resembling a ranged weapon. The Huns had no such hang-ups when it came to impaling your enemies with flying death from a long-ass ways away—these guys rode horses as well as anyone in the world, and they also carried badass composite reflex bows that could punch through two inches of solid wood at a hundred yards. After a brief engagement that involved a hugely unruly long-haired horde of sword-swinging maniacs riding straight on into a solid wall of arrow-heads and subsequently dying painfully and ungracefully, the Vandals bolted and ran the hell out of there at top speed (because their sense of honor did not also apparently look down upon fleeing like cowards in the face of hardship), pursued by an army of fired-up Khal Drogo look-alikes catapulting toward them like Angry Birds.

The third, final, and by far the largest Vandal attack took place toward the end of the day, led by King Gelimer himself. Gelimer's plan was to drive his troops between John the Armenian's vanguard (which by this point had already blitzed through the gates of Carthage and was now chilling out with a cold beer) and Belisarius's main force. Thanks in no small part to his overwhelming numerical advantage, Gelimer's initial attack struck home, crashing hard into the front lines and throwing the Byzantines into chaos. With the battle outcome in question, Belisarius's already-questionable mercenary footsoldiers punked out and fell into complete disarray, most of them dropping their gear and running for their lives like schoolgirls playing Red Rover as the Vandals rushed after them. Belisarius desperately tried to regroup his troops, demanding they stand and fight with honor rather than wimping out on him like dickheads, but luckily for him, just as Gelimer was pursuing the Byzantine army and things were looking bleak, the Vandals came across the total unholy devastation John the Armenian had laid on them earlier in the day. Gelimer became distraught over seeing his brother's corpse, his men lost their nerve at seeing their commanding officer acting like a wussbag, and, despite being outnumbered something like five to one, Belisarius managed to regroup and launch a steel-toed counterattack that not only stopped Gelimer's assault, but smashed his horde and sent them running from the field. The Byzantines sauntered into Carthage and Belisarius threatened any man who looted the city with violent public death.

But Gelimer wasn't done yet. The king of the Vandals spent the next four months seething with rage, plotting his revenge, and desperately trying to convince his troops that he wasn't actually a huge crybaby (note: he was). Eventually Gelimer recalled his brother Zano—a legitimately badass war hero who had just completed the conquest of Sardinia—and the two of them assembled a group of almost a hundred thousand Vandal warriors eager to retake Carthage. When Belisarius heard what was going down, he got a little nervous about having his fifteen thousand men stuck inside a foreign city while a group ten times their size starved them out and hammered them with catapults, and this anxiety got even worse when he also heard that Gelimer had been so damned impressed by the Huns in the previous battle that he was now offering them a huge bribe to betray Belisarius and attack the Greeks during the upcoming battle. The wily Byzantine general doubled Gelimer's offer, temporarily buying the Huns' loyalty back, although at this point he knew these guys were going to end up helping out whoever looked like they were going to stay alive long enough to actually pay them. So, with his forces' loyalty in question and time not on his side, Belisarius knew he had to act. What he did was totally bananas. He took five thousand trustworthy horsemen and rode out to face the entire Vandal army—a hundred thousand men—by himself.

The two forces met in the rocky desert landscape at a place called Tricamerum, a Roman name meaning "Three Camerons" (presumably after Kirk Cameron, Candace Cameron, and Cameron Diaz). The Vandal forces stretched as far as the eye could see in either direction— infantry on either flank, and Zano, Gelimer, and the Vandal cavalry in the center. The Greeks were just a handful of brave warriors— Belisarius, John the Armenian, the Huns, and Belisarius's personal bodyguard of Byzantine heavy cavalrymen known as cataphracts— standing alone in a desperate attempt to prevent Carthage from falling under siege. As you might expect, Belisarius had a plan—this guy remembered how the sight of the dead prince and slaughtered horsemen had really screwed up the Vandals at Ad Decimum, and he was going to try for a repeat performance.

So on the field of Tricamerum, with the entire Vandal army before them, John the Armenian, Belisarius, the Huns, and forty-five hundred other horsemen led a mighty, straight-on cavalry charge into the dead center of the enemy line. Three times they were repulsed after intense fighting, the Huns firing arrows from the saddle to cover the Byzantines' retreat. On the fourth charge, Gelimer's brother Zano fell valiantly in combat, surrounded by the bodies of his enemies, and when King Gelimer saw his other brother's headless corpse fall lifelessly to the ground with a sick thud, he totally pissed his pants again and immediately rode the hell out of there as fast as his steed would carry him. The Vandal army saw their king's banner in flight, driven off by a mere handful of warriors, and they understandably lost all faith in their total moron of a commander. The entire Vandal force packed it in and went home, hanging their heads in shame for their pathetic leadership. The Greeks pursued, cutting them down, whacking guys' heads off by the dozen, and then capturing the Vandal baggage train and making off with vast amounts of royal loot that included everything from the king's crown to the king's daughters. The Vandal Empire dissolved under the weight of Gelimer's idiocy, the territory fell under the rapidly expanding dominion of the Eastern Roman Empire, and Belisarius returned home as the greatest hero his people had ever seen. The huge-ass party that was thrown in his honor would be last official triumph ever given by the Roman Empire.

Remember how I said the emperor hated Belisarius? Well, after receiving his triumph, Belisarius was immediately demoted, and some other jackass was ordered to command the invasion of Italy. When that guy screwed it up beyond all recognition, Belisarius rode in, conquered Sicily, marched into Rome without a fight, defended it from an overwhelming horde of barbarian warriors, then conquered all of Italy from the Goths, impressing them so hard with his badass prowess that the Goths actually offered to make him emperor of the Western Roman Empire (he declined and killed them all instead). After a thirty-year career kicking ass from Persia to Italy, Belisarius retired to a quiet life in Constantinople. He was subsequently called out of retirement twice—once to conquer Spain from the Visigoths, and once to successfully defend the walls of Constantinople from a rampaging army of Bulgar warriors who outnumbered the Greek defenders seven to one. He was then demoted again, lived a life of extreme poverty, died in obscurity, and nowadays nobody's ever heard of him.

SECTION II

MEDIEVAL CARNAGE

*In the face of these dangers to the Fatherland, I fail to eat during the day
and to sleep at night. Tears roll down my cheeks and my heart bleeds
as if it were being cut to shreds. I tremble with anger because I cannot
eat our enemy's flesh, lie down in his skin, chew up his liver,
and drink his blood. I would gladly surrender my life a thousand times
on the field of battle if I could do these things.*

—Trần Hung Đạo, thirteenth-century Vietnamese commander

9

The Last Caliph

The Final Battle for al-Andalus
Carmona, Spain
AD 763

*Let us throw our scabbards into the flame and swear to fall like
soldiers if victory cannot be ours. We conquer or die.*

—ABD AL-RAHMAN, LAST PRINCE OF THE UMAYYAD DYNASTY

FROM THE SAFETY OF THE IMPREGNABLE CASTLE GATES OF
THEIR FORTRESS CITY, HIGH ABOVE THE WAR-TORN SPAN-
ISH PLAINS, THE BELEAGUERED DEFENDERS OF THE MOUNTAIN
STRONGHOLD OF CARMONA STARED DOWN AT THE VAST SEA OF
WARRIORS THAT HAS BEEN BESIEGING THEM FOR MONTHS.

Just as some of his men may have begun to doubt why the hell they
decided to follow a twenty-six-year-old prince in an act of treason
against the caliph, 'Abd al-Rahman ibn Mu'awiya ibn Hisham, the Falcon of al-Andalus, started a totally sweet bonfire just inside the castle
gates. The young warrior slowly drew his scimitar—an ordinary blade
that didn't in any way reflect his royal standing—held it above his head,
and defiantly threw the scabbard into the burning fire. The meaning

was obvious: he had no intention of sheathing his blade again. Either this would be the prince's final battle, or he'd stick his sword so far up his enemies' asses that it would get too bent out of shape to fit back into its sheath.

His seven hundred most trusted horsemen silently followed suit. The fate of al-Andalus was about to hinge on one final suicide charge against impossible odds, with the course of Spanish history hanging in the balance.

Although he was still just a young buck, Prince Abd al-Rahman had been through more bullcrap in the past six years than most people see in their entire lives. He was the last scion of the once-mighty Umayyid Dynasty, and his journey from the lavish, babe-filled harems and be-dazzled palaces of Damascus to the appendage-strewn, blood-slicked battlefields of Andalusian Spain was an odyssey worthy of the most epic poetry and the fieriest guitar solos ever recorded.

It started in the year 750, when Abd al-Rahman's grandfather, the caliph (the supreme ruler of the Islamic world), faced a deadly new challenger—a vicious deathmonger known as Abu al-Abbas the Blood-letter, a dude with an axe to grind into the face of the ninety-year-old Umayyid Dynasty and a few hundred thousand friends to help him do it. Al-Abbas and his fanatically loyal followers, known as the Abba-sids, rose in rebellion against the Umayyids, steamrolled the caliph's army on the battlefield, sacked his capital, and went on a destruct-o-matic rampage that involved the almost complete annihilation of the Umayyid royal family—a bloodbath that involved not just slaughtering every living member of the family, but one that went so far as to dig up the royal tombs, desecrate and torch the corpses of the already-dead Umayyid ancestors, scatter their ashes to the winds, then rewrite the history books to describe the entire family line as "an inept clown car of goat-humping doofuses who ate their own poop."

Prince Abd al-Rahman was living in a quiet little oasis town just east of Damascus when most of this heinous crap went down. The twenty-year-old grandson of the caliph was a decent ways down in the line of succession, and this guy was just chilling outside with his wife and his four-year-old son (yeah, he probably impregnated her when he was fifteen—it's good to be the prince), having a picnic by a swimming pool or something equally idyllic/lame, when suddenly he heard a bunch of bloodcurdling screaming coming from the town at the bottom of the hill. When he ran to investigate, what he saw struck icy fear in his heart—the black banners of the Bloodletter were fluttering through the town. Abbasid horsemen were hacking their way through the populace, blitzing toward Abd al-Rahman's palace on a single-minded quest to deliver the prince a singing telegram from Mister Face-Stab.

The prince did the first thing you'd expect—hide your kids, hide your wife—and then he, his thirteen-year-old brother, and his man-servant Badr (basically an African-born version of Race Bannon, only without all the pterodactyl-punching) made a break for it. Running for his life, the prince narrowly escaped the Bloodletter's horsemen by diving into the mighty Euphrates River and swimming across, but his young brother wasn't so lucky. Struggling against the current, the teenager looked back and saw the Bloodletter's men holding out their arms begging the young prince to swim back. They promised that if he came back, they wouldn't decapitate him on the banks of the river, kick his body into the water, and parade his severed head around the city in triumph. They lied.

Powerless to help his brother, Abd al-Rahman ran. For the next five years, the lone survivor of the Umayyid royal family fled without money, soldiers, a horse, or any friends other than Badr. With roughly every person in the Islamic world trying to kill him, this eighth-century Salman Rushdie fled through Palestine, Syria, Arabia, Egypt, Libya, and Morocco, avoiding government assassins, the tireless soldiers of the Bloodletter, and dozens of cunning bounty hunters, always shooting first when the opportunity presented itself despite what revisionist Special Editions may suggest.

After biding his time and living in the middle of the damn Sahara Desert with a tribe of Berbers, Abd al-Rahman crossed the Strait of Gibraltar into Muslim-controlled Spain (known as al-Andalus) in August of 755 with one thought on his mind—avenge the destruction of his ninja clan, beat the holy Shi'ite out of anyone who stood in the way of his rightful place as the ruler of the Islamic world, and make sure all who opposed him choked to death on his engorged badassitude. Crossing the strait with just three hundred loyal men, the man known as *al-Dakhil* ("The Immigrant") drove his ships to new lands, rallied support, marched on Cordoba, and drop-kicked the Abbasid-appointed emir of Spain into the Mediterranean (well, his torso at least . . . his head stayed behind, nailed to a post on the walls of the city).

Victory had been short-lived. When the newly crowned caliph, Abu al-Abbas the Bloodletter, received word that the rightful heir to the Umayyid throne was now chillin' like a villain in al-Andalus ruling as the emir of Spain, he almost had a damned apoplexy (whatever that is) and started shrieking at his men like Skeletor ordering the destruction of Eternia from his bitchin' skull throne. He immediately bit a chunk out of a gold-plated goblet, called a couple of his chief advisors "boobs" and "nincompoops," and then dispatched the full might of his army to finish the job they'd started outside Damascus. His men crossed the Strait, surrounded Cordoba, and besieged the prince in his new capital.

And so, surrounded, under siege in his fortress, out of options, out of food, and with nothing left to lose, Abd al-Rahman took the one course that was left for him—charge a handful of irate horsemen balls-out down this mountain and take as many of those bastards with him as possible. Undeterred by something as insignificant as being completely encircled by a well-equipped force that outnumbered his defenders many times over, he defiantly gathered the seven hundred most badass, bone-crunching horsemen under his command. His force included stalwart warriors who had flocked to him from across the lands of Islam—Arabs from Yemen and Syria, Moroccan Berbers, dark-skinned African Moors, and Abd al-Rahman's own personal bodyguard of gigantic Visigoths—blond-haired, blue-eyed medieval ass-kickers of Slavic descent whose only loyalty was to the prince who had freed them from slavery under the previous emir of Spain. This brave, undermanned, multinational suicide squad didn't even have an official banner to ride under—instead of a battle flag, they had an ordinary green turban tied around the end of a spear, a humble guidon that was to be resolutely carried straight into battle by none other than a son of the infamous Arab trachea-crushing hellbringer Khalid bin Walid, the man responsible for conquering almost all of Persia and Syria in the name of the Prophet through the sheer force of his own cranium-smashing badassitude. The prince formed his men in a wedge, commended his soul to Allah, and gave Khalid Junior the order to kick ass.

Well as it turns out the last thing the Bloodletter's men expected to see was a screaming, furious onslaught of seven hundred desperate men furiously bearing down at them from a sixty-degree incline in a cavalry charge that for all intents and purposes was like having an Olympic track-and-field gold medalist unleash a spinning hammer throw into your ballsack at point-blank range. The front lines of the Abbasid forces, many of whom barely had a chance to grab their weapons and fall into formation, were blown to hell in a scene that sort of resembled one of those goofy cartoon clips that play on the monitors at the bowling alley after you roll a strike.

Seeing their opportunity to not only survive this suicide charge, but actually somehow win the entire war in one fell swoop of screaming hooves and gleaming steel, the prince's horsemen pressed their attack—straight into the center of the camp where the enemy generals were headquartered. Riding through the tents, causing inexplicable amounts of chaos, Abd al-Rahman and his men cut down the enemy leaders, torched their stuff, slashed apart their catapult crews, and threw the entire besieging army into disarray in a display of mounted carnage worthy of Tennyson poetry or badass Iron Maiden songs. Those brave men who ran to assist their leaders ended up having their hacked-apart corpses pecked at by birds the next day, and the guys who decided to drop their swords and get the hell out of there were unceremoniously ridden down and impaled from behind with scimitars as they fled. Fifteen minutes of frantic sword-swinging mayhem had changed the outcome of Spanish history for the next seven hundred years.

Arab historians claim that when the sparks and dust finally settled on the body-strewn battlefield, seven thousand enemy lay dead at the feet of Abd al-Rahman and his blood-raging band of scimitar-swinging hellions. Naturally, numbers of casualties are almost universally over-inflated across the board, in every country in the world, across every period of history, so it's probably unlikely that every single one of Abd al-Rahman's men killed ten of the enemy on the field that day, but you get the point—this engagement had more in common with one of the *Saw* films than anything resembling a fair fight.

Even though he was a relatively decent guy in his everyday life, Prince Abd al-Rahman wasn't exactly in a mood to be all kind and merciful to the insolent flaming douchebags who had murdered his entire family right in front of his eyes and then (almost literally) urinated on their burning corpses. He ordered that all enemy prisoners have their hands and feet cut off, and then be decapitated. He then personally beheaded the enemy commander, all of the enemy generals, and everyone else he could find, tagged their ears with their names (like the way scientists tag captured tigers), threw all the heads in a bag with some salt, and then had one of his best spies journey to Arabia, sneak into Mecca in the middle of the night, and throw the heads in public places around the city like a nocturnal visit from the Decapitation Fairy. When the usurper caliph—who just so happened to be in Mecca on his pilgrimage at the time—saw the holiest city in Islam littered with the severed heads of all his greatest generals, the Bloodletter allegedly exclaimed, "Praise be to Allah for placing a sea between me and such a demon!"

He never tried to screw with Abd al-Rahman again. Prince Abd al-Rahman and his sons would rule an independent Umayyad Emirate in Spain for seven hundred years.

Abd al-Rahman's wife and son eventually made their way to Spain, as did a few other family members who somehow managed to escape the Abbasid purges. He ruled as emir of Spain for thirty-two years, defeated an invasion by Charlemagne, built the mosque of Cordoba, and set up Spain as a beacon of learning and art, complete with running water, paved roads, public baths, and lighted streets. He encouraged math, science, and art, built a four-hundred-thousand-volume library, and his policy of total religious tolerance made al-Andalus a haven for Muslim, Christian, and Judaic learning alike. He died in 788.

———

Before his first battle against the emir of Spain, Abd al-Rahman rode out to the battlefield on the back of an amazing Spanish steed that was like the equine equivalent of an armor-plated Ferrari 308 GTS with Stinger missiles behind the headlights and those totally dope *Ben-Hur*-style spikes coming out of the wheels. When one of the prince's bitchy allies remarked that if the battle turned badly that horse would be great for running the hell out of there at top speed, Abd al-Rahman went back to the stables, exchanged it for a mule named "Lightning," and then demonstrated his resolve by riding that thing into combat instead.

———

Another "You have killed my family and dishonored the Shaolin temple, now you must die" moment from history came in the thirteenth century, when a warlord named Sumanguru conquered the African kingdom of Mali and had the entire Mali royal family put to death. The only survivor of the massacre was Prince Sundiata, the twelfth son of the king, a child so sickly and weak that Sumanguru decided that decapitating this kid wasn't worth the effort it would take to swing the hatchet. Sundiata was dumped in the wilderness, where he survived and grew strong, and in 1230 he returned to Mali at the head of a huge army, dispatched the usurper Sumanguru like Simba whipping Scar's ass at the end of *The Lion King*, and reclaimed his rightful throne. Sundiata would go on to build an empire so impressive that when his grandson made the pilgrimage to Mecca in 1324 he arrived at the head of an entourage of five hundred slaves, each decked out in priceless jewelry. He brought so much treasure with him that it devalued the price of gold in Cairo, Medina, and Mecca for the next century.

10

THE GREAT HEATHEN ARMY

Ivar the Boneless's Invasion of England
East Anglia, Mercia, Wessex, and Northumbria, British Isles
AD 865–873

Never before has such a terror appeared in Britain as we have now suffered
from a pagan race, nor was it thought that such an inroad from the sea could
be made. Behold, the church of St. Cuthbert spattered with the blood of the
priests of God, despoiled of all its ornaments; a place more venerable than all
in Britain is given as prey to pagan peoples.

—ALCUIN, ANGLO-SAXON MONK

WHETHER YOU CHOOSE TO ANALYZE THEM FROM A SOCIO-ANTHROPOLOGICAL OR A PURELY MILITARY POINT OF VIEW, THE VIKING RAIDERS OF THE NINTH CENTURY AD ARE A HIGHLY INTERESTING GROUP OF WARMONGERING, BLOOD-DRINKING MANIACS WHO WOULD JUST AS SOON SLAM YOUR SCROTE SHUT IN A BEAR TRAP AS EAT YOUR EYES OUT OF YOUR FACE WITH A GRAPEFRUIT SPOON. Sure, it's not exactly a startling, groundbreaking revelation to suggest that the Vikings were pretty much the most face-rockingly hardcore bastards to ever beat a bunch of clergymen to death with their own iron church bells and throw them through a stained-glass window onto some pointy rocks, but it probably bears mentioning nonetheless.

Europe's first contact with the lovable, fun-loving folks known as the Vikings occurred in the year 793 (some folks say 789, but those people are obviously misguided idiots), when a horde of rampaging, pillage-happy bearded Scandinavian murder machines crashed their longships on the coast of the British island of Lindisfarne, threw some monks off a cliff, plundered their monastery, kicked over all their holy water fonts, and sailed off into the sunset with a boatload of gold and women and pieces of saints and probably some other stuff as well. For the next seventy or so years, the people of Ireland, Wales, Scotland, and England got used to this sort of first-degree manslaughter devastation every so often, which was fine and all, but nothing could have really prepared them for the nightmare that occurred in 865, when a hellacious armada of mead-chugging face-crushers landed on the shores of East Anglia in the first organized, coordinated invasion of England by the Viking hordes.

As is the case with many medieval badasses, the info we have on this rampaging army of ham-hock-devouring Viking berserkers is tragically limited. The most coherent source is the Icelandic *Saga of Ragnar Lodbrok*, which was written a couple hundred years later by Viking skalds (warrior-poets) and is so insane-in-the-membrane that it can't possibly be real, except of course that it kind of jibes with the fragments of information the Anglo-Saxons managed to write down before being pillaged out of their last number-two pencils. Naturally, some of this stuff is so gonzo over-the-top that I can't in good conscience leave it out, but as you're reading this please be warned that a good portion of our primary source material is the delirious mead-induced ramblings of Viking warrior-poets who spent their freezing-ass-cold winters trying to come up with the number one A+ craziest tales they possibly could.

The saga begins with a man named Ivar the Boneless—a fierce warrior, a diabolical evil mastermind, and a man so confident with his masculinity that he didn't seem to mind that people went around refer-

ring to him as "boneless." Ivar, who is also known as Yngvar, Invgar, Hingvar, and Imhar, was the son of the excellently epitheted Ragnar Hairy-Breeches, a guy who was so legendary and epic that most historians don't even know if he was a real person or not. According to the skalds, Hairy-Breeches was known as such because he once saved a princess from a giant serpent, a feat he accomplished by boiling his awesome glam-rock eighties leather pants in pitch, stuffing them full of hair, and then submerging them in ice-cold water so the whole thing hardens up together, because this apparently will protect you from the ultravenomous bites of gigantic princess-stealing cobras.

Hair pants aside, we know that Ivar was a member of the Icelandic royal family and a rugged Viking ruler who responded to any threats to his rule with extreme over-the-top violence. Historians are pretty sure Ivar the Boneless is the same Ivar who ruled parts of Dublin in the 850s and carved a name for himself in the chests of his enemies while battling the Irish, Scots, and Welsh up and down the coasts of the British Isles, but the most interesting piece of information—the origin of his badass nickname—is still a mystery. Some people say it was because he was a good seafarer (how "boneless" relates to this is still a mystery to me), or because he was cunning like a snake, or because he was impotent, or because he could do the splits like WHENEVER HE WANTED. Others think it could be from some failure-drenched illuminated manuscript writer who made a boneheaded typo (see what I did there?) and wrote *exos* (Boneless) instead of *exosus* (Detested), thereby forever changing this dude's name from something awesome like "Ivar the Detested" to a moniker that would cause future historians to debate whether this guy needed to pop a Cialis before heading home to his mistresses. It's also been speculated that this guy suffered some sort of degenerative musculoskeletal disorder that forced him to be carried around on his shield by his men and rely solely on his wits, cunning, and diabolicalness to survive. The short answer, I suppose, is that it doesn't really matter.

Now, if the stories are to be believed, as he got older Ragnar Hairy-Breeches started getting all insecure that his son was showing him up as the biggest badass in Iceland—according to the saga, Ivar had just defeated an enemy army that had as its secret weapon a giant evil cow whose horrific Moo of Insanity made warriors lose their tenuous grip on reality and start randomly murdering each other (although, in the saga writers' defense, it doesn't exactly take that much to get Vikings to start randomly murdering each other . . . it's kind of their thing). Ivar outsmarted the bovine beast by sitting down on his shield and having his men hurl him ass-first at the creature, plowing into it death from above-style and knocking both of them down a hill and out of the battle in one of history's first recorded instances of human-assisted flying cow tipping. Daunted by his son's epic beef-vanquishing glory, Ragnar attempted to reassert himself as the most senior badass in the Danelands, demonstrating his awesomeness to everyone by sailing out and trying to conquer the English kingdom of Northumbria with a mere three shiploads of Viking warriors. Since obviously this was an abominably dumbass move it shouldn't come as a surprise that Ragnar's puny force was wiped out, Ragnar was captured, and King Aella of Northumbria executed the Viking maniac by stripping him of his magic hair pants and throwing him in a pit of poisonous snakes that killed him by biting the holy living bejeezus out of him, a manner of death so delightfully eccentric that it would make even the most demented evil genius proud.

Naturally, having his father nibbled to death by tiny vipers and irony didn't make Ivar particularly happy. He and his brothers (whose equally awesome names include Hubba, Halfdan, Bjorn Ironside, and Sigurd Snake-in-the-Eye) got pissed, cracked a pool cue over their heads, immediately put together the largest Viking army ever assembled, and went out to attack King Aella with an armada so immense that it blackened the sea with so many dragon-headed warships that contemporary Anglo-Saxon sources refer to it simply as "The Great Heathen Army."

Now, as we all learned from *Monty Python and the Holy Grail*, during this period of history England was divided into four kingdoms—Northumbria, Mercia, East Anglia, and Wessex. Ivar and his homies landed in East Anglia in 866, and spent the next two years annihilating the local military, hacking apart everyone they could find, and stealing every horse, gold piece, and maiden that wasn't bolted to the ground. After that, the army swept into Northumbria, traveling along an old Roman road and smashing into the Anglo-Saxon kingdom spear-first like an immovable wall of blood-soaked berserking destruction. During this time, the region of Northumbria was being disputed between Ivar's mortal enemy King Aella and some other assclown, and by the time those two bonehead wannabe kings finally decided to get their heads out of their sphincters and work together Ivar's men had already wiped out of half the population, captured the city of York, and locked themselves up behind the wooden stockades of the heavily fortified stronghold. The Northumbrian kings stupidly massed their troops and tried to assault Ivar's base head-on like dumbasses.

After some white-knuckle combat the brave Briton warriors actually managed to bust through the walls, but unfortunately, breaking into the city didn't work out all that well for them—the overeager troops who crammed themselves through the walls suddenly found themselves bearing the brunt of an insane-as-hell counterattack when they were charged by a wall of axe-swinging berserkers who had stripped themselves naked and smeared blood and cream cheese all over their bodies. The berserkers carved their way through the English in a giant spinning tornado of pain and severed limbs and horribleness, the two Northumbrian kings were captured, the army was smashed, and those English warriors who failed to die gloriously with a berserker's axe through their heads were hunted across the countryside and unceremoniously butchered. Northumbria collapsed, Ivar's warriors plundered the countryside, and King Aella was put to death by Blood Eagle.

Blood Eagle, for those of you who aren't down with ninth-century torture methods, is the cool-sounding Viking word for a process that I'd assume has to rank very high on the list of most horrific ways a human being can be killed. The Vikings, in their infinite knowledge of how much punishment a human body can endure before expiring, apparently discovered a way to kill a person by hacking through their rib cage from the back and pulling their lungs out past their spine while they are still alive. Once they'd pulled the lungs out and stretched them out like eagle wings, the Vikings would leave the guy there to bleed to death as a sacrifice to Odin, who seems to appreciate that sort of thing.

After conquering two of the four English kingdoms, Ivar raided Mercia the next year, but eventually agreed to let them off the hook in exchange for a couple boatloads of gold. He then moved south and annihilated the armies of King Edmund of East Anglia. King Edmund himself survived the battle that vaporized his army, so Ivar hunted that lucky bastard down and demanded his surrender. Edmund said he'd never submit to a damned dirty heathen, and would only give himself up if Ivar accepted Holy Baptism and took Jesus Christ as his personal lord and savior. Ivar the Boneless did exactly what you might expect a godless Viking to do when presented with such an option—he captured Edmund by force, beat him with a stick, tied him to a tree, and had his archers use him for target practice until he was thoroughly dead, and then cut his head off and threw it in a hole. The Catholic Church declared him a saint a few years later, but this was probably a small consolation.

Ivar attacked the fourth kingdom, Wessex, in 871, defeating the Wessex king in nine pitched battles over the course of a single year. The most awesome/humiliating of these was the Battle of Ashdown— King Aethelred built a huge wall of tightass fortifications on the top of a steep hill in expectation of a gigantic Viking berserker charge, but when the Vikings saw this they sat back and waited, refusing to charge urethra-first into sharpened stakes like dumbasses. Aethelred eventually got bored sitting around and marched out to battle them, but when the Vikings heard the Wessex troops were on the move, they ran around in a huge circle, got behind the English troops, and took up defensive positions behind those badass fortifications that the English had just worked so hard on. The English, pissed off and frustrated, launched a full-on charge, running uphill into the battlements they'd just built, and despite some epic bravery on the part of the English they were cut down and butchered. Aethelred sued for peace and then immediately died, and his successor, Alfred, knew well enough to pay the Vikings tribute to keep them from attacking him. The Vikings left, the people of Wessex didn't get pillaged too hard, and today we refer to Alfred as Alfred the Great.

Content with the fact that his vengeance ride resulted in the Vikings conquering most of England in a flurry of axe blows to the dome, Ivar retired from the life of dismembering people and went back to rule from his castles in York and Dublin. He died in 873, from causes unknown—some think he died peacefully on his farm, others say he was killed while raiding Ireland, and still others think it might have had something to do with the whole Boneless thing. It doesn't really matter, since pretty much everyone seems to agree that nowadays he's chilling in the halls of Valhalla spending eternity with hot Valkyries feeding him mead and IKEA meatballs all day.

Despite the fact that Iceland was almost completely uninhabited before the Norsemen settled there in the ninth century, recent genetic analyses of the current population have shown that the average Icelander's mitochondrial DNA makeup is roughly 50 percent Scandinavian and 50 percent Gaelic. Historians' best guess is that the Viking raiders stole so many women from Ireland and Scotland that it *altered the genetic makeup of their entire population.*

The Vikings hung around in England for quite a while, but things got kind of bad for them in the year 1002, when the Anglo-Saxon king Aethelred the Unready ordered the bloody massacre of all Norsemen living in the British Isles. Aethelred didn't have a problem ordering this wanton slaughter, but he was, by definition, completely unready for the vengeance the Vikings would lay upon him. Shortly after issuing his fateful decree, Aethelred was attacked by a mammoth Danish force under the command of Ivar's grandson, a dude named Cnut the Great. Cnut obliterated Aethelred's armies, killed Aethelred's son Edmund Ironsides in single combat, drove Aethelred from the throne, and then, to put the cherry on top, married Aethelred's wife, Emma of Normandy (also known as Emma the MILF). Cnut became the first Viking king of England, although it's worth mentioning that his full title was "King of All the English, and of Denmark, of the Norwegians, and of Some of the Swedes."

When Leif the Lucky and his crew of intrepid Norse explorers landed on the shores of Vinland in AD 999, the first European explorers of North America quickly realized that the land they'd just discovered was already inhabited by indigenous peoples, some of whom presumably had discovered the land even before Leif had. The Vikings didn't know what to call these bloodstained tomahawk-chucking natives with the war-painted faces, so they called them *Skrellings*, which was really just the default word the Norse used for fairies, elves, and pretty much anything they couldn't identify. Well, these Skrellings decided they weren't huge fans of having Viking raiders patrolling their land, so they put together a war band and made a concerted attempt to forcibly evict Leif and his buddies by bludgeoning their faces inside out until they passed out and died face-down in a pool of their own blood.

Leif and his homies were just chilling one day when all of a sudden out of nowhere these Skrellings came flying in from every direction, attacking them with slings, axes, bows, and a few strange exotic weapons the Vikings had never seen before. Many of the big ripped Viking warriors decided they didn't want to fight demons or whatever the hell Skrelling people were and started hauling ass outta there at top speed. As these big, bad Vikings were fleeing for their lives only one of the Norsemen decided to make a stand and see whether or not these Skrellings were susceptible to conventional weapons—Freydis Eiriksdottir, Leif's rancorous axe-swinging sister. This hardcore Viking woman was pregnant and pissed off, and she didn't feel like running away from anything. She faced the fleeing Vikings and derisively shouted:

"Why do ye run, stout men as ye are, before these miserable wretches, whom I thought ye would knock down like cattle? If I had weapons, methinks I could fight better than any of ye!"

This pump-up speech went pretty much nowhere (even though it was followed by a hearty "YARRRR!"), and the Vikings didn't even give a little stutter-step as they were rapidly fleeing from the oncoming Skrellings. Well, forget that. Freydis decided to show them she meant business. She grabbed a sword off a dead Viking, got super-psyched up about killing people, ripped open her shirt for some reason, and banged the sword against her chest Tarzan style while screaming like a wounded banshee.

The Skrellings saw this crazy pregnant chick daring them to screw with her and swinging around a bloody sword, and they got so freaked out that they turned and fled. Freydis had saved the day, proving that she had the biggest nuts of all the Vikings in the process. She'd go on to kill five women with an axe in a dispute over distributing the spoils of war, and would eventually have her heroic (and not so heroic) deeds recorded in the *Saga of Leif Ericson*.

11

THE THIRD CRUSADE

Battle for the Holy Land
The Levant
1189–1192

*There is no god but me. I put to death and I bring to life; I have wounded and
I will heal; and no one can deliver out of my hand. I lift my hand to heaven
and solemnly swear, as surely as I live forever, when I sharpen my flashing
sword and my hand grasps it in judgment, I will take vengeance on my
adversaries and repay those who hate me. I will make my arrows drunk with
blood, while my sword devours flesh—the blood of the slain and the captives,
and the heads of the enemy leaders.*

—DEUTERONOMY 32:39–42

EVEN THOUGH THE HOLY CITY OF JERUSALEM HAD BEEN
UNDER MUSLIM RULE FOR SOME FOUR-HUNDRED-ODD YEARS,
FOR SOME STRANGE REASON IN THE YEAR 1098 POPE URBAN
II TOTALLY GOT HIS VESTMENTS IN A WAD ABOUT THE IDEA
THAT JESUS'S OLD STOMPING GROUNDS WERE UNDER THE COM-
MAND OF SOME HEATHEN NONBELIEVERS. So, naturally, he sent
a few hundred thousand Crusaders across the ocean to kick the holy
crapballs out of the Muslims, storm the walls of the Holy City, and cel-
ebrate the liberation of the Church of the Holy Sepulchre by slaughter-
ing every non-Christian they could find until the streets ran waist-deep

with human blood. From that point on, the Christians set up a loosely affiliated series of European-ruled Crusader states that were collectively referred to as "Outremer," which honestly sounds like the name of a space freighter on a bad sci-fi TV series.

Enter al-Malik al-Nasir Salah al-Din aba'l-Mussafar Yusuf ibn Ayyub ibn Shadi—a man whose name is mercifully shortened to Saladin, mostly because nobody really wanted to write all that stuff out back in the days of illuminated manuscripts. Saladin was a badass Kurdish hero who had served as an able subordinate to the sultan of Syria and had been on the front lines when the Sunni Syrian Empire conquered Cairo from its Shi'ite Egyptian enemies, charging at the head of a group of infidel-smiting horsemen awesomely known as the "Burning Coals of Islam." After the fall of Cairo, Saladin was appointed the regional leader of Egypt, mostly because the sultan didn't consider him a threat to the rulers of Syria, but that plan backfired pretty spectacularly when the sultan died and the thirty-eight-year-old Saladin seized control of Syria and Egypt, declared himself the new sultan, and united the entire Muslim world (except for al-Andalus) under the Abbasid caliphate for the first time in over a century.

But Saladin's work was just getting started. For this guy, if it wasn't bad enough that a bunch of non-believing Christian infidels now ruled Jerusalem, some of the Crusaders were really starting to be gigantic pains in the ass about the whole thing—particularly a craptacularly aggro jock asshat named Reynald of Châtillon. Reynald was a grouchy, unflinching zealot Crusader who was a little annoyed that he'd been captured in battle and had been forced to spend sixteen years rotting in the sultan's rather inhospitable penal system, and once this toolbelt finally got free he totally just couldn't play nice and leave well enough alone. From the precipitous heights of the impregnable mountain fortress Kerak, situated high above the main caravan road between Cairo and Damascus, Reynald decided that he was going to avenge himself on his heathen enemies by capturing every trade caravan that passed through his territory and hurling all the Muslim merchants off the towers of his castle (Note: I think Kerak gets its name from the noise they'd make when they hit the ground). The incredibly bitter Reynald then renounced all Crusader treaties with Saladin, built a pirate fleet that raided the Red Sea, and made a bunch of outlandish claims about how his pirate marauders were going to burn Mecca and Medina to the ground, drag the Prophet Muhammad's corpse from its tomb, do a bunch of horrible stuff to it, and then eat pork on a Saturday during Ramadan while putting their feet up on the couch and hogging the remote control. Then, to put the cherry on top, Reynald kidnapped Saladin's sister and held her for ransom. When Saladin calmly demanded her return, Reynald told him that if he wanted her back he should summon the ghost of the Prophet and send him to get her.

Now, Saladin was a guy who's fondly remembered by historians for his uncanny ability to not be a total dick to everyone. This was a dude who couldn't afford to finance his own funeral because he had given all of his personal fortune away to charity, and who once sent his personal doctor and a fresh horse to an enemy commander who had been wounded in combat. But there's a difference between being a decent human being and letting people get away with stuff like kidnapping your family, blaspheming your religion, and threatening your life, and even nice guys can flip their stack of pancakes and start beating asses if they're forced to suffer fools long enough. So when King Guy of Jerusalem (the overall ruler of the Crusader states in Outremer) refused to punish Reynald for his rampant douchebaggery, Saladin figured that it was up to him to kick this Reynald guy so hard in the gonads that his grandchildren would be born impotent.

Saladin called a jihad—a Holy War against the infidel. Then, to show everyone he was serious, he marched a force into Christian territory, wiped out sixty Knights Templar in a single battle, and paraded around Outremer with their heads on pikes. Then he had his fleet hunt down Reynald's pirates, torch their ships, and have them all crucified along the shores of the Red Sea.

Eventually the European forces in Outremer got sick of this Saladin guy and his penchant for going around crucifying people all willy-nilly, and they decided it was time once again to demonstrate that when you mess with the disciples of Jesus-ness you get a two-handed broadsword rammed through your throat. King Guy put out the call for all Christian warriors in the realm to unite and clothesline the enemies of God in one final struggle that would determine the fate of the Holy Land forever. Entire cities stripped their garrisons of troops, and within days the king had mustered the largest Crusader army ever assembled in the Holy Land—twelve hundred knights and eighteen thousand fanatical infantrymen ready for action, a force that consisted not only of every fighting man in Outremer, but every Christian male of fighting age who felt like his religion was something worth dying for. Saladin had slightly larger numbers, sure, but he also knew he didn't have the weaponry to stand up to heavy Christian armor in a straight out hand-to-hand slugfest. So he devised a plan.

Saladin besieged a Christian fortress on the far interior edge of Outremer, well away from the safety of the ocean and directly on the far side of a huge desert. The Crusaders, who were impossibly predictable because of the whole chivalry thing, of course decided to pack up their gear and charge balls-out to relieve the siege—even though this meant marching armor-clad knights and heavy European warhorses twenty miles through the damn desert in the middle of the scorching Syrian summer. Saladin drew the Christians deep into the sands, used his fast-moving light cavalry to cut off their supply lines and deny the Crusaders access to water sources, and then set an ambush at a place called the Horns of Hattin—the traditional site of Jesus's Sermon on the Mount. With the enemy completely surrounded, Saladin waited until the dead of noon, when the Crusaders were all roasting and heatstroking out inside their armor, then launched an all-out attack that crushed the entire male Christian population of Outremer in one fell swoop. The king, Reynald of Châtillon, the Grand Masters of the Knights Templar and the Knights Hospitaller, and the True Cross (a relic from the First Crusade that was believed to be the actual cross Jesus was crucified on) all fell into Saladin's hands. The sultan sold all of his prisoners into slavery, except for the Knights Templar and Knights Hospitaller, whom he just beheaded. Then he personally executed Reynald of Châtillon with a scimitar, because screw that jackhole, but he did let King Guy live, because according to Saladin, "Kings do not kill kings." So he just kept the Christian king in chains for a while and paraded him around like a prized pony any time the sultan wanted people to see how badass he was.

With every single warrior in Christendom either dead or enslaved, Saladin's army easily captured Acre, Beirut, Arsuf, Jaffa, and every other Christian city in the Middle East—including Jerusalem. Aside from the small island castle of Tyre, Outremer was no more.

When news of Saladin's epic conquests reached Europe, it didn't really sit too well with the Christian leaders there—particularly a newly crowned English king known as Richard the Lionheart. Richard, the son of Eleanor of Aquitaine (a badass woman in her own right who had once led a squadron of female knights into battle during the Second Crusade), was a thirty-three-year-old knight who had spent the last fifteen years of his life in near-constant warfare across the French countryside. As duke of the French province of Aquitaine, Richard had battled rival members of the nobility, beat down his own dad (King Henry II of England) and older brother in a succession dispute, and once dealt with a regiment of captured enemy troops by putting out their eyes with red-hot pokers and then having them drowned in the Vienne River. A giant of a man who personally waded into combat swinging a gold-hilted two-handed sword he claimed to be King Arthur's Excalibur, Richard was a righteous steamroller of Catholic justice who pummeled nonbelievers into pulp, lit his post-battle cigarettes by striking matches on the bodies of the dead, and saved the interrogations for the Spanish Inquisition. So when this guy heard that a bunch of godless Muslim heathens had taken Jerusalem by force and decapitated a bunch of monks, he immediately ordered his men to get their gear together and start getting all hyphy about a hardcore Turbo Crusade to the Holy Land. It was time to kick ass and chew gum, and gum hadn't even been invented yet.

In 1189 Richard's army departed aboard an armada of Pisan and Genoese warships. I'd like to think that he listened to Dio's *Holy Diver* album along the way, but in reality it was probably some kind of Gregorian chanting or alt-Christian fusion stuff like "Our God Is an Awesome God." After brief stopovers in Sicily (where he freed his sister from house arrest by the corrupt Sicilian king and ransacked the city of Messina) and Cyprus (where he kicked the impertinence out of some impotent, self-aggrandizing wannabe pseudo-Byzantine emperor and conquered the island for himself), Richard personally rammed an enemy blockade runner with his own flagship troops and then hit the beaches of the Middle East like a war hammer of skull-clubbing righteousness.

Richard got the party started by besieging the Muslim-held city of Acre, bombing the ass out of the city's defenses with a bunch of gigantor siege engines with awesome nicknames like "The Evil Neighbor." During the siege, Richard came down with a nasty case of scurvy, but no wacky pirate diseases were going to stop this madman from getting his cleave on—according to his chronicler, while the Lionheart was laid up in his sickbed unable to swing his twenty-pound battle-axe he took target practice by capping fools off the parapets of Acre with a scoped crossbow. Saladin, distraught from seeing his hard-won coastal fortress being constantly bombarded with granite boulders and dead horses (I guess it was easier to launch dead horses than it was to bury them?), initiated a huge attack attempting to break the siege, but Richard's paladins fought it off, drove Saladin back to the mountains, and then stormed the city, captured the walls, and had all twenty-seven hundred prisoners of war beheaded in full view of the Muslim battle lines.

Richard was just getting started. For this dude, nothing short of the complete conquest of Outremer would be sufficient—anything less would be like eating the bottom part of a cupcake and throwing away the frosting. From Acre, Richard marched his troops south, leading dudes in ninety pounds of armor across the blistering heat of the Middle East, fighting off scorpions, tarantulas, crocodiles, cobras, and a bunch of other terrifying monsters Europeans had never encountered before. The knights who didn't pass out in the desert or get chomped apart by wild poisonous beasts also had to worry about Saladin's raiders, who were riding closely behind the Christian army, butchering any Crusader who couldn't keep up with the pack (they were obviously a little peeved about the twenty-seven-hundred-dead-POWs thing).

Despite these setbacks Richard's forces continued to make good progress, and, seeing that his hit-and-run attacks weren't slowing down the invaders, Saladin decided to make a stand and take on the Lionheart in a pitched battle just a few miles from the coastal city of Jaffa. Even though he brilliantly positioned his numerically superior forces so that they completely boxed in the Lionheart's men, Saladin had fatally underestimated the incalculable getting-pissed powers of the Christian warrior monks. At the Battle of Arsuf, with victory in his sights and the enemy completely encircled, Saladin ordered his light cavalry to see how hard they could piss off the Crusaders' rear flank—a position manned by the Knights Hospitaller, an order of kickass holy knights who (as if they needed any additional reason to despise nonbelievers) took Saladin's whole "I'm going to execute any warrior clerics I capture in battle" policy kind of personally. Saladin knew this, and was hoping to provoke them into an idiotic charge that would draw them away from the main body of Richard's army and into a death trap. Saladin got what he wanted, though it didn't work out quite the way he'd hoped.

Richard ordered the Hospitallers to hold their positions until he gave the order, but honestly it's a little unreasonable to expect a bunch of blue-balled celibate monks with broadswords to keep their cool in the face of overwhelming enemy provocation. On the seventh or eighth feint attack by the Saracen troops, the Hospitallers lost their patience, grabbed their weapons, and rushed ahead in a megaheavy cavalry charge of ultimate godliness +1. Seeing his rear flank suddenly flipping out like ninjas, Richard wisely ordered a general charge, and within seconds the front rank of English spearmen parted and a rampaging horde of trample-happy knights thundered through the gaps in every direction, right into the heart of the Muslim formation. Richard, who at the time of the battle was still recovering from a spear wound he'd received in a previous battle, personally led the attack.

The mashing-hooves double-bladed massacre that followed was a perfect example of why you should never stand in front of a massed formation of heavy cavalry unless you really enjoy having your crotch stomped into reddish-gray goo. The Saracen lines broke in minutes under the weight of heavy armored warhorses, and those who weren't trampled into the sand by two thousand pounds of horse meat in the opening charge were hacked to pieces as they desperately tried to get the hell out of there. Seven thousand Muslim warriors (including thirty emirs) fell before the onslaught, and Saladin himself only barely managed to escape the carnage when the Burning Coals helped him fight through the enemy vanguard. The cities of Jaffa and Darum fell days later, giving Richard complete command of the coastline of Outremer. Saladin had failed to crush the invasion at its source and suffered a near-crippling defeat, and now the Crusaders had a sturdy foothold in the Middle East once again.

Saladin decided to forget that whole head-to-head battle thing and get back to what worked before. He withdrew into the desert, dismantled every structure and fortification larger than an outhouse, and poisoned every well and drinking fountain he could find. He positioned a small elite garrison inside the Holy City of Jerusalem, and then used his fast-moving horsemen to circle around the invading army and launch hit-and-run raids on the Crusader supply lines. As the European army lumbered inland toward Jerusalem, beleaguered by disease, dehydration, and constant arrow storms every step of the way, their numbers dwindled.

This wasn't glamorous or sexy or even particularly exciting, but it worked. In one of the more anticlimactic moments of the entire Crusade, by the time Richard and his exhausted troops nearly reached the walls of Jerusalem, the English king realized he didn't have enough men to secure his supply lines, and without food, ammunition, and reinforcements, he'd never be able to take the city. So he said screw it and went back home without even unsheathing his blade.

Even though he'd punked out right at the gates of Jerusalem, there was still time for one final act of badassitude on the part of Richard the Lionheart. As RTL and the Christians were withdrawing to Acre, Saladin got a little overanxious and launched an attack to retake Jaffa. When Richard heard this, he cranked the e-brake on his red-sailed flagship, hauled ass south as fast as he could, and led his personal bodyguard of Knights Templar on a one-ship amphibious assault of Jaffa just as the last Christian defenders were on the point of losing the interior walls of the citadel. Ditching his leg armor so he could move through the water more easily, Richard and one ship's worth of Templars waded through waist-deep water onto the beach, cutting people apart left and right. Richard and his Templars charged ahead on foot, with arrows sticking out of their armor from so many directions they "looked like the dude from *Hellraiser*" and the small force somehow managed to drive the Muslims from Jaffa, then fight off a coordinated nighttime counterattack by Saladin's men.

And so, with his brother John being a dickweed back home, Jerusalem an impossibility, and his army's reserves dwindling, Richard the Lionheart finally called for peace. The arrangement was that Richard got to keep the coastal cities and plains he had conquered while Saladin would keep Jerusalem and the mountainous regions of Syria and Palestine. Richard, half dead from some horrible disease, limped home after fifteen months of combat. He had lost 90 percent of his men and failed to net the ultimate prize, but nobody could ever talk smack about his bravery or his Lionheartedness. Saladin, for his part, was hailed as the Defender of the Faith for driving out the infidel invaders, and to this day is considered one of the greatest heroes in Muslim history.

Richard the Lionheart has some interesting parallels with fictional starship commander Jean-Luc Picard. In *Star Trek: The Next Generation*, Captain Picard is supposed to be a relentless French asskicker, but he's portrayed by the ridiculously British Patrick Stewart. Richard the Lionheart is also portrayed by Patrick Stewart in *Robin Hood: Men in Tights*, but in reality, instead of delivering Shakespearean speeches the historical Richard spent most of his life on the French mainland and only really visited England long enough to be crowned. Hell, as far as we can tell the guy barely even *spoke* English, and his name technically was *Richard* (pronounced "Ree-SHAR") *Coeur de Lion*.

When it came to the serious business of crusading, Richard wasn't screwing around. Just before leaving for the Holy Land, he called all the warriors of England together and held a three-day tournament to determine the toughest men in the realm. Richard himself participated in the contest, dressing up in full armor with his face hidden behind a heavy steel helm. The gigantic Lionhearted war machine ended up killing a couple guys in the joust and the melee and was only defeated in single combat twice—he took both men to be his chief lieutenants on his quest.

———

Although there's no reference to it in any Western chronicles, Arab historians mention female crusaders fighting against them in the battles at Acre and Arsuf, including women in full armor equipped with longbows and swords. Any woman captured in combat could expect to be swiftly beheaded.

———

Since the Third Crusade had come so close to achieving its goal, the pope called for a sequel in 1202, but by this point crusading had pretty much jumped the shark—the Crusaders got bored before they even reached the Holy Land, so they just sacked the Christian city of Constantinople and called it a day. All told, there were nine major crusades between 1095 and 1272 (plus a bunch of random other ones that are barely worth mentioning), but only the first one managed to actually capture Jerusalem.

———

12

KONO MICHIARI

The Second Mongol Invasion of Japan
April, 1281
Hakata Bay, Japan

Kono Michiari, who jumped on board the enemy ship with lightning speed,
cut his way into the crowded barbarians. He lashed about in all directions,
killing those who stood in his way. His men followed in his footsteps at once.

—NAKABA YAMADA, GHENKO: *The Mongol Invasion of Japan*

BY APRIL 1281, THE WORD "MONGOL" WAS ALREADY SYN-
ONYMOUS WITH GIANT, AWESOMELY MUSTACHED HORDES OF
YAK-MILK-CHUGGING BADASSES CAPABLE OF SHOWING UP AT
A MOMENT'S NOTICE, TORCHING YOUR HOME INTO RUBBLE,
KICKING YOUR DOG IN THE CROTCH, DETONATING YOUR FACE
INTO A CONCAVE FOUNTAIN OF BLOOD, AND RIDING OFF INTO
THE SUNSET WITH YOUR GIRLFRIEND AND YOUR FAVORITE
BEER MUG STRAPPED TO THEIR HORSES. These guys had used
little more than sheer unadulterated spleen-stabbing violence to carve
out the largest contiguous land empire the world had ever seen, Gen-
ghis Khan's grandson Kublai Khan now sat on the imperial throne of

China, and it's fair to say that every single human being in the world started whizzing their kimonos at the mere mention of the unstoppable Mongol Horde.

With the Mongols firmly teabagging the entire continent of Asia and much of Europe, only one Eastern empire stood resolutely against these invincible warriors—the Kamakura Shogunate of Japan. Seven years earlier, Kublai Khan had sent a small reconnaissance force to see what the deal was with these samurai dudes and to find out whether this whole katana thing was really as totally flippin' sweet as everyone said, but in 1274 the Mongol expeditionary force was beaten like a red-headed stepchild riding a rented mule in a heated battle on the beaches near present-day Tokyo.

Now they were back, and this time they weren't playing around.

In 1281, 157,000 Mongol warriors appeared off the coast of Hakata Bay on four thousand gigantic Korean- and Chinese-built heavy warships. It was the second-largest amphibious invasion force ever assembled (eclipsed only by the D-Day landings in World War II), loaded up with invincible Mongols who weren't about to be the suckers who broke up the Great Khan's no-hitter of never being defeated in a full-scale battle.

The Japanese took their own boats out to attack the Mongol fleet but were quickly trounced out of hand in fierce fighting, thanks in large part to the Mongol use of gunpowder cannons on their ships and the Japanese naval strategy of "let's row out there with swords, board their boats, and mess these jackasses up in hand-to-hand combat." The Mongols then attempted to land, but their amphibious landing on the shores of Hakata Bay was met by a fierce counterattack of screaming, ill-tempered samurai. The Mongols were pushed back to their boats, and now a teeming armada of gigantic Mongol warships loomed large in the inlet, patiently preparing for an unstoppable invasion by overwhelming numbers of troops supported by siege weaponry, gunpowder cannons, and the famous Mongol cavalry that had routinely mashed the skulls of armies from Warsaw to Beijing.

It was at this point that a scorchingly gonzo samurai warrior named Kono Michiari showed up with his retinue of five hundred hard-as-adamantium swordsmen. Kono had missed the previous day's fighting, but he was eager to get into the fray and start turning the Mongol Horde into a tornado of dismembered appendages flying about in every direction like dollar bills in one of those awesome phone booths that blow money all over the place. Kono arrived at the defensive wall the samurai were using as cover from the Mongol cannons, and when he heard he'd just missed out on a gnarly battle he got severely pissed off about being left out of the party. Shaking with rage and uncontrollable pumped-uppedness, Kono swore to his ancestors that he would be the first man to see combat the next time it came. So, to that end, instead of camping behind the wall, he ordered his men to set up camp on the OTHER side of the wall—right on the beach, in full view of the enemy armada, showing complete disregard for their cannons or archers, and making it so that every time the Mongols looked to the shore they'd see Kono Michiari standing on the shore crotch-chopping vaguely in their direction.

With nothing better to do before the next battle, Kono pulled out his calligraphy pen and wrote out a presumably badass-as-hell prayer begging the gods for an opportunity to fight the invaders and defend his homeland. When he was done he burned the paper, ate the ashes, and chased it with a little sake. Within minutes some crazy-as-hell giant heron came flying in out of nowhere, grabbed an arrow out of Kono's quiver, and flew off toward the Mongols. Now, while you and I might think this was just some delusional, half-blind nutcase bird building the most unsafe nest ever constructed, Kono Michiari saw it as a sign from the gods that he was supposed to go out there and start kicking ass until all that remained of the enemy fleet was bloodstained splinters and a duffel bag filled with decapitated heads destined to be tastefully mounted on the wall of Kono Michiari's summer home.

So Kono Michiari, being a badass samurai with a code of honor that demanded him never to sheathe his balls, did perhaps one of the most hardcore things in the history of naval warfare—he loaded two tiny, unarmed rowboats up with ten to fifteen warriors each and started rowing toward the Mongol armada. When the Japanese soldiers on the shore saw these twenty or thirty dudes slowly making their way right into the middle of four thousand hulking Mongol warships in broad daylight, they immediately started cheering. They knew what was up. The Mongols, of course, had no idea what in the hell was going on and they rationally came to one of two logical conclusions—either these guys were coming to surrender, or they were coming to negotiate on behalf of Japan. They couldn't be coming to attack. That would be too crazy.

So the Mongols sat back and let the pair of tiny ships row their way right up to their admiral's flagship.

As soon as the two rowboats pulled alongside the largest and most ornate-looking enemy vessel in the harbor, Kono Michiari drew his katana and *chopped the mast of his own ship down* with one clean strike of his sword. Kono's lumberjack skills were so finely tuned that the mast fell against the side of the enemy flagship, and as soon as it was in place the samurai commander ran up the mast and sprinted to the deck of the Mongol warship, screaming his battle cry, the names of his ancestors, and probably some other stuff as well. As the Mongol crew stood there with their jaws hanging open, Kono Michiari dropped the first idiot he saw by cleaving the dude head to groin with one swing of the sword.

I don't have to tell you that the Mongols weren't exactly pushovers. This was a group of people who had literally conquered nearly the entire known world, and quite honestly I'd rather have Danny LaRusso crane-kick me in the fruit stand than try to go sword to sword with just one of these guys, let alone face off against an entire flagship crewed by the admiral's elite honor guard, but Kono Michiari was so balls-out you'd think this guy had a malfunctioning codpiece. Even when the Mongols regrouped, grabbed their weapons, killed Kono's uncle with a dart through the eye, and started charging out of every hatch and doorway on the sprawling ship like a medieval Asian *Under Siege*, this guy refused to back down—he had been training his entire life for this exact moment, and for this utterly-fearless swordsman facing hundred-to-one odds was exactly the way he wanted it. Michiari waded his way into the enemy ranks, swirling his blade around in every direction, lopping off whichever human body parts came within arm's reach as he carved the ship a new communal asshole. Despite being nearly a foot shorter than most of his enemies (I am speculating here, based on contemporary sources that constantly refer to this guy using terms such as "diminutive"), this hardcore armored warrior cleaved a swath of bloody annihilation across the deck of the ship, slowly working his way aft, pausing only to parry sword blows, wipe the blood off his blade, or light a cigar with an arc welder. Leading the charge and creating a nice crimson path of diced Mongol for his soldiers to follow, this Toshiro Mifune–grade asskicker took an arrow through the elbow and another in the shoulder but these painful wounds to major joints in the body didn't even slow him down. It was impossible to get rid of this determined samurai badass—he was like the sword-swinging equivalent of glitter. Or herpes.

Heading sternward, Kono Michiari's blade continued to strike true in every direction. With no room to use their bows and no horses to help them, the Mongols didn't stand much chance against the heavily armored, katana-swinging warriors, and before long Kono found himself climbing to the quarterdeck, where the enemy admiral stood, mouth hanging open, protected by his most trusted, strongest warriors.

Everything got quiet as Kono Michiari found himself face-to-face with the biggest, most jacked human being he had ever seen—the captain of the admiral's honor guard, a man hand-selected for his ferocity in battle, his immense size, and his ability to open beer bottles with his biceps and/or teeth. The behemoth Mongol slowly drew an exceedingly huge two-handed sword, cracked his neck, and put on his best "prepare to die" face.

Michiari dropped him in two moves.

The whole thing was over in minutes—before any of the other Mongol ships could figure out what to do, Kono Michiari and his thirty men had already slaughtered the entire crew of the Mongol flagship, captured the admiral, and set the ship on fire, and now these frighteningly efficient samurai were rowing their asses back to the shore as fast as their exhausted sword arms could carry them. The black smoke rising from the burning hulk prevented the Mongol ships from directing accurate fire at the samurai rowboats—arrows, darts, and cannonballs splashed down around them, but Kono pressed on and returned home safely, his prisoner still intact and his attack such a legendary accomplishment that it's still included in Japanese history books today.

The ferocity of Kono Michiari's raid inspired other samurai to attempt similar things, and these ridiculous attacks forced the Mongol fleet to withdraw out of Hakata Bay to regroup near the island of Takashima, wait for reinforcements, and coordinate their next move. They wouldn't get the chance—a few days after Kono Michari tore up the Mongol flagship, a massive typhoon rocked the Japanese islands with driving rains, high seas, and ferocious winds. Forced out of the safety of the protected bay and unable to land on the shore, the entire Mongol fleet was utterly annihilated in a single night. This storm, known to the Japanese as the *kamikaze* (meaning "divine wind"), obliterated most of the Mongol ships, battering them to pieces with hurricane-force winds and giant rolling waves that flipped entire ships upside down *Poseidon Adventure* style. Those who didn't drown shipwrecked on shore, where they were promptly butchered by opportunistic samurai looking for severed heads to add to their collections. Of the 157,000 men on board the armada ships, 60 to 90 percent of them slept with the fishes. The rest packed it in and went home to get some sleep.

Chinese alchemists discovered gunpowder in the ninth century, when they were looking for an elixir of immortality and accidentally discovered a substance that directly caused more human deaths than any invention in history. Even though this crap was the exact opposite of an invincibility potion, they apparently thought the stuff was pretty cool anyway, so they used it to make fireworks. Eventually one enterprising Chinese dude decided this explosive shiznit would work well as a weapon, too, so he used it to invent the flamethrower in 919. The first true cannons didn't start to emerge until the thirteenth century.

After his famous one-man killing spree aboard the Mongol Super Star Destroyer, Kono Michiari was wisely recruited by the shogun to help deal with a band of renegade outlaw pirates who had been terrorizing the bays and inlets of western Japan. Needless to say, he sliced those scurvy cockmonkeys into pirate kebabs and then used their mangled corpses to decorate the front of his pirate-hunting ship like how the Reavers used to do it on *Firefly*.

In the West, the Mongols were defeated for the first time at the Battle of Ain Jalut in 1260 when they faced off against the die-hard warriors of the Egyptian Mamluk Dynasty. The Mamluk commander, a slave-soldier named Baybars, lured the Mongols into a trap with a false retreat (some sources debate the "falseness" of the retreat, but Baybars swore he *totally* meant to do that), then ambushed them from three sides with a considerable horde of livid Egyptians who captured or killed the entire Mongol force. True, it helped that the Egyptians outnumbered the Mongols roughly six to one, but everyone was so pumped that the Mongols were actually killable that at this point troop ratios were only a minor detail. Baybars became a hero overnight, and when the sultan failed to show adequate appreciation for his slave-general's tremendous victory over the Mongol Horde, Baybars had that jerkwad assassinated and took over as sultan himself. Now that's how a badass gets a promotion.

⊷⊷⇒ KARANSEBES: HISTORY'S DUMBEST BATTLE ⇐⊷⊷

Keep firing, Assholes!

—DARK HELMET IN *Spaceballs*

Toward the end of 1788, Emperor Joseph II of Austria marched a multinational force across the Balkans in an effort to attack the Ottoman Turks in Transylvania and force them out of Europe once and for all. He took 174,000 men into Turkish-occupied Romania, promptly lost 33,000 of them to disease, and then accidentally engaged his forces in one of the most idiotic battles ever fought. Apparently, one night a group of Imperial Austrian Hussars crossed the Timlis River to scout for the enemy, but ended up running into a gypsy party bus and getting all distracted and crunked up on booze and cute girls. When the main body of the force—mostly Hungarians, Lombards, and Slovaks—showed up to see what the hell was going on, the Hussars (who weren't in the mood to share their party) formed a defensive perimeter around the booze casks and cleavage and drove the intruders out by whacking them in the face with the flats of their swords. At some point during this drunken dispute, a shot rang out, and the next thing you know the dark moonless night was filled with hundreds of muzzle flashes and musketballs. The Austrian officers, trying to keep the already absurd situation from getting even more out of hand, only made things worse when they started screaming "Halt! Halt!"—since Lombards, Hungarians, and Slovaks don't speak a hell of a lot of German, they thought they were hearing cries of "Allah! Allah!" and immediately turned and opened fire on the "Turks" who had somehow snuck up on them.

Meanwhile, back on the other side of the Timlis, the rest of the emperor's army awoke to the sound of gunfire and the screams of dying men, figured the Turks were upon them, and opened fire in the direction of the muzzle flashes across the river. Before long, tents were burning, riderless horses were darting through the camp, and the entire army panicked at the mayhem around them and bolted the hell out of there, leaving behind a wake of burned, shot, trampled, and drowned corpses. When the grand vizier of the Ottoman Empire showed up for battle the next morning, he stumbled upon the carnage and was left trying to piece together the previous night's events like those dudes in *The Hangover*. It wasn't long before he realized he'd routed an entire European army and killed ten thousand enemy soldiers without actually even being present on the battlefield.

13

ALBA GU BRÀTH

The Scottish War of Independence
1303–1314
Scotland and Northern England

We fight not for glory, nor for wealth, nor honor, but only and alone we fight
for freedom which no good man surrenders but with his life.

—ROBERT THE BRUCE

IT'S A WELL-ACCEPTED FACT AMONG EVEN THE MOST DIA-
BOLICALLY BORING STUFFED-SHIRT HISTORIAN-TYPES THAT
ROUGHLY EVERY SINGLE EUROPEAN WAR DURING THE MIDDLE
AGES CAME ABOUT FOR ONE OF TWO REASONS: THEY'RE EI-
THER OVERLY FERVENT DISPUTES ABOUT WHICH WEALTHY NO-
BLEMAN WAS MOST DESERVING OF BEING THE KING OF SOME
PARTICULAR COUNTRY, OR THEY'RE EQUALLY OVERZEALOUS
DEBATES ABOUT WHOSE ABSTRACT INTERPRETATION OF THE
TRUE NATURE OF GOD IS THE MOST ACCURATE. The War of Scot-
tish Independence is no different—while its name and final purpose
might indicate that it was about something slightly more important

than a boring debate over legal semantics, it did in fact start off as yet another succession dispute that took a wrong turn at Piccadilly Circus and somehow ended up on a bullet train to Crazytown.

It all started in 1296, when some barely-worth-mentioning king of Scotland beefed it and died for some reason that has nothing to do with this story. Now, it was bad enough that this tragically deceased monarch bequeathed the throne to his two-year-old daughter (you'd be surprised how many arrogant pretentious noblemen don't particularly enjoy being ruled over by someone who isn't toilet trained), but when the new infant baby queen subsequently died of illness a few seconds after her dad, the higher-ups in the Scottish nobility did a brain-meltingly idiotic thing and asked the worst possible person on the planet to arbitrate their succession dispute—King Edward I of England, a rank old bastard who flossed his teeth with the de-meated bones of his brutally dismembered enemies and had about as much respect for Scottish nationalism as I have for Kevin Federline's music career. Edward, also known as "Longshanks" (an obvious reference to the time in 1258 when he got sloshed and whipped his dong out at a wedding), and responded to this wishy-washy, "oh, please tell us how we can differentiate our bungholes from a garbage disposal" nonsense like a boss—he grabbed the Scottish crown, authoritatively stuffed it on his own head, and emotionlessly told the assembled crowd, "Okay, idiots, I choose myself to be king of Scotland. Succession problem over." When the Scottish nobles had a problem with that (seriously, what numbnuts *didn't* see that coming?), Longshanks invaded Scotland, slaughtered every human being in the city of Berwick, kicked the Scots' asses at the Battle of Dunbar, arrested most of their nobility, installed loyal Englishmen to rule over every important thing north of London, and then stole the Stone of Destiny (a giant Pet Rock that served as the symbol of Scottish royalty), took it back to London with him, and installed it underneath his coronation chair in Westminster Abbey, where it sits to this day.

Everything was coming up Longshanks. That is, of course, until he found himself on the wrong side of a notorious outlaw known as William Wallace.

The man known as "The Wallace" (because, as we all know, whenever you're talking about badass sword-swinging Highlanders *there can be only one*) was a true believer Scotsman who really didn't appreciate having annoying English bastards all up in his business all the time. According to the backstory laid out for him by a traveling medieval minstrel named Blind Harry (who admittedly probably didn't see this all go down firsthand, har har har), it all started one day when Wallace was out drinking beer and fishing in the town of Lanark. On his way home, William ran into five drunk-ass English soldiers who demanded that Wallace hand over his entire day's catch. Wallace offered to give the jerks half of his haul, but they told him that if he didn't fork over the damn trout then they would have him executed for treason. Wallace responded by bashing one of the dudes in the face with his fishing pole, stealing the guy's sword, using it to hack all five men to pieces, and then using those pieces as bait to catch even larger fish. He then leisurely strolled back to town so he could cook up dinner at his girlfriend's place because he was just a good boyfriend like that. When the English sheriff came by her house to arrest Wallace, his girlfriend said she had no clue where he was. Since "aiding and abetting" was a much bigger deal back then than it is today (and "due process of the law" a much smaller one), the sheriff had Wallace's girlfriend executed on the spot.

Mistake.

Now, take a minute and picture the sort of dudes who compete in the Highland Games—those beer-chugging, log-hurling, beard-wearing haggis eaters who easily lob eight-hundred-pound kegs of whiskey two thousand feet through the air and then head-butt small woodland creatures to death with their bald, tattooed foreheads. Then picture a guy who breaks those suckers' faces apart in a bare-knuckle boxing match nine out of ten times without even breaking a sweat and you're starting to get the idea of the sort of psycho asskick-a-tron Bill Wallace was. Judging by the fact that this sword-swinging maniac carried a six-foot-long claymore into battle with similar results to those produced by a gas-powered chainsaw, many historians believe that this dude was close to seven feet tall, a detail which is extra-impressive when you consider that the average human around this time stood about five foot four. What we do know for sure is that nobody could take this outlaw warrior in single combat without getting their skulls detonated like an overripe cantaloupe, he personally took down some of England's toughest knights in single combat, he could drink his weight in scotch without making a fool of himself, and his crazy unabashed kilt-wearing is the utter definition of being excessively balls-out all the time (he probably had to wear a kilt because no mortal pants could contain his massive brass nuts anyway). Oh yeah, and now he was really, really pissed.

Wallace went into a souped-up turbocharged berserker rage, killed the sheriff with a steely death stare and a judo chop to the neck, dismembered that asshole's corpse, and then slaughtered the entire garrison at Lanark with his dick and half a broken-off beer bottle. From there he began an unstoppable death crusade against the English, recruiting an unruly band of disenfranchised badass Highlanders as he rampaged across the countryside utterly ruining any Englishman unfortunate enough to be alive. At the Battle of Loudoun Hill Wallace and a few buddies ambushed a two-hundred-man English cavalry detachment, jumping down from some rocks, knocking them off their horses, and then wearing their faces around as hats. At the Battle of Ardrossian Castle Wallace managed to capture a heavily fortified, well-defended English stronghold despite having absolutely no siege weaponry—he simply stood outside the garrison walls mooning at the defenders, and when the garrison marched out to beat his ass Wallace's men came out of nowhere, caved their brains in with tire irons, and then set the whole place on fire. As news of Wallace's victories got around it inspired the Scottish people to get their freedom on and start kicking ass, and before long roughly every armed commoner, outlaw, and peasant north of Edinburgh was sprinting across the countryside to join his ranks. In just a few months William Wallace had gone from some random surly outlaw to a full-on rebel leader, assembling a sizable army of rugged, brain-eating Scotsmen ready to tear the English limb from limb and then deposit those limbs somewhere that wasn't part of Scottish soil. This unruly angry mob besieged and captured several English strongholds across Scotland, including the historical seat of power at Scone Castle, and tossed the English out of Scotland on their asses.

While this was all going down Edward Longshanks was off crusading and/or joyfully exterminating the people of France, so when he heard about what was going on back home he was obviously a little miffed that his jerkass generals couldn't get their faces out of their sphincters long enough to quell this puny outlaw band of disgruntled papists. He had a bunch of his senior officers executed Darth Vader style, ordered the survivors to launch a full-scale attack on Wallace's makeshift army ("You are in command now, *Admiral* Piett"), and then sat back and put his feet up on the backs of some French POWs, confident that his men could get the job done.

They didn't.

At the Battle of Stirling Bridge, a strong, well-equipped, well-trained, professional English army drew up battle lines against William Wallace's pitchfork-and-torches peasant mob, ready to end this silliness once and for all in a barrage of arrows and bloodstained broadswords. Outnumbered over five to one by armored dudes with steel weaponry, Wallace still refused to back down. He just stood there, calmly watching as the English crossed the narrow bridge, and then, as soon as the first part of their army was on Wallace's side of the river, ordered his men to charge out of the woods and hammer them from all sides like a pack of rabid hell wolves attacking an unconscious man made completely out of beef sirloin. As the English stupidly attempted to bring their heavy cavalry across the hilariously small bridge (it was barely wide enough for two riders to travel side by side) Wallace collapsed the structure (he'd sabotaged it before the battle), sending a few dozen knights plummeting down into the river below, stranding the rest on the far side of the river, and cutting off the English vanguard's only reasonable escape route. The Scots ran up and massacred the English without mercy, and then to celebrate the victory Wallace had a super-sweet scabbard, belt, and matching sandals made out of the dried skin of the slain English commander—which is kind of morbid and yet also undeniably badass at the same time.

With the English army now in disarray, Wallace pressed the attack. He drove the routed army all the way back to England, then he even launched a campaign across the border into Northumberland, raiding, pillaging, and burning English settlements wherever he could find them. Wallace pushed as far south as Cockermouth, which means very little to me in terms of geography and is really only mentioned here because Cockermouth is probably the greatest name for a city in the entire history of the world, but you get the point. After several months strong-arming the already defeated English army, Wallace returned to Scotland with incredible quantities of booty and fame, which in turn presumably helped him get incredible quantities of booty from hot Gaelic redheads any time he felt like it. Wallace was knighted by Scottish nobleman Robert the Bruce, and the new Sir The Wallace was given the prestigious title "Guardian of Scotland and Leader of Its Armies," which is a pretty great title if you ask me.

Okay, well now the 'Shanks was *really* riled up, and it was now becoming painfully obvious that if he wanted this whole "kill all Scots" thing done right he was going to have to do it himself. King Edward abruptly ended the war in France, called his troops home, and committed the full might of his considerably menacing army to battling the rebellion. In 1298 he crossed thirty thousand Englishmen and Welshmen into Scotland, intent on a final badass showdown with the Goliath Scots bastard who had spent the previous couple years annoyingly killing all of his peeps. At the Battle of Falkirk, six thousand Scotsmen once again made a desperate stand against the invaders, utterly oblivious to the fact that the odds were worse than the male-female ratio at a Magic: The Gathering tournament. Then, just to make the situation somehow even worse, just as things were starting to get interesting Wallace was betrayed and abandoned by his cavalry on the battlefield—Longshanks had bought them all off before the battle with promises of wealth and land and shady prescriptions for medicinal marijuana. Wallace's remaining infantry, though brave, couldn't stand up to the ludicrous numbers of longbowmen and heavy cavalry that Longshanks was able to field. Despite killing the master of the English Knights Templar in single combat, Wallace lost the battle and was forced to flee to France so he could hook up with Sophie Marceau for a while.

After trouncing Wallace's oversized soccer riot with a few billion arrowheads Edward continued on, defeated Robert the Bruce in a subsequent battle (sending the Bruce fleeing to Ireland, where he had no trouble finding people to commiserate with about how the English kings are total dicks sometimes), and reasserted his iron-fisted dominance over Scotland once more. Wallace returned a few years later to continue the fight, but before he could really get going his own men handed him over to Edward in exchange for some cash and a high five. Wallace was convicted of treason, and the English dragged him naked through the streets, cut off his balls, beheaded him, disemboweled him, set his organs on fire, dismembered his corpse, and then publicly displayed different parts of his body in grocery stores and mall parking lots across England and Scotland.

Even in death, however, William Wallace still managed to incite the people of Scotland to kill the English—when the Scots went to work the next morning and saw their beloved national hero's severed limbs hanging from a rope in the town square they got EVEN MORE PISSED, took up arms again, and carried out their deceased leader's mission by going around killing English soldiers wherever they could find them. Robert the Bruce, pumped about the recent turn of events, returned from Ireland, formed a huge army of totally stoked kilted bastards, and was crowned king of an independent Scotland in 1307.

Edward Longshanks, who by this point in his thirty-year career of unceremoniously thumping the Scots up and down the British Isles with a steel-toed boot was known by the badass moniker "The Hammer of Scotland," responded to King The Bruce in the same way he'd always responded to uppity clansmen who didn't know their place—by preparing to curbstomp the sedition out of them with the mashing hooves of a couple thousand heavily armored war horses. 'Shanks marched across the River Forth into Scotland for a third time, but, luckily for the Bruce, the ultra-hardcore, ultra-old English king died of extreme decrepitness before he could face Robert on the field of battle. In true badass fashion, with his dying words Edward Longshanks told his son to press the attack, never stop kicking Scotsmen in the kilt, stay off drungs and always brush his teeth at least twice a day, and then he requested that his dead body be carried out onto the battlefield in front of the English army so that even in death Edward Effin' Longshanks could strike fear into his enemies' hearts.

King Edward II did not do any of those things. Instead, he ran home like a punk and spent the next seven years being utterly incompetent and useless. While he was doing that, Robert the Bruce launched a masterful guerrilla war in Scotland, eventually recapturing every Scottish city that had been under English control.

It was only after he stopped receiving taxes from the Scots that Ed Junior (also known as "Shortshanks," "Dongshanks," or "Edward the Assclown") finally decided he probably needed to deal with this situation, so in 1314 he marched north with the single largest army ever personally commanded by a reigning English king—a massive throng of infantry accompanied by thousands of heavy knights and those same longbowmen who had messed Wallace's troops up so murderously a few years earlier. Robert the Bruce only had about seven thousand men and five hundred horses under his command, but this guy proved that it's not the size that matters—it's what you do with it. Bruce knew he was outnumbered by a ridiculous margin, so he chose his battlefield wisely—setting up in the middle of a dreary Scottish bog outside Edinburgh with very little ground for the English heavy cavalry to ride through. As if that wasn't enough of a terrain advantage, he then covered every piece of dry land out there with caltrops, thumbtacks, whoopee cushions, and camouflaged pit traps that opened up into spike-filled holes. Once this was done, Bob the Bruce rode out in front of his army and started trying to encourage his men with a badass speech about duty, honor, etc., but then suddenly, out of nowhere, some psycho lunatic English knight named Sir Henry de Bohun came charging all the way across the battlefield, by himself, leveling his lance right at the face of the Scottish king in a turbo-brave display of crippling idiocy. The thirty-nine-year-old Scottish ruler took one look at this jackass, sidestepped his charge, and split the dude's skull with a single powerful swing of his royal battleaxe. That pumped up the Scots about a thousand times more than any lame speech possibly could.

Despite being badly outnumbered, Robert the Bruce's tactics proved beeftastically successful against the moronic Edward II, whose hemorrhoidal battle plan consisted basically of pulling out a sword and half-heartedly yelling "CHARGE!" while spinning around in a circle. The English troops rushed ahead, hampered by the booby-trapped bog, and blitzed straight on into the Scottish *schilton*—basically a Macedonian-style phalanx of kilt-wearing blue-painted psychos carrying gigantic wooden spears they'd whittled into points with their beards. The horses didn't want to charge into the spear wall, so the cavalry was ineffective, and these mobile death hedges mercilessly shish-kebabed their way through the English lines with little resistance. Then, just when it looked like things couldn't possibly get worse for young Edward II, a second force of cheesed-off Scots came out of the woods and surprise-attacked the back of the English army from the direction they least expected it— the English king only escaped painful sword-induced death when his personal bodyguards bravely cut their way through the ambush and dragged him out by his ear.

The English ran home and didn't bother returning. Scotland would maintain its independence for the next four hundred years, only relinquishing its autonomy when James Stuart, the reigning king of Scotland, was crowned king of England as well and figured it would be easier to manage his dominion if he just combined everything together.

Twelve Highlanders and a bagpipe make a rebellion.

—SCOTTISH PROVERB

Just before Robert the Bruce died of leprosy in 1329 he asked to have his heart carved out of his chest cavity and carried into battle by Sir James Douglas on the next Crusade, a fact that only makes me love this guy more. The Douglas honored the king's wishes, naturally, and just before he was killed in battle against the Moors he is said to have whipped the heart of Robert the Bruce out of his backpack and chucked it at the swarm of enemies surrounding him.

———

In the seventeenth century, when wars were being fought with muzzle-loading gunpowder muskets, a badass Scots mercenary named Alasdair MacColla devised a tactic known as the "Highland Charge." Basically, the Scots would line up across from their enemies, both sides would fire a volley of musket balls at each other in the standard fashion of early modern warfare, and then, when the enemy went to reload their muskets (a process that could take anywhere from twenty to forty seconds depending on how skilled the musketeer was) the Highlanders would drop their guns, unsheathe steel broadswords, and run full speed at the enemy, trying to butcher them into pieces before they could get their weapons reloaded. As you can imagine, this was effective as hell— the British only managed to counter this brand of terrifying attack by adopting the bayonet.

———

Longshanks's son, the inept King Edward II, ended up marrying Isabella, the She-Wolf of France—a take-no-prisoners hellion who became famous for being the only queen of England to ever order the execution of the king. Married together in an attempt to stop all the wars between France and England, it wasn't long after their marriage that Ed started dissing his French princess in public, telling everyone she was just some stupid bimbo and he didn't really like her that much anyways. When she complained about her treatment he tried to have her assassinated, so Isabella went home to France, started shacking up with some other guy, raised an army, came back, overthrew the king, tossed him in the Tower of London, and had all of his friends executed in subatomically brutal ways—one particularly unsavory dude was hanged, disemboweled, had his entrails burned, was then beheaded, drawn, and quartered, and had his parts distributed across England. After he'd witnessed her wrath, Izzy then had Edward dragged out into a field and murdered by being stabbed in the ass with red-hot pokers. Their son, Edward III, would eventually take over as king and have Isabella placed under house arrest, where she'd spend the rest of her days living in a huge awesome castle.

14

TRIAL BY COMBAT

Jean de Carrouges vs. Jacques Le Gris
Paris, France
December 29, 1389

I do hereby charge that during the third week of this January past, one
Jacques Le Gris, squire, did feloniously and carnally know my wife,
the Lady Marguerite Carrouges, against her will, in the place known
as Capomesnil. And I stand ready to prove this charge by my body against his
and to render him either dead or vanquished at the appointed time.

—SIR JEAN DE CARROUGES

WHEN MOST PEOPLE THINK ABOUT MEDIEVAL WARFARE, THEY
PICTURE GIGANTIC ARMIES OF DUDES IN PLATE MAIL WILDLY
SWINGING SWORDS AND SPEARS AROUND LIKE SPASTIC MANI-
ACS WHILE HORSES TRAMPLE HELPLESS PEASANTS, GUYS WITH
TORCHES EXTOL THE VIRTUES OF SETTING THATCHED-ROOF
COTTAGES ON FIRE, CROSSBOW BOLTS MORPH THE ATMOSPHERE
INTO A SWARMING MASS OF POINTY DESTRUCTIVENESS, MEN
GET THEIR FACES MELTED INTO GOO BY CAULDRONS OF BOIL-
ING OIL, AND ROCKS THE SIZE OF CATTLE ARE CATAPULTED
OVERHEAD BY TOWERING TREBUCHETS, TAKING MINIVAN-SIZED
CHUNKS OUT OF THE SIDES OF FORMIDABLE CASTLE WALLS.

Well, sure, all of this stuff is pretty awesome (unless of course you're one of those poor suckers with a pitchfork and a dopey hat and some asshole in full chain mail is jamming a burning torch in your eye while a horse kicks your wife in the stomach), but some of the most vicious battles to take place during this period weren't full-scale struggles between colossal armies of pikemen but much more personal affairs—no-holds-barred arena deathmatches where two men with serious beef, implacable hatred, and almost no respect for the due process of law aired out their grievances with longswords, lances, and boots to the crotch while thousands of bloodthirsty fans cheered from the stands like they were sitting on the fifty-yard line at the Super Bowl. Trial by combat was the medieval World Series of Vengeance, where two men were so emphatically convinced of the righteousness of their cause that they were willing to battle it out on the field of combat and let the Almighty Himself decide who was just and honest and good, and who deserved to be shanked in the throat until dead.

The last trial by combat ever officially authorized by the government of France took place in 1389 between Sir Jean de Carrouges and Jacques Le Gris, two hardass old bastards with serious irreconcilable differences that could only be solved in the sort of delicate manner that involved publicly trying to kill each other with swords in front of a live studio audience.

Back in what they used to call the "good old days," Carrouges and Le Gris were homeboys. Both men served under the lordship of Count Pierre of Alençon, they used to get together for beers after work, and they'd occasionally go to Le Gris's estate for mutton sandwich barbecues on the weekend, but over the years, the two buddies eventually had something of a falling-out. Whereas Sir Jean Carrouges spent most of the mid-fourteenth century fighting on the front lines of the Hundred Years' War, battling the English in Normandy and participating in an expedition where he teamed up with the Scottish and spent several months raiding and ravaging English villages, Jacques Le Gris stayed home, attended networking power luncheons, joined the company softball team, hit on everyone's wives at the annual holiday party, and otherwise preoccupied himself with seeing exactly how far he could shove his head up Count Pierre's ass.

Since corporate life wasn't much different in feudal times than it is today, kissing ass got Jacques Le Gris a hell of a lot farther than Jean de Carrouges's towering deeds of awesomeness, and it shouldn't have been that much of a surprise in 1389 when Sir Jean de Carrouges came home from his most recent campaign and discovered that even though he'd spent the last thirty years wading through knee-high piles of dead Saracens and Englishmen for king, country, and glory, it was Jacques Le Gris who had been promoted to a lofty position of wealth and luxury as Count Pierre's new right-hand man.

What did surprise him was when when Jean's wife told him that while he was out fighting the English, Jacques Le Gris had come over to his house, tied up Lady Carrouges, and brutally had his way with her against her will.

Well, surprise isn't the right word. Enrage probably is.

The ensuing trial was a joke. According to French law, the case was to be brought before Count Pierre, and Pierre of course acquitted his favorite vassal before the lawyers had even finished unpacking their briefcases. But Carrouges's rapidly-boiling-over death-fury wasn't about to be placated so easily. The grizzled knight went over the count's head, riding his horse straight into Paris and appealing his case to King Charles IV himself. With no way to officially determine the truth (this was back before DNA testing and *Law & Order: SVU*), Jean demanded vengeance the badass old-school way—through judicial combat. If Sir Jean won, then Le Gris would be proven as a no-good rapist bastard. If Le Gris slew Carrouges, not only would Le Gris be proven innocent of all crimes, but Carrouges would be dead and Marguerite would be dragged out in the street and publicly burned at the stake as a liar. Since Charles IV was like eighteen at the time and was really in the mood to see some badass Medieval Times stuff go down, he did the whole "so let it be written, so let it be done" thing and the next thing you know Sir Michael Buffer was asking people whether or not they were ready to rumble.

The dispute would be settled once and for all on a sand-covered 240-by-60-foot field on the grounds of the priory of Saint-Martin-des-Champs monastery in Paris, in front of thousands of screaming groundlings, the king himself, most of the senior nobility, and the black-clad Lady Marguerite de Carrouges. Sir Jean would battle his enemy with cold steel, fighting not only for his own life, but for bloody revenge and for the life of his beloved Marguerite.

It went down with an eerie similarity to a jousting event at a Ren Faire. The overflowing crowd of lowly peasants clutched their ballpark popcorn and oversized, ludicrously priced plastic beer mugs anxiously, roaring like bloodthirsty lions as Sir Jean de Carrouges thundered across the sand-swept battlefield on the back of his fourteen-hundred-pound armored warhorse, his awesome-looking helmet plume fluttering like a righteous feathered mullet in the cold December wind. Through the narrow visor slit of his reinforced steel helm, this vengeance-hungry knight carefully aimed the tip of his heavy lance at the torso of his archnemesis, his mind firmly intent on driving the metal point of the brutal weapon straight through the heart of that bastard before him, impaling him like a corn dog.

The two armored knights slammed into each other with the same force as a car crash, only in this case instead of a nice fluffy air bag popping up to cushion the tremendous blow, they were each greeted by the brazen tip of a medieval lance plowing into their shields with enough velocity to dent reinforced steel. Both men reeled in their saddles, but it was going to take a hell of a lot more than a love tap to the sternum with a metal spike to settle the ultimate blood feud between these two honor-bound knights.

Carrouges inspected his lance for cracks as he circled back around for a second pass. The din of the crowd was barely audible over the thundering of horse hooves, the clanking of plate armor, and the beating of the knight's own heart as the two men closed again. This time, with only seconds before a second earth-rending impact capable of liquefying internal organs, Le Gris suddenly raised his lance, aiming the tip of his deadly instrument of brain-stabbing misery directly at Carrouges's helmet visor. Streaking toward his opponent at twenty-five miles an hour, Jean didn't even have time to get his shield up—all he could do was duck his head and hope for a glancing blow.

With a metallic clang Le Gris's lance caught the rounded part of Carrouges's helm and slid off, sending visible sparks flying—much to the delight of the assembled spectators, who threw up a satisfied cheer while these two maniacs tried to violently demolish each other in a judicial spectacle that's way more awesome than anything that ever aired on Court TV (seriously, imagine how badass it would be if alleged baby killers had to prove their innocence by face off against Nancy Grace in a Vulcan knife fight).

The armored warriors urged their tired steeds on for a third time. The impact of this collision was even more chest-implodingly violent than the first two. Both knights' lances, burdened by the stresses associated with being involved in three fifty-mile-per-hour head-on collisions in under five minutes, exploded into wooden shrapnel, leaving only their steel tips embedded in the other's shield. Both men remained firm in their saddles somehow, their implacable hatred outlasting the structural integrity of their weapons.

The knights ditched their shattered lances and beat-to-hell shields, drew gigantic battleaxes from their saddles, and started smashing the hell out of each other on horseback. Using a combination of gourd-splitting one- and two-handed blows, this medieval version of *American Gladiators* involved both dudes hacking at each other like crazy for a while, each trying to either knock the other man from his horse or lop off some vital appendage that would damage the other's ability to fight back. After deflecting several hate-fueled swings, Le Gris made a feint to strike at Carrouges's head, and then slammed his battleaxe down hard into the neck of Carrouges's horse with enough force to nearly decapitate the beast, finding a weak spot in the animal's plate barding and sending both the horse and Sir Jean crumpling to the ground. This would have probably been considered a dirty trick in the more honorable duels of the time period, but fourteenth-century judicial combat had even fewer rules of engagement than a drunken unlicensed backyard MMA cage-fighting bout—chivalry had no place on this battlefield, ball-punches were totally legal, and PETA hadn't yet established its offices in Paris.

Jacques Le Gris circled around and spurred his warhorse toward his fallen foe, axe held high for a final killing blow that would forever exonerate him from those horrible baseless claims against his family's honor (roasting marshmallows for delicious after-battle s'mores while Marguerite burned at the stake would just be an added bonus). He charged in, closing quickly on his dismounted opponent, but just as he ripped off an axe blow earth-shattering enough to split a uranium atom into a thermonuclear detonation, Jean de Carrouges dove out of the way of the attack—not only avoiding the kill shot, but also planting his own axe into the underbelly of Le Gris's horse in the process. The wounded beast crumpled, throwing Le Gris violently from the saddle, pitching him face-first into the sand.

Both men were in their fifties at this point, but Jacques Le Gris was bigger, stronger, and in much better health than Jean de Carrouges, who had been worn down from injuries sustained during decades of constant battle. If his imposing size wasn't enough, Le Gris was also far wealthier than Sir Jean, so he could afford the best gear and the sturdiest armor France had to offer.

But Le Gris was also a guy who had stayed home boning his friends' wives while Carrouges was marching through a blood-drenched battlefield decapitating enemy warriors with an endless series of armored headbutts, and even though the exhausted war hero was half dead, suffering from a fever, and probably experiencing some postconcussionlike symptoms, Sir Jean was more than ready to bust out a display of raw badassitude that would rival Michael Jordan's performance in game 5 of the 1997 NBA finals.

Both warriors drew their swords, stepped forward, and began battering each other right in front of the royal viewing box, parrying, slashing, and hacking, looking for weaknesses in their enemies' armor while the teenage king and the black-clad Marguerite looked on anxiously and the court jester yelled out some of the more memorable one-liners from SoulCalibur and Street Fighter II.

The battle raged back and forth, but then, with a sudden mighty blow, Jacques Le Gris knocked Carrouges's sword back and buried the point of his blade into Carrouges's thigh, punching through the armor and driving the steel hard into Sir Jean's leg.

Rather than panicking, the sight of his own wound only succeeded in making Jean de Carrouges angry. It was like Bruce Lee getting slashed across the chest by that guy with the bear hands, tasting his own blood, and then FLIPPING THE HELL OUT.

Carrouges lifted his own blade, shouted a battle cry, and resumed his attack with a newfound ferocity. Le Gris withdrew his sword from Carrouges leg and blocked the blow, but in his righteous fury Carrouges battered Le Gris with a flurry of hammerlike strikes and then, when Le Gris least expected it, Carrouges grabbed his archenemy by the helmet and slammed him headfirst into the dirt. Carrouges then kicked the sword from his flailing enemy's sweaty mitt, rolled him over, straddled him, and unsheathed his dagger. Sir Jean tried first to stab his wife's rapist through the visor of the guy's helm, but when Le Gris evaded, Carrouges went for a more direct approach—he smashed the visor lock with the hilt of his dagger and flipped up the faceplate to expose Jacques Le Gris's sweating visage. Carrouges, now in control, shouted one word at his enemy: *Confess.*

Le Gris said nothing. Jean de Carrouges stabbed him through the throat with a six-inch blade, killing his archnemesis immediately. Flawless victory. Fatality.

A hush fell over the crowd as they came to the solemn realization that a man had just died before their eyes. Sir Jean waited a second, then slowly, deliberately, pulled himself to his feet, blood still flowing from the wound in his leg. The knight turned, faced the crowd, and with one move raised his sword and shouted in a loud, clear, triumphant voice, "Have I done my duty?"

The crowd went nuts.

Sir Jean de Carrouges received honors from the king, then limped over to embrace his wife. He would become an official knight of the crown and receive land and wealth from the estate of Jacques Le Gris, and he and Marguerite would go on to have three sons over the course of their next ten years together. Meanwhile, Jacques Le Gris's body was stripped of its armor and hung in chains outside Paris alongside various traitors, bandits, and murderers. The last judicial duel ordered by the Parlement of Paris was over.

In medieval Europe, oaths of friendship, marriage, and fealty were formalized with a ceremony that involved the two oath takers clasping their right hands together. Oaths of hatred and vengeance, such as those sworn before a judicial combat, were taken by clasping left hands. This is why it feels so weird to shake hands with your left.

If trial by combat is the most badass way to arbitrarily prove guilt or innocence, then trial by ordeal is probably the most horrible. Dating back to the days of Hammurabi, trial by ordeal was when an accused person would be tied to a board, weighted with rocks, and then thrown into a river—if they lived, it was a sign from God that they were innocent. If they drowned, it had to be assumed that they were guilty (not that it mattered, since they were dead anyway). The advent of medieval torture put an interesting spin on the ordeal—in England, the accused would either stick his arm up to the elbow in a kettle of boiling water for five seconds or grab a red-hot poker and hold it for five seconds (prisoner's choice). If the prisoner showed any signs of pain, he was deemed guilty and would immediately be beheaded on the spot. Trial by ordeal was officially outlawed by the Catholic Church in 1215—they deemed it too inhumane, so they mercifully did away with it and replaced it with the Inquisition.

Some medieval sources claim that later in life Marguerite was overcome with crippling guilt and announced that she was lying about the whole rape thing. I'd argue that sticking your neck out there and risking being burned at the stake would be a good enough reason not to make such a wild unsubstantiated accusation, but I guess the short answer is that we'll really never know the truth. The official verdict of the king was that God had given Jean de Carrouges the strength to win the duel, thereby proving Le Gris's guilt, and if the backward medieval judicial system was good enough for him, I guess it's good enough for me.

A HISTORY OF DUELING, AS TOLD THROUGH THIRTEEN BADASS DUELS

1. THE HORATII (667 BC)

Nobody put an emphasis on the glory of man-to-man combat quite like the ancient Greeks and Romans. Their love of single combat was so great that the Romans actually once staked their entire future as a nation on a duel—during a dispute with the nearby town of Alba, the two young city-states decided to settle their war by staging an all-or-nothing badass duel for ultimate control of the Italian peninsula. The Romans sent three brothers known as the Horatii, while the Albans sent *their* best three-man tag-team brother duelists, the Curiatii. In the initial bloodbath, two of the three Horatii were slain and all three Curiatii were wounded. Surrounded by three enemies, the lone surviving Horatius stood his ground, fought bravely, and managed to somehow kill all three Curiatii in one ten-ton display of badass swordsmanship. After saving the city's honor, the surviving Horatius returned home only to find his sister crying because he was still alive (she'd been engaged to one of the now-dead Curiatii and had been secretly hoping they would win). A good stoic Roman, the last Horatius got mad and stabbed her as well. Since the Senate understood where he was coming from, they commuted his murder sentence from "death" to "we all get to hit you with sticks for a while," and everyone called it a day.

2. BATTLE OF BADR (AD 624)

In Arab custom, large-scale battles were kicked off by each army's greatest champions walking out into the middle of the battlefield and fighting each other in a no-holds-barred deathmatch in full view of both armies. Before the Battle of Badr in 624, one of the key battles in the early history of Islam, the Prophet Muhammad sent out his toughest warrior, Ali ibn Abi Talib, to take on the toughest warriors the army of Mecca had to offer. Armed with the holy sword Zulfiqar—a badass two-pronged forked scimitar that sort of functions like the Excalibur of Islam—Ali killed not one, but three men in single combat, one after the other. The Muslims were so pumped by his victories that they won the battle despite being badly outnumbered.

3. VIKING JUSTICE (C. AD 930)

One of the most volatile Vikings to ever live was the omega-insane Egil Skallagrimsson—a fire-breathing berserker warrior, poet, and all-around psychotic bastard whose limitless battle-rages and video-game-grade killing sprees were only made more intimidating by the fact that he had some weirdo musculoskeletal disease that gave him a gigantic, imposing, eggplant-shaped head. Despite his disturbing vegetablelike appearance, Egil married a lovely Viking maiden named Asgerdr (pronounced either "ass girder" or "ass guarder" depending on the translation), but when his new wife's rightful inheritance was confiscated by a Norwegian berserker named Atli the Short (who really hated Egil), Egil immediately decided to meet in the dueling circle to settle their beef once and for all. In the rabid roid battle that ensued, both men's shields were smashed into splinters and their weapons were blunted, so, in a furious fit of insanity, Egil threw down his weapons, tackled Atli like Lawrence Taylor destroying Joe Theisman on *Monday Night Football*, and killed the guy by BITING HIS THROAT AND TEARING OUT HIS JUGULAR WITH HIS TEETH. This display of toothy testosterone cemented Asgerdr's inheritance for good, since nobody would have ever wanted to cross Egil after having witnessed that crap.

4. The Iron Monkey Steals the Peach (1127)

In 1127 a lesser-ranking nobleman named Guy of Steenvoorde was accused of leading a conspiracy that assassinated the count of Flanders, so one of the count's top lieutenants—the awesomely epitheted Herman the Iron—challenged Guy to one-on-one judicial combat to the death. Herman was unhorsed in the initial joust, but before Guy could spear Herman with the lance while he lay on the ground, Herman killed Guy's horse and pulled him down as well. The two men fought bitterly, breaking their weapons, losing their shields, and resorting to fierce hand-to-hand combat. Guy got the better of it, pinning Herman to the ground and bashing him in the face with a gauntleted knuckle sandwich, but as he was getting his face rearranged Herman reached down, grabbed Guy's nads with a steel-plated fist, and, summoning all his strength for the brief space of one moment, he hurled Guy from him; by this motion tearing all the lower parts of the body so Guy, now prostrate, gave up, crying out that he was conquered and dying. Guy wasn't a guy any longer, and the recently eunuched knight was hanged for conspiracy the next morning.

5. The Elephant Duel (1592)

As the heavily outnumbered warriors of Siam desperately fought off a full-scale invasion by the Burmese army during the Battle of Nong Sarai in 1592, King Naresuan of Siam suddenly looked out across the blood-spattered battlefield and caught sight of the king of Burma charging full speed toward him. Because these two men had intensely hated each other since childhood—and each king just so happened to be mounted on the back of a gigantic badass war elephant—they obviously decided to settle their differences the old-school badass way. The two elephants charged, smashing together in a thunderous crash of pachyderm tusks. The warriors climbed out onto the heads of the animals, fighting with swords in a battle so over-the-top awesome that both sides actually stopped fighting each other so that they could watch it. The men bobbed and weaved, hacking furiously while the elephants kicked and tusked at each other. After a heated battle, King Naresuan harnessed his inner getting-pissed powers, smacked the Burmese king's weapon away, then swung his sword down

HARD on his enemy's collarbone. There was a brief pause, where both men stood motionless atop the heads of their elephants like a Kurosawa samurai duel, and then the Burmese king totally fell in half—he'd been bifurcated from his right shoulder all the way through to his left hip Darth Maul style. The top half of him fell to the ground. The rest collapsed where it was. Blood fountain. War over.

6. Don't Mess with the Jubei (c. 1650)

In the late seventeenth century an eyepatch-wearing Japanese ninja/samurai warrior named Jubei visited a wealthy feudal lord, and the lord's top champion challenged Jubei to a friendly sparring match. The two men took up wooden swords, stood across from each other, and then proceeded to lash out simultaneously with lightning-quick strikes in a quick-draw dueling style known as iaijutsu. In one movement, both men drew their weapons and struck, each stick hitting home almost simultaneously, and then Jubei stood back and bowed. The other samurai brought his weapon back up, not fully understanding what was going on, and lunged at Jubei once more. Again, the swords clashed in a single strike that was almost too quick for the human eye, and again, Jubei stood back and bowed. The samurai was totally hateful now—"Why the hell are you bowing, you douche!" Unfazed, Jubei was just like, "Well, because I owned your ass, fool, so deal with that." Well, the moron samurai was immeasurably pissed at this point, because he seriously thought both fights were stalemates (idiot). Jubei calmly informed the samurai that if he honestly thought both fights were even, then he was obviously an incompetent ass-head, so the samurai pulled out his sword and challenged Jubei to fight for real. Jubei rolled his eyes, sighed, and promptly sliced the dude in half with one swing of his blade. This duel was the basis for that awesome scene in *The Seven Samurai*.

7. La Maupin (c. 1690)

One of the most badass sword fighters in French history was a hard-core, face-eviscerating woman named Julie D'Aubigny, better known simply as La Maupin (which, by the way, is French for "The Maupin"). A master swordswoman with ten dueling kills to her name, La Maupin was a ridiculously-awesome chick who was also the lead contralto in the world-renowned Paris Opera, and who once took the Holy Orders just so that she could sneak into a convent and bang a nun. Well, one time

La Maupin showed up to a royal ball at the palace of King Louis XIV dressed in an opulent scarlet tunic and immediately started dancing with all the hottest chicks she could find. This was fine and all, but when La Maupin had the audacity to tongue-kiss a particularly fine-looking blonde countess right in front of the entire royal family, three ham-faced noblemen got a little bent out of shape about it and told Maupin she needed to start acting like a lady and stop macking on all the hot babeage. La Maupin offered to take it outside, drew her musketeer-style rapier, killed all three men in three consecutive duels, then came back to the party while the trio of poseurs were still lying bleeding in the street like dogs. When some guy asked her what the heck just happened she told him she was glad she was wearing a red dress because it was great at masking the blood of her enemies.

8. The Wrath of Mary Read (1720)

During her adventures sailing around with Anne Bonny plundering ships in the Caribbean during the Golden Age of Piracy, the fierce female pirate Mary Read found herself falling in love with the ship's navigator, a nerdy dude who was much more comfortable staring at naval charts than he was holding a musket or swinging a cutlass around. Well, one day one of the bigger, douchebag asshole pirates started talking smack to the navigator, and the poor guy, feeling obligated to defend his manliness, challenged the pirate to a duel the following morning—a challenge the cutthroat gleefully accepted. Well, Mary Read, a high-octane chick who had served as a front-line infantry soldier under the Duke of Marlborough during the Wars of the Spanish Succession, wasn't about to sit back while her new boyfriend got butchered into beef jerky nuggets—she went straight up to the cutthroat, insulted his mother, his place of birth, and his stupid gigantic ears, and challenged him to a duel right then, right there. He accepted, the two went ashore, and Mary Read cut that fool down with her cutlass in front of the entire crew.

9. Jackson Shot Second (1803)

The seventh president of the United States, Andrew "Old Hickory" Jackson, fought in 103 duels during his lifetime, and despite being hit with so many musket balls that his entire body allegedly "rattled like a bag of marbles," this guy still managed to live to be seventy-eight years old. His most famous pistols-at-dawn moment came when some flagrantly incompetent asshelmet named Charles Dickinson thought it would be really hilarious to write in to the local newspaper about how Jackson was a dumbass and his wife was a voracious cock-mongering slutbag (or something along those lines). Jackson, undeterred that young Mr. Dickinson had already killed twenty-six men in duels, not only challenged Dickinson to a gunfight, he let Dickinson take the first shot—when the men hit eight paces, turned, and heard the command to fire, Jackson just stood there and let Dickinson put a bullet right in his chest. Jackson looked down at the gaping gunshot wound, touched it, licked his finger, and then shot Dickinson right in the chest, killing him on the spot.

10. HAMILTON VS. BURR (1804)

America has its fair share of political animosity these days, but it's still nothing quite like it was in 1804 when the sitting vice president of the United States got into a gunfight with the former secretary of the treasury. Aaron Burr, the Democratic-Republican VP (this is back when Democrats and Republicans teamed up and collectively hated the Federalists), apparently got his knickers in a bundle when Federalist Party leader Alexander Hamilton (you know, the guy on the ten-dollar bill) talked a bunch of smack about him in the newspapers, called him out on Twitter, and put up some obscene cross-stitching making fun of him on Pinterest, so Burr decided the best way to deal with this mudslinging smear campaign was for the two men to meet up in New Jersey and shoot each other. Burr and Hamilton dressed up in their nicest clothes, went to Weehawken at 7:00 a.m., stood back-to-back, then stepped out ten paces, turned, and fired. Hamilton "threw away" his shot by firing up into the air—a typical tactic that allowed the duelist to keep his honor without actually inflicting death. Burr felt no such compunction; he capped Hamilton in the liver, fatally wounding him.

11. THE HOT-AIR BALLOON DUEL (1808)

One of the weirdest duels ever fought took place in France in 1808, when a Monsieur de Grandpre and a Monsieur Le Pique settled an argument over a woman by going up in two hot air balloons, armed with muskets, and shooting at each other until one person put a hole in the other's balloon. Grandpre won, putting a round through Le Pique's balloon, sending the unfortunate suitor plummeting a half-mile to his death below.

12. ZAITSEV VS. KOENINGS (1942)

One of the most acclaimed sniper duels in history took place in the ruins of burned-out Stalingrad at the height of history's bloodiest battle, as two of the deadliest marksmen to ever live played a cat-and-mouse game where one mistake meant a bullet in the brain. Zaitsev, Russia's most famous sniper, had already killed over two hundred men during the Battle of Stalingrad, so the Germans decided to put him in his place—they sent Major Koenings, their top countersniper, straight from Berlin to take him down. Koenings had the advantage: There was a ton of propaganda out there describing Zaitsev's exploits, so Koenings knew exactly what to expect, but Zaitsev knew nothing about Koenings's habits, style, or tactics—just that he was coming, and he was very very good. Koenings found a good perch and started picking off Russian snipers, sending a message to Zaitsev, who came to meet the challenge. As the fight for Stalingrad raged around them, the two men waited it out for three days and nights, moving under cover of darkness and lying motionless during the day while artillery exploded overhead. Finally, on the fourth day, Zaitsev's good friend Danilov spotted the German with his binocs and said, "Let me point him out for you." Danilov stood up and took a bullet in the shoulder, and when he did Zaitsev's quick eyes saw a slight glint underneath a sheet of iron in the middle of no-man's-land—sunlight reflecting off a telescopic sight. Zaitsev lined it up and took the shot. He never missed.

13. NOLAN RYAN VS. ROBIN VENTURA (1993)

There may have been more exciting MMA bouts, boxing matches, hockey fights, or basketball brawls, but as far as I'm concerned no sports duel has ever been more badass than when the Ryan Express beat the hell out of Robin Ventura in front of a sellout home crowd on national television. Nolan Ryan, an eight-time All-Star, Baseball Hall of Famer, and the all-time MLB leader in career strikeouts and no-hitters, was a forty-six-year-old living legend on August 4, 1993, when a wild pitch nicked the arm of twenty-five-year-old Chicago third baseman Robin Ventura. Ventura, a career .267 hitter, stupidly charged the mound full speed looking to coldcock a baseball icon twice his age. Ryan responded by gritting his teeth, slapping that punk in an under-arm headlock, and bashing Ventura repeatedly in his stupid face with a vicious barrage of relentless bare-knuckled fists. When the dust settled on the ensuing benches-clearing brawl, Ventura was ejected for being a douchebag while Ryan simply got up, readjusted his uniform, stepped back on the mound, and didn't give up another hit for the rest of the game. He recorded the win, 5–3.

15

THE HUNDRED YEARS' WAR

A Century of Battle
The Kingdom of France
1337–1453

From this day to the ending of the world, but we in it shall be remembered—
we few, we happy few, we band of brothers; for he today that sheds his blood
with me shall be my brother; be he ne'er so vile, this day shall gentle his
condition; and gentlemen in England now-a-bed shall think themselves
accurs'd they were not here, and hold their manhoods cheap whiles any speaks
that fought with us upon Saint Crispin's Day.

—WILLIAM SHAKESPEARE, *Henry V*

THE NEVER-ENDING DEATH FEUD FOR CONTROL OF MEDI-
EVAL FRANCE STARTED IN 1328, WHEN KING CHARLES IV OF
FRANCE STUPIDLY UP AND DIED BEFORE HE'D HAD THE CHANCE
TO IMPREGNATE HIS WIFE WITH A HUMAN MALE CHILD THAT
COULD INHERIT THE THRONE. His reproductive failure and subse-
quent death put a rather abrupt end to over three hundred years of rule

by the House of Capet, and, more pertinently, kicked off a gigantic raging maelstrom of crap that would result in over a century of warfare and bring about the utter destruction of nearly half of his country.

At its heart, the Hundred Years' War was a senseless pissing contest over who should have succeeded Charles as the new King of France. The king of England, Edward III, was the son of King Charles's sister (Isabelle, the aforementioned She-Wolf of France) and, according to English succession law, Edward by right should have become king of France. But the French understandably weren't too keen on being ruled over by a guy who was also the king of England, so they cited some old law claiming that succession could not be passed down through the female line (the time-honored "No Girls Allowed" rule) and issued the crown to Charles's cousin Philip of Valois instead.

This wouldn't work out very well for them.

To further complicate matters, Edward III was not only the king of England but also the duke of the French Duchy of Aquitaine—a title that had been passed down to the kings of England since Richard the Lionheart inherited it from his mother Eleanor of Aquitaine (see how it all fits together?). So, what this essentially means is that Ed could do whatever the hell he wanted to do with England, but Aquitaine was part of France, and as a duke, Ed needed to swear fealty to Philip of Valois and pay taxes to the French king. As you can imagine, the Edmeister wasn't exactly happy about forking over his hard-earned cash to the man who had stolen his rightful crown out from under him, so instead of filling out a 1040EZ form that year Edward co-opted the French fleur-de-lis onto his personal coat of arms, started calling himself the king of England and France, and went around talking to everyone in a terrible fake French accent. Philip responded by annexing Aquitaine, declaring Ed an outlaw, banning corned beef, and hiring a bunch of privateers to plunder English shipping, burn the cities of Portsmouth and Southampton, and bring a bunch of English fishermen back to Calais so they could be mutilated in public in front of cheering French crowds.

That was it.

Now, at this time in history, France was the largest, richest, and most powerful kingdom in all of Europe. King Philip ruled over five times as many subjects as King Edward, he had the pope imprisoned in the French-controlled city of Avignon, and his fanatically hardcore heavy cavalry units had trampled the family jewels of all who opposed them for the last couple of centuries. To put it in perspective, in 1337 there were more knights serving in Philip of Valois's heavy cavalry than there were people living in the city of London.

But Edward III didn't give a flaming crap—the vengeance-seeking king of England sold his crown to the Belgians for some extra cash, raised a mercenary army with his own private funds as well as the English treasury, and sailed across the Channel on the first of many expeditions designed to pummel the disobedience out of his no-good cousin and pry the bloody crown from his cold, dead hands.

The first major battle of the war came in 1340, when the English navy caught the entire French fleet with their sails down in the port of Sluys, massacred the French defenders with longbow arrows and broadswords to the face, burned most of their ships, and hung the French admirals from the yardarms of King Philip's personal flagship. Edward III had initially been worried about the possibility of a French invasion of England, but in one day of fighting he fully annihilated his enemy's entire navy, crippling their ability to launch attacks on the island of Britain, taking complete naval control of the Channel, and clearing the way for the endless series of full-scale invasions of France that would follow. The battle was such a disaster that the court jester was the only guy brave enough to break the news to the French king, and I'm pretty sure that guy ended up like the cute green chick that enraged Jabba the Hutt with her terrible dancing.

The next major expedition to France came in 1346, when King Edward landed an army on the shores of Normandy and immediately started wantonly burning, pillaging, and looting everything he could get his hands on. Leaving behind nothing more than a smoldering swath of carnage and misery where there once used to be bustling villages is a good way to get the enemy's attention, and it wasn't too long before Philip of Valois's army of plate-armor-clad heavy knights caught up to Eddie outside the town of Crécy-en-Ponthieu, eager to bitch-slap the English back down to size and then use their femurs as toothpicks.

Edward III of England only had eleven thousand men with him for the Battle of Crécy, over half of whom were archers who wore no armor and carried nothing more than a six-foot Welsh longbow and a pathetic little dagger that was about as effective against heavy armor as a fondue fork. Edward positioned these archers in a V formation at the top of a hill, then had them slam sharpened stakes down into the ground in front of them so that enemy horses wouldn't charge, but these guys still weren't exactly all that thrilled when they looked down the hill and saw thirty thousand French knights on horseback wearing plate armor and carrying giant ominous steel lances. The French knights were world renowned for their unbelievable asskicking powers—not only were these men trained at birth to destroy any and all opposition without mercy, but the horses themselves were trained to bite, kick, and trample the enemy in hand-to-hand combat. Being outnumbered three to one by these guys wasn't exactly a picnic, especially when all that's standing between you and a broadsword to the ribcage is a wooden stick and the shirt on your back.

But Edward was a righteously badass dude who had learned well from Grandpa Longshanks, and a few years earlier he had implemented a law that required all English yeomen to practice archery once a week—so by the time the Battle of Crécy rolled around, these guys were pulling eighty to a hundred pounds of draw strength on their longbows, and on a good day each archer could shoot ten arrows a minute capable of puncturing steel plate at sixty yards. And Edward had five thousand of them in defensive positions atop a hill. He wasn't worried.

The French launched fifteen separate cavalry charges uphill through the mud toward the British lines, each one galloping forward seeking glorious combat with the under-equipped, outnumbered enemy. It was like assaulting a World War II German machine gun nest by riding straight at it on a bicycle across open ground.

The French charge reached English lines only once, and it was immediately wiped out by a counterattack led by Edward's son, the seventeen-year-old Edward the Black Prince (so named because of his badass black plate armor). The French lost ten thousand men, including the king of Bohemia, the Duke of Lorraine, ten counts, a couple dozen earls, and fifteen hundred other members of the aristocracy. The entire French nobility had been moked out in one afternoon by a couple thousand middle-class Englishmen, and the French countryside was now free to be pillaged and plundered whenever and wherever the English saw fit. Edward lost a hundred men in the battle, mostly due to them collapsing from exhaustion because they were so tired of killing Frenchmen.

The Hundred Years' War continued on like this for quite some time. The main problem was that no matter how many times they were shot to hell by arrows, the French responded to every battle simply by lining up their knights in a row and charging like dumbasses straight on into a never-ending storm of English arrows. At Crécy, the French charged the English infantry, ignoring the archers, and were wiped out. A few years later, at the Battle of Poitiers in 1356, the French decided to change up their tactics, and instead of charging straight into the longbows on horseback they dismounted, ran across a mud-covered field on foot toward the longbows, and still got mowed down by arrows. Seven thousand Englishmen annihilated a force of twenty thousand French knights, and a counterattack by the Black Prince and his men-at-arms resulted in the capture of the French king, who was later ransomed back to France for mad cash. Thirteen years after that, at the Battle of Najera, the French commander added a little Latin flavor by sending Spanish knights to charge into the Black Prince's archers, and, well, you know how it went. By the end of the decade, England would own territory all across the northern and western coasts of France.

Both sides took a break for a while because of internal rebellions, civil wars, and the Bubonic Plague, but then in 1415 they decided to pick up right where they left off when Edward III's great-grandson, Henry V, declared himself the legit heir to the throne and invaded France with a huge army. King Charles VI of France sent troops to stop this further incursion into his lands, and at the Battle of Agincourt, he decided that the best way to proceed would be to mass a huge force of heavy cavalry and charge straight on at the English longbowmen. Forty thousand French knights were massacred by ten thousand Englishmen—the bodies of knights and horses were said to have been piled up so high that a man couldn't see over the top of them. Shortly after Agincourt, there was a Battle of Herrings, where French knights charged a baggage train containing barrels of dead herrings and were shot to hell by English longbows. It really was just getting that ridiculous.

Finally, sick of being shot by arrows and almost completely out of knights to hurl aimlessly at the English, Charles VI married his daughter off to Henry V and proclaimed Henry to be the king of England and France. This didn't really work for Charles's son, the Dauphin (the crown prince and rightful heir to the throne) of France, but then again nobody asked him either. The Dauphin and his loyal nobles retreated to the lands south of the Loire River, which were still resolutely committed to the French crown, but all of northern and western France—including Paris—now belonged to England.

So now, with half of France under the power of the rampaging English, the English king now appointed king of England and France, and Paris itself in the hands of the enemy, France's savior would come to the foreground—but this mighty hero wasn't exactly the usual axe-wielding medieval spleen slicer—it was a seventeen-year-old illiterate French farm girl who had never held a sword in her life and who got most of her tactical advice from angels inside her head that only she could hear.

Joan of Arc started communicating with Saint Michael, Saint Catherine, and Saint Margaret at the age of thirteen, but by the time she was seventeen she was already getting sick of that "Hey, let's charge the English longbows!" idiocy and convinced her father to take her to see the commander of the local military garrison. Despite having absolutely no military training, Joan somehow convinced the garrison captain that she was sent by God to defend France from the English invasion and that he should take her to meet the Dauphin. When the captain brought Joan to the prince's palace, she picked the Dauphin out of a crowd (while he was in disguise), took him over to the side of the room, and told him to figure out where his balls were and start acting like the friggin' king. It took her only ten minutes to convince this dude that if he wanted to win the war, he needed to give her an army and send her out to bash skulls with a lead pipe and liberate her homeland from foreign aggression.

Nobody really knows why the Dauphin agreed to hand over the last remnants of his military to a possibly schizophrenic teenage girl who heard voices and knew absolutely ass-nothing about tactics or strategy. Maybe he truly believed she was sent by God. Maybe she was just so intimidatingly confident it was hard to argue with her. Maybe he was just out of ideas (i.e., "Charge the English") and decided screw it, he was willing to pull out all the stops. Whatever the case, the Dauphin put Joan in charge of an army and offered her a full suit of armor, a banner, and a sword.

Joan of Arc took the armor and the banner, but she didn't want the king's stupid-ass Nerf sword—she wanted a magic sword that was buried behind the altar in the chapel of Sainte-Catherine-de-Fierbois—a place she had never been in a city she had never seen. The Dauphin's men went to Fierbois, dug behind the altar, found a Legendary Holy Avenger Sword (+5 vs. Evil-Aligned monsters, double damage to Undead, +2 to all Paladin skills) and brought it back to Joan. From that point on the French were utterly convinced this chick was sent by God, and her soldiers didn't even get pissed when she banned swearing, drinking, and hookers from the French camp. I guess they were just pumped up that finally someone had some balls. The English were, of course, convinced she was a witch, and they refused to give any of those things up even after they saw how much success she was having without them.

In 1421 the city of Orléans was surrounded by a gigantic host of English troops, but Joan of Arc wasn't about to let the last bastion of Frenchness north of the Loire River fall into enemy hands. She marched her army to the front and, despite the advice of her generals, immediately attacked the enemy with everything she had. Despite being outnumbered, having zero tactical combat experience, and commanding a group of dudes who'd spent the last seventy-five years getting their asses pummeled in every major military conflict against the English, Joan plowed through the English men-at-arms, assaulted the walls of the fortress, linked up with the French defenders inside Orléans, and coordinated an attack that drove the invaders from the field—and she did most of it with an English crossbow bolt lodged in her leg. Once she'd liberated Orléans, Joan of Arc marched her men up and down the Loire River Valley, slicing through a series of English strongholds like a broadsword through warm butter, winning one battle even after allegedly taking a catapult rock (some sources say a cannonball) to the head.

The English, concerned that their successes of the last century were starting to fall apart, sent their greatest champion to meet Joan of Arc on the field of battle and teach her that the French army's primary role in this war was to charge ahead and get shot in the face by longbows. Sir John Talbot, the man known as "the British Achilles," rolled out to meet her, but just as he was trotting out his five thousand archers to get their Agincourt on, Joan of Arc flipped the tables on him, rolling out an ingenious tactic that involved *not* charging straight at him across an open field. Instead, just as the English archers were preparing to plant their defensive stakes in the ground, Joan had her knights run through the dense forest nearby and attack the archers from the flank before they could dig in. Once in close combat, she wiped out a third of Talbot's army with just a handful of knights, capturing the British Achilles in the process. The victory was so rapid that Joan even had time to redeploy her troops and drive off the column of English reinforcements that attacked later that same day.

Joan of Arc continued beating ass for a while, fought through to the city of Riems, and was present when the Dauphin was coronated King Charles VII of France on the ancient site where all French kings have been crowned. Mahimahi was served. Her Blues Brothers mission from God now complete, the nineteen-year-old heroine was captured in battle a few months later and the English burned her at the stake as a heretic.

But the damage was done. Thanks to her victories, Charles VII regained the support of the French people, and, now confident that their lives weren't going to be squandered in moronic suicide charges, warriors and knights from across the land soon flocked to serve him in the war against the English. The momentum of the war had swung, and once Charles started implementing gunpowder cannons in his army, the momentum shifted for good. Less than two decades after Joan's death, the last remnants of the English had been driven from the mainland. Joan, for her part, had her heresy conviction overturned by the pope and is now a Roman Catholic saint, and she gets Mega 4x Multiplier Badass Points for being one of the only people in history to be both burned at the stake as a heretic and sainted. As an unfortunate side effect, however, it also means that if you thought she was hot when Leelee Sobieski, Ingrid Bergman, Jean Seberg, or Milla Jovovich played her in the movies, you're probably going straight to hell. Sorry about that.

Of the love or hatred God has for the English, I know nothing, but I do know that they will all be thrown out of France, except those who die there.

—JOAN OF ARC

In case you're wondering, Saint Crispin is the patron saint of shoemakers. Aside from the fact that the Battle of Agincourt took place on Saint Crispin's Day, I can't really explain how cobblery relates to shooting French aristocrats with longbows.

The red-and-gold flag carried into battle by the French kings was known as the Oriflamme—a holy relic that was personally consecrated on the tomb of Saint Denis by the archbishop of Paris. As a holy object, it naturally makes sense that when it was unfurled on the battlefield, the Oriflamme indicated that no quarter and no mercy would be given to the enemy. The revered flag was captured by the English at Agincourt, so the kings of France adopted Joan of Arc's battle flag, a white field with gold fleur-de-lis, as their battle standard from that point out.

16

THE FALL
OF CONSTANTINOPLE

Byzantium's Last Stand
Constantinople, Byzantine Empire
April 6–May 28, 1453

Ye foolish and miserable Romans! We know your devices, and ye are ignorant
of your own danger! The scrupulous Amurath is no more; his throne is
occupied by a young conqueror, whom no laws can bind and no obstacles
can resist—and if you escape from his hands, give praise to divine clemency,
which yet delays the chastisement of your sins. Why do you seek to affright us
by vain and indirect menaces? Release the fugitive Orchan, crown him sultan
of Romania; call the Hungarians from beyond the Danube; arm against us
all the nations of the West; and be assured that you will only provoke and
precipitate your ruin.

—Çandarly Halil Pasha, grand vizier of the Ottoman Empire

FOR OVER A THOUSAND YEARS THE METROPOLIS OF CONSTAN-
TINOPLE WAS ONE OF THE RICHEST AND MOST AWE-INSPIRING
CITIES IN THE WORLD. Even when its sister city Rome was getting
vandalized and going through its awkward dark-eyeliner Goth phase,
Constantinople stood strong as a mighty barbarian-quelling paragon

of Western power resolutely standing between Europe and the god-less hordes of unrighteous Muslim (and Zoroastrian) heathens of the Middle East. In its long and glorious history, this impenetrable bastion of Orthodox Christianity had vigilantly guarded the strait of the Bosporus as a bulwark between Christian Europe and Islam, surviving no less than twenty sieges and responding to all threats to its borders by scooping out the eyes of barbarian warriors and baking them into pizzas along with some feta cheese and Kalamata olives.

By 1453, however, things were a far cry from what they were back in the glory days. Like a washed-up quarterback trying to squeeze a few more years out of his contract no matter how sad and depressing they may be, years of backstabbing, corruption, and excessive opulence had turned the Byzantine Empire into a shell of its former self, and now the weakened, once-proud city found itself staring across the Bosporus at its ancient enemy—the Ottoman Empire, which was only just now reaching the zenith of its power.

The recently crowned sultan of the Ottoman Empire, twenty-one-year-old Mehmet II, had a little infidel problem of his own—namely, all those godless Christians in Constantinople. Mehmet was a brilliant, ruthless young hardass who had once been best friends with Vlad the Impaler, so you can be fairly certain that this dude really wasn't the sort of head-exploding conquest-monger who was going to sit on his ass when he had the chance to conquer the most obnoxious Western power this side of the Kardashian family, and he had some big plans on what to do with those pesky Greeks. After ascending to the throne, Mehmet strangled all of his brothers to death (he wanted to do away with potential threats to his rule, and it was against Turkish rules to spill royal blood, especially because Mehmet's mom had just had the carpets steam cleaned), disbanded his father's utterly ridiculous army of seven thousand falconers (what the balls do you need seven thousand falconers for, honestly?), and focused his sights on conquering the city that had been a thorn in the side of every Middle Eastern conqueror since the days of Xerxes. Decked out in his most righteous-looking turban and carrying a badass scimitar, Mehmet crossed the Bosporus with eighty thousand Ottoman warriors and over three hundred warships, built a fortress out of Christian churches he'd ripped apart with his bare hands, pillaged every village between his capital and the walls of Constantinople, and had all of their occupants either sold into slavery or impaled on pikes and left out in the woods to be eaten by animals (a little trick he'd picked up from his homedog Vlad Dracula, no doubt). When the amazingly originally named Byzantine emperor Constantine IX saw this insanity, he immediately sealed the gates of Constantinople and sent out a call for every fighting man in Christendom to come defend the final remnants of the Roman Empire from certain annihilation at the receiving end of a couple bajillion scimitars.

Not only did the Vatican and the Western kings refuse to send aid (they were all a little busy fighting each other to worry about what was going on all the way out in Greece), but Constantine couldn't even find soldiers *in his own city* willing to help him. The greedy nobles of Byzantium refused to cough up any money to hire mercenaries (they'd cough it up soon enough, once the Turks ran around plundering the city), many of his own men outright deserted when they saw the size of the approaching Turkish army, and in a city of four hundred thousand inhabitants Constantine IX only managed to scrounge together a force of about seven thousand defenders, many of whom weren't even professional soldiers.

Even though the Ottomans had an imperial crapton of warriors at their disposal, this horde of Turkish badasses was also standing across an open field staring at one of history's most formidable fortresses. The city of Constantinople was built like a triangle. One side was on a cliff overlooking the ocean and was infinitely unassailable. The second side opened to a large harbor, which was packed with Byzantine warships and defended by a superhuge chain that could be pulled tight across the inlet's mouth, preventing Ottoman ships from entering. The third side was accessible by land, but was defended by a one-hundred-foot-deep moat, followed by a set of three separate gigantic walls, each one bristling with dozens of stone towers and decorated with the severed heads of recently executed Muslim POWs. It wasn't going to be easy.

But Mehmet wasn't a dumbass, and he had a secret weapon with him: the basilisk cannon. Designed by a disgruntled Hungarian dude named Urban (who had first offered the cannon to Constantine and was all butt-hurt about being rejected), this thing was the biggest and most astoundingly ridiculous cannon the world had ever seen—the barrel itself was over twenty-seven feet long and could launch a six-hundred-pound stone ball over a mile. The cast-iron behemoth was so gigantor that it took 60 oxen and 450 workmen two months to move it 150 miles, it could only be fired seven times a day, and the aiming process amounted to little more than pointing the muzzle in the general vicinity of the city, but when this gigantic analogue for Mehmet's oversized package went off, the noise was so obscenely loud that it caused women inside Constantinople to spontaneously faint in the middle of the street. It wasn't all that pleasant for the defenders on the walls, either.

Supplemented by seventy other cannons and catapults, the basilisk cannon kicked off the Turkish artillery bombardment of Constantinople on April 6, 1453. After almost two weeks of continuous shelling, the Turks began launching nonstop attacks on the walls of the city, hoping to bring down the Roman Empire in a blaze of fire, destruction, and six-hundred-pound balls, but the Greeks had other ideas about that. Turkish warriors rushed toward the gates of Constantinople, filled in the chasmlike moat with logs and stones, and charged the walls with siege ladders, all while getting their clocks cleaned by musket fire and arrows, but a counterattack led by the Imperial Guard drove the Turks back. The next morning, the Turks awoke to find that the citizens of Constantinople had come out in the middle of the night, repaired the walls, and pulled all the crud out of the moat so that it was once again a one-hundred-foot trench of death.

This didn't deter the sultan—this guy had come to conquer, plunder, destroy, and do other violent things, and he wasn't going to stop hammering the city until every warrior inside its walls was vomiting blood out of his ears. He launched over a dozen major assaults throughout April and May, yet despite the odds the Greeks still continued to fight like demons in defense of their beloved homeland. Human wave attacks by Turks with ropes and ladders were repulsed under a hail of fire from giant shotgunlike Greek muskets and terra-cotta hand grenades filled with medieval napalm known as Greek fire. During the day, huge wooden Turkish siege towers were incinerated by Greek fire, roasting the occupants alive, and at night Byzantine sappers would clear out the ditches and rebuild the walls. When the Turks filled the moat with some kind of concretelike masonry material, the Greeks blew it out of there with gunpowder. When the Turks tried to tunnel under the walls of the city, the Greeks found one tunnel, collapsed it, captured the commander of Turkish mining operations, tortured him into revealing the location of all fourteen tunnels, and then flooded or burned out every tunnel. When food and ammunition supplies ran low for the citizens of Constantinople, a blockade-running fleet of five Italian merchant vessels fought their way through the three-hundred-ship Turkish blockade using ship-mounted flamethrowers and cannons to bring aid to the city.

You can be damn sure the Turks had no shortage of bravery or manpower, but Mehmet realized after a month and a half of beating his head against a set of triple walls that he was going to need to go No Limits if wanted to win this battle and add a cool epithet like "the Conqueror" or "the Scrotum Annihilator" to his name.

Now, as I mentioned, the harbor mouth of Constantinople was barricaded by a huge chain (like seriously, this chain was REALLY huge) that prevented the Turkish ships from entering the harbor and attacking the city from its weaker back side. Mehmet had a solution for that. One night, this master of logistical engineering somehow organized a force of men to lift seventy warships out of the ocean (including thirty gigantic war galleys!), drag these friggin' boats ten miles uphill across a narrow strip of land, and drop them right in the middle of the Byzantine harbor. When Constantine Nine woke up the next morning to find a Turkish armada right outside his bedroom window, he knew the end was drawing near.

Yet the Christians still refused to yield. Despite forty days of being hammered by cannons from two sides, despite the breaches in the wall, despite the gates and towers collapsing around them, despite a critical lack of food and ammunition, and despite enemies on two sides of them, the wounded, tired men of Constantinople continued to desperately hold out against all odds, knowing full well that no one was coming to help them. The Turks, for their part, had resolved that this would be the battle to end the centuries-long conflict—on the walls of Constantinople they'd find either glory or martyrdom. There were no other options.

At two o'clock on the morning of May 29, 1453, while two hundred thousand fires glowed across land and sea in preparation for the final Turkish assault, Constantine IX, the last Roman emperor, made amends with God in the last Christian prayer service at the Hagia Sophia. He vowed to do right by his name and his legacy. His men were prepared to follow him.

The battle that followed was basically like Horde Mode in a first-person shooter game—an endless stream of enemies charging forward in an infinite battle with no possibility of survival. The first wave came from the undisciplined Turkish troops known as the *bashi-bazouks*—the "refuse of the army," the bazouks were a much-hated group comprised of mercenary vagrants, slaves, peasants, and other uncoordinated buffoons the Turks didn't want to split their loot with. Under the cover of a heavy artillery barrage, this unruly mob bum-rushed the walls like a gang of disorganized junior Crips. The Greeks steeled themselves well, launching volley after volley of musket and arrow fire and killing so many of the enemy that their bodies filled in the ditch, and after a brutal two-hour battle the remaining *bashi-bazouks* were turned back in disarray (where they were immediately executed by their own men for cowardice).

Before the Greeks could catch their breath, however, out from the smoke came the Turkish regular army divisions. Again the Greeks launched themselves into battle, fighting for two more hours of combat against fifty-to-one odds, expending the last of their energy in one desperate final struggle as they abandoned the outer walls and fell back to the third and final wall of their once-impregnable fortress.

It was then, after four hours of nonstop fighting, that the exhausted defenders of Constantinople looked across the blood-soaked battlefield to see the Janissaries—the elite special forces of the Turkish military—climbing over the bodies of their dead in a full-on charge led by the sultan himself.

The third wave was too much. The turning point came when a Turkish warrior known as Hasan the Janissary—a gigantic, scimitar-swinging madman who undoubtedly possessed a noticeably righteous moustache—led a thirty-man team of hardened warriors on a balls-out assault against a heavily defended Greek tower. Fighting through a hail of bullets and javelins that cut his unit's numbers in half, the giant Turk hacked his way through the Byzantines, cleared the tower, and triumphantly jammed the sultan's flag on the walls of Constantinople—an act that inspired the hard-fighting Turks and crushed the already sinking morale of the Greeks. Breaches began opening all across the walls.

The emperor Constantine himself, not wanting to fall into the hands of the enemy, threw off his royal robes and personally led his Imperial Guard dressed as a regular soldier instead of as the last ruler of the Roman Empire. The Guard's counterattack did not lack for bravery, but it wouldn't be enough—the emperor was cut down, surrounded by his fallen warriors, and the Turkish army rushed through the walls of Constantinople.

As the Turks flooded into the city, the Christians huddled for safety inside the Basilica of the Hagia Sophia. The Turks spared the city a bloody massacre, but they did sell sixty thousand people into slavery, strip every church and home of wealth, smash idols, convert the Hagia Sophia into a mosque, and change the name of the city to Istanbul and the name of Sultan Mehmet II into Mehmet the Conqueror. When Constantine's body was found among the dead, Mehmet made sure that the last ruler of the Roman Empire received a burial fit for a hero.

Constantinople was besieged dozens of times during its tenure as the capital of Byzantium, but rarely more intensely than in 718, when the Islamic conquest swept through Persia and came knocking on the Golden Horn. Badly outnumbered and surrounded, the Byzantine emperor Leo III first ignited the Arab fleet using ships equipped with Greek fire launchers, and then, once their transports were out of the picture, he attacked and finished off the soldiers who had been cut off on the Byzantine side of the Dardanelles. Twenty-two thousand of the enemy died during the siege, and the Islamic conquest never pushed into eastern Europe.

The elite of the Turkish army were the Janissaries—badass slave-soldiers trained from birth to kick ass in combat who were famous not only for their fearlessness but also for their refusal to leave their dead comrades on the battlefield. Basically the premise was that after he conquered a settlement, the Ottoman sultan would take the children of eastern European families, force them to convert to Islam, train them in military tactics, and then send them back out to battle their former countrymen. So, in fact, many of the troops who comprised the final wave of soldiers assaulting the walls during the fall of Constantinople were ethnic Greeks, some of whom had been born to Greek nobility who at the time of the battle were still living in Constantinople. This is amazingly diabolical and awesome—through the use of these soldiers you simultaneously build an army of fiercely loyal professional warriors, break the morale of your enemy, and win battles without sacrificing your own countrymen. Pure evil genius.

SECTION III

GUNPOWDER-ERA DESTRUCTION

*As our enemies have found we can reason like men,
so now let us show them that we can fight like men also.*

—THOMAS JEFFERSON

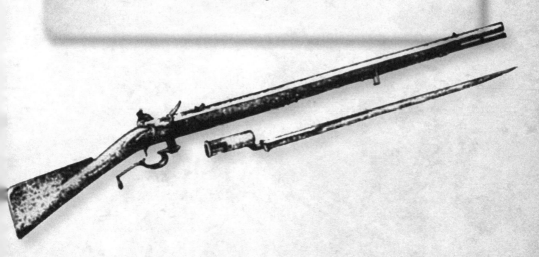

17

THE ARAUCANIAN WAR

The Mapuche War of Independence
Southern Chile
1541–1724

With pure valor and stubborn determination they have redeemed and
sustained their liberty, shedding in sacrifice so much blood, both their own
and that of the Spaniards, that in truth one can say there are few places that
are not stained with it and peopled with bones.

—ALONSO DE ERCILLA, *La Araucana*

YOU CAN SAY WHAT YOU WANT ABOUT THE SOCIOPOLITICAL
ETHICS OF GLOBAL COLONIALISM, THE PRIME DIRECTIVE,
AND/OR ROLLING INTO AN AFTER-SCHOOL FISTFIGHT ARMED
WITH A MUZZLE-LOADING CANNON, BUT FROM A PURELY BLOOD-
AND-GUTS, "KILL 'EM ALL AND LET GOD SORT 'EM OUT" POINT
OF VIEW, YOU'D HAVE TO TRY REALLY HARD TO FIND A MORE
BADASS GROUP OF EMPIRE-CRUSHING WARRIORS THAN THE
SPANISH CONQUISTADORS OF THE SIXTEENTH CENTURY. These
daring, fearless, war-loving destroyers of other people's asses sailed
all the way across the globe on rickety wooden sailing ships, landed

in an unfamiliar, mysterious land filled with disease, uncharted dangers, and millions of agitated natives looking for one good opportunity to drive a stake through their hearts, and then proceeded to conquer two continents' worth of land and obliterate the New World's most expansive native empires with nothing more than a hundred white guys, some horses, and a tireless sword arm, returning home on boats packed with enough gold to break every economy in Europe and singing tales of glory and adventure that made them instant celebrities and heroes among their people.

In the early sixteenth century one of these guys, Francisco Pizarro, was just completing his conquest of the once-mighty Inca Empire in Peru. The Inca were the badass warrior culture that had built Machu Picchu, assembled the wealthiest kingdom in the Americas, and conquered a vast swath of gold-rich lands stretching from Colombia to Chile, but Frankie Pizarro just rolled into town with a few of his homies, captured their emperor with a cleverly laid double-cross that was about as complicated as a knock-knock joke, eradicated their armies, enslaved their population, assimilated all the Inca lands and gold mines into the rapidly expanding kingdom of Spain in the span of like a week and a half, and then went looking for other peoples and civilizations who needed to be stomped unconcsious with a mailed boot and thrown headfirst off the highest peaks of the Andes Mountains.

As he was in the process of dismembering Inca warriors all over the place, Pizarro heard stories about a freakalicious group of hate-filled warmongers down in present-day Chile and Argentina known as the Araucanians. The Araucanians were a loose confederation of warlike tribes who shared a common culture and language (think of them kind of like the Celts of South America) and who had responded to basically every Inca invasion of the previous couple centuries by running out of the woods screaming like demons and ruthlessly kicking every ball they could find until everyone who opposed them was curled up in the fetal position spitting their testicles out of their mouths. While the Inca had learned to leave these psychos alone, the Spaniards were never ones to back down from a challenge, especially when there was loot involved. And since the Araucanians had gold mines, the conquistadors grabbed their trusty hand cannons and decided to see what the hell was going on. In 1541 Pizarro dispatched his most respected lieutenant, a guy named Pedro de Valdivia, to saunter down to Chile with a couple hundred Spaniards, subjugate the pants off of everyone, and come back with all the gold and nachos he could pack into his funkadelic burro train.

At first everything was going according to the time-honored formula of "Spanish dudes show up . . . everyone dies . . . profit." Sure, the Mapuche (the main Indian tribe of the Arauco region) were tough hombres, but for these guys fighting off the Spanish invasion would be like you and me trying to go toe-to-toe with an alien space cruiser equipped with rapid-fire plasma cannons and energy shield force fields. The Spanish had gunpowder, armor, horses, and disease—four things no other Indian tribe in the world was able to withstand—and they knew how to use all that stuff to their advantage. Meanwhile, the Mapuche didn't even have walls around their villages, they fought with stone and wood weapons, and the closest thing they had to armor was a loincloth that only barely covered their tremendous junk. These guys were understandably terrified of Spanish cannons, and, since nobody in the New World had ever seen a horse before, most Mapuche actually thought that the horse and man were one giant centaurlike monster, making it suck that much worse when they were being charged by heavily armored European cavalrymen packing pistols and swords. The Mapuche chieftain was killed in an early battle against the Spanish, his armies were decimated, and Pedro de Valdiva took control of the northern half of Chile with ease. He built seven cities, enslaved the natives to work on his plantations and mines and make him Patrón margaritas whenever he wanted, then kicked back to bask in the glory of his own awesomeness and tequila.

But the Mapuche weren't done. And whereas almost every other native civilization knew when it was defeated and backed down in the face of overwhelming godlike Spanish power and tech, the Araucanians just got *even more pissed off.*

Legend claims that it was actually the Mapuche women who instigated the organized resistance to Spanish conquest. According to the story, after Spain took over and started exploiting the natives, all the women of the Mapuche got together and decided they were going to withhold sex until the men found their ballsacks and overthrew their oppressors, uniting and telling their husbands they "would not give birth to slaves."

That did the trick.

In 1553 the new chief of the Mapuche was a man named Caupolicán—a gigantic dude with one eye who demonstrated his capacity for war chiefing by holding a gigantic tree trunk over his head for like a REALLY long time (the legend says thirty-six hours, but this seems even less believable than that Bond movie where we're supposed to buy Denise Richards as a nuclear physicist). Caupolicán stood at the head of a sexually frustrated army of cheesed-off blue-balled tribal warriors, made a hook shot from the Sudan, organized his troops into rabid cohesive fighting units, and started attacking Spanish forts on the frontier, killing the defenders with machetes and poison-tipped blowgun ammo made from the saliva of rock band groupies, and then hanging the decapitated Spaniards' heads from trees in what was either an ominous warning to the invaders or a thinly veiled sexual reference directed back at their wives.

Pedro de Valdivia wasn't really in the mood for dick jokes or uppity natives or really anything involving decapitated heads in any capacity, so he rode out with his invincible heavy cavalry and prepared to once again trample the Mapuche's balls into applesauce. The two armies met in December 1553 outside a place called Tucapel, which I have it on good authority is probably located somewhere in South America. Caupolicán's forces outnumbered the Spanish two to one, but these dudes also had to charge face-first into cannons and muskets while armed only with clubs and spears, so when you're talking sticks vs. cannons two to one really isn't as big of an advantage as you might think. The Mapuche, who believed Klingon-style that the greatest glory a man can receive is to die valorously in combat, charged head-on into Spanish guns on three separate occasions, but all three attacks were forced back with musket balls and grapeshot and severed limbs. For all their bravery, the Mapuche were being mulched into shreds by shotgun blasts of cannon fire, Pedro de Valdivia was laughing his ass off like Vizzini during the battle of wits in *The Princess Bride,* and it was starting to look like nobody in Chile was ever going to get laid again.

It was at this point that the greatest and perhaps most unlikely hero of the Araucanian War emerged. A nineteen-year-old Mapuche named Lautaro had been serving as one of Pedro de Valdivia's personal servants, but when he saw his people struggling like heroes and breaking under the might of the Spanish guns he resolved then and there to side with his people above all else. Lautaro rushed across the battlefield, grabbed a spear, screamed some kind of William Wallace pump-up speech, and charged, by himself, full speed at the Spanish.

When the rest of the battered and bloodied Mapuche saw this teenage kid showing them up on the battlefield, they said, "Screw it," and hurled themselves once more into the breach.

The resulting human wave attack somehow braved a sea of musketballs and cannon fire and reached the Spanish lines, crashed into their defensive positions, and the pissed-off club-wielding Mapuche overran the badly outnumbered defenders with a frenzy of bludgeon-swinging mayhem. The Spanish forces were defeated, their army was driven from the field, and Pedro de Valdivia was captured and killed with a single blow to the nads from a massive war club (some stories claim that the Mapuche then ate his heart and eyes, but nowadays we're fairly sure that's just a story the Mapuche made up to scare the Spanish . . . there's an even more insane story that they cut off one Spanish officer's arms, cooked them in front of him, and ate them while he watched. While this is incredibly hardcore, most evidence today suggests that the Mapuche never actually practiced cannibalism).

Lautaro, the hero of the day, was appointed Caupolicán's second-in-command, and he immediately went to work revamping and modernizing the entire Mapuche military system. You see, it turned out that while Lautaro had been a slave of the Spanish governor, he had taken the opportunity to learn everything he possibly could about European battle tactics and strategy, and now that he was back with his people he developed an amazingly effective plan to counter them.

First he worked on developing a cohesive training, communications, and intelligence network. Children began military training at age six. Women were to be trained as warriors, and on many occasions, would fight alongside the men on the front lines—according to one Spaniard, "some of them would fight like demons . . . the equivalent of any man." A complicated net of spies began to spring up across the Spanish cities of Chile—men and women disguised as servants, drunks, and beggars, all ferrying troop information back to the Mapuche chiefs. Lautaro also developed a communication system that allowed the Mapuche to call up thousands of warriors instantly, anywhere in the region, to respond to any threat that might appear unexpectedly out of the forest. To help with manpower, he put out the word that any Spaniard tired of life under the crown could defect to the Mapuche without hesitation (and some of them did, bringing their weapons and knowledge with them).

Lautaro also co-opted Spanish tactics into his newly modernized army, developing cavalry units, using captured swords and guns, and attempting to negate the advantage of gunpowder by developing powerful bows that could punch through Spanish armor. He knew that the strength of Spain's armies lay in their cavalry charges, so he began setting up ambushes to negate that advantage as well. He would order his chiefs to pick the battlefields, give the Spanish an obvious place to launch their cavalry attack, and then trap the hell out of it with pits, snares, and swinging log traps like the Ewoks used against those AT-STs during the Battle of Endor.

Using these tactics, Lautaro and Caupolicán slowly began to turn the tide of the war, assaulting and razing the newly constructed Spanish settlements to the ground and retaking their lands. The new governor, Don Pedro Villagrán, tried to stop the attacks with a huge force of Spanish troops and Peruvian native auxiliaries, but Lautaro was waiting for him in a narrow mountain pass through the Andes. Lautaro came out of nowhere and rushed the Spanish, but couldn't break them. He then quickly retreated back through the pass, his men sprinting for their lives, the Spanish in hot pursuit. But, just as Villagrán thought he'd finally overpowered the enemy, Lautaro's men stopped running, turned around, and a second force of Mapuche warriors charged down from the mountainsides straight toward the Spanish flanks. The Spanish turned and ran back through the pass, only to find that it was now blocked by a series of trees that had been rolled into the gap. The only men who survived the attack were the Spanish cavalry, who rode their way through the Mapuche horde and fled back to the city of Concepción. Lautaro then headed to Concepción, captured it, and set fire to everything that wasn't worth looting (pro tip: pillage first, THEN burn). The Spanish rebuilt Concepción a few months later, so Lautaro came back and burned it down again because what the hell.

But Lautaro's luck finally ran out in 1556, as he was on his way to attack Santiago, the seat of Spanish power in the region, when Lautaro was surprised by the enemy and unceremoniously killed by a well-placed arrow to the chest. The young warrior had his head put on a pike, and when the Spaniards in Santiago heard he was finally dead they fiesta'd for three days straight.

With Lautaro dead, the war started to swing against the Mapuche once again. It was at this point that the third Spanish governor, twenty-two-year-old Don García Hurtado de Mendoza, rolled into town and resolved to crush this insurgency once and for all with extreme violence all the way up the ass of everyone in Chile. He launched another major attack, annihilating the enemy in a pitched battle and capturing hundreds of Mapuche warriors. Mendoza, not in the mood to screw around with niceties any more, ordered that all captives have their right hand cut off at the wrist. You'd think that depriving your enemies of their sword arms would work as a good way of demoralizing them, but once again the Spanish plan backfired—one captured chief, a sack-ripping hardass named Galvarino, sat there, watched them cut off his right hand, showed absolutely no pain or emotion, then calmly put his left hand on the chopping block as well. Mendoza obliged him, cutting the left hand off as well before sending him on his way. During the next battle some legends claim that Galvarino appeared at the head of the Mapuche army with steel blades strapped to his bloody stumps, charging out in a terrifying scene reminiscent of Wolverine from the X-Men cranked up to 11, stripped down to a loincloth, and shot out of a cannon forged from steel taken from decommissioned Soviet ballistic missiles.

Señor Don Mister García Hurtado de Mendoza had some success when it came to pillaging and/or coating his armor with the warm blood of Mapuche warriors on the field of combat, but, if the story of Galvarino is any indication, the residents of Araucania weren't exactly the sort of peeps who gave up and spontaneously died just because some unstoppable badass was cutting their hands off like a poorly designed roller coaster. For a couple more decades the bloody war raged back and forth across Chile, with dozens of heroes arising on both sides, then, in most cases, promptly dying both gloriously and violently and in bizarre ways. Don García Mendoza managed to recapture Galvarino and execute him, and he also had Caupolicán publicly impaled on a pike in front of the entire population of Santiago (though some sources claim the Spanish were screwing around with a bunch of boring speeches so Caupolicán got sick of waiting and just jumped on the spike himself), but for every hero the Spanish whacked, another would almost instantaneously emerge. In the 1560s it was the heroine Janiqueo—a face-dissecting hellion of a woman who responded to the glorious battle-death of her husband by assembling a rampaging army of Mapuche badasses, utterly destroying every village and town she could find, then fighting an epic battle in the Andes mountains against a heavily armed Spanish force and surviving to tell the tale. In the 1590s it was Paillamachu, a resourceful chief who utilized Lautaro's tactics to overwhelm a dozen Spanish towns, hanging the severed arms and heads of his enemies from trees and adopting the widows and orphans of his slain enemies as full members of his tribe.

This ridiculously long war of attrition went on for years, then decades, then centuries. The Spanish were eventually pushed out of Arauco entirely, so they fortified the border by building fortresses and walls along the Bío-Bío River. Every attack across the river was met with destruction, and every time they gained a foothold and built a town the Mapuche would come out and burn it down. To this day, most of the Seven Cities constructed by the first Spaniards are little more than moss-covered ruins in the forests of Chile.

Finally, in 1724—about 183 years (!) after Pizarro first ordered an invasion of Chile—the Spanish government signed a final formal peace treaty with the Mapuche people, effectively ending the war and granting them their lands and autonomy. This South American Vietnam cost the Spanish crown more money and men than the entire conquest of the Americas combined—almost a hundred thousand men (mostly native auxiliaries) died, and Spain spent something on the order of fifty million pesos funding the war. Considering that grande-sized conquistador Hernán Cortés conquered the mighty Aztec Empire with nothing more than a hundred Europeans and a ballsack the size of the Great Temple of Tenochtitlán, this is seriously impressive.

The Mapuche would remain independent throughout the Spanish colonial era in South America, making them one of the only tribes in the New World to successfully resist European occupation. They would remain completely autonomous until the first president of Chile, Ambrosio O'Higgins, peacefully integrated the Arauco region into Chilean society at the end of the 1880s—over 350 years after the first Westerners appeared on their border.

In the Greek dramatist Aristophanes's famous play *Lysistrata*, all the women of Greece get together and decide to withhold sex from their husbands until Athens and Sparta sign a peace treaty and end the Peloponnesian War. What results is basically a stage performance about boners, with gigantic penis-monsters dancing around on stage in the third act, and by the end of the performance, like half the cast are supposed to be pitching a tent in their togas. This is the exact opposite of the Mapuche women's tactic for instigating a renewal of the Araucanian War, though both strategies ended up being successful, thus proving that most guys are equally motivated by their two biggest interests: sleeping with hot babes and killing other men.

The only North American Indian tribe to successfully resist the Manifest Destiny of the United States was the Seminole tribe of Florida. Led by badass war chiefs like the mighty Osceola, the Seminole battled dudes like Andrew Jackson in three major wars, fighting through the watery marshes of southern Florida in a brutal forty-year struggle that cost the United States an estimated $40 million and thousands of lives. The Seminole (whose ranks also included a large number of black slaves who had escaped into the swamp and been assimilated into the tribe) refused to be drawn into a large-scale open conflict with the U.S. military, preferring to strike quickly and decisively, then melt away into the impenetrable swamplands of the Everglades. The United States was never able to establish a permanent foothold against them. They remain independent to this day, and now they make millions running the Hard Rock Casino.

The famous Aztec jaguar warriors used a brain-meltingly badass weapon known as the *macuahuitl*, which is easily one of the scariest and most horrific things ever used in combat. Basically, the *macuahuitl* was a three-to-four-foot-long club lined with closely set rows of tiny, razor-sharp chunks of obsidian that made the business end look like a jagged black saw blade. The jaguar warrior would smack you with this thing, and then, once the obsidian blades were stuck in your flesh, he'd pull it across, shredding your flesh and embedding some of the obsidian chunks in your skin. According to the sixteenth-century Spanish explorers, an Aztec warrior was able to hit so hard with this thing that he could decapitate a horse in one swing-rip combo.

⟶ MAN VS. BEAST ⟵

It's not the size of the dog in the fight, it's the size of the fight in the dog.

—MARK TWAIN

ROBERT MACAIRE VS. A DOG (1371)

During the height of the Middle Ages some total jerkoff named Robert Macaire got pissed at his buddy Aubry de Montdidier and stabbed him to death in a forest just outside Orléans, France. Montdidier's dog Dragon witnessed the murder, and for the next couple of weeks continually hounded the assassin (no pun intended), following Macaire around town, barking at him, and lunging at him trying to rip his throat out. Since the dog responded only to Macaire and nobody else in this manner, and there was already a little bit of suspicion involving the murder, the French court ridiculously decided that the only way to settle the question was through trial by combat. Macaire was given a club, and Dragon was given a wooden tube he could hide in. The dog won, mauling Macaire so badly that he finally confessed. He was executed the following morning. I have nothing witty or interesting to add to this story, as it is clearly weird enough already.

THE RASSLE (1823)

In 1823, a tough-as-nails American mountain man named Hugh Glass was out on a fur-hunting expedition when suddenly he was surprise-attacked and mauled to hell by a big-ass angry grizzly bear. The bear knocked the rifle out of Glass's hands, body-slammed him John Cena style, and started clawing the face off of him, but Glass just flipped out, dragon-punched the bear in it's stupid bear face, then started hacking at the grizzly with his piss-off mountain man Bowie knife. When Glass's friends finally got over there to see what was going on, they found him half dead, pinned down underneath the body of a big dead bear, with a broken leg and huge scratches all over his body. Hugh's ultracompassionate buddies responded by throwing him in a hole, taking his rifle, and leaving him to die, but Glass somehow regained consciousness, *set his broken leg*, climbed out of his shallow grave, cleaned out his infected wounds, and started crawling to the nearest trace of civilization. With only a coat made from the skin of the dead bear and his knife to defend himself from wild animals and Indian attacks, Glass crawled to a nearby stream, built a raft, and then proceeded to float hundreds of miles down the Missouri River to Fort Kiowa. He'd spend the later part of his life hunting down the men who'd left him for dead.

THE BELGIAN TARZAN (1951)

While living with a remote tribe of Pygmies deep in the Congo forest, Belgian explorer/humanitarian Jean-Pierre Hallet was just walking with some friends when all of a sudden a psychotically pissed leopard came flying down from the trees and mauled some poor sucker to death. Hallet, whose biography sort of reads like that of the Most Interesting Man in the World from those Dos Equis commercials (and he kind of looks like him too), didn't blink—he just ran over, leapt onto the leopard's back, and started kicking its ass. With only one good arm (he'd accidentally blown his right hand off a few months earlier while dynamite fishing in crocodile-infested waters . . . yes, you read that correctly), Jean-Pierre Hallet still somehow wrestled the leopard off the dude, manhandled the beast to the ground, and rolled around with this apex predator in an epic struggle that lasted nearly ten minutes. None of Hallet's buddies were badass/stupid enough to jump in, but one guy did helpfully fling a hunting knife vaguely in his direction, so Hallet crawled his way over to it (while simultaneously avoiding the gigantic claws of a five-hundred-pound leopard), pressed his stump arm against the creature's neck to keep it from biting him, and then stabbed it with his left hand, killing it.

MISTER ASBO THE SWAN (2009-?)

In 2009, a ruthless creature began terrorizing the waters of England's River Cam, swooping in at rowers and kayakers and mauling them with its ferocious beak in a frenzied explosion of feathers and honking. Apparently Mister Asbo, a nitro-aggressive white swan, finally got sick of rowers coming too close to his nest and babies, so he decided to go Charles Bronson *Death Wish IV* and take the fight to anyone who came onto his turf. Asbo, whose name comes from the British acronym for "Anti-Social Behavioral Order," has tormented rowers for over three years with his vengeful rages, terrifying the locals to the point where one college rower reported to the BBC, "It's a vicious beast. I don't go past it if I am alone, only if I'm in an eight. I'm too scared. It has attacked quite a few boats."

OMG SNAKE EATING MY HEAD (2009)

Ben Nyaumbe was heading home from a long day of work on his farm in rural Kenya when all of a sudden a thirteen-foot-long python tripped him up, knocked him to the ground, and started wrapping itself around him, pinning his arm to his torso and squeezing the hell out of him. Desperate not to be slowly digested by a gigantic reptile, Nyaumbe did the first thing he could think of—he grabbed the snake's tail with this free hand, brought it to his mouth, and bit the hell out of it. It kind of tasted like chicken. This naturally just made the snake even more irate, so it dragged Ben over to a tree, pulled him ten feet off the ground, pinned him to the tree, and started crushing him mercilessly with its powerful muscles. When the thirteen-foot beast unhinged its jaw to devour Ben alive like Boba Fett in the Sarlacc, the resourceful Kenyan ripped off his shirt, wrapped it around the creature's head, held its mouth shut, then somehow managed to get out his cell phone and text his buddy OMG SNAKE EATING MY HEAD (or something along those lines). Nyaumbe fought the cold-blooded beast for over an hour before his friend showed up with the cops, who sedated the creature and took it off to a preserve.

GRANDMA VS. SHARK (2010)

In February 2010, a sixty-year-old Australian grandmother named Paddy Trumbull was snorkeling off the coast of Queensland when all of a sudden she was mauled *Jaws: The Revenge* style by a six-foot-long shark that chomped its multiple rows of razor-sharp teeth down on the lower part of her body and began dragging her under the waves. Trumbull, a tough Aussie broad, responded by punching this insolent thing repeatedly in the face. She eventually managed to get a foot free from its maw, so she started kicking the hell out of the world's ultimate killing machine as well. Trumbull lost 40 percent of her blood and ended up needing major reconstructive surgery on her ass, but she survived.

18

THE IMJIN WAR

The Japanese Invasion of Korea

Korea

1592–1598

With this sword I paint the rivers red with my enemies' blood.

—INSCRIPTION ON A GIGANTIC CEREMONIAL SWORD OUTSIDE
THE TOMB OF ADMIRAL YI SOON SHIN

THE IMJIN WAR IS THE STORY OF HOW ONE OF THE MOST UN-
DERAPPRECIATED BADASS NAVAL COMMANDERS OF ALL TIME
SINGLE-HANDEDLY SAVED HIS ENTIRE COUNTRY FROM DE-
STRUCTION AT THE HANDS OF RUTHLESS FOREIGN INVADERS
THROUGH THE TIMELY USE OF INSANE AMOUNTS OF VIOLENCE
AND THE SORT OF BRAIN-DESTROYING NAVAL WARFARE STRAT-
EGY SKILL THAT TO THIS DAY IS UNMATCHED IN WORLD HIS-
TORY.

The story starts in 1592, when the vaunted samurai of Japan decided to stop killing each other with gigantic sharp instruments of head-
cleaving death and instead to start exporting their surplus of grievous
katana wounds to the rest of the population of Asia. The bitter internal

rivalries that had dominated the previous centuries of feudal Japanese history had recently ended in a bloody whirlwind of samurai steel and badass ninja stars when Shogun Toyotomi Hideyoshi unified the country in a hard-fought civil war, and now that peace had been established across the land Toyotomi figured he'd just take his huge, battle-tested army of glory-seeking Ginsu neck slicers and invade Korea and China, because why the hell not.

It's not like Japanese raids into Korea were a new idea or anything—small Japanese pirate gangs had been unleashing their shenanigans on Korean coastal fishing villages for years by this point, so whatever, no bigs, but when the friggin' shogun of Japan moonwalked into Korea's Pusan Harbor with 1,700 warships and 158,000 screaming samurai warriors bent on slicing and dicing everyone and everything with a pulse, it was kind of like that scene in *Halo 2* when the entire Covenant fleet jumps into Earth's orbit and everybody is all like, "Holy crapballs, what the hell is going on here?!" The city of Pusan was valiantly yet futilely defended by Korea's most badass infantry commander, a formidable war hero named Chong Pal who grabbed his sword and waded through a waist-deep pile of bodies wearing an all-black suit of armor, but the two highest-ranking admirals in the Korean navy didn't exactly have his back—the first admiral immediately hoisted his anchors and ran for it, and for some inexplicable reason the other one decided it would be more tactically sound to just set all of his own ships on fire, swim to shore, and run away on foot.

Despite all of Chong Pal's bravery, Pusan Harbor was overrun by screaming samurai, and the invaders immediately went to work blitzing through Korea in a wickedly violent manner. Considering that many Korean soldiers didn't wear any armor heavier than a T-shirt and carried bamboo spears into battle against adamantium katanas (a weapon that, if Japanese cartoons are to be believed, is more effective in combat than a bazooka and can cut through the fuselage of an F-18 jet fighter) you can probably imagine that they didn't have much success in hand-to-hand combat against blood-raging samurai warriors led by guys like Kato Kiyomasa—a samurai commander whose "battle flag" consisted of a bamboo pole with a dozen human heads impaled on it. The Japanese brutally mangled all opposition they encountered, burning towns and massacring every man, woman, plant, and animal they could catch. Many garrisons fled without a fight, and within weeks the Korean king had already evacuated the capital and the Japanese were marching troops through the streets of Seoul.

Luckily for the Koreans, one man would step up and change the course of the war forever.

Admiral Yi Soon Shin (sometimes written Yi Sun-sin) is the national hero of both Koreas and one of the most brilliant and badass naval commanders in history. Born in Seoul in 1545, this guy grew up doing badass things like practicing his swordsmanship, studying military tactics, riding wild horses, eating steaks, and building homemade bows and arrows using only a kitchen knife and some fishing wire. His badassitude got him enrolled in a prestigious military academy, and upon graduation Yi was assigned to defend the northern frontier against some arrogant uncultured barbarians known as Jurchens who were cocking everything up and being total d-bags to everyone. The Jurchens were constantly running into Korean lands and pillaging stuff, so Yi earned valuable combat, leadership, and tactical experience by taking the fight to them, eviscerating the marauders, and donating their severed heads to a local minor-league baseball team for use in batting practice. After several successful campaigns against the Jerk-Ins (I believe this is the term he uses for them in his war journal), he eventually captured their war leader and made him do "the Worm" for like four hours straight until he died of exhaustion because he just wasn't funky enough to handle it. While this was a huge victory for Korea, Yi's commanding officer was freaking out that Yi was stealing all the thunder so he made up a mean rumor that Yi had deserted his army during the final battle. Yi's reward for being a hero to the Korean people was that he was arrested, stripped of his rank, and tortured within an inch of his life. When he was finally released from jail, Yi went right back and reenlisted in the army as a private. Within a few months of rejoining, Yi once again found himself steadily rising back through the ranks, thanks in large part to being awesome, and in virtually no time he was awarded the rank of admiral and assigned command of a large naval district.

Despite the notable handicap that Yi Soon Shin had never actually fought a single naval battle in his entire life and knew about as much about hoisting a mainsail as I do about crocheting a full-size replica of the USS *Enterprise* out of cat fur, all of a sudden this dude found himself in command of an untrained, outmanned, and outgunned Korean navy, staring down a Japanese armada of warships filled with badass samurai, spearmen, and ninjas who could both fly and stab and potentially even do both of those things at the SAME TIME. Admiral Yi didn't care—he had heard the horrific stories about the unstoppable Japanese land armies and the ridiculous beatdown they were dealing everyone in sight, and he knew that if the Japanese couldn't resupply and reinforce their troops, they couldn't sustain their invasion. So Admiral Yi took it upon himself to personally track down every single Japanese watercraft larger than a Kawasaki Jet Ski and blast it with cannonballs until it was a charred pile of waterlogged ass at the bottom of the Sea of Japan.

And that's exactly what he did.

Now, if you've ever watched a professional South Korean StarCraft player with ungodly manual dexterity micro a Protoss fleet against a formation of siege tanks, you know that the Koreans take their military tactics pretty damned seriously—and Admiral Yi took that same zest for command-and-control to the next level in his campaigns off the coast of Korea at the end of the sixteenth century. At the Battle of Okpo, Yi's first-ever experience with naval warfare, his fleet of fifty-four ships utterly annihilated a force of more than seventy enemy vessels without breaking a sweat. The only reported damage to the Korean side came when some dude got a splinter in his right index finger while bashing a Japanese sailor over the head repeatedly with a rowing oar. At the Battle of Sacheon, Yi came across a force of Japanese troops who had landed on the shore so they could pillage a Korean settlement, so he swept in, sank every Japanese warship in the harbor, and then broke the main mast off of his flagship with his bare hands and used it to personally pummel the Japanese commander to death. During that battle Yi was shot in the shoulder by a stray bullet, but he didn't even flinch. He just sucked the bullet out of his wound and spit it with enough velocity to explode two Japanese battleships, then high-fived Korean Poseidon and ate dinner using a trident as a fork.

Throughout 1592 Admiral Yi Soon Shin continued to sink enemy vessels all over the place, carefully striking enemy transports bringing critical food, ammunition, and troops to the front lines. In ship-to-ship combat Yi relied on the firepower of his cannons and ordered his men to avoid hand-to-hand combat with the Japanese—Japan's naval tactics hadn't improved much since the days of Kono Michiari rowing his boat into the middle of the Mongol fleet armed only with a katana and a tempered steel ballsack, but by this point the Koreans had adapted to the more Western-style approach of "Let's sit back here and blast these jerks and their dinghies into flotsam with gigantic cannonballs."

To this end, Yi built something called "turtle ships," which sound kind of lame but were actually totally awesome. Fast-moving warships with reinforced metal plating completely covering the top deck to protect the sailors from enemy arrows and gunfire, these plates also had big-ass steel spikes sticking out of them so if any ninjas tried to fly on board they'd get impaled like when you knock Scorpion or Sub-Zero off the bridge level in Mortal Kombat. Each turtle ship carried about thirty guns, and the front of it was shaped like a badass dragon that shot a flamethrower out of its mouth, had a smoke screen that came out of its nose, and could be used as a battering ram to crunch enemy ships into driftwood. Yi used these early-model ironclads to barrel straight through the enemy lines, pinball around their formation Arkanoid style, ram the enemy flagship, then set the Japanese commander on fire with a dragon-headed blowtorch before he could coordinate a counter-attack and/or figure out how the hell he was supposed to stop this gigantic steel-plated nautical bowling ball.

All of this fiery mayhem eventually got Admiral Yi noticed by the shogun himself, and in August of 1592 Toyotomi personally ordered his three greatest admirals to team up, assemble a ridiculously huge eighty-two-ship armada, hunt down Admiral Yi, and feed him piece by piece to a school of rabid piranha-sharks with friggin' laser beams attached to their heads. On the fourteenth of August, 1592, the armada spotted six Korean ships hauling ass through a narrow strait, running full speed away from the Japanese. The Japanese warships pursued them, racing through the strait in a nice, orderly, single-file line, only to emerge from the other side and find a semicircle of Korean battleship broadsides ready to face-hump them with cannonballs from three angles. The Japanese fleet, stuck in a trap that would have given Admiral Ackbar an aneurysm, was completely annihilated. Two of the top three admirals in Japan were captured and beheaded, dozens of captains swallowed their Frisbees and committed seppuku, and the Koreans spent the next couple days combing the coastline for shipwrecked enemy sailors who upon being rescued were of course immediately filleted into bite-sized chunks of human sashimi.

Back on land Japan was still running things, but thanks to Admiral Yi the shape of the battle was changing. Encouraged by promising reports that the Japanese fleet was utterly unable to get reinforcements to the front lines, Korean guerrillas started attacking supply routes on land as well. Groups known as righteous armies—grassroots partisan forces comprised mostly of pissed-off peasants and kung fu Buddhist monks—started hammering lightly defended Japanese garrisons, supply depots, and transportation lines across Korea. The Koreans had found their fighting spirit, and, bolstered by newfound confidence in their powers of beating ass, they finally stopped running from the seemingly invincible Japanese onslaught. Heroic stands were made at places like Haengju, where twenty-three hundred warriors held a mountain fortress against thirty thousand Japanese. Massive formations of *ashigaru* (Japanese peasant spearmen rather than samurai) charged up a steep mountain toward the citadel only to recieve a bunch of arrows, artillery shells, rocks, and Shaolin flying side kicks to the face for their trouble. When ammo got low, the women of the city collected rocks in their aprons and ran up and down the line, passing them off to men who either discharged them from slings or hurled them at the Japanese the old-fashioned rock-to-the-face way.

Facing stiffer resistance, unable to bring more troops to the battlefield, and unable to protect the supplies they already had in place, the Japanese lines were spread too thin. Their ammunition ran perilously low, their men went hungry, and it only took one tack hammer to the sack to finally break their invasion once and for all.

That tack hammer was a Chinese military general named Li Rusong.

Li Rusong was a Ming Empire commander who had spent the last couple years battling Mongols in the wilderness to the northwest of China, and this guy really wasn't in the business of suffering fools. Not long after Japan captured Pyongyang, Li showed up with a huge force of Chinese and Korean infantry, surrounded the city, positioned troops outside every gate, and gave two orders: Number one was that any man who retreated in battle was to be beheaded on the spot. Number two was that no Japanese soldier should be offered mercy for any reason.

Li bombarded Pyongyang with artillery, then launched an all-out attack against the badly outnumbered Japanese defenders. The Japanese naturally stood their ground and dove headfirst into combat against incredible odds. When their outer defenses fell under the onslaught, they withdrew to the inner citadel, holding off the attackers with rifle fire from their makeshift fortifications and charging out with their katanas, but eventually the overwhelming Chinese onslaught was too much. When darkness finally fell, the last surviving defenders of Pyongyang swam across the river and escaped, and they didn't stop heading south until they'd reached Pusan Harbor.

The two sides made peace, but their agreement lasted about as long as the full-series run of *Firefly* and the next thing you know the Japanese were suddenly ready to have more of their ships reduced to firewood by Admiral Yi. Unfortunately for the Koreans, in the time between the fighting, the Japanese had managed to put a double agent into the Korean court, and that jerk convinced the king to order Admiral Yi to move his armada to a dangerous area known as the Chilchon Straits. When Yi received the order he immediately saw the plan for the dysfunctional baloney it was and refused it, reportedly giving the messenger the finger and then slapping him full in the face like a little bitch. For his insolence Yi Soon Shin was once again stripped of his rank, imprisoned, and tortured within an inch of his life. Command was given to some jackass named Won Gyun, who was so staggeringly incompetent it's a miracle the guy managed to put his pants on. Won moved Admiral Yi's combined force of 169 battleships and thirty thousand sailors to the Chilchon Straits, directly into the trap that was laid for him by the Japanese. In the span of only a few hours Japanese Commando Samurai Ninja Marines annihilated the entire armada and chopped Won Gyun up into shark chum. Only thirteen ships and two hundred men were able to escape the carnage, and they only did so by bravely running away at top speed as soon as the Japanese started wasting everyone in sight. The king then put Admiral Yi back in charge because at this point it was abundantly obvious that not just any idiot could lead the Korean navy to victory against the Japanese war machine. When Yi retook command of his navy and saw the dire situation before him, he is reported to have calmly said the following:

"I still have thirteen ships. As long as I am alive, the enemies will never gain the Western Sea."

So in 1597 Admiral Yi and his thirteen ships found themselves on the run, hunted by the entire Japanese navy. At the Battle of Myeongnyang, Yi Soon Shin came face-to-face with a fleet of three hundred Japanese warships, all bearing down on him and filled to the brim with angry, screaming, katana-wielding samurai warriors. Yi wisely positioned his tiny force to block a narrow strait Themistocles style in an effort to deny the Japanese the chance of completely enveloping him. The Japanese poured into the strait at top speed and ran head-on into a strong current that slowed them down considerably, leaving them exposed to fire from the Korean ships. During the course of the battle, Yi constantly repositioned his fleet in an effort to keep the Japanese marines at a distance and prevent them from boarding. His cannons bombarded the enemy, and when the smoke cleared he had sunk 123 Japanese ships and killed over twelve thousand enemy sailors, including the admiral in overall command of the Japanese navy. Yi's losses totaled three wounded and two killed.

This improbable victory broke the back of Japanese morale and marked a major turning point in the war. The Koreans once again fought bravely, and finally, at the Battle of Noryang, over 150 Korean and Chinese vessels finished the job on the Japanese navy, defeating an armada of 500 enemy ships as they attempted to retreat back to Japan. While giving pursuit, Admiral Yi was shot in the chest and died, Horatio Nelson style, at the moment of his final victory. His last words were, "Do not weep, do not notify my men of my death. Beat the drum, blow the trumpet, wave the flag for advance. We are still fighting; finish the enemy to the last one." The remnants of the Japanese fleet would limp back to its homeland, and they wouldn't bother to return for another three hundred years.

———

Before accepting a newly forged katana, samurai would test the sharpness of the blade by decapitating a convicted criminal and chopping up the beheaded corpse. There were sixteen distinct cuts that were made to the body to test various sword strokes—the easiest was "cutting the sleeve" (slicing off the hand at the wrist), while the most difficult was the "pair of wheels" (slicing the body in half at the hips in one swing). I think we can all agree that this is pretty messed up.

———

The Koreans employed a uniquely badass weapon known as the *hwacha*. One of the first documented pieces of antipersonnel artillery, the *hwacha* was basically a wooden board with like a hundred bottle rockets strapped to it and an arrow at the end of each bottle rocket. When a fuse was lit, all the arrows would light simultaneously, sending out a hundred-arrow wall of death straight at anything that moved. The weapon, I believe, is named after the sound the gunners made when firing it—*hwacha!*

———

During the Battle of Namwan, one Japanese samurai named Okochi Hidemoto performed some seriously nuts acts of ballztastic badassitude. The first man to assault the walls of the city, Okochi leapt down into a crowded courtyard, drew his blade, and shouted his name and ancestry in the traditional Japanese custom. Then he killed three dudes, one of whom was charging in on a horse, put their heads in a bag, and kept running. Hidemoto was later swarmed by five or six enemy warriors, who knocked him to the ground, cut him badly across the chest, and severed a couple of Hidemoto's fingers. Somehow, swarmed on all sides, the righteously pissed samurai managed to fight off his attackers, pulled himself back up, killed a couple of them, and then came toe-to-toe with the Korean commander. The big Korean warrior cut Okochi Hidemoto six times in the epic sword battle that ensued, but the samurai eventually got the better of his enemy, dropped him with two slashes across the chest, and took his head, breaking the morale of the defenders in the process.

19

JAMES MACRAE

The Cassandra Takes On a Pirate Armada
Off the Coast of Madagascar
August, 1720

Me? I'm dishonest. And a dishonest man you can always trust to be dishonest.
It's the honest ones you want to watch out for, because you can never predict
when they're going to do something incredibly stupid.

—CAPTAIN JACK SPARROW, IN *Pirates of the Carribean:*
The Curse of the Black Pearl

FEW THINGS MADE EIGHTEENTH-CENTURY SAILORS BLAST A
LOAD OF GRAPESHOT INTO THEIR TROUSERS WITH GREATER
FEROCITY THAN THE SIGHT OF A GIANT OMINOUS BLACK FLAG
FLUTTERING IN THE BREEZE FROM THE MAST OF A BADASS WAR-
SHIP TEEMING WITH UNSHAVEN, HOOK-HANDED, CRANIUM-
SLASHING, BALL-STOMPING PIRATE ASS DESTROYERS. So you
can probably imagine what was going through the mind of James Mac-
rae, captain of the East India Company ship *Cassandra*, when he saw
not one, but two Jolly Rogers pulling into the harbor off Johanna Is-
land and floating toward him on a warm afternoon in August 1720.

Macrae and his crew had pulled into port on a tiny island off the coast of Madagascar looking to replenish their stores of food, casks of water, and kegs of top-shelf Bacardi, but now they all of a sudden found themselves neck-high in a screaming pile of crap without their inflatable water wings.

Macrae hailed another East Indiaman that was in the port, the *Cassandra*'s sister ship *Greenwich*, but the coward asshole captain of the *Greenwich* was like, "So long, suckfaces, I'm out of here . . . enjoy having your colon annihilated. See you in hell." Macrae screamed untold obscenities at the *Greenwich*, even going so far as to fire a volley at her while she ran for her life like a little bitch, but she evaporated in a cloud of smoke like something out of a *Scooby-Doo* re-run and left *Cassandra* alone to deal with all the big scary pirate-types.

Cassandra now found herself boxed in by the vessels of two of the Golden Age of Piracy's most successful cutthroats: the *Fancy*, commanded by Edward England, and *Victory*, under John Taylor. Neither of these men was particularly known for being a real-life analogue of Barney the Dinosaur dancing an Irish jig under a full-on double rainbow all across the sky, a detail you could probably divine from the fact that they were both murderous effing pirates who would just as soon pull your nose off with a claw hammer and use it for fishing bait than piss on you if you were on fire. Macrae and his crewmen weren't exactly hardcore SAS paratroopers with rocket launchers for arms and cybernetic muscle implants allowing them to vault over small dinosaurs with a single ridiculous leap, but confronted with their own mortality these men also weren't the kind of chumps who were going to sit back and let a group of scurvy assholes eviscerate them with cutlasses either. Macrae unflinchingly ordered his men to load their cannons, and as soon as *Victory* was within range *Cassandra* turned and blasted her with a devastating broadside.

The initial impact of being pounded by dozens of giant balls sent *Vic-*

tory reeling, and a second cannonade from *Cassandra* tore into her and blew off part of her mainsail. The pirates dropped twenty sets of oars into the water in an attempt to row their damaged ship close enough to board Macrae's vessel, but a third volley of lead death blew those oars into splinters. This trio of broadsides still didn't deter the pirates from their mission to slit the throats of every sailor aboard *Cassandra* (if anything, it just made them more angry), and the now-crippled *Victory* continued to limp toward them like an unstoppable shambling undead nautical zombie. Around this time the other pirate warship, *Fancy*, pulled into range and released a volley of her own at *Cassandra*. Fragments of the deck exploded out under the force of the cannonballs hurtled throughout the ship with deadly velocity, killing several of Macrae's men as they furiously attempted to reload their weapons, but before *Cassandra* could even wheel about for a broadside on this new opponent the badly damaged *Victory* had already pulled in close enough to unleash another bombardment of her own, nailing her from both sides with gigantic balls. It wasn't looking good.

For over two hours Macrae traded fire with *Fancy* and *Victory* as these mighty sailing ships pummeled each other relentlessly, but despite expert gunning and masterful maneuvering on the part of her captain the situation aboard *Cassandra* was becoming increasingly desperate. *Cassandra*'s surviving crewmen were pouring musket as well as cannon fire on the rapidly closing pirate ships, hurling over homemade bombs when the pirate ships got close enough, but casualties were quickly mounting and Captain Macrae knew that his men wouldn't stand a chance in close-quarters combat with those bloodthirsty, heavily armed scalawags. He ordered his ship to pull about and sail full speed toward the shore, where his men could hopefully escape into the dense jungles on the island's interior, but Captain England of the *Fancy* was quick to realize what Macrae was attempting. *Fancy* moved to take the angle and cut *Cassandra* off, but in her haste she struck a shoal and became lodged in the sand. *Cassandra* attempted to go around *Fancy*, but then she too became grounded on a sandbar, wedged into the surf mere feet from the pirate vessel. From point-blank range, the two vessels exchanged several brutal broadsides, pulverizing the hell out of each other in a brutal display of naval demolition as their sailors took potshots at anyone brave enough to stick his head above decks. Ammunition was running low on board *Cassandra*, and even though he had taken a glancing blow from a musket ball off the skull and was bleeding profusely from a massive head wound, Macrae still had his men loading the cannons with chains, nails, broken beer bottles, handfuls of rifle bullets, really hard loaves of bread, and anything else they could find to shoot at *Fancy*.

Both ships were basically just held together by their rigging at this point, and to make matters worse for James Macrae, *Victory* was limping toward the immobilized *Cassandra*, unleashing volleys of musket fire and shouting insults about the crew's collective mothers. When the pirates on board *Victory* threw their hooks over the side of *Cassandra* and prepared to haul themselves on board, Macrae knew that the battle was lost. He was completely outnumbered by bloodlusting pirates on both sides of him and his surviving crewmen didn't exactly resemble the cast of *WrestleMania X*, so he ordered the men to throw a double load of powder into the cannons, and when they fired their final volley, he used the smoke screen and ensuing havoc to cover his crew's escape. The men scrambled to their rowboats and escape pods or swam to shore, where they then ran deep into the tropical jungle of Johanna Island. Pirates swarmed over the decks of *Cassandra*, slashing the throats of any wounded or dying men they came across, and plundering the cargo hold of nearly $150,000 worth of precious goods from India and China. But their real vengeance still eluded them.

Unfortunately for our hero, pirates don't give up that easily—especially after taking a beating like the one Captain Macrae had ever-so-deservedly laid upon them. Squads of pirates combed the jungles of the island searching for the captain and his men, intent on avenging their fallen brethren. Macrae's starving, war-weary, wounded crew evaded these patrols, living off the land deep in the inhospitable jungle for ten days before Macrae finally decided to say, "Screw it. I've had enough of this bullcrap." Then, in one of the most brazen display of brass balls ever recorded, Captain Macrae put on his full dress uniform, polished his sword, cleaned off the bullet wound on his head, and confidently strode toward the coast. A large group of pirates was standing on the docks, completely astonished that the man they had been searching for so intently was now walking right up to them like he owned the joint. The captain marched right up to the pirate commanders like he was approaching an ATM, stated his name and rank, unflinchingly demanded the return of his ship and cargo, and requested safe passage for himself and his crew.

Obviously the pirate captains didn't know what to make of this. On one hand, the man standing before them was personally responsible for the deaths of over a hundred pirates and had crippled two of their best ships. Many of the pirate crew believed he deserved to be tied to the mast and beaten to death with herrings. But on the other hand, everyone also had to respect the enormous ballbag of badassitude that Macrae evidently possessed. Luckily, as it turned out, quite a few of the pirates aboard *Fancy* and *Victory* had actually once served under Captain Macrae, and they all remembered him as being a fair and just leader who commanded the respect of his men. So eventually the pirates decided that they couldn't possibly commit the cold-blooded murder of a man like this. They kept his ship, but allowed safe passage for his men, returned one-half of the food and water supplies aboard *Cassandra*, and sailed off, leaving him with the half-destroyed *Fancy*. Macrae and his men performed some emergency repairs and then set off with little more than a skeleton crew to operate the ship. For forty-eight days the starving, dehydrated, half-dead men sailed on a barely seaworthy vessel, finally reaching Bombay in October 1720, where they were greeted as heroes by the local British administration. For his amazing courage, and his effort killing a hundred pirates and making the journey home while losing just thirty-seven of his own men, Captain Macrae was promoted by the East India Company and eventually became the governor of Madras, an extremely prestigious post within the British Empire.

Keelhauling was the pirate practice of tying a rope around your waist, throwing you off the front of the boat, and then dragging you underneath the ship until you drowned or were cut to death by razor-sharp barnacles. I'm not a doctor or anything, but that doesn't sound like a super fun way to spend your afternoon.

While in office in India, James Macrae fought corruption and ruled justly, and he eventually retired to Scotland an incredibly wealthy man. One year after this battle, Captain John Taylor would use Macrae's ship, *Cassandra*, to capture the single greatest pirate treasure in history, liberating two million dollars' worth of diamonds and goods from some obscure yet wealthy Portuguese count. Taylor, a badass in his own right, would later receive a pardon from the Spanish crown and retire to live a life of luxury in South America. Everyone wins, except Captain Edward England, who was marooned on a desert island by his men after a mutiny a few days later.

20

THE RANI OF JHANSI

Rani Lakshmibai in the Indian Rebellion of 1857
Jhansi Province, British India
May 1857–June 1858

Thus the Maratha Queen, tall in stature,
handsome in person, young, energetic, proud
and unyielding, from that moment indulged
in the stern passion of anger and revenge.

—SIR GEORGE FORREST, *The Indian Mutiny, 1857–1858*

PEOPLE GENERALLY LIKE TO REFER TO THE WARRIOR QUEEN RANI LAKSHMIBAI AS INDIA'S VERSION OF JOAN OF ARC. Sure, there are plenty of obvious similarities between the two young warrior maidens who came out of nowhere to lead their people in their efforts to skewer Englishmen through the torso with a bunch of keenly sharpened metallic objects, and the fact that Rani Lakshmibai is considered a martyr for the cause and revered by her countrymen even to this day lends her quite a resemblance to the Limey-cleaving Maid of Orléans. Personally, however, I would argue that she's more akin to being the

William Wallace of India than anything else—and not only because this never-say-die blood factory was tall, charismatic, and more than capable of personally sawing your brain in half with a giant two-handed sword, but because she was also incredibly successful in leading her overly oppressed comrades in a valiant, brutal rebellion against British occupation of their homeland.

Born in 1835 in the state of Jhansi in northern India, Rani Lakshmibai was just a young child when her mother died, leaving most of the child-rearing duties to her incredibly busy father, the king of Jhansi. As a member of India's elite warrior caste, Dad knew the value of being able to lop people's helmets off with one swing of a blade, so he decided to forgo the b.s. curriculum usually foisted upon Indian women at this time and instead opted to teach her how to do badass shizzle like ride elephants, jump over fire pits on horseback, sword-fight, shoot a crossbow, load a musket, read, and write. Training in the arts of war every waking moment, Lakshmibai quickly became an unstoppable snowplow of sari-wearing destruction and passed on the secret art of scrotal annihilation to any other women of the court who thought it would be totally flippin' sweet to kick people's asses. Before long, the rani managed to assemble a hyperloyal personal bodyguard of mecha-tough women courtiers who doubled as organic wood chippers capable of slicing and dicing people apart like a paper shredder ripping through a necktie.

As soon as she was old enough, Lakshmibai was married off to some guy, as was the custom in the day. But a quiet, demure lifestyle wasn't in the cards for this caustic chick. A few years into the marriage, she had a son, who died at four months old, and then she almost lost her husband just a year and a half later. In the wake of these tragedies, the new queen of Jhansi adopted a new son to serve as heir to the kingdom as soon he was old enough to rule. In the meantime, she'd serve as his regent and bifurcate the cranium of anyone who wanted to screw with him by suplexing a whirling circular saw on their heads.

Now the big dogs in India during the mid-nineteenth century were a power-hungry ultracapitalist megacorporation known as the British East India Company. If it helps, you can think of these guys as being like something out of Shadowrun, *Blade Runner*, *Neuromancer*, or any of the other hundred billion cyberpunk dystopian sci-fi futures where superpowerful evil companies spend the majority of their spare time plotting world domination, screwing over other equally evil corporations, and developing diabolical schemes—only these guys were real, omnipresent, and supported by private armies equipped with bizarro future tech that far outstripped anything possessed by the indigenous peoples they were currently dominating. Basically, if you ruled a province in India in the 1850s, you had two options: do what these guys say, or be forcibly replaced by someone who will. And when the East India Company heard that the brand-new king of Jhansi was an adopted young boy with no royal blood, the high-ranking company officials declared the throne to be "lapsed" and the region to be "totally boned." The Rani was deposed, given a small pension, and told to keep her mouth shut and deal with it if she knew what was good for her.

But Rani Lakshmibai wasn't the sort of warrior chick who was going to sit around and take a heaping handful of disrespect without replying with a bindied head butt of vengeance. First, she tried the go the legal yet less violent bureaucratic route, filing a formal appeal in the British courts, and going to trial to assert the legitimate right of her and her adopted son to rule. This failed, of course, because the courts were being run by the exact same people who were currently trying to screw her over, which is kind of a bad combination when you're looking for impartial justice.

But the British dissing of the rani wasn't just an isolated incident: it was just one in a series of dick moves the East India Company was pulling on the Indian people. With essentially no oversight at all, the EIC continued to be totally evil, overtax the populace, and—even worse—systematically slaughter Indian cows and chop them up for food, something that was kind of a problem for the Indian people, since a chief tenet of the Hindu religion is that cows are sacred and should never be brought to harm, but mostly just because honestly nobody in the country could really stand those guys anyways. So, as you can probably expect, in June 1857 the entire Indian army mutinied against the forces of colonial Britain. Seeing an opportunity arise at the perfect moment, the twenty-two-year-old Queen Lakshmibai formally declared open revolt five days later, gathered an army of loyal supporters, attacked the British fort at Jhansi (the same palace that had just been stolen out from under her), recaptured her homeland, and massacred every British man, woman, and child she could get her hands on (which was pretty much all of them).

I should mention that many sources aren't particularly clear about the rani's involvement in the massacre—some people claim not only that she wasn't there, but that she was officially reinstated as queen of Jhansi by the British after she came out and publicly decried the violent murderfest as being bad and wrong and also wrong and bad. Historians have a tough time figuring out where the truth is in this story, so feel free to go ahead and believe whichever version makes you like her better.

Whatever the case may be, Rani Lakshmibai quickly solidified herself as ruler of Jhansi, built up her defenses, and quite honestly a lot of Indian and British people were mulched into clam chowder in the process. During the turmoil and destruction surrounding the Great Indian Rebellion of 1857, Lakshmibai consolidated her small kingdom, trained the men and women in her service in the arts of combat, and on two separate occasions personally repelled large-scale invasions from jackass rival regional Indian lords looking to swoop in during the anarchy and claim her dominion for themselves. Some reports indicate that she personally charged into battle on horseback on countless occasions, leading cavalry charges with her child strapped onto her back, a sword in each hand, and the horse's reins in her teeth. That's hardcore. I picture this going down kind of like a nineteenth-century version of Ripley incinerating the alien queen's egg baskets with a blowtorch duct-taped to a machine gun while carrying Newt around in her other arm and kicking some face huggers in whatever passes for a nutsack on their anatomy.

Seeing that the loyalist forces were unsuccessful in taking down this flesh-ripping chick and her heavily entrenched, highly disciplined army, British general Sir Hugh Rose launched a full-scale invasion of his own, bringing a couple thousand men and cannons to blow Jhansi to hell until the people there had the good sense to surrender. Despite facing a crippling, ultra-high-tech force that would have explodiated the balls off of most other city-states in about ten seconds, Rani fought tenaciously, holding out for two full weeks against the onslaught, clinging to survival just long enough for a twenty-thousand-man-strong relief column to arrive from a nearby allied rebel province and charge straight into the flank of the British army. She had succeeded in holding out to defend her city.

Unfortunately for the rani, the relief column soldiers hadn't really had much experience with heavy artillery, and when the first couple cannon shots blew the hell out of their ranks they all dropped their weapons and ran away. Awesome.

Having put all her eggs in the "massive horde of gun-toting dudes coming to my aid" basket, and now seeing that the situation was utterly hopeless, the rani evacuated as many people as she could in the middle of the night, abandoning the village and retreating to link up with another rebel group nearby. Combining her forces with that of the remaining rebels, the rani continued to fight her way through what was increasingly becoming a hopeless effort to overthrow colonial rule in India. She led her warriors to defeat the Indian maharaja of Gwalior after he defected from the rebel cause and sided with the British, but she was killed in battle during a counterattack by the British Eighth Hussars Regiment while trying to rally her troops. Fulfilling her dying wish not to let her body fall into British hands, her followers built a funeral pyre in the middle of the battlefield and burned her on the spot where she fell. The rebellion would end up being quashed by the British, and India would remain a colony until 1948.

Rani Lakshmibai's son survived the war, but when faced with a few thousand bayonet points the kid quickly renounced his throne and spent the rest of his life living on a British pension (there are worse ways to retire, I suppose). As a result of her personal leadership, ferocity in combat, and uncompromising tenacity, Sir Hugh Rose would later be quoted as saying that she was the bravest, most fearless, and most dangerous rebel commander of the entire Indian uprising.

Over the years, the queen of Jhansi has become a near-mythical hero among the people of India for her role in kicking ass during the 1857 rebellion. She fought bravely, refused to surrender, and died the death of a martyr for freedom. She now has a couple of statues in her honor, is included in all Indian history textbooks, met Flashman a couple of times, and is so synonymous with being an asskicking chick that when the Indian National Army put together an all-female infantry unit during World War II they had the good sense to name it after her.

⇢ WOMAN WARRIORS ⇠

Every century has produced heroes who have sacrificed their lives
for their country. If they had remained at home to die by the fire,
would their names have been inscribed on bamboo and silk
to live eternally in Heaven and on the Earth?

—Trần Hưng Đạo

PRINCESS PINGYANG (617 AD)

When the utterly incompetent emperor of China's Sui dynasty decided that the best way to protect his reign was to execute his only capable general out of sheer high school jealousy and pettiness (he was bitter that General Li Yuan got all the attention just because he drove a sweet car and single-handedly won a bunch of wars against the barbarians), General Li got over his hurt feelings, assembled his loyal troops, and divided command between himself and his twenty-year-old daughter Zhao. Zhao went to work recruiting peasant soldiers, bribing bandits and mercs to join her cause, and castrating anyone dumb enough to defy her by rolling over their groins with a pizza wheel, and when the emperor marched out to face the so-called "Army of the Lady," Zhao throat-stomped the entire Sui army into meat slurry without even taking her sandals off. With the imperial army crushed, Zhao linked up with her dad's force and participated in the final assault that deposed the corrupt emperor once and for all and installed her father as the first emperor of a new dynasty known as the T'ang. Zhao was appointed Princess Pingyang, and when she died of illness three years later she was given a funeral fit for a general.

ANGELIQUE BRULON (1799)

While it was fairly common for liberated eighteenth-century women to travel the land fighting battles disguised as men, Angelique Brulon of France didn't really see the point of cutting her hair and taping down her boobs, so instead she just grabbed a gun and fought alongside the men without even attempting to conceal her womanhood. Serving in front-line combat duties in Corsica during the wars of the French Revolution, this iron lady rose through the ranks from private to sergeant major, won a medal for her swordfighting skills, and survived being badly wounded at the Battle of Calvi in 1799 when she led the assault on an enemy fort, fighting first with a rifle, then battling her enemies with a sword "with the courage of a heroine." When Brulon took a nasty cut to her sword-swinging arm during one battle, she pulled a dagger wtih her left hand, uttered a line from *The Princess Bride,* and continued hacking/slashing like a maniac until all around her died just from witnessing this insanity. Later in her career she would be awarded the French Legion of Honor by Napoleon III.

Nakano Takeko (1868)

During the thirty-day siege of the Japanese castle of Aizu, one dedicated warrior woman decided she wasn't about to sit back on her kimono sipping flower-infused tea while her husband and his men had all the fun fighting and dying gloriously in a losing battle against impossible odds. Nakano Takeko organized the women of the castle, armed them all with *naginata* (basically a big stick with a cutting blade on the end of it), and personally led a suicide charge straight-on against a vastly numerically superior formation of Japanese imperial soldiers armed with modern bolt-action rifles and cannons. The men opposing Takeko hesitated for a minute, unsure about pulling the trigger on a group of cute girls, and their split-second delay bought Nakano and her women enough time to close in to clobbering distance with the enemy formation and start lopping off heads and dongs and anything else that happened to be hanging around. Takeko is said to have killed five or six of the enemy with her *naginata* before finally being shot down at point-blank range.

Flora Sandes (1914)

Flora Sandes was a tough-as-hell old British chick who took the stereotypical Victorian attitudes toward women, ramrodded them down the tube of a howitzer, and blew them straight through the heads of anyone who stood across from her on the battlefields of World War I. This battle-axe of destruction was the only British woman to officially serve with an infantry unit in WWI, the first woman to ever be commissioned as an officer in the Serbian army, and a torso-eviscerating, grenade-chucking demon-dame who performed so many intense acts of badassitude that she's now considered a top-shelf Jose Cuervo war hero in both her homeland and her adopted country of Serbia. Orignally part of a Red Cross team dispatched to the Balkans to help assist wounded soldiers, within a year Sandes was decked out in a Serbian army uniform, running through no-man's-land, charging enemy positions with a fixed bayonet. Sandes fought in dozens of battles, sometimes administering first aid and field dressings "between shots," and when the forty-year-old sergeant major wasn't bayoneting people through the eyes or crawling under barbed wire while machine gun fire whizzed overhead, she published a book and convinced the British government to buy new uniforms to replace the tattered rags her war-weary unit was sporting. Back in England she became a role model to women across the country, while her comrades in Serbia knew her simply as "Our Brother."

"FIGHTING GIRLFRIEND" (1943)

When her beloved husband of sixteen years was killed in action fighting the Germans during the Battle of Kiev, fearless Ukrainian kill-bot Mariya Oktyabrskaya sold all of her worldly possessions, bought a Soviet T-34 medium battle tank with her own money, painted the words "Fighting Girlfriend" on the side of it in Cyrillic, and hauled ass straight out to the front lines looking to link up with the first tank regiment she could find. She ended up with the Twenty-third Guards Tank Brigade, an elite Russian unit that wasn't sure what to make of her at first, but Mariya quickly earned their respect in her first battle when she ignored a few million pounds of danger and blitzed straight into the enemy positions, wasting Nazi antitank guns and lighting up armored vehicles in every direction. She participated in a number of battles in 1943 and '44, took part in the largest tank battle in world history (the Battle of Kursk), and on two separate occasions was cited for bravery for getting out of her damaged tank in the middle of a gunfight and performing repairs to it while bullets whizzed past her face. While certainly ballsy, this really isn't a recommended practice, however, and the third time she tried a midcombat repair job, Senior Sergeant Oktyabrskaya was struck and killed by shrapnel. She was posthumously declared a Heroine of the Soviet Union.

LEIGH ANN HESTER (2005)

On March 20, 2005, a convoy of about thirty civilian supply trucks was driving through the Iraqi countryside just minding its own business and singing Johnny Cash songs when all of a sudden a hail of heavy weapons ripped out from a row of irrigation ditches just off the side of the road, knocking several vehicles out of action and disabling the two U.S. Humvees that were escorting the convoy. With the column sufficiently suppressed, a group of about thirty Baath Party insurgent fighters advanced on foot toward the convoy, but right as these jackasses are getting ready to start taking hostages, all of a sudden three Humvees from the Kentucky National Guard came flying onto the scene out of nowhere, .50-cals blazing. Sergeant Leigh Ann Hester rolled out of the lead truck, rifle at the ready, and blitzed straight into the battle. Firing with her rifle and her Scarface-style underbarrel-mounted M203 automatic grenade launcher, Hester and her team destroyed the band of insurgents, killing twenty-seven enemy fighters, wounding three more, and capturing another. None escaped. Sergeant Hester would be the first woman ever awarded the Silver Star for valor in combat.

21

GETTYSBURG

The Battle of Gettysburg
July 1–3, 1863
Gettysburg, PA

The hoarse and indistinguishable orders from commanding officers, the screaming and bursting of shells, canister and shrapnel as they tore through the struggling masses of humanity, the death screams of wounded animals, the groans of their human companions, wounded and dying and trampled under foot by hurrying batteries, riderless horses, and the moving lines of battle—a perfect hell on earth never perhaps to be equaled, certainly not to be surpassed, nor ever to be forgotten in a man's lifetime. It has never been effaced from my memory, day or night, for fifty years.

—PRIVATE WILLIAM ARCHIBALD WAUGH,
TWENTY-SECOND MASSACHUSETTS INFANTRY

THE FIRST TWO YEARS OF THE AMERICAN CIVIL WAR OF NORTHERN AGGRESSION BETWEEN THE STATES ARE BASICALLY THE STORY OF CONFEDERATE GENERAL ROBERT E. LEE'S ARMY OF NORTHERN VIRGINIA MORE OR LESS KICKING THE UNHOLY BALLSACK OFF OF A SEEMINGLY BRAIN-DEAD SUCCESSION OF IN-CREASINGLY LESS COMPETENT UNION COMMANDERS UNTIL SUCH POINT THAT NEARLY EVERY PERSON NORTH OF THE MASON-

DIXON LINE WAS WONDERING WHY THE HELL THE UNION ARMY WAS BEING LED INTO COMBAT BY A BUNCH OF ASSCLOWNS WHO WERE UNFIT TO SERVE AS CAST MEMBERS ON *SESAME STREET*. Despite constantly being outnumbered by better-equipped federal armies with almost unlimited resources, manpower, and weaponry, Lee somehow repeatedly overcame ridiculous odds, won battle after battle against the Yanks, and kicked their asses up and down northern Virginia in a display of raw badass prowess that has never been seen again on American soil.

By July of 1863 Lee was getting a little bored with repeatedly bludgeoning his enemies to death with their own incompetence on his own turf, so he opted for a change of scenery and decided to take the fight to the enemy and invade the North instead. He marched his men through Maryland and Pennsylvania with a simple plan—wreak havoc, capture Union supply depots, cut Yankee railroad ties to the western front (where a Union general named Ulysses S. Grant was doing a far superior job of stomping out rebel sedition), encircle Washington, D.C., and deal the North a crushing blow that would destroy its will to fight once and for all, then go home and sip on some sweet Virginia whiskey.

Lee wasn't really looking for a fight in the quiet Pennsylvania town of Gettysburg. The Southern commander was flying a little blind, since his master cavalry commander J. E. B. Stuart was out raiding enemy depots instead of providing basic reconnaissance, so when Lee dispatched elements of A. P. Hill's corps to Gettysburg to execute a raid on a shoe factory (many of the badly undersupplied rebs had marched all the way from Richmond to Pennsylvania barefoot—not exactly ideal when you're looking at twenty-mile hikes every day for a week), he didn't realize that an afternoon shopping trip would end up kicking off the largest and most epic battle ever fought in the Western Hemisphere.

Defending Gettysburg on June 1, 1863, were the troopers of General

John Buford's First U.S. Cavalry. Buford was a tough-as-nails old soldier with a bushy Sam Elliot mustache who'd leveled up his stats fighting the Sioux out west, and when he saw rebel troops heading into his town he immediately ordered his men to dismount, take cover behind a stone wall, and open fire. He was badly outnumbered, sure, but Buford's weaponry helped level the playing field a little—the First Cav was armed with breech-loading rifles that allowed them to fire almost twice as fast as infantrymen with standard muzzle-loading rifles, and his fearless troops immediately started laying down a field of death on the advancing enemy. It took the Confederates a few minutes to regroup and mount a more organized attack, buying Buford a little time for reinforcements to arrive. He was reinforced by a division commanded by John Reynolds, a guy who was shot to death immediately upon arriving at the battlefield, and was subsequently succeeded by Abner Doubleday, the dude who invented baseball. Doubleday was only a stopgap middle reliever, though, and when Confederate reinforcements continued to roll in he was forced to retreat and take a position just outside the town at a place appropriately known as Cemetery Ridge. He'd eventually be pulled in favor of the right-hander from Pennsylvania, Winfield Scott Hancock.

With elements of their forces now committed, the two armies—who were a hell of a lot closer to each other than either had previously realized—converged on Gettysburg, and before you know it a dispute over Reeboks suddenly became an epic battle involving 150,000 men in a timeless struggle for life, liberty, and the pursuit of tasteful footwear.

On the morning of the battle's second day the U.S. forces were deployed along Cemetery Ridge, entrenched behind a stone wall on an embankment that overlooked about a mile of open field. The ridge was anchored by large hills on either side—Culp's Hill to the right and Little Round Top to the left. Lee had ordered one of his corps commanders, Richard "Old Baldy" Ewell, to take Culp's Hill on the night of the first day, but Ewell didn't really feel like it so he sat back and let the Union dig fortifications there instead because that seemed like a much wiser idea to him anyways. Ewell had recently taken over for the amazingly hardcore cask-conditioned oak-barrel-aged double-malt badass General Stonewall Jackson, a seemingly invincible Virginian who was so good at killing Yankees that the only way he could be stopped was when some of his own men accidentally shot him to death. Having Ewell filling in for Stonewall at Gettysburg was kind of like bringing Ryan Leaf into an overtime playoff game after Peyton Manning goes down with a season-ending musket-ball-related injury. Meanwhile, as a side note, "Old Baldy" was also the name of Union commander George Meade's horse, a marginally-intelligent beast that was arguably about as effective an officer as Ewell during this battle.

Faced with this situation Lee decided that rather than marching across the open field like a dumbass he'd launch a two-pronged attack on Culp's Hill and Little Round Top, hitting both sides simultaneously while keeping A. P. Hill's corps back to ensure the Union didn't send too many men to reinforce their flanks. If the operation was executed quickly and correctly, it could theoretically have flanked the federal army, driven them from the field, and left nothing standing between the Army of Northern Virginia and a running groin kick at Abraham Lincoln's Oval Office.

The hardest fighting on the second day took place on the Little Round Top side of the field. It started when an overly ambitious Union general named Dan "The Man" Sickles saw the Confederates advancing on him, disobeyed orders, and moved his troops forward, taking up positions in a wheatfield with a peach orchard anchoring one flank and a large group of ominous rocks known as Devil's Den on the other. In some of the most brutal fighting of the entire war, the rebs threw everything they had at Sickles's troops. For several hours men from Georgia,

Mississippi, South Carolina, Texas, and Arkansas hurled themselves against men from New York, Pennsylvania, and Vermont, fighting, advancing, capturing the enemy positions, high-fiving each other, then being driven back by counterattacks. The battle was so gruesome that at one point the First Minnesota suffered 82 percent casualties after charging a force twice their size to prevent their position from being overrun. Sickles got his leg blown off by a cannonball and his corps was shattered by relentless attacks, forcing him to eventually pull back to Cemetery Ridge.

While all that was going on, some rebel troops under General Evander Laws swung around Sickles's flank, captured Devil's Den, and then noticed with surprise that when Sickles had moved up he'd unwittingly left the heights of Little Round Top completely undefended. Since LRT overlooked the entire Union army, it was a pretty bitchin' place to set up cannons, so Laws logically ordered his men on an all-out charge to take the hill. Union commander George Meade noticed this unfortunate development at almost exactly the same moment as Laws, and sent five regiments from his reserves running off on a King of the Hill race to the top.

The Union troops got there first, and they had roughly ten seconds to prepare for the onslaught. On the extreme flank of the Union army was the Twentieth Maine Infantry—some 360 men under the command of Colonel Joshua Lawrence Chamberlain who now had almost instantaneously gone from chilling out in the back of the battle to holding the line against a force that outnumbered them almost ten to one.

Chamberlain ordered his men to take cover behind boulders and pile up rocks where they could, but within minutes a terrifying rebel yell came up through the woods as Laws's Alabama boys appeared through the brush. The Twentieth Maine fired everything they had into the onslaught as the rebels scrambled over boulders, racing up the hill into the teeth of withering fire, charging full speed toward the Twentieth Maine like an army of hard-charging SEC linebackers looking to decapitate an unsuspecting QB and then do a hilarious sack dance over his headless corpse.

At first the Alabama boys were pushed back by the unexpectedly strong resistance—after whupping up on the bluebellies for the last two years, they thought most Yankee infantry formations were about as formidable as a stuffed animal tea party at a Justin Bieber concert and were caught off guard by the unexpectedly massive cast-iron ballsackage now opposing them. It was going to take more a few gunshot wounds to the face to keep a bunch of insane Alabamans from trying to kill them, though, and four more times the exhausted yet determined rebels charged up the steep hill, straight into the enemy, firing their rifles and shrieking like wildmen while musket balls shredded the woods around them. On a couple occasions, the Alabamans made it to the peak and crashed into the Union lines, bayonets at the ready, but each time they were thrown back by fierce hand-to-hand combat as men swung fists, canteens, car batteries, tin pots, and rifle butts in a desperate attempt to club their hated enemies into bone dust.

After an hour and a half of nonstop asskickings all around on Little Round Top, things really weren't looking great for Joshua Lawrence Chamberlain—half his men were dead, the other half were wounded and wished they were dead, and those survivors still in fighting shape were so low on bullets that they were either taking rounds off of dead soldiers from both sides or just pointing their fingers and yelling "Bang!" really loud. What's worse was that somewhere unseen at the bottom of the hill, the rebels were reorganizing for yet another attack, one designed to break the line, capture the hill once and for all, and in doing so possibly end the war in one final cavalcade of rifle fire, Rebel Yells, and ridiculously-dead Yankees. The soldiers of the Twentieth Maine were brave, but they knew they weren't going to be able to hold

off another charge like the ones they'd already just miraculously managed to hurl back.

So Colonel Chamberlain, a schoolteacher in his regular life (kind
of like Tom Hanks in *Saving Private Ryan*), completely out of ammo
and with the entire fate of the Civil War hinging on his ability to

hold this line without being horribly mutilated beyond recognition, ordered the most kickass thing he could think of—he told his exhausted, wounded men to fix bayonets and prepare to stab their way into American history.

As the bloodied men from Alabama reformed their lines and began making their sixth full-speed charge up Little Round Top, they were greeted by the last thing they thought they'd ever see—a hundred guys from Maine running screaming toward them in a makeshift battle line, hollering like madmen, bayonet points glinting in the afternoon sun. This was the last straw for the Alabama boys—these exhausted warriors had already marched twenty-four miles that morning, reaching G'burg just in time to be sent straight into the battle and charge up a damned mountain five times in a row while guys shot bullets in their faces, and the sight of a hundred-bayonet-point phalanx was enough to make even these hardcore Southern-fried badasses throw up their hands and say "Screw this." The entire Fifteenth Alabama was killed or captured on the slopes of Little Round Top.

Old Baldy, meanwhile (the man, not the horse), didn't even get going on his end of the pincer attack at Culp's Hill until 6:30 p.m., well after the fighting was over on Little Round Top and the fate of the day had been decided. Man, that guy was worthless.

On the third day of the battle, Robert E. Lee made the biggest tactical mistake of his otherwise untarnished career. Lee, who may or may not have been having a stroke at the time, decided that if the Union troops were as strong on the wings as they seemed, they had to be soft in the middle like an Everlasting Gobstopper. So he reasoned that a full-on attack by three divisions of infantry launched at the dead center of the Union lines would split the Yankee forces in half, roll them up, and pulverize them into a meaty blue sludge once and for all. So, after a two-hour artillery barrage by 143 Confederate guns did its best to pepper the Union troops on Cemetery Ridge with enough shrapnel to set off every metal detector in Pennsylvania, Lee ordered fifteen thousand troops from Virginia and North Carolina to form a battle line a mile long, fix bayonets, and march a mile and a half across open ground toward the enemy infantry and artillery positions. Along the way they could expect not only to be fired on by the twenty thousand troops across from them, but also to be bombarded with cannon fire from Little Round Top and possibly even Culp's Hill. Every man out there knew this would totally suck, but that victory in the war would depend on their success here. They didn't even complain.

With the battle cry "Up, men, and to your posts—don't forget that you are from Old Virginia!" General George E. Pickett assembled his troops.

At three p.m. on July 3, 1863, a sea of gray marched out from the woods and began its 1.5-mile suicide charge toward a wall of blue-clad guys with heavy rifles and obnoxious New England accents. Marching in total silence, staying in lockstep with parade-ground precision, their battle flags waving in the breeze and bayonets shining in the hot Pennsylvania sun, the brave, doomed men of the Army of Northern Virginia looked out at an immovable wall of blue uniforms across the battlefield, knowing that for most of them this would be their last march.

At six hundred yards the Union artillery opened up with everything they had, ripping the Confederate troops a new one with cannonballs from Cemetery Ridge and Little Round Top. The Confederates closed their gaps, men stepping up to take the place of their fallen comrades.

At three hundred yards, Union riflemen—stacked six ranks deep— stood up as one from behind the stone wall on Cemetery Ridge and opened fire in one hellacious volley. They were joined by more cannons, this time firing canister shot, which is basically the cannon equivalent of a shotgun blast. Entire companies of men disappeared, but the Confederates still pressed on like they didn't even give a crap.

At two hundred yards, the rebels picked up the pace, their badly mauled units determined to charge the length of two football fields right into the teeth of withering fire and cannons capable of spraying dozens of fist-sized pellets with every blast from their muzzles, oblivious to the nightmarish amount of biblically apocalyptic death going on all around them.

The Confederate charge only reached the wall in one place—a small clump of trees known as The Angle. Led by daring Virginia general Lewis Armistead, who personally charged up the hill at the head of his men, rallying his troops by placing his hat on the end of his sword and holding it high above him. With a Rebel Yell the Southerners crashed into the Yankee lines, desperately striking out with sabers, pistols, bayonets, punches, and point-blank rifle shots to the face. The Union troops fell back under this unremitting onslaught of chicken-fried face-stabbing as the furious rebels battled to avenge the horrific destruction they'd just marched through. The front rank of Union infantry crumpled beneath their assault, as did an artillery battery, but despite Armistead's bravery it was too little, too late—Union gunfire had utterly crippled Pickett's Charge, and there were no Confederate reinforcements left to help him exploit the breach. Armistead's men were counterattacked by the Seventy-second Pennsylvania, Nineteenth Massachusetts, and Forty-second New York (marking the first and only time in history that people from Massachusetts, New York, and Pennsylvania ever agreed on anything), Armistead was shot while trying to turn the captured Union cannons around on their former owners, and his entire force was either wiped out or captured.

There were no Confederate officers left to order a retreat—every brigade and regimental commander involved in Pickett's Charge was dead, dying, or captured—but the soldiers got the point. The battle was lost. Of the fifteen thousand men who marched out, only five thousand stragglers returned, most of them badly wounded. The hardened core of the Army of Northern Virginia had been completely wiped out in a single afternoon. As the shattered units limped back to Confederate lines, Lee himself rode out to meet them, telling his men, "It's all my fault," because it kind of was.

Despite this brave yet horrific death charge, the casualty numbers at the Battle of Gettysburg are actually somewhat comparable—twenty-three thousand U.S. to twenty-eight thousand Confederate were killed or wounded. But, much like the Spartans at the Battle of Leuctra, the Southern states were so badly hurting for manpower (there were thirteen million more people living in the North than the South) that they simply could not afford to take losses on that scale. Pickett's Charge would be the Confederate Crécy—their losses were too great to replace, and, while the war would go on for three more years, the South would never have a chance of invading the North again. The tide of the war—and U.S. history—had dramatically shifted forever.

When fighting broke out at Gettysburg, a local resident named John L. Burns promptly grabbed his old-school flintlock musket, turned off his reruns of *Matlock,* and ran out to the front lines. Burns, a seventy-two-year-old geezer who had fought in the Mexican-American War and the War of 1812, joined up with the Seventh Wisconsin, fought with the "Iron Brigade" throughout the first day of the battle, and was wounded by three musket balls to various parts of his person. He survived the battle, shook hands with Abraham Lincoln afterward, and then calmly went back to his house for a Natty Ice.

———

As the Confederates withdrew back across the field of Pickett's Charge, the Union troops began chanting "Fredericksburg! Fredericksburg!" mostly because they were still marginally bitter about the whole Battle of Fredericksburg thing that had gone down a few months earlier. The short version of the story is that Union general Ambrose Burnside—an epically muttonchopped man who lives on in history not because of his generaling skills but rather because he's the guy who gave his name to sideburns—attempted a rampagingly stupid full-scale assault straight on toward a five-deep formation of Confederates who were entrenched behind a huge stone wall at the top of a hill. In a series of murderous, increasingly futile death marches, the Union troops were relentlessly mowed down, suffering thirteen thousand casualties without accomplishing anything useful.

———

After the war, Joshua Lawrence Chamberlain became the president of Boudoin College and served as a four-term governor of Maine. During the war he'd survived twenty battles, had six horses shot out from under him, was wounded six times, and was cited four times for bravery, including receiving the Medal of Honor for his actions on Little Round Top. He personally oversaw the surrender of the Confederate infantry at the end of the war, ordering his men to present arms in respect as the enemy laid down their weapons.

Since I'm going to be referencing this a lot in the upcoming chapters, I think it probably makes sense to give you an idea of what I'm talking about when I refer to unit sizes and military ranks. Exact numbers vary greatly from time period to time period and country to country, but this is the basic idea:

Unit	Makeup	Strength	Commander
Field Army	2–5 corps	50,000+	General
Corps	2–5 divisions	20,000–50,000 men	Lieutenant General
Division	3 + brigades	10,000–25,000 men	Major General
Brigade	3+ battalions	3,000–5,000 men	Brigadier General
Regiment*	3–5 battalions	1,000–3,000 men	Colonel
Battalion	3–5 companies	500–800 men	Major or Lieutenant Colonel
Company	3–5 platoons	100–250 men	Captain
Platoon	2–4 squads	16–44 men	Lieutenant
Squad	—	4–10 men	Corporal or Sergeant

*Aside from certain specialized arms such as cavalry and paratroopers, the regiment designation is largely archaic today. Many modern military units still maintain regimental numbers, but this is mostly due to tradition and not because these are cohesive fighting units.

22

SAMURAI SHOWDOWN

The Ikedaya Incident
Kyoto, Japan
July 8, 1864

Not one of the paper screens was left intact, all of them having been smashed to pieces. The wooden boards of the ceiling were also torn apart where men who had been hiding under the floorboards were stabbed with spears from below. The tatami mats in a number of the rooms, both upstairs and downstairs, were spotted with fresh blood. Particularly pitiful were arms and feet, and pieces of facial skin with the hair still attached scattered about.

—NAGAKURA SHINPACHI, ASSISTANT VICE COMMANDER
OF THE SHINSENGUMI

THE SHINSENGUMI OF THE LATE TOKUGAWA SHOGUNATE WERE KIND OF LIKE THE S.W.A.T. TEAM IN AMERICAN POLICE DEPARTMENTS, IF INSTEAD OF JUST BEING CALLED IN TO DEAL WITH BANK ROBBERIES AND DRUG DEALERS THEY HAD ABSO-LUTELY NO OVERSIGHT AND WERE ALLOWED TO RUN WILD AROUND THE CITY KILLING CRIMINALS AND TRAITORS AT THEIR DISCRETION WITH SWORDS AND BAD LANGUAGE WHEN-EVER THE HELL THEY FELT LIKE IT. Personally commissioned by the shogun at a time when allies of the Tokugawa Shogunate were being decapitated by renegade ronin and having their severed heads spiked on bamboo stakes on the daily, this last-ditch special police force consisted of one hundred of the most high-octane badass swordsmen in all of Japan, all of whom were equipped with a decent salary and a license to kill and set loose on the streets of Kyoto with one simple order: hunt down and kill traitors without mercy or any annoying paperwork to fill out afterwards. The shogun named this elite special police kill team Shinengumi, meaning "Newly Selected Corps," which is a pretty tame moniker considering that these guys ended up being the most feared paramilitary organization in Japanese history. My guess is that it was just to throw off the enemy, kind of like how SEAL Team Six officially goes by "Special Warfare Development Group" rather than "United States Navy Overseas Human Mutilation Factory."

The Shinsengumi were commanded by an unflinching hardass named Kondo Isami—a peerless swordsman so scorchingly hardcore that Toshiro Mifune played him in a movie once. Kondo wore an awesome-looking black robe with a white skull emblazoned on it, making him basically the Meiji Restoration's equivalent of Frank Castle the Punisher, and just like the borderline-psychotic comic book vigilante he shares his apparel with, Kondo was a battering ram of street justice who responded to criminal infractions not with a courtroom full of due process, but by simply grabbing the heaviest weapon he could find and using it to batter the wrongdoers into a bloody mess in the most violent and disgusting manner humanly possible and messing them up so bad they'd need a forensic dentist and a voodoo seance to identify the body. This penchant for wantonly massacring the enemies of the shogun rightly earned Kondo a reputation as a man you didn't want to screw with, and you can be damn sure that any time he walked into a bar he got his drinks for free and everyone in the joint that didn't want to be murdered just dropped their sake bowls and ran out of there hysterically crying.

The son of a peasant, Kondo had been training in martial arts since he was fourteen, and by 1864 he was believed to have killed at least sixty men in sword fights. Kondo was completely fearless, unfazed by even the most comical fountains of gore (he once claimed that he decapitated a dude so hard the guy's arterial blood spray splashed onto the roof of the house behind him and that it was *totally hilarious*), and under his able tutelage the Shinsengumi had become the toughest organization of face-wrecking scrotum kickers the city of Kyoto would ever see. One hundred of the most amazing swordsmen in the country, handpicked by Kondo and hardened by incessant training, constant battle against the enemies of the shogun, and a disciplinary code that basically stated that any kind of boneheaded screw-up was punishable by seppuku. Hell, one time the friggin' Shinsengumi *accountant* screwed up on his tax returns or something, so Kondo ordered him to commit ritualistic sword-related suicide for "the crime of miscalculation." So yeah, it was that kind of party.

But if Kondo Isami and the Shinsengumi were willing to disembowel one of their own members just because the poor incompetent joker forgot to round up the remainder on the long division he was doing by hand without a calculator, you can only imagine how they reacted in early July 1864 when they started hearing rumors that there was a cabal of heavily armed anti-shogun ronin warriors plotting a violent coup against not just the shogun, but the emperor himself. Not exactly willing to sit around while a group of seditious assclowns plotted to kidnap Emperor Komei, burn down the city of Kyoto, and massacre a few dozen of the shogun's best friends, these guys started scouring the city looking for the jerkburgers who would dare even *think* about committing such a treasonous act of heinous douchebaggery.

Kondo and the Shinengumi eventually found some suspicious-looking dude wandering around on the street, grabbed him by the balls, and tortured the information they needed out of him—first by whipping him a few dozen times, and then by hanging him upside down from a chandelier, driving spikes into the soles of his feet, putting candles on the spikes, and then letting the hot wax drip down on the guy's feet while he hung there. Nobody with a central nervous system would put up with that crap for long, and eventually this shady bastard spilled the beans about how there were a dickload of conspirators holed up in some local teahouse plotting dastardly deeds of kung fu treachery and curling their molester mustaches sinisterly. The dude wasn't sure where the rebels were hiding, so the Shinsengumi decided to split up and started canvassing the entire city.

At 10:00 p.m. on the evening of July 8, 1864, Kondo Isami and nine of the most badass swordsmen in Japan quietly walked up to the front door of the Ikedaya Inn—a charming, peaceful little teahouse that was about to become the scene of a katana-swinging deathmatch worthy of even the most obscenely badass Kurosawa and Tarantino flicks out there. Kondo knocked twice on the door, his face locked in an expression of icy, Clint Eastwood–style pissedness. When the inn's proprietor slid the door open, Kondo authoritatively stepped onto the soft tatami mats in the Ikedaya's entryway, pushing his way past the small old man in front of him. This was one of many inns he'd inspected this evening, but he refused to let his guard down ever for any reason, no matter how much of a wussbag the innkeeper seemed to be. He alertly looked side to side, scanning for signs of anything out of the ordinary, his hand lightly resting on the grip of his sword, his eye pulsating with badass fury. Satisfied that everything was kosher in his immediate vicinity (or whatever the Japanese version of kosher is), he took one step toward the stairs leading up to the second floor.

The inn's proprietor barely had a chance to scream a warning to the men upstairs that they were about to get their asses filleted like a blow-fish before Kondo flipped the old man to the mat with a badass jujitsu throw, drew his blade, and charged up the stairs. Three of his best men followed close behind, eager for some awesome samurai beatdown action. Kondo raced up the steps, sword at the ready, sprinted to the paper screen door at the top of the stairs, flung it open in an incredibly dramatic fashion, and commandingly shouted that anyone who moved was going to get shanked in the balls with a katana until they died from massive blood loss from the scrotum.

Kondo and his three men froze when they saw what was waiting for them on the other side of the screen: thirty-five ronin warriors, all armed with katanas, and all just drunk enough on sake to consider putting up a fight.

The tense standoff only lasted a few moments. One of Kondo's men pulled himself together and approached the nearest traitor, preparing to arrest him, but right as the Shinsengumi officer extended his arm to grab the conspirator, the dude whipped out his sword and cut Kondo's man down with one swing.

It was on.

Without flinching, Kondo and the two surviving men with him readied their blades and took on all thirty-five ronin by themselves in one of the most epic sword battles you can possibly imagine. Thirty-eight men, mostly unarmored, wailing on each other with samurai swords, nobody holding anything back, nobody asking for mercy, and damn sure nobody receiving it. Guys on both sides were leaping, flying, and being thrown through the paper walls of the inn, tables were smashed into splinters by swords and bodies, blood was spraying everywhere, warriors were screaming with anger and agony, and sparks were flickering in the night as katanas clashed into each other with enough force to break the blades apart or cut a man in half with one blow. A couple of the Shinsengumi from downstairs ran up to see what was going on and joined the swirling melee, which soon started to spill over to the downstairs and outside.

Kondo's well-trained, battle-hardened Shinsengumi samurai warriors seemed completely unfazed by the fact that they were outnumbered roughly ten to one in a close-quarters combat scenario surrounded by guys with two-foot-long blades sharp enough to rip a man apart with one hit, and they battled with the mad-dog ferocity you'd expect from a detachment of the emperor's most balls-out warriors. The Shinsengumi tore into the traitors, hacking the would-be nineteenth-century terrorists into tiny pieces any time they made the slightest tactical mistake, constantly keeping their defenses up against attacks from every direction. Kondo's family sword, a +5 Ancestral Masterwork weapon named Kotetsu, sliced through some of his foes' blades like Hanzo steel, and on one occasion one of his men was even documented as cutting a man's sword arm off at the wrist and then cleaving the poor disarmed sucker shoulder-to-hip, leaving half of him unceremoniously slumping down to the tatami floor mat.

It wasn't long before the traitors started to realize they were getting the worst of this teahouse beatdown, and the more weak-spirited and drunk among them decided they weren't in the mood to have their heads bifurcated by immensely pissed samurai. So hey, maybe that "Let's kidnap the emperor" idea wasn't so smart after all. They started to make a break for it. Some of the fleeing ronin pushed their way down the stairs, charging for the exit, while others simply leapt out the second-story windows to the courtyard below, figuring that the possibility of breaking an ankle was a hell of a lot better than the certainty of having an insane madman cut your arm off and rack you in the balls with your own dismembered fist. Even some of the traitors who stood their ground somehow accidentally ended up on the first floor, as there were a couple accounts of guys getting bodyslammed down, *breaking through the floorboards*, and crashing down through the ceiling into the room below only to hop up and continue fighting.

But Kondo and his team were ready for anything—this guy wasn't about to let a single one of these John Wilkes Booth wannabes walk away intact on his watch, and before going into the teahouse he'd already positioned the rest of his squad around the building with the express purpose of dismembering anyone who tried to escape. When these eager Shinsengumi officers saw the ronin rushing toward them trying to run like bitches, they gleefully drew their weapons and started screaming their battle cries. The next thing you know the arterial blood spatter had spilled out into the street, the courtyard, and throughout both floors of the teahouse.

When the dust and blood mist finally settled, there were eleven rebels dead, twenty-three captured, and one (the leader) who stabbed himself in the aorta seppuku style after being mortally wounded. The Shinsengumi calmly walked out from the main doors of the teahouse, covered in the out-of-control blood spray of their enemies, clutching swords that in some cases were so shredded they "looked like bamboo whisks" and in other cases were so bent out of shape that they wouldn't fit back into their scabbards. Kondo's troops reassembled into parade ranks, and without a word they marched in file back through the streets of Kyoto toward their headquarters while the citizens of Kyoto gaped at them in stunned silence with serious WTF looks on their faces. During the battle one of the Shinsengumi was killed (the guy at the very beginning), two were wounded, and one guy collapsed from an attack of tuberculosis that came on after he'd gotten a little excited while lacerating a couple traitors in half and went into an uncontrollable crazy coughing fit so intense/awesome he spit blood and almost barfed.

After the massacre at the Ikedaya teahouse the rest of the traitors hastily mounted a half-assed attack on Kyoto, assaulting the imperial capital head-on with two thousand disorganized men who were immediately eviscerated by the Shinsengumi and fifty thousand of their closest Tokugawa Shogunate buddies in a fight that took place just outside the Forbidden Gates of the Imperial Palace. For their actions at Ikedaya, the one hundred men of the Shinsengumi were made *hata-moto*, official samurai retainers of the Tokugawa, and were given lavish rewards, increased salaries, and the sort of prestige that you can only get by cutting down thirty-five traitors in fifteen minutes during a bad-ass close-quarters room-to-room sword fight. They continued to be the most feared organization roaming the streets of Kyoto right up until the unit was dissolved by the shogun in 1868.

One time eight Shinsengumi were enjoying the services of a geisha house when suddenly a gang of twenty gigantic sumo wrestlers came running up outside the house armed with iron-reinforced war clubs (these guys had been friends with a dude a Shinsengumi officer had pureed earlier that day for *Judge Dredd*-style reasons that may or may not have been legit). The Shinsengumi rushed to the window, and when they saw what was going on all eight men responded to the twenty thousand pounds of WrestleMania outside their hotel by leaping from the second-story window, *wakizashi* swords at the ready, and slicing them apart in a down-and-dirty, no-holds-barred street fight. Despite a couple club wounds to the head, the ronin killed eight sumo wrestlers and chased the rest of them off, all without losing a single man.

The battle at Ikedaya is sometimes credited with delaying the Meiji Restoration by nearly a year, but no amount of ronin decapitation was going to stop the freight train of samurai resentment against the Tokugawa shogun and his perceived spinelessness when dealing with the Western powers. Finally, in 1868, under extreme pressure from the emperor and some of the country's most powerful samurai lords, the Tokugawa shogun abdicated his position, restoring full military power over Japan to the emperor. With the rug pulled out from under them, the Shinsengumi were declared outlaws, and over the course of the next couple months most of them were systematically hunted down and killed.

23

VON BREDOW'S DEATH RIDE

The Prussian Cavalry at Mars-La-Tour

August 16, 1870

Mars-La-Tour, France

On taking my position with my battery nothing was to be seen of the Prussian cavalry. Where in the world had these cuirassiers come from? All of a sudden they were upon my guns like a whirlwind, and rode or cut down all my men save only one . . . it was only by the skin of my teeth that I myself escaped as the mass of furious horsemen swept past me, tramping down or sabering the gunners. But it was a magnificent military spectacle, and I could not help exclaiming to my adjutant as we rode away, "Ah, quelle attaque magnifique!"

—GENERAL HENRI, CHIEF OF STAFF, XI CORPS, FRENCH ARTILLERY

MAJOR GENERAL FRIEDRICH WILHELM ADALBERT VON BRE-
DOW'S ORDERS WERE CLEAR—THE INFANTRY AND ARTILLERY
ACROSS THE WAY HAD TO BE BROKEN, NO MATTER WHAT THE
COST. The fate of the war depended on it.

Crap.

The situation couldn't have been more dire if it were taking place in the control room of a planet-killing laser orbiting the Earth. Early victories in the Franco-Prussian War had successfully split the French military into two disorganized army groups—one in Metz and one in Chalons, a hundred miles apart—and a quick end-run flanking maneuver by an enterprising corps of Prussian troops under the command of a dude known as the Red Prince had effectively blocked the two units from consolidating. Through intense forced marches and that blazing foot speed the Germans are so famous for, the Red Prince had somehow got behind the French lines, positioned his men on the only road leading from Metz to Chalons, and now, with a war-ending victory just out of reach, he only had to stare down half of the French army and hold out against impossible five-to-one odds long enough for the rest of the Prussians to show up and complete the divide-and-conquer encirclement and destruction of the French military.

The Red Prince had given the French a good fight, but hours of constant battle were taking their toll on the Prussian forces. Still waiting for reinforcements, his numbers dwindling, the Red Prince realized that the French were preparing one final, fierce counterattack to demolish his beleaguered corps once and for all, break out, and regroup with their buddies in Chalons. The French had already massed artillery and infantry on their right flank and began bombarding the Prussian positions, softening them up for the final Pillsbury Doughboy love tap that would send the Germans giggling all the way to hell. If the Red Prince was going to hold, he needed a crazy-as-hell preemptive strike to cockpunch the French counterattack before it could even get started—because once they got their troops moving, it was going to be like trying to stop that boulder at the beginning of *Raiders of the Lost Ark* with your face.

The unenviable task of launching a horseballs-out suicide attack into the teeth of the strongest enemy positions on the field fell to Major General Friedrich Wilhelm Adalbert von Bredow's heavy cavalry brigade. Bredow, a forty-year veteran with a bushy white mustache and one of those awesome pointy German helmets, had been serving in the Prussian military since his sixteenth birthday, and this guy wasn't a total dumbass—you don't survive four decades of constant warfare without being able to know the difference between a glorious decisive attack and a "kiss your sack goodbye" suicide charge, and he had no delusions as to which option was being presented to him today. Von Bredow was to take eight hundred men from the Seventh Magdeburg Cuirassiers and the Sixteenth Lancers—two regiments that had already been beaten to hell during a charge earlier in the day—and run them two thousand yards across open ground without any infantry or artillery support, then hurl them saber-first into an entrenched enemy position loaded with disagreeable Frenchies armed with bolt-action rifles, heavy artillery, and multibarreled prototype Gatling guns called *mitrailleuses* that were capable of spewing out 150 rounds per minute of .512-caliber ammunition. This attack would have been suicidal even in the 1600s, back when old-school muskets were about as accurate as a rubber band gun fired from a moving train, took thirty seconds to reload, and were just as likely to blow up in your face as they were to actually launch a projectile at your enemy. In 1878, against a modernized European army, it was insanity. Much like Commander Shepard preparing to go through the Omega 4 Relay, von Bredow understood what was being asked of him—a suicide attack—yet he knew his men would do whatever it took to win the day. When asked by his subordinate for clarification as to what in the holy hell they were getting ready to do, von Bredow simply stared ahead into the bristling, artillery-packed French lines and said, "It will cost what it will."

But Friedrich von Bredow wasn't just some random glory-seeking young douchebag who had fallen out of a douche canoe into a river of douche and been swept away by the current—he was a cagey vet, and this hardcore old bastard wasn't about to just randomly chuck his boys into a meat grinder in some kind of hideously idiotic Tennyson-style Light Brigade death charge. Instead, von Bredow found a weird terrain advantage on the battlefield that he could exploit to his advantage—he took his men, marched them in a long narrow column through a deep valley where the enemy couldn't see them, then, when he'd stealthed his way as close as he could to the enemy positions without being detected, the Prussian officer gave the order to form up and attack. His troopers, acting as one, charged up the gunsmoke-covered ridge, wheeling as they marched with parade-ground precision, forming a massive battle line of Prussian badassitude galloping straight toward the flank of the French positions.

Spurred on by the wild cheer erupting from the Prussian battle lines as they watched this obscenely magnificent act of battlefield bravado, the heavy cavalry brigade charged out from the cannon smoke and barreled down on the French positions, their banners whipping in the breeze as they lowered their spears toward the enemy. It would take only two minutes to cover the last twelve hundred yards to the French positions, but it would be the longest two minutes of Friedrich von Bredow's already eventful life.

The French opened up with everything that they had, desperately trying to wheel their artillery and wipe out this bonkers cavalry formation that had basically just deep-strike teleported right on top of them seemingly out of nowhere. *Mitrailleuses*, rifles, and canister fire from cannons ripped into the massed cavalry formations, bringing down man and horse alike, but it wasn't enough—von Bredow's men charged ahead like heroes, undaunted by the death around them, and with an incredible explosion of thundering hooves, gleaming lance points, and umlaut-laden profanity the formation smashed into the French artillery in a murderous German death tsunami.

Now, a cannon blast of hundreds of tiny steel balls is seriously effective at shredding up cavalry, but your typical artilleryman becomes significantly less effective when he's forced to swing his ramrod around like a club while pissed-off dudes on gigantic warhorses stampede around him attacking indiscriminately with revolvers and sabers. The Prussian heavy cavalry brigade cut the French artillery apart in a freakout blood rage, leaving behind nothing more than a blood-colored patch of trampled grass and broken cannon parts as it rampaged through their lines.

The nearby French infantry formations that formed the second rank of their formation figured "Screw this" and opened up with their rifles on the melee, hitting friend and foe alike, and once the Germans were done making mincemeat of the artillery they just kept rolling and plunged into the infantry line, scattering the troops and cutting down everyone in a frenzy of horse bites, trampling hooves, and powerful, arm-severing saber strokes, as the mass of infantry dissolved into a bunch of broken-apart mooks with horseshoe imprints on their foreheads.

As all this was going down, von Bredow saw even more French artillery sprinting toward him, rolling a fresh set of cannons and *mitrailleuses* into position to attack. Von Bredow ordered his men to keep on rolling, issuing yet another charge, this one at the new line of enemy artillery. The artillerymen immediately crapped their trousers and tried to bolt for it, but haha dumbass good luck outrunning a dude on a horse while you're dragging a five-hundred-pound cannon around like a jackass. The cuirassiers chopped them up too and added them to the pile.

But soon a new challenger entered the melee—a well-rested, full-strength French cavalry brigade had noticed the copious amounts of hell breaking loose, formed up into a wedge, and galloped into the fray, crashing hard into the decimated and exhausted Prussian troops, blindsiding them midhack.

What follows is the last epic cavalry melee in military history. Almost three miles behind the now-shattered front lines of the French positions, surrounded by dead and wounded men from both sides, shrouded in white smoke, five hundred blood-raging Prussians were swarmed by almost three thousand French dragoons and cuirassiers, armed with carbine rifles, revolver pistols, and sabers. Both sides were hacking and/or slashing like old-school knights back in the good old days of the Middle Ages, wailing on each other with that special "I hate you to death" mentality that pervaded French-German relations in the nineteenth and twentieth centuries. The Prussians, surrounded and pressed on all sides in the all-out no-holds-barred barroom brawl on horseback, struck back furiously, hacking and slashing with their straight-bladed swords despite extreme exhaustion. The French, who carried curved sabers, fought primarily by stabbing at the joints of the Prussian armor, finding weak points and exploiting them with finesse, while their German enemies preferred the brute strength of a manly sword blow. Both sides fought like Tong Po and Van Damme trading broken-glass-laced face punches at the end of *Kickboxer*, and the remnants of the French infantry didn't exactly make life easy for either of them—the shattered companies had already witnessed the terror of melee combat with an ill-tempered dude on horseback firsthand, and were so shellshocked (hoofshocked?) that they were now just firing their rifles randomly into the fray without much regard to whether they were hitting friends or enemies. Thanks a lot, jerks.

Seeing that Von Bredow's Wild Ride was quickly becoming Von Bredow's Death Ride, the Prussian general (who, by the way, was in his late fifties out there trading sword blows with young punks in their twenties) finally ordered a retreat. The only surviving bugle player he could find had already taken a bullet in the horn, so when that kid blew the thing it sounded like cats having sex while dying, but the Prussians got the point. Pursued by the French cavalry and hounded by rifle fire, the Prussians retreated, dodging cannon explosions along the way as the shattered remnants of von Bredow's troopers bolted back to friendly lines.

Of the 800 men who participated in Von Bredow's Death Ride, only 104 Cuirassiers and 90 Lancers returned. Despite the heavy losses (almost seventy-five percent casualties), their mission had been an incredible success—the French artillery was decimated, their carefully planned counterattack was thrown into disarray by a swirling tornado of hooves and steel. His balls-out suicide charge had bought the Prussians the time they needed—two more Prussian corps showed up shortly after, nearly blundered the entire operation, and then eventually got their act together and completely boxed the French into the fortress at Metz. Emperor Napoleon III, his forces now split in two, marched out from Chalons to try to break the siege of Metz and was subsequently surrounded in the city of Sedan. Napoleon tried to crib von Bredow's style, ordering a death charge of his own, but his attack was completely shredded like a sentient block of *fromage* trying to assault a cheese grater. Both French armies surrendered, the emperor was captured, and France was forced to sign a humiliating peace treaty (it's worth noting that they'd eventually try to avenge this with the Treaty of Versailles after World War I, and we all know how that worked out). Friedrich Wilhelm Adalbert von Bredow became a national hero overnight, and the French military commander who'd had his army-wide counterattack thwarted by a fifty-six-year-old man was arrested, court-martialed, and sentenced to be executed for criminally negligent incompetence (though he eventually escaped prison, fled to Spain, and was never really heard from again).

Von Bredow's success was enough to convince the European powers that cavalry wasn't a total waste of time, since apparently a bunch of dudes riding around on horses in a suicide charge was still apparently considered a viable method of combat in the age of machine guns. This is a big reason why many European armies went into World War I with expensive, well-equipped mounted armies that ended up being about as useful to them as a liberal arts degree.

One of the most badass cavalry units ever assembled was the Winged Hussars—a hardcore brigade of Polish and Lithuanian heavy cavalry who charged across eastern Europe in the sixteenth century decked out in a nearly musketproof suit of plate armor with a gigantic set of feathered wings coming out from the back. The Hussars (whose completely badass motto was "Kill First, Calculate Later") routinely charged straight into enemy formations five times their size, undaunted by even the most ridiculous odds. Some of the Hussars upped the "wow factor" by stuffing severed heads down the tips of their weapons and charging into battle with a lanceful of heads, which sounds pretty gnarly/badass. The Winged Hussars' finest hour came during the Battle of Vienna in 1683, when the badass King Jan III Sobieski of Poland led the single hugest and most balls-out cavalry charge in history. Their wings fluttering and zipping like creepy, spear-flinging birds of prey, over three thousand Winged Hussars (plus several thousand additional European cavalry troopers) plowed unexpectedly into the soft meaty flank of a much larger Turkish cavalry force, battered them mercilessly, plundered their supply train, and chased the Sultan's army all the way out of Europe.

24

RORKE'S DRIFT

The Battle of Rorke's Drift
Rorke's Drift, South Africa
January 22–23, 1879

Our men at the front wall had the enemy hand-to-hand, and, besides,
were being fired upon very heavily from the rocks and caves above us
in our rear . . . such a heavy fire was sent along the front of the hospital,
that although scores of Zulus jumped over the mealie bags to get into
the building, nearly every man perished in that fatal leap; but they rushed
to their deaths like demons, yelling out their war-cry of "Usutu, Usutu."

—REVEREND GEORGE SMITH, ACTING CHAPLAIN, RORKE'S DRIFT

IN 1879, A SOUTH AFRICA–BASED ENGLISHMAN NAMED LORD CHELMSFORD HAD A LITTLE BIT OF A ZULU PROBLEM. Mainly, that problem was that the Zulus were just across the border from South Africa, and these guys apparently didn't have any respect for the queen or Saint George or warm beer or any of those other things that British people really seem to like for some reason. So, as you might guess, Lord Chelmsford decided that the best way to deal with this situation was to march across the Buffalo River, invade Zulu territory without the formal consent of the home government, and win glory for himself by bringing the uncivilized tribesmen of Zululand under the just and rightful subjugation of Queen Victoria of England. You know, because it was for their own good to learn about the magic of pants.

Well, it turns out that Lord Chelmsford wasn't really a good student of history, and this Douche-a-tron 9000 apparently didn't appreciate the fact that the Zulus were the most powerful tribal African empire ever assembled—a blood-and-guts warrior culture of face-shanking violence dating back to Shaka Zulu, one of the most ferocious, Boss Hogg gangsta hardcore military commanders who ever lived. The Zulu guys could fall into formation, run fifty miles in a day, fight a full-scale battle, then still have the energy left over to hunt and forage for their own food before going to sleep and doing it all over again the next day. These guys were as tough as overcooked beef jerky or those Big Bites that have been sitting on the heat rollers at the 7-Eleven down the street since 1987, and they really weren't all that keen on being overly hospitable to a bunch of red-coated jerkwads marching all over their territory killing people like they owned the place or something. The Zulu chief Cetewayo, outraged by this assault on his hard-conquered property, put together a huge army and prepared to crush the British by jumping on their heads Mario Brothers style and then feeding their flattened corpses to savanna lions.

Chelmsford's column, which consisted of seventeen hundred British soldiers, plus local soldiers, militia, and native auxiliaries, was sneak-attacked by Cetewayo's massively superior Zulu army at a place called Isandlwahna. Encircled in a tactically complicated double-envelopment maneuver reminiscent of Hannibal's attack at Cannae, Chelmsford's peeps were massacred beyond recognition (though Chelmsford himself conveniently wasn't present for the battle). The Zulus, armed only with short stabbing spears and animal-hide shields, fearlessly charged straight on into tight-knit formations of professional soldiers armed with top-of-the-line rifles, overran the British positions, and showed no quarter in a furious frenzy of groin-shanking ferocity and ritualistic disembowelment. Only eight Europeans survived the bloodshed—six members of the Natal Police (local Boer and South African citizen-soldiers) and two British soldiers made a break for it on horseback, shot through all their ammunition, fought their way out with swords, and had to swim their horses back across the Buffalo River to safety.

While this was a mighty victory for Cetewayo and his still-badass Zulu Empire, one blood-hungry Zulu warrior wasn't exactly thrilled with the outcome. Prince Dabulamanzi kaMpande (say that three times fast) was a little cheesed off that he'd been held in reserve during the battle, and by the time his mighty force of forty-five hundred glory-seeking Zulu warriors were actually unleashed on the battlefield the British were already dead on the battlefield being ritualistically eviscerated according to Zulu custom. But the resourceful prince knew about another small outpost of British troops—a tiny, understaffed supply depot just fifteen miles from Isandlwahna that would be ripe for the massacring. So, upset that his men didn't have the glorious opportunity to "wash their spears" in the blood of their enemies, kaMpande decided to go off on his own, disobey a direct order from Cetewayo not to attack, and immediately sprint his men fifteen miles across the African brush toward Rorke's Drift.

The first stop on the South African side of the Buffalo River, Rorke's Drift was a tiny, two-building Catholic mission that had been commandeered by the British to be used as a supply depot during the invasion. It was garrisoned by the men of B Company, Second Battalion, Twenty-fourth (Second Warwickshire) Regiment of Foot—reserve troops who weren't exactly thrilled to hear that the entire rest of their regiment had been utterly annihilated in spear-to-face combat by a mob of merciless African tribesmen with a few thousand axes to grind and no shortage of faces in which to grind them. They were even less happy when they heard that 4,500 Zulus were coming to finish the job, rushing straight at the 139 British troops of Rorke's Drift—a number that included the medical, supply, and administrative staff, as well as the 36 men confined to the hospital with malaria and other horrible debilitating tropical diseases. The senior officer in the depot was Lieutenant John Chard of the Royal Engineers, a man who had never actually even seen combat and who had only been sent there to repair the ferry across the Buffalo River (this is the "Drift" in "Rorke's Drift"—the "Rorke" was obviously some Irish guy).

The men of the Twenty-fourth had about two hours to prepare for the imminent attack. Retreat wasn't an option—the Zulus could travel twice as fast as the British on foot, and if there's one thing the Olympics should teach you, it's that Europeans should never screw with the Africans when it comes to long-distance foot races.

Rorke's Drift consisted of two thatched-roof buildings—one was being used as a hospital and the other as a storeroom—and had no other walls or natural defenses, but as any IT guy will tell you, engineers have done more with less.

Lieutenant Chard, assisted by Company B's awesomely named commanding officer, Lieutenant Gonville Bromhead, immediately began psyching up his men for the defense. First, the guys dragged a bunch of two-hundred-pound bags of corn out of the storeroom and constructed a three-foot high wall that linked the hospital and the storeroom in one cohesive defensive perimeter. Then they dragged out boxes of biscuits and assembled a five-foot interior wall as a second line of defense, with a smaller, four-foot corn-bag wall inside of that as a third, final line of defense. Next they punched holes in the walls of the buildings to use as gunports, distributed ammunition, gave rifles to the sick and wounded men in the hospital just in case, fixed bayonets, and prepared for the fight of their lives.

Just minutes later the hills around them began to bristle with thousands of Zulu warriors. The battle-hungry Zulus beat their shields with spears, the sound reverberating through the valley like thunder, and began their prewar chants and battle songs—a practice that, if you've ever watched the amazing movie *Zulu* (which is acted by actual Zulu warriors, many of whom were direct descendants of men who fought in the actual battle), is totally terrifying.

The Zulus opened the battle with gunfire from the hills—Zulu snipers, hiding in the bush, using rifles they'd either captured in battle or bought or seized from local settlers. With sniper fire pinning the British troops down all along the perimeter, the first wave of Zulus attacked—six hundred warriors sprinting straight up toward the corn-bag wall, screaming their battle cries, brandishing their scary-as-hell assegai spears. The Brits, outnumbered four hundred to one, desperately opened fire with their Martini-Henry rifles—modern weapons that fired a modern cartridge bullet rather than that ramrod black powder nonsense, but that had to be reloaded after every shot—firing desperately against the onrushing mass of humanity. Still, the Brits put out a withering fire, finally breaking the Zulu charge a mere fifty yards from the corn-bag wall and forcing the decimated wave of attackers to scatter for cover.

But there was no time to bask in the glory of their victory—as soon as the Brits looked around, they noticed that the entire rest of the Zulu force had moved up from every side, closing in on the British perimeter. The frontal attack had been nothing more than a diversion, and, according to some sources, just a suicide attack so that their commander could test the firepower of the British lines. Which is pretty much nuts.

The second Zulu charge attacked at the corners of the two main structures, fearlessly running at modern rifles while armed only with spears and hide shields that offered about as much protection against a bullet as a loincloth and a papier-mâché sailor's hat. The Zulus were mauled by the nonstop fire, but there were too many of them—the formidable tribesmen reached the walls on both sides, and all-out hand-to-hand combat ensued at the wall. Lieutenant Bromhead, who had wisely kept a platoon of troops in reserve, launched a counterattack with bayonets, charging at the walls in an insane-in-the-membrane display of raw testicular might. During the intense hand-to-hand melee that followed, a Swiss soldier named Ferdinand Schiess proved himself so femur-shatteringly tough that he would eventually become the first non-British citizen to ever received the Victoria Cross—despite being shot in the foot a few days earlier, Schiess still charged in, got amazingly cranky about having his hat shot off, and responded by bayonetting four men to death in the span of a minute to exact revenge and hold the line.

The Zulus were pushed back at the storehouse, but fighting still raged around the hospital. With the outer walls crumbling around them, the sick men in the hospital—many of them still in bed unable to move—fired through holes and windows in the structure, desperately trying to hit anything that moved, but the onslaught was too much. The walls were crumbling around them, and before long the Zulus breached the corn-bag wall and broke into the hospital. The British fought bravely, struggling room-to-room with an overwhelmingly powerful force as the Zulus torched the thatched-roof structure and stabbed at the sick and wounded, the British desperately fighting from their sickbeds as the enemy swarmed around them.

At this point Private Henry Hook of the Twenty-fourth proved himself to be an uncontrollably ultimate badass. Fueled by an unstoppable amazerballs awesome sauce with mozzerella dedication to killing Zulus, Hook fired through all of his ammunition, fixed a bayonet, and then single-handedly proceeded to bar the door to the main hospital building with just his ballsack and a six-inch spike of sharpened steel attached to an unloaded rifle standing between him and a few thousand rampaging enemies with spears and torches. As the building burned down around him, Hook somehow blocked, then barricaded the doors, stabbing anything that moved, first with the bayonet and then with a captured Zulu spear. As Hook dodged stabs from every direction and fought back with anything he could find, his platoon mate, Private John Williams, busted through the plaster hospital wall with the butt of his rifle and started single-handedly fireman-carrying sick and wounded men out of the burning building into the courtyard, where they then had to speed-limp fifty yards back to the second line of defense (the biscuit box wall). With flames raging all around him and Zulus breaking in through the windows and doors, Hook still held the door, buying time for everyone to escape, then running back out after them, amazingly somehow emerging alive and only slightly well-done.

At this point the hospital was nothing more than a bonfire illuminating the evening sky, but the storehouse and biscuit wall were still holding despite the Zulus' repeated efforts. Zulu warriors charged out through the hospital, rushing the interior wall, taking heavy losses from gunfire but closing to hand-to-hand range, stabbing over the five-foot wall at the hedge of bayonet-swinging Brits just on the other side. They were only pushed back by a fury of point-blank rifle shots and bayonets.

As the epic fight dragged on into the night the Zulus kept on coming, the battle raging through the firelight of the burning hospital as the exhausted Zulus continued to hurl themselves fearlessly at the British. Inside the second line of defense, Lieutenant Chard was still running up and down the line, blasting in every direction with both rifle and revolver, encouraging his men to hold the defenses at all costs. The outpost's only doctor, surgeon James Reynolds, continued working, fixing the badly wounded men all around him despite miserable working conditions, undeterred by the fire, the battle cries of the Zulus, or the bullets zipping past his head from every direction. All around them, battle raged—bayonets and spears swinging through the air, Zulus being shot point-blank in the grillpiece, British being dragged off and ritualistically disemboweled according to Zulu custom, and men double-killing each other, being stabbed and then sticking the other guy before finally dying. Near the storehouse, the Zulus broke through a small cattle corral, forcing the British to abandon the second wall and fall back to their last line of defense—a small, cramped wall of cornmeal bags that would be the site of their last stand.

Inside the tiny, shoulder-high circle of corn bags, the British formed up in three ranks, Lieutenant Chard confidently screaming for each rank to volley-fire in order while the other two reloaded. The Welshmen and Englishmen of the Twenty-fourth laid down a crippling hail of bullets, those soldiers who were too wounded or sick to work a rifle constantly running or crawling up and down the ranks distributing ammunition, the men fighting on, oblivious to the fact that their rifle barrels were now too searingly hot to touch without melting their hands.

When sunlight broke over the hills surrounding Rorke's Drift the following morning, Lord Chelmsford's relief column was surprised to see smoke and fire coming from the tiny outpost. The column had been dispatched to investigate the site of the Isandlwahna massacre, but they hadn't heard anything about fighting at Rorke's Drift, so they marched in to see what the heck was going on.

As they got close, the men of Chelmsford's column saw the bodies of six hundred Zulu warriors spread out across the battlefield. The next thing they noticed was Lieutenant John Chard and the men of B Company, Second Battalion, Twenty-fourth Regiment walking out to greet them, carrying a cask of rum they'd "requisitioned" from the storeroom building. The men of Lord Chelmsford's column broke ranks, without orders to do so, and ran out to congratulate them (and help them deal with their surplus booze situation).

In the 158 years since the Victoria Cross has been awarded, only

1,356 people have ever received the United Kingdom's highest award for personal valor in combat. Eleven of them were issued for the heroic actions at the Battle of Rorke's Drift. It would be the most ever awarded for a single engagement in Britain's history. To this day, B Company, Second Battalion of the Royal Welsh Regiment is known as the "B (Rorke's Drift) Company."

The man who first unleashed the true power of the Zulus was the mighty warlord Shaka. In addition to inventing the multipurpose assegai spear and the iconic Zulu shield, this much-feared, wildly eccentric war leader also revolutionized African tribal warfare through his use of complex tactical formations and a brutal disciplinary code stating that any man under his command who showed pain, complained, or dropped his weapon during *training* would be executed on the spot as a coward (he also claimed he could "smell" witches, went into battle dressed in blue monkey fur, and once had seven thousand people executed for "not looking sad enough" when they heard that Shaka's mother had died). When defeating rival tribes, the Zulu lord would give the vanquished douchebags two options— join the Zulus or receive a catastrophic puncture wound to the brain. Most of his victims took the more appealing option, meaning Shaka is one of the few military commanders who finished many of his wars with a bigger army than he had when he started. When Shaka Zulu assumed control over the entire Zulu nation in 1817, it had 350 warriors and 1,500 citizens. Ten years of nonstop battle later he commanded 40,000 warriors, 250,000 citizens, and ruled two million square miles of territory for his people—the largest and most powerful sub-Saharan African empire in history.

SECTION IV

INDUSTRIAL-AGE MAYHEM

*Even though large tracts of Europe and many old and famous States
have fallen or may fall into the grip of the Gestapo and all the odious
apparatus of Nazi rule, we shall not flag or fail. We shall go on to the end.
We shall fight in France. We shall fight on the seas and oceans.
We shall fight with growing confidence and growing strength in the air.
We shall defend our Island, whatever the cost may be. We shall fight on the
beaches. We shall fight on the landing grounds. We shall fight in the fields
and in the streets. We shall fight in the hills. We shall never surrender.*

—Winston Churchill

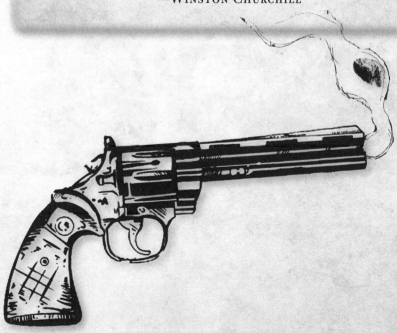

25

THE GUNFIGHT AT THE O.K. CORRAL

The Old West's Greatest Shootout
Tombstone, Arizona
October 26, 1881

You sons of bitches, you've been looking for a fight and now you can have it!

—WYATT EARP

IT WAS TWO O'CLOCK IN THE AFTERNOON ON OCTOBER 26, 1881, WHEN FOUR HARDASSES WITH NONSTOP BAD ATTITUDES STRODE DOWN THE MAIN STREET OF TOMBSTONE, THEIR LONG BLACK COATS AND INESCAPABLY BITCHIN' WAXED POWER 'STACHES BLOWING IN SUPERSLOW MOTION AS THEY SAUNTERED ON LIKE THEY JUST DIDN'T GIVE A DAMN. These were men on a mission, and that mission was to confront the dangerous gang of cattle-rustlin' scumbag outlaws that had turned their town into a crime-ridden cesspool, dispense a six-pack of old-school justice from the polished barrels of their revolvers, and save the cross-examinations for the county undertaker.

Dramatic pump-up music played somewhere in the distance as the lawmen made their way toward the now-infamous O.K. Corral. They knew there would be at least an equal number of hardened criminals waiting for them—tough, heavily armed, foul-smelling old sons of bitches who'd rolled into town looking for booze, hookers, poker, beef jerky, and a hell of a lot of trouble—and were about to get a nice heaping dose of the latter.

One of the gunslinging, outlaw-obliterating badasses casually sauntering toward a close-quarters gunfight with bloodthirsty Old West gangsters was the legendary lawman/asskicker Wyatt Earp. A former railroad worker, horse thief, prison escapee, brothel enforcer, and Dodge City lawman, Earp had taken his talents to the silver-mining boomtown of Tombstone, Arizona, in the fall of 1879. Looking to turn his life around, spend some time with his family, and quite possibly even find a profession that didn't involve punching sketchy dudes in the face or shooting their nuts off with a half-inch of burning-hot led delivered at high velocity, and hopefully even make a little extra coin in the process.

Wyatt and his brothers Virgil, Morgan, James, and Warren tried their hand at a couple gigs that didn't require a nice heaping dose of brute physical violence directed toward the faces of anyone who messed with them. They really did. But when their stagecoach line and gambling saloon didn't end up fattening their wallets the Earps were forced to fall back to their ways of generating income with their fists. And, to be totally honest, the tall, powerfully built Wyatt really just wasn't happy unless he was pistol-whipping some sobriety into a bunch of drunk assholes, smashing whiskey bottles over their heads, then throwing them 'stache-first through those awesome swinging saloon doors and unceremoniously face-planting them into the street outside. So, when Wyatt's older brother Virgil took the job as city marshal of Tombstone (essentially the chief of police for the city), Wyatt and

Morgan naturally had to join up, become deputy marshals themselves, and get back into the family business of pimp-slapping dillholes unconscious any time they failed to show adequate respect for the law.

As you can probably imagine, silver-mining frontier Old West boomtowns tended to attract their fair share of desert rabble, seedy characters, and hardened, foul-smelling criminal douchebags, and Tombstone was certainly no exception. But while the Earps didn't really mind the fact that there was no shortage of evildoers' heads to crack, back in the early 1880s they had a pretty serious problem with one particularly vicious, highly organized gang known as the Cowboys—a murderous association of lawless cattle thieves who terrorized the populace and were more hated than Troy Aikman and Jerry Jones riding a shimmering chariot made of melted-down Super Bowl trophies being pulled across the goal line by Michael Irvin and Emmitt Smith.

The Cowboys' primary racket involved riding down into Mexico (only a few hours' journey south), stopping at the first border town they could find, killing a bunch of Mexicans in cold blood, stealing anything of value, and then riding back into town on stolen burros so they could sell their loot to unscrupulous merchants in Tombstone for a 100 percent profit. Since these crimes were taking place out of the country, nobody really had jurisdiction over this uncontrolled dickishness, and these Cowboy fellows really made a hell of a living running a nineteenth-century organized crime faction that would have made Tony Soprano proud.

So Wyatt, Virgil, and Morgan Earp, together with Wyatt's good friend Doc Holliday—a wildly unstable, tuberculosis-ridden Georgia dentist who, when he wasn't murdering people or fleeing murder warrants, practiced his sadistic craft of maxillofacial deconstruction at a time in history when root canal operations more closely resembled something out of the Spanish Inquisition—decided that, jurisdiction or no jurisdiction, they were going to crack down on this Cowboy nonsense and restore order in Tombstone a half-dozen .45-caliber bullets at a time. Since they had no legal grounds to arrest the Cowboys for stuff they were doing outside of the city, the Earps awesomely decided that the best way to get these bastards was to piss them off as hard as they could and basically provoke them into doing something they could get arrested for. So basically every time you turned around some Cowboy was getting harassed by the law, filing a police brutality claim, and then subsequently being brained in the dome by the concussive force of an Earp-brother pistol-whip administered sharply and compellingly to the cranial region.

Everything eventually came to a head on the night of October 25, when the leader of the Cowboys, a grizzled old son of a bitch named Ike Clanton, headed into town with his friends Frank and Tom McLaury, refused to check his guns at the door (because of all the bullet-related deaths in town, Virgil Earp had understandably issued an ordinance banning all weapons within the city limits), and then headed off to the bars to get emphatically drunk on rotgut hootch and raise all kinds of hell. The Earps, seeing a decent opportunity to once again provoke the Cowboys into doing something arrest-worthy while inside city limits, immediately headed out to screw with them and ruin their lives. First, Doc Holliday followed Ike Clanton into a rowdy saloon and started calling him a bunch of inappropriate names in front of some cute girls while simultaneously insinuating that perhaps Ike's mother might have been a woman of somewhat loose morals. When Ike finally had enough and went after Doc in a fit of furious murderous drunken rage, Virgil Earp immediately flew in outta nowhere and clubbed that jobber in the skull with his pistol midlunge, sending the asshole hilariously sprawling to the nasty hardwood saloon floor. Virgil then grabbed Ike by his ear and dragged his drunk ass off to night court. Meanwhile, Wyatt found Tom McLaury in a different part of town and gave him a total BS traffic ticket for improperly tying up his horse in a no-parking zone.

When Tom protested, Wyatt coldcocked him in his illiterate punk jaw with a right hook, sending the outlaw crumpling to the deck with one mighty swing.

This may come as something of a shock, but it actually turns out that randomly pummeling the holy hell out of an Old West outlaw gang is a good way to get yourself a fight, and the next morning Wyatt Earp woke up from a relaxing evening of getting wasted and sleeping with his ex-prostitute mistress to hear news that Ike Clanton had telegraphed the surrounding area for help, and that he, Tom McLaury, and a couple other armed outlaws had spent most of the morning hours running around town talking a bunch of smack about how the next time they saw him they were going to saw Virgil's Earp derp face in half and shove the top part up Morgan's ass until he died from it.

That, incidentally, was exactly what Wyatt Earp wanted to hear. He rounded up his brothers, deputized Doc Holliday a temporary marshal (*Police Academy 4*–style), and went down to the O.K. Corral to give Ike Clanton exactly the fight both men were looking for.

When Doc Holliday and Wyatt, Virgil, and Morgan Earp finally sauntered up to the gates of the O.K. Corral, they found five similarly pissed-off outlaws waiting for them. Ike Clanton was there with his son Billy, and this Green Goblin father-son crime duo were joined by Tom and Frank McLaury and a guy named Billy Claiborne. Most of them were packing heat, which, if you'll recall, was illegal and punishable by face-punching, and I don't even want to get into the Old West Earp-style punishment for loitering, unregistered moustaches, and chewing tobacco within fifty yards of a schoolhouse. Virgil told the Cowboys to throw up their hands and grab some sky so the Earps could disarm and arrest them. The Cowboys had no inclination to comply.

What followed was the sort of badass, ultratense Old West standoff so intense that it would be in danger of making even Clint Eastwood's Man with No Name show the slightest glimpse of a human emotion.

The Earps and Cowboys stood there, mere feet from each other, giving each other badass death stares so withering they would melt butter, each man waiting for the other to flinch first. The sun beat down on their backs as their fingers hovered above the grips of their pistols. The only sound was the pounding of the men's cold hearts, the rustling of a tumbleweed blowing by, and the trilling of whatever instrument it is that they use to make that awesome showdown music in badass western movies.

Everything happened in the blink of an eye. Billy Clanton and Frank McLaury drew their pistols so fast it caused a sonic boom, but Wyatt Earp was just as fast. Billy leveled his weapon at Wyatt's head, but the most badass Earp knew that Frank McLaury was a better shot and a more ruthless cold-blooded killer, so instead of aiming at the guy about to decapitate him with a .45 from five feet away, Earp brought up his weapon and snapped off a shot at Frank instead. The bullet struck McLaury in the stomach. He stumbled forward, firing wildly and hitting Doc Holliday in the side. Billy's shot at Wyatt zipped past the lawman's ear *Matrix*-style. The other Billy, Billy Claiborne, stood there just long enough for the words "screw this" to run through his mind, and immediately dropped his gun and ran for it like a giant flaming wussbag because holy crap who in their right mind wanted to be in the middle of this nonsense.

By this point everybody had drawn their steel and the gunfight was on big time. Virgil fired his gat and missed, but Morgan got off a round that struck Billy Clanton in his shooting hand. Morgan was then immediately shot through the shoulder by Frank McLaury, who was still in the process of dying from a painful bullet wound to the gut, but despite his entire arm radiating with searing pain Morgan somehow steadied himself and returned fire, striking Frank in the head, killing him instantly.

Meanwhile, the two unarmed men in the fight—Ike Clanton and

Tom McLaury—tried to figure out what the deuce to do. Ike, still drunk from last night, ran straight up to Wyatt screaming about how he didn't have a gun, please god don't kill me, I think I wet myself, etc., so Wyatt threw that dipstick to the ground, kicked him in the ass, and told him to get the hell out of there. Ike ran for it.

Instead of pleading for his life like a punk, Tom McLaury sprinted to his horse and went straight for the Winchester rifle in his saddle holster. He pulled it out and fired a round off, but Doc Holliday, already wounded by a grazing shot from Frank McLaury, whipped a Doom II–style double-barreled sawn-off Super Shotgun out from under his coat and emptied both chambers, killing Tom with a few dozen pellets of buckshot at extreme close range, then ditching the shotgun, quick-draw pulling his nickel-plated pistol, and firing wildly at Ike as the elder Clanton sprinted away from the battlefield.

Meanwhile, Billy Clanton, reeling in pain from after being shot in the hand by Morgan, fell to a knee and continued spraying bullets around with his off-hand, drilling Virgil through the calf before being shot himself in the stomach by either Wyatt or Morgan.

The whole shootin' match was all over in roughly thirty seconds. Frank and Tom McLaury were dead, Billy was mortally wounded (he died from blood loss while still trying to reload his weapon), and Virgil, Morgan, and Doc were all wounded. Wyatt was the only combatant to emerge unscathed, despite the fact that all accounts have him standing tall throughout the battle and making no attempt to take cover or evade the gunfire swirling around him.

But the story of the Gunfight at the O.K. Corral doesn't end with this brief yet badass high-noon showdown—the Earps were actually arrested and tried for murder, but were acquitted because it was a righteous kill both in the legal sense and in the sense that it was totally bitchin'. But, more important than that whole adorable Old West due process thing, there were still plenty of angry Cowboys left out there:

dangerous men like Johnny Ringo, Curly Bill Brocius, Ike Clanton, and Billy Claiborne, who weren't going to let such an epic bullet-storm beatdown go unavenged. The Cowboys turned out in force for the McLaury/Clanton funeral, swore bloody high plains vengeance on the Earps, and then went out to 7-Eleven for Xtreme Revenge Slurpees and go-go taquitos so they could scheme their next moves on full stomachs.

It didn't take long for these guys to spring into action, and when the Cowboys went down the revenge path, they went big. First, Virgil was shot five times with a shotgun while walking down the street. (He survived somehow, lost the use of his arm, and eventually became a one-armed sheriff out in California somewhere. Here's a pro tip for all you aspiring hardasses out there: Any time you're confronted by a one-armed sheriff with five shells' worth of shotgun pellets embedded in his body, you immediately drop your weapon and lay down on the ground with your hands behind your head.) Then, in March of 1882, Morgan Earp was shot twice in the back while he was in the middle of the best game of pool of his life, killed (probably) by a Cowboy named Frank Stillwell who didn't have any relation to Ike Clanton or any of the other dead Cowboys, but who was really just pissed out of principle. A third bullet from Stillwell's hand cannon struck inches from Wyatt's head, punching through the wall like that scene from *Pulp Fiction* where that one idiot wannabe tries to cap Jules but the bullet is deflected by the ultimate force field of badassitude that I assume surrounds Samuel L. Jackson at all times.

The Cowboys should have finished the job when they had the chance, because this wasn't over. Not by a long shot. Now Wyatt Earp was *really* mad. Before, he was just annoyed. Now he was the sort of angry you get when you can't even remember how to speak in complete sentences and any words that do happen to escape your lips are accompanied by a shotgun blast explosion of spittle.

Realizing that the only way this feud was going to be over was if he was the last man standing, Wyatt put his wounded brother Virgil, Virgil's wife, and everyone else Wyatt cared about on a train to California, strapped together all of his gear in a badass pump-up montage, and prepared to settle the score with the outlaws once and for all. He didn't have to go far. As Wyatt was preparing to see his brother off he immediately Spider-Sensed trouble—both Ike Clanton and Frank Stillwell were there, scoped sniper rifles at the ready, waiting in ambush to finish off Virgil before he could skip town and escape their vengeance. Earp saw through the plot, spotted the two men in their sniper perches, narrowed his eyes, spit, and got the drop on Frank Stillwell, sneaking up behind his brother's assassin and annihilating that asshole at extreme close range with two rounds of buckshot and all six .45-caliber slugs in his revolver. Ike, once again scared pissless, ran for it, because that yellow-bellied assclown once again couldn't handle being in the presence of a real man.

That was it. Wyatt put together a vigilante posse consisting of himself, Doc, his brother Warren, and two random guys named Sherman McMasters and Turkey Creek Jack Johnson (the Jack Johnson with the iron balls and the whiskey obsession, not the Banana Pancakes guy), and these over-the-top cold-blooded human tornadoes went out on a twenty-megaton special sauce vengeance ride to kill the hell out of every Cowboy they could get their hands on until the only thing left of the gang was a series of pine boxes stuffed with whatever parts of the dead men the coroner managed to recover. Nobody knows exactly what happened or how many men were blasted out of existence during this cross-country Frank Castle–style Wyatt Earp American Revenge-a-Thon 1882, or what the actual details of this nationwide manhunt were, but basically, it amounts to this—if you were part of the gang, you were gonna die. Badly. And in a painful way you almost certainly would not enjoy. Known Cowboys like Indian Charlie, Florentino Cruz, and some guy named Freis all turned up facedown in ditches across the

Arizona territories, killed by Colt Peacemakers or double-barreled shotguns fired at nearly point-blank range—cops couldn't really match ballistics or bodily fluids or do any other cool CSI stuff back in the day, but it was pretty achingly obvious what was going down here. Shortly after those three bought the farm another Cowboy, Johnny Ringo, was found dead at the base of a tree, dead from a single gunshot wound in the skull. Curly Bill turned up a little after that—according to the story, Curly had gathered all of his Cowboy buddies and stupidly tried to set an ambush for the Earp posse, but despite a hail of bullets flying in every direction Wyatt Earp (who had a Steven Seagal–style immunity to bullets) stood straight up, walked right toward Curly Bill without flinching (as the dude was shooting at him!), put his shotgun straight against Curly Bill's chest, and pulled the trigger. As Curly Bill went flying backward like he'd taken a fatal gunshot wound in a John Woo movie, Wyatt calmly drew his pistol and capped some other outlaw named Johnny Barnes who just happened to be in the vicinity at the time. Ike Clanton was killed in 1887 while fleeing the law for some unrelated crime, which was good enough for Wyatt, so with the federal marshals closing in to arrest him for incredible amounts of spree murder Wyatt simply escaped the law, laid low in Colorado until the coast was clear, and the spent the rest of his days running saloons in California with his girlfriend (who, I have it on good authority, is one of those "hooker with a heart of gold" stories we've been hearing so much about over the years). He got off scot-free and lived until 1929.

Wyatt Earp worked as a shotgun messenger for Wells Fargo back at a time when "riding shotgun" actually meant rolling around the backcountry with a twelve-gauge in your lap. With bandits and stage robbers crawling all over the Old West, most coaches (especially Wells Fargo wagons, which were usually loaded with cash) employed guys to sit next to the stagecoach driver and make sure that anybody who got any wild ideas about making off with the cash received a big faceful of lead.

Despite what its reputation implies, Tombstone's city name actually has nothing to do with the Earp brothers' penchant for gunning down dirt-bags and varmints every time one or both popped their heads up. Instead, it comes from the first settler of the region—an ex-Army scout named Ed Schieffelin who had come out to Arizona looking for gold and was deri-sively told by the locals, "The only rock you'll find out there is your tomb-stone." Schieffelin found eighty-five million dollars of silver instead, and, awesomely enough, named the city totally out of spite.

Wyatt's parents were apparently pretty frisky people, because there were nine Earp kids in total: Newton, Mariah, James, Virgil, Martha, Wyatt, Morgan, Warren, Virginia, and Adelia. The eldest son, James, suffered a serious wound during the Civil War that left him with minimal use of his left arm, meaning he wasn't part of any of his brothers' crazypants shootouts (although he did move to Tombstone with his brothers and helped them run their saloon). Warren participated in the vengeance ride but was later killed in an unrelated barfight. Newton, Wyatt's half brother through his father's first marriage, also served in the Civil War, and while he shared his brothers' love of saloonkeeping, he's one of the few Earp brothers to never work in law enforcement. None of the daugh-ters seems to have done anything noteworthy except get married and live in Illinois.

26

THE TWENTY-ONE SIKHS

The Battle of Saragarhi
Khyber-Pakhtunkhwa, British India
September 12, 1897

Outnumbered and surrounded and still the men fought on
With a stubbornness and pride for which the Sikhs have long been known.

—GANEEV KAUR DHILLON, "THE BATTLE OF SARAGARHI"

THE BALLBUSTING DEFENSE OF THE TINY YET CRITICAL BRIT-
ISH FORTRESS AT SARAGARHI IS ONE OF THE MOST STORIED
TALES OF SKULL-CRUSHING BRAVERY IN THE ALREADY BADASS
MILITARY HISTORY OF THE SIKH PEOPLE. The middle-finger-
until-death response of the ferocious twenty-one men who bravely held
their ground against impossible odds is often held up as the ultimate
example of Sikh badassitude, which is really saying something considering that these balls-out Indian hardasses have stories about stuff
like a dude who ran around pureeing enemy soldiers apart even after
being mostly decapitated by a broadsword to the throat. Yet despite
this superhuman showdown being a valiant, head-cleaving last stand
worthy of the Spartans at Thermopylae and the basis for a national hol-

iday among Sikhs, this tale of twenty-one warriors going horde mode against roughly the entire male population of Central Asia in a single battle remains largely undocumented in Western military histories. This is their tale.

The story starts near the end of the nineteenth century (or, as the British like to call it, "The Good Old Days"), when the sun never set on the British Empire and the queen convinced one-quarter of the world's population that drinking tea at 4:00 p.m. was "totally bodacious" and/ or "off the chain" (they used lots of outdated terminology back then). The British Raj was ruling over India, providing enlightened governance in exchange for shiploads and shiploads of valuable natural resources, and the empire oversaw the defense of the subcontinent by way of a series of awesome mountain fortresses positioned along the border between present-day Pakistan and Afghanistan. While it wasn't particularly well fortified or heavily garrisoned, the outpost at Saragarhi was a seriously critical communications relay position between two major British forts. It played a crucial role in the first line of defense of British India against the tribal warriors of Central Asia—the Orakazai and the Afridi—and these warriors knew that if they ever wanted to wreak havoc on the subcontinent and punch the raja in the crown jewels, they were going to need to get past this defensive outpost first.

On the morning of September 12, 1897, signalman Gurmukh Singh of the Thirty-sixth Sikh Regiment looked out into the horizon and, to his surprise, saw regimental battle flags. Like, a crapload of them. A sea of colors, swirling dust, and more enemy soldiers than you could shake a kirpan at, even if you'd built some kind of mechanical rig designed for the sole purpose of shaking kirpans at things. Unable to get his Rain Man on and count how many troops were in the horde of warriors rampaging his way, Singh just quickly tallied up the regimental flags and signaled the alarm. When he rushed down from his tower and found his commanding officer—a lowly havildar (sergeant) named

Ishar Singh—he put the estimate of the number of assailants at somewhere between ten thousand and twenty thousand riflemen. Oh, plus an unknown amount of heavy artillery. And probably some other dangerous stuff in addition to that.

Havildar Singh called his garrison together for an emergency meeting. Standing before him in the tiny courtyard of this small, mud-and-stone garrison was the entire detachment of the Thirty-sixth Sikhs assigned to the defense of this critical strategic outpost—all twenty men of it. Calmly, honestly, with no fear in his voice, the noncommissioned officer told his troops that they were most likely the last and only bastion of defense between that teeming throng of bloodthirsty warriors and the heart of India herself—these twenty-one soldiers were the only people even remotely in a position to slow down a coordinated tactical strike that was guaranteed to take the British and Indian defenders by surprise and wreak havoc across the land. He also told them that even though he knew how much lay at stake here, he wasn't about to order his men to their deaths in a hopeless battle they had no chance of surviving. The men had a choice to make—stand here and defend India against this invasion, hold back the assault as long as possible, and die valiantly in battle; or abandon their position, retreat up the mountain to the nearby Fort Lockhart, where a more sizable British force was stationed, and essentially give the enemy a clear path straight into the heart of India. He put it to a vote among the men. Since they were all going to fight, serve, die, or flee together, they needed to stand as one.

All twenty men voted to stay.

Gurmukh Singh relayed word of this ungodly massive sneak attack to a nearby British fort as the doomed Sikhs fortified their mud-walled fort as best they could and braced themselves for the onslaught. The calm before the battle was kind of like the moments before the Battle of the Hornburg at Helm's Deep, only with Orakazai instead of Urukhai. And, you know, Sikhs are roughly a thousand percent more badass than elves. Finally, at 9:00 a.m., the first of the enemy came into range of their weapons. Havildar Singh issued the order to fire at will, and the twenty-one men of the Thirty-sixth Sikhs began to bust out one of the most epic last stands in history.

The Orakazai and Afridi did the sort of thing you'd expect from an overwhelmingly powerful force assaulting a tiny podunk outpost garrisoned by a force they outnumber roughly five hundred to one—they charged balls out, Emperor Xerxes style, looking to overrun the defenders by hurling wave after wave of their own men at the walls. It didn't work out so hot for them. This gigantor horde of ass-kicking maniacs thought they were going to completely bulldoze the Saragarhi Sikhs like a Ford F-350 mega-extendo-cab pickup truck being dropped out of a plane onto a bucket of plastic green army men, but the admittedly hardcore Orakazai quickly realized that these weren't any chump douchebags manning the defenses here—these were gnarly gnarlington high priest Vatican assassin warlock F-18s ready to deploy their ordinance to the ground, and all these Sikhs came here to do was WIN. On two separate attacks the Orakazai hurled themselves at the walls of Saragarhi, climbing the walls on ladders, laying heavy rifle and cannon fire into the fortress, and on both occasions the twenty-one defenders shielded themselves with their giant bulletproof balls, kicked down the ladders, and barfed out enough rifle fire to drive the attackers back. This is completely insane, especially considering that the Sikhs didn't exactly have access to heavy machine guns or assault rifles back in 18-freaking-97—these out-of-their-mind warriors were using bolt-action rifles, and were somehow firing them so retardedly fast that ten thousand trained warriors with guns found themselves unable to push their way through this ridiculous curtain of leaden-deathy evilness. Meanwhile, when he wasn't taking potshots from the signal tower with his scoped rifle, the garrison's signalman, Gurmukh Singh, was operating his signaling equipment and informing the nearest British outpost (just barely visible in the distance beyond the ridge) exactly what was going on, how many men the enemy had, and what sort of equipment they were carrying. No sweat, right?

While the Vegas books probably would have set the over/under for the duration of this fight at about fifteen minutes, five hours into the combat the Sikhs were still managing to hold out against all odds. Sure, they'd taken a few hits here and there, but even the wounded men were propped up on the battlements laying down fire on the attackers as best they could. Completely surrounded by a mob of troops, these guys continued to dish out withering gunfire with ball-crippling accuracy. Eventually, while the Sikhs were completely overwhelmed by attacks on all sides, a team of Orakazai sappers breached a particularly lightly defended section of the outer defenses, snuck in, and set fire to the fort. Their positions concealed by the smoke and flames, and the Sikhs concerned with extinguishing their burning fortress, the rest of the enemy troops managed to charge in and break through the outer walls of the fort, rushing into the courtyard.

With their own fortress walls crumbling and smoldering around them in an inferno of suck, the Sikhs continued to stand by their initial assessment of "You fools are only getting through here over our dead bodies." Havildar Singh ordered his men to fall back to the inner section of the fort, barricade the walls, and continue laying down fire on the attackers, who were now swarming over the walls. Singh himself didn't make it back—in an effort to buy his men time to fall back he drew his kirpan dagger, charged into the horde, and died valiantly in hand-to-hand combat against an impossible swarm of rifle-swinging tribesmen.

So even now, seven hours into the battle, with their commander dead, their ammunition dwindling, and their fort burning down around them, the Sikhs continued to stick it to the Orakazai with everything they could muster. It didn't take long for the enemy to find the weak point in the inner defenses—a rickety wooden gate that was already on fire—yet still, even when the tribesmen shot up the gate, stormed the wall, and entered the main building of Saragarhi, they blitzed through only to find a determined handful of pissed-off Sikhs standing there with fixed bayonets and vicious scowls. There wasn't going to be any Gandalf the White riding in on a hurricane of fireballs this time . . . these Sikh hardasses were going to have to take matters up into the points of their blades and finish this like men.

Seeing enemies inside the tower, signalman Gurmukh Singh issued his last communications to the British, dropped his signal gear, and took up his rifle, laying down sniper fire on the enemy troops swarming over his friends below. He is credited with killing twenty men by himself, and it is believed that when he ran out of bullets he fixed his bayonet and charged down into the fray shouting the battle cry of the Sikhs: "He who cries 'God is Truth' is ever victorious." When British troops reached the position later, they found 21 dead Sikhs and somewhere between 180 and 800 dead tribesmen. The number is debated because when the British showed up there was a second round of fighting over the fort, and it was difficult to say how many enemies were killed in which engagement, but we do know that nearly every single Sikh rifleman was completely out of ammunition, exemplifying the British ideal of fighting "to the last man, with the last round." The Sikhs had started with four hundred rounds each.

The white-knuckle defenders of Saragarhi were slain to a man, but they had held their position all day and well into the evening, delaying the massive onslaught just long enough for the British to get over there and reinforce the position. After Saragarhi, the Orakazai moved on to the nearby Fort Gulistan, but the delay at Saragarhi had cost them the element of surprise—the men at Fort Gulistan were ready for them, and they held the attack back while freshly arrived British heavy artillery dropped a few hundred high-explosive shells right into the middle of the oncoming army.

When the story of the Sikhs at Saraghiri was recounted to Parliament, it received a standing ovation from every member of the British government. All twenty-one Sikhs received the Indian Order of Merit, the highest military award available to them at the time, and their families each received a plot of land and five hundred rupees in cash. (The 2011 exchange rate lists five hundred rupees as being equal to about $10.85 in U.S. dollars, but it was probably worth a lot more back in 1897—though I'm only basing this on the fact that in 1987 five hundred rupees was nearly enough to buy two Blue Rings, and those were by far the most expensive items in *The Legend of Zelda*.) The tale was mentioned by UNESCO as being as one of eight great stories of collective bravery in human history, and to this day, every September 12 the people of India celebrate Saragarhi Day.

We may sorrow for the sacrifice of these brave soldiers, but the Sikh nation, while it lasts, will never forget the glory of the defence.

—LIEUTENANT COLONEL JOHN HAUGHTON, COMMANDANT, THIRTY-SIXTH SIKH REGIMENT

One of the most badass saints of the Sikh religion was a hard-as-hell guerrilla warrior known as Baba Deep Singh. In 1757, when the Mughal warlord Ahmad Shah Durrani blitzed in from Afghanistan, conquered the Sikh holy city of Amritsar, and desecrated the Golden Temple of God by blasting it with cannons and filling the sacred pools with cow guts, this seventy-five-year-old, ultrabearded hardass pulled his well-worn thirty-pound sword off the wall and just started walking toward the enemy with the look of unquenchable pissed-offedness in his eyes. At every village along the road to Amritsar, armed Sikh warriors rushed out to join him in his vengeance quest, and when the motley band finally reached the Golden Temple, this Dr. Frankenstein pitchfork mob of Sikh badassitude hurled themselves at their hated enemies with the sort of enthusiasm you'd expect from a bunch of guys who'd just had the holiest site in their religion redecorated with bovine guts. According to the legend, during the battle Baba Deep Singh took a wound to the neck so grievous that he had to hold his head with his hand to keep it from falling off, but this guy wasn't going to let something like *being mostly decapitated* stop him from liberating his temple with extreme violence. Baba Deep Singh eventually bled out and died on the floor of the Golden Temple of God, but not until he and his men had driven the enemy from the field. The Golden Temple was reconsecrated by Sikh priests, and the spot where Singh fell is now a shrine where pilgrims come from across India to pay their respects to one of their religion's greatest martyrs.

The symbol of Sikhism is the kirpan, a small dagger that signifies the courage of the First Five Sikhs and serves as a constant reminder that Sikhs should be willing to defend the weak and oppressed. Most Sikhs carry a kirpan dagger with them at all times (either a full-sized dagger or a small pendant on a necklace), though it is considered extremely disrespectful to draw it from its sheath in any situation where you aren't actually planning on using it.

SAMUEL WHITTEMORE (1775)

As the British were returning from the Battle of Lexington in the opening days of the American Revolution, an eighty-year-old veteran of the French and Indian War named Samuel Whittemore positioned himself behind a stone wall, waited in ambush, and then single-handedly engaged the entire British Forty-seventh Regiment of Foot with nothing more than his musket and the pure liquid anger coursing through his veins. With a cry of "You damn kids, get offa my lawn!" Whittemore rose up from behind a stone wall and fired off his musket at point-blank range, busting the nearest guy so hard it nearly blew the guy's red coat into the next dimension. Then, with a company of Brits bearing down on him, Wittemore quick-drew twin flintlock pistols and popped a couple of locks on them (caps hadn't been invented yet, though I think the analogy still works pretty well), busting another two limeys a matching set of new assholes. Then, just to prove that this eighty-year-old madman still wasn't done kicking the crap out of everyone, he unsheathed an ornate sword he'd taken from the body of a French officer during the French and Indian War and proceeded to stand his ground in hand-to-hand combat against a couple dozen trained soldiers a quarter of his age. Whittemore was shot through the face by a .69-caliber bullet, knocked down, and bayonetted thirteen times, but amazingly, when his friends rushed out from their homes to check on his body, they found the half-dead, ragingly bloody octogenarian still trying to reload his weapon. He survived the war, finally dying in 1793 at the age of ninety-eight from extreme old age and awesomeness.

NED KELLY (1880)

In June of 1880, semilegendary folk hero/crazy person Ned Kelly captured the hearts of Australians everywhere when he and his gang of outlaw bush rangers took a bunch of hostages in a pub and tried to blow up a passenger train full of cops. The homemade bombs didn't go off, and the pub was soon surrounded by cranky police who weren't all that keen on being blown up, but Ned Kelly and his men weren't about to go down without a badass last stand—they kicked open the door and Army of Twoed it into the hot Aussie sun, busting into the outback wearing full suits of plate armor Kelly had constructed himself out of plowshares, bolts, and the blood of kangaroos he strangled to death with his bare hands. He and his gang, each wearing ninety-six pounds of homemade Killdozer, clanked out, guns blazing, fighting a hopeless battle against an entire county's worth of police officers. In the carnage that ensued, every member of Kelly's gang was killed and Ned was shot nearly a dozen times in his unarmored arms and legs, yet somehow continued to press on, firing his rifle with one arm until he was finally (and understandably) dropped by a close-range shotgun blast to the knees. He somehow survived this as well, but was captured, arrested, and thrown in jail. Ned's battle with the cops made headlines across the country the next morning, and Kelly was instantly catapulted to national celebrity because, as we all know, Aussies are insane, unruly, anarchy-loving people who hate police and laws and organized society (for reference, just look at Australian Rules Football—it's a perfect demonstration of the fact that "Austrialian rules" are synonomous with "absolutely no rules"). This armor-plated madman's Butch and Sundance last stand story was so ridonkulous that thirty thousand people went out that day and signed a petition calling for leniency and mercy for this misunderstood psychopath. He didn't get it—he was convicted of mega-murder and hanged from the neck until dead. His last words were, "Ah well, I suppose it has come to this . . . such is life."

SERGEANT YORK (1918)

Caught alone in the open and ambushed by almost an entire regiment of German soldiers in the forests of eastern France during World War I, American sergeant Alvin York didn't even make an effort to dive out of the way of the dozen or so full-auto machine guns that were shredding the vegetation around him—he just stood there calmly, pulled out his bolt-action Springfield rifle, and started shooting every German he could see. Which was a lot of them. According to the account of the story he recorded in his diary, "I didn't have time to dodge behind a tree or dive into the brush . . . I had no time nohow to do nothing but watch them-there German machine gunners and give them the best I had. Every time I seed a German I jes teched him off . . . jes like we often shoot at the targets in the shooting matches in the mountains of Tennessee; and it was jes about the same distance. But the targets here were bigger. I jes couldn't miss a German's head or body at that distance. And I didn't. Besides, it weren't no time to miss nohow." After York single-handedly "touched off" two dozen Krauts and annihilated an eight-man bayonet charge with his Colt 1911 pistol (a weapon that only holds eight bullets, by the way), the machine gun fire suddenly stopped. A

German major rose up from the trenches with both hands in the air, pleading (in perfect English), "If you don't shoot anymore, I will make them give up." York, a pacifist at heart who had no desire to continue killing, accepted the surrender. As the German POWs were being marched back to the American HQ, an American general walked up and said, "Jesus Christ, York, I hear that you captured the whole German army!" York responded, "No sir, just 132 of them."

Leo Major in Zwolle (1945)

One quiet night in 1945 a one-eyed Canadian infantryman named Leo Major and his buddy were sent out to do some recon in the Nazi-occupied Dutch town of Zwolle, report back on enemy numbers, and, if possible, establish contact with the local Dutch resistance. Unfortunately, not long into the mission, Leo Major's buddy was spotted and killed by a freak shot from a German machine gun, setting off one of the most epic blood rages ever recorded. The eyepatch-wearing Canadian Nick Fury completely flipped his gourd, strapped three machine guns onto his back, grabbed a huge sack of hand grenades, and charged into the quiet town, heavy weapons blazing, flinging grenades around like he was throwing high-explosive rice at a really dangerous wedding. Leo Major ran around like a berserker madman, creating such a clusterhump of explosions, fires, and dead bodies with his one-man rampage that the German garrison was convinced that they were being assaulted by the entire Canadian Army. At one point during his mad lone-wolf onslaught of righteously epic Nazi destruction, this one-eyed juggernaut kicked in the door of an SS officer's club, killed four high-ranking enemy commanders in a spray of machine gun fire, and then ran across the street and burned down the local headquarters of the Gestapo before anybody knew what the fructose was going on. By the time the sun rose on Zwolle the next morning, the entire German garrison had evacuated, Zwolle had been single-handedly liberated by a single psychotic one-eyed Canuck, and Leo Major was declared the official hero of the city. Not bad for a night's work.

SEAL Team Six in Granada (1983)

In October of 1983 thirteen SEALs from the famous ultra-elite counterterrorist force Team Six rescued Grenadan governor-general Sir Paul Scoon when Scoon, his family, and nine members of his staff were taken hostage in his mansion in Grenada. SEAL Team Six fast-roped down onto Scoon's tennis court from a helicopter while the Grenadan army shot machine guns and antiaircraft cannons at them, but the SEAL operatives, completely un-fazed by staring death in the face while suspended in midair from small black ropes, charged ahead, wasted everything in sight like in that scene at the end of *Commando*, and freed the queen's representative on Grenada by storming the mansion and clearing it of enemy troops in a whirlwind of bullets and concussion grenades. After securing all the hostages un-harmed, the SEALs, realizing they were cut off from from their extraction point by a rapidly-growing horde of enemy military forces, then proceeded to hold the position against a full-on counterattack by basically the entire Grenadan army at once. These thirteen bad-as-hell warriors held their position despite staring down tanks, APCs, and grenade launchers while armed with little more than sniper rifles and small arms, somehow hold-ing out in the mansion long enough for air support and marines to break the siege. Scoon, all thirteen SEAL team members, and all of the hostages made it out.

HILL 776 (2000)

In March 2000, during the final days of the Chechen War, one obscenely-badass ninety-man Russian Spetsnaz paratrooper unit under the com-mand of a colonel named Mark Yevtukhin was dropped into a critical position behind enemy lines on a ridiculously-dangerous mission. Colo-nel Yevtukhin's orders were clear—capture and hold Hill 776, a crucial mountain pass through the Caucasus, and seal off the only mountain path the Chechens' were using to escape the country. Yevtukhin's Spetsnaz paratroopers moved to the position, overwhelmed the defenders there, fortified the position, and dug in for the fight of their lives as eighteen hun-dred rebel fighters rushed them in a desperate all-out attempt to break out of the trap. With no reinforcements coming any time soon, and heavily armed enemy troops swarming around them from all sides, the Russians battled like demons, pouring fire into the Chechens day and night, hour after hour, driving them off in hand-to-hand combat on several occasions when the enemy got close enough to get falcon-punched in the face with a combat knife. For three days and nights the Russians held off every-thing the enemy could throw at them, but on the fourth morning, with the Russian force dwindling to just thirty survivors and a fresh mob of over a thousand fanatical warriors charging straight into them, it quickly be-came obvious the line would not hold against such an impossible crush of humanity. As the Chechens swarmed into the Russian positions, engaging the desperate, exhausted survivors in brutal close-quarters battles, Colonel Yevtukhin called down an artillery strike, giving the artillery gunners his own coordinates and raining death on everything on Hill 776. Only six of the ninety paratroopers made it out alive, but when the smoke cleared over seven hundred of the enemy lay dead on the hill before them. The Chechens were so impressed by this bold act of bravery that they named a street after the Russian unit in the Chechen capital of Grozny—no small gesture considering how much these two groups hate each other.

27

The Charge of the Australian Light Horse

The Battle of Beersheba
Beersheba, Palestine
October 31, 1917

It was growing dark, and the enemy trenches were outlined in fire by the flashes of their rifles. Beyond, and a little above them, blazed the bigger, deeper flashes of their field guns, and our own shells burst like a row of red stars over the Turkish positions. In front, the long lines of cavalry swept forward at racing speed, half-obscured in clouds of reddish dust. Amid the deafening noise all around, they seemed to move silently, like some splendid, swift machine. Over the Turks they went, leaping the two lines of deep trenches, and, dismounting on the further side, flung themselves into the trenches with the bayonet.

—Lieutenant-Colonel R. M. P. Preston, Australian Light Horse

The eight hundred men of the Fourth Australian Light Horse Brigade looked out at the imposing walls of the desert fortress of Beersheba. Between them and their distant objective lay four miles of wide-open, coverless terrain—a veritable shooting gallery for the thousands of rifles, machine guns, and heavy artillery pieces that guarded this strategically important city. Their mission was simple—charge forward, attack the town, and capture it intact. Blitzing on horseback toward automatic weapons amounted to little more than a suicide mission, but no one present on this day questioned his duty. Every man aligned on this fateful battlefield knew that this would be his final charge and his finest hour. They were determined to make sure it was one that would be remembered for years to come.

With the clusterhump of World War I slowly grinding down to a disgusting bloody halt in western Europe, the Allies were hoping that a major victory against the Ottoman Empire in Palestine would break through the stalemate and turn the tide of war in their favor. Success on the Palestinian front, however, would hinge on the capture of Beersheba. Situated on the extreme right of the Turkish flank, and therefore a critical target, this heavily defended town was also home to nineteen full-functioning water wells. In case you didn't know, Palestine is about as hot as Lucifer's balls, and with the British headquarters situated two hundred miles away in Cairo, Egypt, supply problems were a total pain in the nuts. Drinkable water was at a premium in the British army, which was kind of a problem. Without it people tend to, you know, die horrific, excruciating deaths, and the Brits were trying to avoid that if at all possible.

The element of surprise was on their side. The Turks certainly had to suspect an attack would be coming on this crucial position, but they couldn't have predicted the direction of the attack. You see, Beersheba is located on the edge of a desert, and the Turks correctly assumed that nobody in their right freaking minds would ever have been foolish or suicidal enough to ride through the white-hot, searing sands of Palestine and attack the fortress from the desert side. Unfortunately for the Turks, nobody has ever accused the Aussies of being in their right minds—these tough-ass bastards spent all day riding sixty miles through the harsh, unforgiving Judaean Desert, and this evening they were prepared to attack the town from the side the defenders least expected.

Still, even from this angle the Turkish defenses were more formidable than an axe-swinging Minotaur, and the Light Horse wasn't exactly designed (or equipped) for the sort of utterly balls-out mission they were about to undertake. You see, cavalry in World War I worked great in terms of getting soldiers from place to place quickly, but most sane people didn't still fight on horseback. The general tactic was to ride to the scene, get off the horse, and fight as regular infantry. If it helps, just think of the horses as giant hair-covered Humvees that yell really loudly and crap all over the place. Hell, the men of the Australian Light Horse didn't even carry lances or sabers or anything. For this mission, these crazy warriors simply sharpened and polished their Pattern 1907 bayonets—almost two-foot-long, single-edged blades more akin to Short Swords +1 than a proper cavalry saber—and psyched themselves up about spending Halloween 1917 going Michael Myers on their long-time foes.

Now the Turks had encountered British cavalry before, but only in their aforementioned function as dismounted infantry. So when the Turkish and German commanders at Beersheba saw the Aussies amassing in the desert, their orders were simple—wait for these jerks to get off their horses, and then ram some hot lead up their urethras at high velocities. So eight hundred Australian cavalrymen galloped forward, spurring on their epic mounts, pushing it to the limit (and also to the max), and the Turks held. And held. And held. As the cloud of dust and the thunderous sound of hooves grew louder, and the shocked defenders caught the glint of the evening sun reflect off the blades of the badass Australian bayonets, a sickening feeling welled up in the pits of their stomachs—they realized all too late that these psychos rapidly charging toward them had absolutely no intention of stopping until they'd reached into the eye holes of the city's defenders and manually turned their faces inside out.

The Turks began firing wildly at the crazy whackjobs with the pointy guns, desperately trying to fend off the onslaught before they found out firsthand what it was like to be disemboweled with a weapon that had been obsolete since the days of William Wallace. But the Aussies are freaking nuts. These men came from a murderous land filled with übervenomous creatures including not just every flavor of poisonous snake and arachnid, but also killer box jellyfish, platypuses with neurotoxin-infused stingers, and a kind of tree capable of stinging a person to death (seriously). These guys faced perilous danger every time they went into the woods to take a leak, and the men of the Australian Light Horse were convinced they were more than ready for whatever the Ottoman Empire could fling at them. They didn't even flinch as machine gun bullets and artillery shells ripped past their heads—instead they flipped out and charged through blistering heavy-weapons fire, their only goal to reach the enemy trench line with their appendages intact enough that they could swing their bayonets and cause some massive carnage.

With a tremendous crash the horses leapt over a row of barbed wire and then somehow vaulted across two rows of enemy trenches (no small feat of awesome in and of itself—these trenches were four feet wide by ten feet deep, and filled to the brim with angry, badass Turkish riflemen). As soon as they'd passed through the machine guns' field of fire, the Aussies leapt down from their horses and dove headlong into the Turkish fortifications, bayonets at the ready. Hordes of crazy Aussies brutally slashed their way through the defensive positions, hacking at the shocked defenders with their short swords and basically ruining the lives of anybody unfortunate enough to be standing in their path. The Turks are a tough as hell group of people, but witnessing something like this in person would pretty much ruin anyone's day. Turkish morale was crippled, and after a quick and incredibly bloody knife fight, Beersheba was firmly in the blood-soaked hands of the Australian Light Horse.

Of the eight hundred cavalrymen who participated in this unbelievable charge, the Australians suffered just thirty-one troopers killed and thirty-six wounded. They captured 750 Turks, nine artillery pieces, three machine guns, and tons of other munitions and supplies. Even more important, they seized seventeen of the nineteen wells intact, recovering ninety thousand gallons of fresh, drinkable water from the town. In addition to giving the army a chance to stave off death by dehydration, victory at Beersheba turned the Ottoman flank, allowing the British army to eventually roll up the enemy forces and defeat them once and for all. Jerusalem fell two months later, and all of Palestine crumbled soon afterward. The defeat in Palestine caused the Ottoman Empire to drop out of the war, and ultimately caused the destabilization and collapse of a five-hundred-year-old empire dating back to the days of Mehmet the Conqueror. With the stalemate still holding strong in the west, this was a major moral victory for the Allies as well as a military one. The Great War would be over within a year.

Nowadays there is some debate as to whether launching the intrepid cavalry charge at Beersheba was the most tactically brilliant move the Allies could have undertaken during the Palestine campaign. Many revisionist military historians with too much time on their hands complain that this amazing charge was a lot of wasted effort (historians just love to argue about hypothetical nonsense from the safety of their studies, nitpicking the actions of steel-balled hardasses scrambling in the actual field of war), and that this suicide dash could have just as easily have blown up in everybody's faces. Sure, while galloping full speed toward a half-dozen machine guns might not have been the smartest idea anyone ever came up with, nobody in their right minds could ever doubt the bravery or toughness of the men of the Australian Light Horse—these guys were stone-cold hardasses who took a seemingly foolhardy suicide attack and turned it into the last great cavalry charge in history.

The greatest individual Aussie hero of World War I was Albert "Hard Jacka" Jacka, a tough-as-hell warrior who proved himself to be a cut about your average already-insane Australian person during the seriously harsh fighting of the Gallipoli campaign. When the trench in front of Jacka was infiltrated and overrun by a determined wave of gunslinging Turkish troops, the Australian private knew that he needed to do something quickly or the entire position would be lost in a blaze of fire, smoke, shrapnel, and flying Aussie parts. First, he tried to take a section of men out on a direct assault, but it didn't work out too well—Jacka popped up, ready to rock, but when the two men with him leapt up to follow him they both took bullets to soft parts of their bodies within seconds. Jacka grabbed both of them, dragged them back to safety, then sprinted across the field in a balls-out one-man bum-rush, leaping feet-first into the enemy trench and clearing it out with his bayonet-equipped bolt-action rifle. For the next fifteen minutes, the Turks led a massive counterattack to retake the position, but the Aussie Jacka'ed them all up and held the trench by himself, fighting off anyone who came close to him in an unbelievable onslaught of gunfire, rifle butts to the dome, and general bayonety stabbingness. Australian reinforcements didn't arrive until dawn, because it wasn't until the sun came up that Jacka's buddies realized that he had actually defied the odds, single-handedly taken the position, and driven off the enemy. When his commanding officer reached the captured trench, he found Jacka sitting there by himself amid a knee-high pile of bodies with a cigarette in his mouth. All he said was "Well, I got the beggars, sir."

28

THEIR FINEST HOUR

The Battle of Britain
Southern Britain and the English Channel
July–October 1940

The Battle of France is over. I expect that the Battle of Britain is
about to begin. Upon this battle depends the survival of Christian civilization.
Upon it depends our own British life, and the long continuity of our
institutions and our Empire. The whole fury and might of the enemy must
very soon be turned on us. Hitler knows that he will have to break us in this
island or lose the war. If we can stand up to him, all Europe may be free
and the life of the world may move forward into broad, sunlit uplands.
But if we fail, then the whole world, including the United States,
including all that we have known and cared for, will sink into the abyss
of a new Dark Age made more sinister, and perhaps more protracted,
by the lights of perverted science. Let us therefore brace ourselves to our duties,
and so bear ourselves that, if the British Empire and its Commonwealth last
for a thousand years, men will still say, "This was their finest hour."

—WINSTON CHURCHILL

IT DOESN'T TAKE A PH.D. in political science from some
pretentious-sounding university and a decade of experience with
Model UN to realize that things were looking pretty ridiculously
terrible for the United Kingdom in July of 1940. Over the course

of the previous eleven months, the German dictator Adolf Hitler (you may have heard of him before) rolled his Panzers all over Europe's collective balls, conquering Czechoslovakia, Poland, Denmark, Holland, and Belgium in roughly the amount of time it takes most people to apply for medical school. The British force that had been arrayed against him in France got their groin racked so hard by the Nazi Blitzkrieg that they were lucky to escape France with their lives (a feat they only accomplished when basically every British ship bigger than an inflatable inner tube hauled ass across the Channel to evacuate them from the beaches at Dunkirk), and in the span of a few short explosion-intensive weeks the United Kingdom went from being a world power calling the shots in Europe to suddenly finding itself staring twenty-one miles across the Channel at a solidly Fascist continent populated by a couple of million seemingly unstoppable German soldiers, tanks, aircraft, and artillery guns all eager to come across the sea and lay a beating on everyone who didn't think National Socialism was *das Größte* (the "bee's knees").

Luckily for England, it wasn't going to be all that easy for those anxious hordes of murder-happy Panzer-riding Hun *Übermenchen* to cross the Channel and start goose-stepping their jackboots all over the queen's crown jewels—the British still had the most kickass navy in the world, and all the Germans managed to scrounge together for their amphibious invasion of England were a couple hundred crappy little unarmed barges that were sitting ducks for British attack planes, and were about as useful in ship-to-ship naval combat as a ball-point pen in a sword fight. What the Germans did have, however, was the largest and most technologically advanced air force the world had ever seen, and they weren't afraid to use it to bomb the crap out of everything in the United Kingdom. So, long story short, if Hitler wanted to put his wiener schnitzel in Churchill's morning tea, he was going to need to take out British Fighter Command, establish air superiority over the Channel, and then have his bombers and fighters blast a path of destruc-

tion leading from the beaches of Normandy all the way to 10 Downing Street.

The job of pummeling the Brits into meaty little gibs fell to Reichsmarschall Hermann Goering—Hitler's second-in-command, the founder of the Gestapo, the chief ranger of all national parks in Germany, and a World War I fighter ace so tough that he's the guy who took over command of Manfred von Richthofen's squadron after the Red Baron's untimely fiery bullet-riddled death. Goering had three air fleets at his disposal—over two thousand ultramodern fighters and bombers manned by hardened veterans who had already ripped democracy a new one in Spain, Poland, France, and Holland, and this dude was more than prepared to jam every one of these suckers full throttle up England's ass colonoscopy camera style. All that stood between the Reichsmarschall and total Nazi domination of Europe was about seven hundred fighter aircraft and the thirteen hundred pilots of the Royal Air Force—inexperienced teenagers outnumbered almost three to one by the most hard-boiled veteran airmen on Earth, with nothing less than the fate of the free world at stake. No pressure.

The Battle of Britain technically started in July, when German aircraft started shooting up British destroyers and convoy ships in the Channel, but on August 15 Hitler declared that he was going to "kick it up a notch, BAM!" and ordered the Luftwaffe to execute "Eagle Day"—a magical happy fun time when the skies of Great Britain would be darkened by endless waves of Heinkel and Dornier twin-engine bombers raining fire and destruction on every English structure bigger than a bread basket until the only thing left standing in Great Britain was Nelson's statue in Trafalgar Square blown up in such a way that it would look like he was giving everyone the finger. All three Nazi air fleets attacked England at once, hammering the entire country in a three-pronged pincer attempt to flatten its radar defense outposts and bring the isle to its knees with one swift Rochambeau to the funbox.

Endless fleets of bombers soared overhead throughout the day, ominously lumbering toward their targets, but instead of Britain crapping their pants at this vulgar display of airpower and immediately surrendering as Hitler and Goering expected, the RAF rose to the challenge and decided they were going to stick eight barrels of .303-caliber machine gun ammunition down Hitler's esophagus if it was the last thing they did before exploding into flames. Daring, fearless British pilots flew dozens of missions on August 15, hammering the German bomber waves with everything they had in a daylong series of epic plane battles, each British pilot doing everything in his power to stop the Nazis from blowing the ass out of his homeland. The German air fleets were mauled out-of-control crazy by endless strikes from hard-flying Spit-fires diving straight into their formations in a bloody stream of tracer fire and contrails, and despite the well-coordinated three-pronged attack, Goering's men completely failed to do any major damage to British airfields or radar systems. The British had faced down nearly everything the Luftwaffe had to offer, and they were still standing.

While it never hurts to have a cadre of foolhardy warriors willing to sacrifice their lives to blow the crap out of German bomber planes, the real key to British success in the Battle of Britain was in their intricate network of radar systems and communications. Now, sure, radar isn't as sexy as Nikola Tesla's aircraft-melting death rays or a double-deluxe BBQ bacon cheeseburger made out of rhinoceros meat, but this device was way more useful as a secret weapon of World War II than any ri-diculous steampunk zeppelin that shoots laser-guided stealth rockets or even that Vulcan-gun-armed cyborg Hitler from Wolfenstein 3D.

As you might have noticed, the sky is a pretty big place, and be-fore there was radar fighter pilots really didn't know where the hell the bad guys were. This kind of made it difficult to fight them (seri-ously, try playing Ace Combat sometime without looking at the HUD or the radar), so as a result, back in the day squadrons of pilots used to just fly around like jackasses all day patrolling the skies, wasting time, energy, and fuel in an often fruitless search for something worth killing. But with these newfangled radar stations set up all along the English coast (and a communications relay system that linked their data into a central command structure), British Fighter Command could now coor-

dinate concentrated attacks on incoming bomber raids, allowing their pilots to put the maximum number of machine guns on enemy formations as quickly and efficiently and badassfully as possible.

An interesting thing about these radar stations is that since almost every RAF man in the United Kingdom was pressed into pilot or ground crew service, the radar bases across England were largely crewed by the Women's Auxiliary Air Force. From a central underground headquarters in the basement of a girls' boarding school outside London, WAAFs would receive data from ground spotters and radar stations (also manned by WAAFs), plot enemy movements on a huge map, and then radio coordinates and orders to airfields, pilots in the air, and antiaircraft gun batteries, coordinating hundreds of vehicles traveling at two to three hundred miles per hour while also providing pump-up words of encouragement to RAF pilots in sexy British accents even as German bombers strafed the WAAF radar stations and dropped ordinance so close to their positions that the windows were exploding in on them (as a radar station burned around one WAAF, she famously remarked to her commanding officer that "the course of the enemy bombers is only too apparent to me because the bombs are almost dropping on my head!").

Of course, being a pilot in the air wasn't exactly a picnic either—these were teenagers or guys in their early twenties hurtling three hundred miles an hour in a freezing-cold unpressurized cockpit, closing to within two hundred yards of the enemy, then hammering a two-second burst of fire—eight machine guns barfing out ninety-six hundred rounds per minute of .303-caliber ammunition in a desperate attempt to blow a few hundred holes in the enemy's fuselage and/or brain. World War II fighter aircraft didn't have power steering, either, so air combat in 1940 wasn't like delicately manipulating the analog stick on an Xbox controller in order to leisurely slide your crosshairs into place—if you wanted to get your Hawker Hurricane into position to blast that Nazi biznatch who just rocketed past your cockpit, you had to manhandle the thing as if you were playing tug-of-war with a yeti, and you had to do it while pulling a couple Gs, rolling upside down, trying to keep the sun out of your eyes, and desperately attempting to stay focused through the icy cockpit windshield at a dot the size of your thumbnail (which of course was also traveling a couple hundred MPH as well and also trying to kill you with bullets). Then consider that you we're five miles in the air, listening to your wingmen die screaming horrible deaths on your radio headset, and your body was shoehorned into a cramped coffinlike cockpit where one mistake (or one random mechanical failure) meant that you—and the couple hundred pounds of aircraft fuel and ammunition you were sitting on top of—were going to be spending the last few seconds of your life spinning to the ground on fire like a burning piece of space junk on re-entry. If you were lucky enough to survive all that and make it back to your home airfield (assuming the airfield was still there and hadn't been bombed into a smoking crater), you could look then forward to a brief smoke break while fearless ground crews rearmed your plane as bombs exploded all around them. Then try doing that four or five times a day, every day, for a couple months straight, and you can start to get a feel for what these pilots were up against.

From August through September, the daring, overworked pilots of the Royal Air Force flew huge numbers of missions like every single day, kind of like the *Battlestar Galactica* episode "33," only for real and with less Katee Sackhoff and Grace Park. As these battles continually raged through the skies the British developed effective tactics for thwarting the endless German waves of heavy bombers—essentially they would scramble when they got the call from Fighter Command, and then the squadrons with the faster, more maneuverable Spitfires would take on the German Bf-109 fighter escorts while the bigger Hawker Hurricane squadrons ripped past the fighter screen and tried to cause anarchy among the German bombers. In keeping with my sub-conscious, apparently-unstoppable compulsion to reference *Star Wars* in pretty much every damn chapter of this book, the Spitfires were like X-Wings and the Hurricanes were Y-Wings. Using coordinated coun-terattacks on these seemingly endless German heavy bomber waves, the RAF still managed to post a two-to-one kill ratio in the early part of the campaign despite being heavily outnumbered every time they took to the skies.

Of course, that's not to say that the Germans didn't have plenty of badass acts of heroic bravery going on for their side either—their daring-bordering-on-suicidal bomber pilots were taking behemoth twenty-six-thousand-pound twin-engine aircraft and screaming 270 miles an hour across the British countryside at altitudes of fifty feet and lower—so close to the ground that the bomber pilots sometimes navigated by *reading the street signs below them*—and even after their missions went awry there were still accounts of downed bomber crews stripping the machine guns off their wrecked aircraft and getting in-volved in intense firefights to defend their crash sites. And, speaking of firefights, it's also worth mentioning that one enterprising German deck gunner once stripped the MG off his Dornier-17 and replaced it with a flamethrower (this sounds awesome, but ultimately it didn't work all that great—the flamethrower had trouble igniting at high al-titudes, and just ended up spraying oil on the Hurricanes that were chasing him down like the car in Spy Hunter), which is some seriously above-and-beyond-the-call-of-duty-for-the-sake-of-badassitude-style stuff. To top it off, the Luftwaffe's best pilot was a totally righteous dude named Adolf Galland who had lost most of the eyesight in his left eye during a horrific fiery plane crash in 1935, yet still ended up scoring 104 enemy aircraft kills during the course of the war, includ-ing 33 in the Battle of Britain alone. Galland also had a custom ashtray installed in the cockpit of his yellow-nosed Bf-109 so he could smoke cigars while he was blasting the hell out of rookie RAF pilots. I like to picture this one-eyed cigar-chomping hardass looking like Kurt Russell in *Escape from New York* even though in reality he looks more like a German Clark Gable. It also bears mentioning that the commander of their night bomber fleet was a cranky three-hundred-pound German nicknamed "The Elephant" who wore a monocle and looked like the comic relief villain from some black-and-white World War II TV series, which is of course awesome.

The Germans were eventually smart enough to figure out that their daytime raids on RAF airfields weren't really paying off too well, so starting around mid-August they began coming back around at night and bombing industrial targets like fuel refineries, repair facilities, and aircraft factories. The RAF were getting nailed day after day, losing roughly the equivalent of a squadron of Hurricanes a day during this period of the campaign, and before long their fighting effectiveness was being severely affected by fatigue, endless fighting, and constant bombing on their positions. Things were going downhill in a hurry.

Well, this tactic was working great for the Germans until August 24, when some totally lost off-course German bomber accidentally tea-bagged London with a few hundred tons of high explosives in the middle of the night. Well, sure, it was one thing to hammer military targets nonstop all the time, but badass world leaders like Winston Churchill don't just sit around when you go around blowing up civilians in their capitals like some kind of turbocharged jackass—they get vengeance. Churchill responded to the attack on London by sending long-range bombers to Berlin *the next night*, shoving it down Hitler's stovepipe in a daring show of his gigantic brass balls.

This was a huge dickslap to Hitler and Goering, who looked like total assclowns to the German public for letting enemy bombers get all the way to the capital. They responded the way you'd expect a Nazi to, which is by venting their fury on the innocent bystanders, grocery stores, and hot dog carts of England. From September 7 on, the Germans switched the focus of their attacks from military to civilian targets, bombing London almost nightly in a period of the battle known to the Brits as the Blitz.

Okay, well, the loss of civilian life was incredibly tragic and all, but let's look at this like a sociopath for a second—every bomb that was landing on the taco truck down the street was a bomb that wasn't landing on a Fighter Command radar station, and this much-needed break in the attack actually allowed the RAF to almost completely rebuild their airfields and reform their previously half-dead air force into a coherent fighting organization once again. And, whereas Hitler thought that bombing civilian targets would break Britain's will, in actuality it only served to make them EVEN MORE PISSED (and, incidentally, more sympathetic to neutral countries like the United States).

After the attack shifted to the citizens of London, the RAF redoubled its efforts to rip Hitler's aircraft out of the skies, an effort that culminated in a massive air battle on September 15, when another "Eagle Day"–style megafleet attacked the United Kingdom in an over-the-top display of German airpower. In a battle where nearly every RAF squadron in active service was simultaneously deployed, the British fought off four separate waves of German bomber flights, machine-gunning every Kraut they could find and taking out sixty enemy aircraft—mostly heavy bombers—while losing just twenty-three of their own.

The day after the battle Hitler postponed the invasion of Britain indefinitely—the fighting and bombing would continue for another couple months, but the world's biggest air battle was now completely lost, thanks in no small part to his unerring ability to bungle up military operations right at the moment of their final success. For the rest of the war, the führer would have to contend with Britain constantly threatening German holdings in France, and his inability to put the UK out of action in 1940 resulted in the United Kingdom serving as a springboard for the combined British-American invasion at Normandy in 1944—an attack that would help contribute to the downfall of the Reich.

The most famous German bomber pilot of World War II was Hans-Ulrich Rudel, an utterly unstoppable Ju-87 Stuka dive-bomber pilot who put up video game-style kill numbers and to this day remains the most decorated combat aviator of any nation in the history of warfare. Diving out of the sky in his slow two-seater attack bomber, Hans-Ulrich Rudel flew twenty-five hundred combat missions—more than any pilot ever, for any country, in any period of time. The stats speak for themselves—he is credited with personally destroying 11 enemy aircraft, 519 tanks, 1,000+ trucks, 4 trains, 70+ landing craft, 2 cruisers, a destroyer, and the Soviet battleship *Marat*—a six-hundred-foot warship he cracked in half with one well-placed bomb down the smokestack. Rudel survived being shot down twice behind enemy lines, kept flying even after losing his leg in combat, received his country's highest award for military valor five times, survived the war, escaped to Argentina, and later served as a consultant on the American development of the A-10 Warthog ground-attack aircraft.

Most of the RAF pilots and crew were British, but there were plenty of badasses from across Europe and the Commonwealth helping out the cause as well. For instance, the highest scoring unit in the battle was 303 Squadron, which was made up entirely of Polish expats who had fled the Nazi invasion in 1939, and the top-scoring ace of the Battle of Britain, Josef Frantisek, was a Czech. Fighter Group Number 11, the unit that defended London and bore the brunt of the fighting, was commanded by a New Zealander; the minister of aircraft production—the dude who doubled the number of Spitfires and Hurricanes the British factories were churning out—was a Canadian guy known as "The Beaver"; and every pilot's ready room in the UK had a poster prominently displayed describing South African superace Adolph Malan's "Ten Rules for Air Fighting."

⊷⇒ ACE IN A DAY ⇐⊷

FRITZ OTTO BERNERT (APRIL 24, 1917)

A World War I German infantryman who was wounded four times in front-line trench warfare across France, when Fritz Otto Bernert lost the use of his arm after taking a bayonet to the triceps he decided, Screw this, I'll become a pilot instead, because it's not like you need both arms to fly a plane, right? Bernert, who was also so superblind that he needed eyeglasses the size of a telescope to see anything (not an easy feat back in the days of open-topped biplanes), nevertheless ripped apart the skies over France during Bloody April in 1917, trashing five British aircraft in a single day on April 24—all in the course of about an hour—and achieving the coveted, incredibly rare honor of becoming an "Ace in a Day." The half-crippled pilot would be wounded and shot down a couple more times during the war, but still lived long enough to die of the Spanish flu in 1918.

RAYMOND COLLISHAW (JULY 6, 1917)

Canada's most famous flying ace, Raymond Collishaw was a daring World War I pilot who battled the enemy in a badass-looking squadron of all-black Sopwiths known as "Black Flight." Collishaw, who was known for undertaking dangerous bombing runs in enemy territory and for having once survived an air duel with the Red Baron, became the first person in history to kill six enemy planes in a single day, fragging a half-dozen German Albatrosses into flaming wreckage in the skies with some nifty flying above France in July 1917. Collishaw would end the war with sixty two kills, collect so many medals that wearing his uniform gave him back problems, and go on to fight against the Communists in the Russian Revolution. He spent the later years of his career serving as air marshal of the Canadian air force.

DUKE HEDMAN (DECEMBER 25, 1941)

Before Christmas 1941, Robert "Duke" Hedman of the Chinese air force's First American Volunteer Group (better known as the "Flying Tigers") was mostly known for hanging out in the Tigers' ready room playing the piano badly with a cigarette hanging from his lips and a cold beer on the baby grand. But in the skies above Rangoon on that fateful Christmas Day, Hedman suddenly found himself toe-to-toe with a huge formation of deadly Japanese aircraft closing in on his position. Undeterred by ridiculous odds, Hedman dove straight in for the attack and quickly proved he was much more than just the evening's half-drunken musical entertainment. Hedman hurled his awesome shark-face-painted P-40 Warhawk straight into a formation of Japanese Ki-21 Sallys, firing his cannons from 150 feet out, blasting them to hell from ranges so close that he had to swerve to evade the breaking-apart pieces of the exploding enemy aircraft after he sniped them to pieces. Hedman killed four enemy planes in a row before a bullet shattered his canopy, showering him with broken glass and embedding itself in the headrest beside him, but even that holy-crap near-death experience didn't stop this Flying Tiger from peeling out of formation on his way home and shooting down a Ki-43 Hayabusa fighter that was pissing off one of his wingmen.

Takeo Okumura (September 14, 1943)

This badass Japanese Zero pilot had come close to achieving Ace in a Day status during his very first battle, downing four crappy little Chinese bi-planes during a full-on deathmatch air duel in 1940, but it was in the skies above New Guinea that Takeo Okumura put on the deadliest display of Japanese aviation badassitude ever recorded. In a frenzy of gunfire and full-throttle destruction, Okumura recorded ten aircraft kills over three sorties, downing an F4U Corsair, two P-40 Warhawks, five F6F Hellcats, an SBD Dauntless, and a B-24 bomber in just one day of psychotic emperor-loving aeronautical devastation. For setting the Japanese single-day kill record, this guy received an awesome-looking ceremonial katana from his commanding officer, which, quite honestly, is way more badass than any medal you could possibly get if you ask me. Unfortunately, Okumura wouldn't get a chance to be the first pilot to ever take out another plane with a fly-by sword attack—he was killed in action eight days later.

Emil Lang (November 3, 1943)

The Soviet attempt to retake Kiev from the Nazis in November 1943 began with nonstop Russian bombing raids in the skies above the Ukraine—an opportunity that provided the perfect hunting ground for Knight's Cross recipient and 144-kill German superace Emil "Bully" Lang. Lang, whose badass callsign was "Black-7," flew multiple sorties against Soviet Il-2s and Pc-2s, meeting bombers and fighters alike with a nonstop donkey punch of large-caliber ammunition to the sensitive areas, lowering the throttle only long enough to refuel, rearm, or change aircraft to one that wasn't so badly shot up it couldn't generate lift. Lang, a former Lufthansa commercial airline pilot who had given up on the idea of in-flight safety and was now shredding the atmosphere in a turbocharged Focke-Wulf 190 Murder-Tron 9000, is credited with single-handedly breaking up an entire Soviet heavy bomber formation on his own. During a mere twelve hours of combat he recorded eighteen kills—a single-day record that will probably never be broken.

CHUCK YEAGER (OCTOBER 12, 1944)

One of America's most famous and badass aviators, the great Chuck Yeager, was flying his P-51 Mustang in an escort mission to support bombing operations over Germany when suddenly his flight of B-29s came under attack by a formation of menacing-looking Bf-109s with inhospitable attitudes and nothing nice to say. As Yeager fearlessly dove into the fray, two of the enemy planes peeled out, but Chuck smoked them like bratwursts before pulling hard on the stick, screaming into a 180-degree half loop, and nailing the other three as they clumsily tried to line up for their run on the bombers. The five kills had all happened in the span of about five minutes. After the war Yeager would work as a USAF test pilot, where his job primarily involved strapping himself into prototype jet aircraft to see if they could be flown without exploding, and he would later achieve fame for becoming the first man to fly faster than the speed of sound.

MUHAMMAD MAHMOOD ALAM (SEPTEMBER 7, 1965)

The only person to ever achieve Ace in a Day status in the cockpit of a fighter jet, this Pakistani wing commander shredded his enemies from the controls of an F-86 Saber during the relatively obscure 1965 Pakistan-India War. Flying low over the treetrops on a search-and-destroy mission, Commander Alam engaged a squadron of Indian air force fighters while screaming through the skies at 550 miles an hour, performing hair-raising maneuvers a mere one hundred feet from the ground. The Pakistani ace first took out two unsuspecting enemy aircraft *Top Gun* style with a pair of AIM-9 Sidewinder air-to-air missiles, then closed to gun range and shot down three more with his cannons before anybody could even figure out what the face-eating mother hell was whomping their asses so hard. The entire thing was over in about two minutes, so Alam went home, had a cup of coffee, and then received whatever Pakistan's version of the Medal of Honor is called.

29

PAVLOV'S HOUSE

Sergeant Jacob Pavlov vs. the German Sixth Army
Stalingrad, USSR
October–November 1942

Pavlov's small group of men, defending one house,
killed more enemy soldiers than the Germans lost in taking Paris.

—LIEUTENANT GENERAL VASILY CHUIKOV,
COMMANDING OFFICER, SOVIET SIXTY-FOURTH ARMY

THE BATTLE OF STALINGRAD WAS THE SINGLE BLOODIEST
BATTLE IN HUMAN HISTORY. Over the course of six months of
nonstop, ultra-over-the-top-in-a-bad-way combat, this unfathomably
violent blood fiesta ended the lives of two million people, almost single-
handedly obliterated an entire generation of Russian and German men,
and reduced a modern, sprawling industrial city to shrapnel-riddled
rubble unfit for human habitation. To put the scale of this carnage in
perspective, it's like taking every article on Wikipedia, turning each
one into a person, and then shooting them all in the head. It's a number
that's larger than the populations of Monaco, Bermuda, Estonia, Iceland, Lichtenstein, the U.S. Virgin Islands, and the Federated States

of Micronesia combined, yet, despite all of this devastation and trag-edy, in the middle of this blood-scorched wasteland of miserable ass-sucking awfulness, one man proved himself a hero equal in epicness to the battle that raged around him—a lowly sergeant from some un-known village in Russia who almost single-handedly tipped the scales in the battle that changed the course of World War II in Europe.

Jacob Pavlov of the Forty-second Regiment, Thirteenth Guards Division, had been little more than a proud yet insignificant peasant farmer at the beginning of the war. But at Stalingrad his iron-willed ability to kick the crap out of Fascist Nazi Deutschbags with a skill that has never been witnessed by human beings before or since altered the course of the battle, and, with it, the course of World War II itself.

On the afternoon of September 28, 1942, Sergeant Pavlov was crouch-running his way across a snow-covered, smoke-swept field to-ward an ordinary-looking four-story apartment building on the edge of Solechnaya Street, part of what used to be downtown Stalingrad be-fore downtown Stalingrad simply became a festering pile of rubble and Nazis. Facing the burned-out husk of what once was the town square, this sturdy building had somehow withstood the bomb-riddled horri-bleness that had leveled almost the entire rest of the city, but aside from that (and, you know, the MG42s spewing a steady stream of lead death out of every other window), it was otherwise relatively unremarkable. Bullets zipped past his helmet as Pavlov charged across the coverless field, his PPSH submachine gun spewing rounds everywhere, while one by one the German machine gun teams methodically cut down his squad as it raced across the open ground. By the time Pavlov got anywhere near the house, all that remained of his thirty-man platoon was himself and two other men. This didn't seem to bother the sturdy peasant warrior, and Pavlov wasn't exactly the sort of unstoppable assreaming maniac who would come all the way across a bullet-strewn field just to die or surrender to the enemy like some total dumbass (not that he could have expected mercy from the Germans anyways). Another couple bursts of fire from his submachine gun (and a few close calls) later and he slammed his back up against the brick and mortar exterior and lobbed a pair of expertly placed grenades right through the windows of the building, dropping them conveniently on enemy weapon emplacements. The Germans who weren't blasted into bite-sized morsels dropped their rifles and ran for it, and Pavlov, by virtue of the fact that he was the only noncommissioned officer who wasn't currently either dead or screaming for a medic, suddenly found himself the senior ranking member of his platoon. He ordered his two surviving men to clear the building while he began administering first aid to a few wounded Russian POWs and civilians he found inside. Within minutes, the quick-minded sergeant had organized a defensive position, set his men on watch for counterattacks, and was firmly in control of a tiny, crumbling, unremarkable apartment building two hundred meters from the Volga River. His orders were simple—do not let the Germans take this structure. Do not let them reach the river. Hold until death. Keep holding after death, if possible.

After a superfun night fighting off repeated counterattacks, Pavlov's platoon was reinforced to twenty-five men the following morning. There were nearly a dozen civilian men and women trapped in the hardened military bunker that at one point used to be their home, and Pavlov wisely had everyone—soldiers and civilians—busting their ass to turn this ordinary apartment building into a fortress of impenetrable deathdealing awesomeness. Within a few hours, every approach to the building was cleared of debris and cover, sprinkled with land mines, and redecorated with thousands of feet of barbed wire. Every window in the structure was sandbagged and stocked with enough weapons and ammunition to make David Koresh's Branch Davidian compound look like a magical rainbow Disney princess castle in Mister Rogers's Land of Make-Believe. Pavlov's men cut glory holes in the wall just big enough to fit the barrel of a machine gun through, they ripped out the middle of the building's interior so that in the heat of battle they could throw machine guns, ammo, and grenades back and forth to one another even if they were on different floors, and then they booby-trapped the hell out of the place like a bunch of big beefy, bearded Soviet Macauly Culkins. The platoon also dug a ten-foot-deep communications trench back to the Volga that eventually allowed them to sneak a ridiculously huge wheeled antitank artillery piece into the basement, and which also allowed them to ferry food, ammunition, and medical supplies back and forth between the Russian lines and Pavlov's fortress. By the time they were done, this was the sort of place that would have withstood the zombie apocalypse.

Of course, the main difference between the Battle of Stalingrad and the zombie apocalypse is that the swarm of humanity rushing toward Sergeant Pavlov was highly intelligent, well coordinated, organized, and trained in the use of hand grenades, mortars, and automatic weapons. This made things a little more complicated, and defending an apartment building with twenty-five lightly-armed guys against full-strength regiments of German infantry shooting at you day and night from every possible angle was about as much fun as hiring Pyramid Head from the Silent Hill games to perform interpretive dance at your child's birthday party. Despite the unrelenting onslaught of charging Fascists, Sergeant Pavlov tirelessly urged his men to shoot until their gun barrels melted, kick ass, and never stop kicking ass until there were no more asses left in the universe. Repairs to the structure were made by the light of day, and at night the tracer fire poured out by the twenty-five men in the fortress was so intense that their murderous kill zone was visible across the entire battlefront. It was pretty demoralizing for the enemy, but to the Russkies it stood out like a beacon of heroic resistance against the Nazis, and a detail that earned Pavlov the code name LIGHTHOUSE.

The Germans hurled everything including the kitchen sink at this dude, but for some ungodly reason they just couldn't slow this insane juggernaut of proletariat asskicking down. And even though bodies were piling up and they still couldn't take the building, the Germans also couldn't just chill out and ignore the dude, either—Pavlov's House overlooked the main road approach to the Volga, and the Germans couldn't win the battle unless they were able to cross that river. So they kept throwing guys at him, and Pavlov kept killing all of them.

When the Germans weren't occupying his bullets with the fleshy parts of their abdomens, Pavlov was personally out on the roof with a pair of binoculars sexting coordinates to Soviet artillery guns, which then in turn rained death down on the Nazi positions. At one point the Germans got so fed up with this jerk that they called in a full panzer division, rolled their tanks so close to the house that they basically jammed their gun barrels through the windows and shot point-blank into the living room, but even this failed miserably—Pavlov saw them coming and had already cleared out the main floors, moving his anti-tank weaponry into the basement. As the Panzer commanders stared into the smoke looking to see how much carnage they'd created, suddenly Soviet gunners blasted straight up from the basement, through the floor armor of the tanks, and blew the Frankenberries off everyone inside. The panzers that were being held in reserve were then shot down through the thin armor at the tops of their turrets by marksmen on the roof with PTRS antitank rifles. Dozens of rounds of high-explosive armor-piercing ammunition the size of a baby's fist showered down on the tank formation, ripping right into the hull, where the bullets ignited the ammunition stores and sent the tanks up like TNT sticks inside a case of hand grenades. By the time the panzers figured out what the hell was blowing the *scheiße* out of them they were already too close to the structure, and they couldn't raise their turret guns high enough to shoot back. The Russians picked them off like ducks in a shooting gallery.

Just keeping this daily regime of Nazi-capping insanity up for a couple days is impressive, but for TWO FULL MONTHS the men of the Forty-second Regiment, Thirteenth Guards Rifle Division held their ground. The soldiers inside represented eight ethnicities from across the Soviet Union—Russian, Kazakh, Georgian, Uzbek, Tajik, Ukrainian, Jewish, and Mongolian—and with every man wounded and exhausted, and the building crumbling around them from the mortar, artillery, and machine gun fire that hammered it nonstop, these guys resolutely fought on against all odds. Jacob Pavlov, for his part, never seemed to lose his sunny, ever-cheery disposition, and even though this guy was a low-level sergeant he not only inspired his own beleaguered unit, but the entire Red Army—his balls-out defense was a propaganda-machine-fueled beacon of heroism amid a war that up until now had seen the Germans putting their dicks in mashed potatoes from Warsaw to Moscow. Always looking for ways to improve morale, during the defense Pavlov found an old phonograph machine in a blown-out apartment—it only had a single record, and nobody knew the tune, but he and his troops played that song until they'd memorized every note and the record disintegrated into vinyl dust.

As the most ferocious battle of World War II raged around them, men fighting street-to-street and house-to-house, the Nazi onslaught continued on this makeshift fortress. Pavlov's men constantly cranked machine gun fire in every direction, and while the Germans were well-known for their strategic blitzkrieging-your-ass-off abilities, toward the end of the battle for Pavlov's house it was kind of like the commander of the Sixth Army threw all that tactical nonsense out the window and started taking his operational cues from *Zapp Branigan's Big Book of War*—he simply hurled wave after wave of his own men at the Russians in a fight not too dissimilar to the Nazi Zombie survival mode in Call of Duty. It allegedly got to such a point that during breaks in the fighting the Russians had to run out of the house and kick over piles of bodies just so that they'd have clear firing lanes toward the enemy, which is of course insane and also kind of awesome. Before long the place was covered with so many skulls and bones that it was starting to look like the cover of a Warhammer 40K codex—I feel like there's probably some kind of Yakov Smirnoff, "In Soviet Russia, house keels YOU!" joke to be made here, but it seems to be eluding me at the moment for some obnoxious reason.

Jacob Pavlov's troops held the position for an unbelievable fifty-nine days. By that point the Battle of Stalingrad was nearly decided—Pavlov and the other defenders of this vital city had held long enough for a fresh Soviet army group to arrive from Siberia, encircle the German Sixth Army and utterly annihilate it where it stood. The defense of Stalingrad proved to be the turning point of World War II—the back of the Nazi invasion of Russia had been broken, and from that point on the Germans would be on the defensive as they retreated all the way back to Berlin. And, in the middle of all of this, for two months, one sergeant had held the high-water mark of the German invasion of Russia. The Germans never advanced past him, never took the building, and never overran his position, despite outnumbering his force by a factor of about a hundred thousand to one. Sergeant Jacob Pavlov survived the battle, fought through the rest of the war, was present during the fall of Berlin, and was awarded the title Hero of the Soviet Union, the country's highest honor for military bravery. The building he defended is still standing today and is a national landmark in Russia.

But, despite all that, the greatest testament to Pavlov's defense is this—when the Russians captured the Sixth Army, they noticed that German commander General Friedrich von Paulus's personal map of the battlefield had the structure circled in red and with the handwritten word "Castle" next to it.

The Russians' maps had simply labeled it "Pavlov's House."

———

The Soviet Union was in the unique situation of having more people than weapons, so in some battles Soviet conscripts were given a rifle with one clip of bullets, sent into combat, and told to use that clip to kill a German and take his gun. The dudes in the second and third waves line weren't quite so lucky—they were only handed a handful of bullets and told to take the rifles off their dead comrades from the first wave.

———

The city of Stalingrad, which housed the valuable oil refineries that kept the Soviet tanks and trucks operational, was initially garrisoned only by the Soviet 1077th Anti-Aircraft Regiment—an all-female unit of Russian peasant women and girls whose only jobs up until this point in the war involved firing flak rounds as flights of German bombers passed miles above their heads. Despite being heavily outgunned and badly outnumbered, the women of the 1077th refused to evacuate, held their ground, and fought like badasses, lowering their turrets to zero elevation and hurling antiaircraft shells at German tanks. Despite their tenacity, the women were no match for the battle-hardened troops of the German Sixteenth Panzer Division, but they fought to the end, the last women dying at their guns.

———

One unique weapon that helped Pavlov in his desperate defense was the PTRS antitank rifle. A noticeably gigantic forty-five-pound bipod-mounted rifle that measured seven feet from stock to muzzle, this thing fired a gigantic 14.5-millimeter tungsten-carbide core round that was capable of penetrating twenty-five millimeters of armor from five hundred meters away. Used throughout the war by Soviet forces, the PTRS was excellent at taking out trucks, lightly armored cars, and low-flying aircraft (but only if you were a damn good shot), and could even punch through the weak spots of some tanks provided you were either an amazing shot or ballsy enough to get uncomfortably close to it before pulling the trigger. The PTRS was especially popular in the fighting for Stalingrad, where Russians routinely used it to shoot through solid brick walls like that totally sweet gun from the movie *Eraser*.

30

LAST STAND OF THE
TIN CAN SAILORS

The Battle off Samar
October 25, 1944
Strait of Samar, Philippines

This will be a fight against overwhelming odds
from which survival cannot be expected.
We will do what damage we can.

—LIEUTENANT COMMANDER ROBERT W. COPELAND,
COMMANDING OFFICER, USS *Samuel B. Roberts*

UNITED STATES NAVY TASK GROUP TAFFY-3 WAS NOT DE-
SIGNED TO ENGAGE ENEMY WARSHIPS IN COMBAT. Comprised
of just six carrier escorts (basically just ordinary merchant ships, each
equipped with a flight deck and a complement of thirty aircraft), three
destroyers, and four destroyer escorts, Taffy-3's primary mission during the American operation to retake the Philippines was to hang
around off the coast of Leyte Island and launch ground attack aircraft

to support the infantry assault. If a submarine or two came knocking on the door looking for a nice meaty carrier to deep-six, or some stray squadron of Japanese fighter-bombers stuck its nose where it didn't belong, the destroyers were equipped to handle it.

So, naturally, when Rear Admiral Clifton "Ziggy" Sprague, Taffy-3's commander, received a frantic radio call from one of his reconnaissance pilots reporting that the largest and most heavily armed assortment of surface-sailing battle cruisers ever assembled was bearing down on a collision course with Taffy-3, he was a little concerned. Unfortunately, there wasn't a damn thing he could do about it—the Japanese superbattleship *Yamato* was out there, accompanied by three massive battleships, eight cruisers, and eleven destroyers, bearing three-four-zero, range twenty miles, closing fast on his position at thirty knots.

Huh?

Five minutes later, a trio of armor-piercing shells eighteen inches in diameter threw up a towering wall of water just off the bow of Sprague's flagship. It had been launched by the *Yamato*, the largest battleship ever built in the history of naval warfare—seventy-two thousand tons of steel-plated intimidation equipped with massive cannons that could launch a bullet the size of a Volkswagen over fifteen miles. This heavily armored, virtually indestructible behemoth of imperial justice outweighed the entire Taffy-3 task force *by itself*, and those planet-killing guns it was popping off like bottle rockets were more than baller enough to completely vaporize any ship in the American task force with a single round. Meanwhile, the biggest guns in Taffy-3 were the Mark 12 5-inch/38-caliber guns mounted on the decks of the destroyers and destroyer escorts—midsized crew-operated cannons designed for use against aircraft and lightly armored targets like surfaced submarines. A direct hit from one of those things couldn't have even dented the cooking utensils on the *Yamato*.

Of course, it's not as if that was going to stop the Americans from giving this massive Japanese battleship fleet a hell of a fight.

It should be mentioned here that there was a hell of a lot more at stake here than just those six carrier escorts (although these were to be defended at all costs). Earlier in the day a masterful Japanese feint had succeeded in drawing the entire U.S. Third Fleet away from the Philippines on some wild-goose chase snipe hunt into the middle of nowhere, and with Third Fleet's unexpected departure the only thing keeping this gigantic Japanese armada from donkey-punching the two hundred thousand American soldiers and marines fighting on Leyte Island in the kidneys with artillery shells the size of refrigerators were the tiny antisubmarine warships of Taffy-3. Defeat here would give Japanese admiral Takeo Kurita's battleships a free run to annihilate the landing craft and troop transports currently ferrying reinforcements and supplies to the island, massacring an entire division of U.S. Marines in their ships, crippling the operation to retake the Philippines and quite possibly turning the tide of the war in the Pacific back against the Allies.

The men of Taffy-3 weren't about to let that happen.

Sprague's carriers turned east into the wind so they could launch their fighters, then the entire Taffy-3 group turned south and ran toward Leyte as fast as they could go, zigzagging between enemy shells while roughly half of the Japanese navy took potshots at their asses. The destroyers all started pumping black smoke out of their smokestacks in a desperate effort to conceal the carriers from enemy gunners, hanging tight around the ships they'd been ordered to protect as salvos from the unstoppable enemy armada churned up the water around them so hard it looked like they were sailing through a glass of Alka-Seltzer, but it quickly became obvious that running wasn't going to be enough—the Japanese cruisers could easily haul ass at twice the speed of the carrier escorts, and their guns were more than enough to shred the unarmored carriers as if they were paper targets in a shooting range. And they were closing in fast.

Then, suddenly, out of the black smoke spewed forth by the destroyer screen, burst the bow of the DD-557—the U.S.S. *Johnston*. A fifteen-thousand-ton Fletcher-class destroyer on a one-ship suicide run straight into the teeth of the most heavily armed surface fleet ever assembled. It was commanded by Captain Ernest E. Evans, a Cherokee Indian who had vowed never to take one step back from the Japanese no matter how miserable a situation he found himself in, and now that

he was presented with the opportunity to stick it to the enemy this infinitely hardcore warrior brave was launching a freakishly dangerous lone-wolf suicide attack head-on against a twenty-three-ship armada, hoping that his desperate effort to ruin their assses would delay the enemy long enough for his task force to escape.

Still way out of range for her little five-inch guns or torpedoes, *Johnston* determinedly zigzagged at flank speed through a barrage of concentrated fire from twenty-three enemy ships, knowing full damned well that she needed to cross twenty miles of open water to get within range and that a single hit from any enemy ship would rip her hull a new one and send her careening to the ocean floor in minutes. Still, seemingly completely oblivious to any form of danger, Captain Evans raced on.

Six squadrons of American fighter-bomber aircraft screamed through the air over *Johnston*, making their way toward the Japanese fleet despite a hail of tracer fire and airburst shrapnel exploding all around them. Undaunted by a sky full of explosions, bullets, and other horrible crap capable of disintegrating the fuselage of even the toughest aircraft like a wet paper towel in a bowl of sulfuric acid, the Avenger attack craft and Hellcat fighters streaked in at two hundred miles an hour, strafing the enemy ships with everything they could bring to bear—which wasn't all that much, considering that these planes had been kitted out for antipersonnel and antisubmarine warfare and the ground crews hadn't had time to rearm them with something more useful. But the American pilots didn't give a crap—with literally five hundred heavy machine guns and antiaircraft cannons ripping up the skies around them, Avenger pilots were dropping depth charges on heavy cruisers and Hellcat fighters were diving out of the clouds to strafe armored battleships with .50-caliber machine guns, just hoping that maybe they could maybe just shoot someone important or knock out some critical piece of exposed equipment.

Back on the ocean surface, *Johnston* had somehow miraculously made its way through the carnage and closed within range to begin its attack. Desperate for delicious vengeance and single-mindedly intent on doing as much damage as its armament would allow, *Johnston* opened up on the lead Japanese heavy cruiser, blasting all five of her five-inch guns at the *Kumano*, a hulking warship that outweighed the little *Johnston* by a factor of seven. Undeterred, *Johnston* ripped off two hundred rounds of five-inch ammunition in just five minutes, hammering the enemy superstructure, destroying a couple of her heavy gun mounts, and then following that flurry of blows up with a ten-torpedo salvo that smashed into *Kumano*'s balls, ripped her hull up, and blasted off her bow, splitting the cruiser force's flagship nearly in half. First blood had been drawn, and it was Little Mac getting the Star Power uppercut on Mike Tyson himself.

Having now expended all of her torpedoes—the only weapons capable of legitimately damaging the enemy heavies—*Johnston* cranked the emergency brake, turned about, and started screaming ass back toward Taffy-3, still blasting hundreds of rounds from her five-inch cannons at anything with a rising sun emblazoned on the hull.

Unfortunately, *Johnston*'s luck finally ran out, and, at extreme close range with the enemy she took a direct hit from the ridiculously massive Japanese battleship *Kongo*. Heavy sixteen-inch shells punched through *Johnston*'s hull, destroyed a boiler, and cut the American ship's speed in half. Another round from a heavy cruiser then smashed into the crippled American ship, igniting a magazine of forty-millimeter antiaircraft ammunition that exploded and spewed shrapnel across several decks, and then yet another round from some other enemy ship slammed directly into the ship's bridge, snapping the mast and destroying her communications and radar capabilities. Captain Evans lost two fingers and took a ridiculous spray of white-hot burning metal shrapnel to his face, chest, and hands, but this tack-eating hardcase just got up, dusted himself off, walked out to the deck like he didn't even notice half his body was burning, and kept shouting orders, commanding his ship even though his shirt had been blown off like when James T. Kirk fought the Gorn lizard man captain on the surface of that asteroid.

Overhead, the Avengers and Hellcats continued their strafing attacks, diving down at high speeds on the enemy, releasing their ship-humping bomb loads, then pulling out of their dives and trying not to black out from the ferocious amount of Gs that were trying to crush their skulls. The cruiser *Suzuya* was hit with two air-to-ground bombs and badly damaged, pulling out of formation alongside the similarly crippled *Kumano*. Even the pilots whose bomb bay holds had been loaded with propaganda leaflets and other useless objects found a way to contribute to the battle—these guys opened their (empty) torpedo bays and made fake torpedo runs on the enemy cruisers—the Japanese, of course, didn't know that these pilots weren't carrying weapons, and were forced to take evasive maneuvers just in case, throwing them off their game and buying the American fleet just a little more time to make their escape.

Inspired by the example of the *Johnston*, the rest of Taffy-3's destroyer screen soon decided, Screw it, these guys aren't going to have all the fun, we're also going to join the fight and get in on some of this sweet sweet asskicking goodness. The American destroyers *Heerman* and *Hoel* threw themselves through the smoke screen into battle, joined by the destroyer escort *Samuel B. Roberts*—a supertiny, superslow, lightly armed, virtually unarmored antisubmarine ship that under any other circumstances would stand up about as well in toe-to-toe surface combat with an imperial battleship as a paddle-operated swan boat crewed by two guys with steel helmets and nine-millimeter handguns. To give you some indication of scale here, the splashes of water thrown up by off-target Japanese battleship rounds were taller than the mast of the *Roberts*.

As the second American attack wave closed to torpedo range, they passed the crippled *Johnston*, still trying to limp back to the carriers. The bleeding, half-dead Captain Evans was standing at attention on the deck saluting them as they hurtled toward almost-certain death. After the destroyers had passed him, Evans gritted his teeth, got pumped up out of his mind, and ordered the *Johnston* to turn around and go *back into the fray*, bringing up the rear of the formation and providing covering fire with whatever ammo was left in her five-inch guns despite the ship basically just being held together by duct tape and bumper stickers at this point.

The American destroyers steamed flank speed through the deadly spray of enemy artillery shells straight into the midst of the Japanese formation, their assortment of antiaircraft and antisubmarine guns blazing for everything they were worth. The *Hoel* launched her torpedoes at the battleship *Kongo* but missed, then started trading point-blank salvos with the gimongous imperial cruiser *Haguro*—a losing proposition on the best of days, let alone when you're outnumbered twenty-three to three. The *Heerman* charged straight into four Japanese battleships, hitting them with a barrage of fifty-four-pound shells from its five-inch guns, and then fired seven torpedoes at the behemoth *Yamato*. The imperial flagship, seeing more than a half-dozen torpedoes streaking through the sea toward her, peeled off to evade, a maneuver that sent the ship—and Admiral Kurita—sailing out of the battle in the wrong direction. Kurita, observing the battlefield in his rearview mirror and realizing he wasn't going to be around to command and control the action, simply ordered a "general attack," meaning basically every Japanese captain was on his own to figure out what the hell he was supposed to be shooting at. *Heerman* then hit the battleship *Haruma* with another torpedo barrage, damaging her hull with a high-explosive underwater kick to the junk. The little *Samuel B. Roberts* got involved as well, closing with the heavy cruiser *Chokai*, hammering it with torpedoes, and trading gunfire with it at point-blank range. The *Roberts* was so small that at such a close range, the *Chokai* couldn't depress its guns low enough to hit it, allowing *Roberts* to get in some sweet shots at *Chokai*'s soft peanut-buttery underbelly.

As the swirling ship-to-ship free-for-all melee ensued, with three tiny American destroyers engaging a dozen enemy heavy cruisers and battleships at extreme close range, Captain Evans noticed that a group of five Japanese destroyers—ships comparable in size and weaponry to the *Johnston*—had peeled off from the enemy formation and were preparing to make a torpedo attack on the American carriers. *Johnston* was crippled and without electrical power (the engine had to be hand-cranked by two strong men while ocean water seeped into the engine room around them), but Evans knew she was the only ship with any prayer of making it there in time. He ordered his ship to turn and attack, diving straight into the formation, guns blazing, firing madly despite being outnumbered five to one by ships in much better fighting shape than his. In his desperate charge, Evans successfully threw the entire Japanese destroyer column off course as they reacted to the heavy shells pounding into their hulls, distracting their aim and sending their entire torpedo complement sailing well wide of the American carriers.

Back in the gun battle now engulfing the seas off Samar Island, the destroyer escorts *Dennis*, *Raymond*, and *John C. Butler* also steamed ahead and joined their sister ship *Samuel B. Roberts*, powering straight into the teeth of the epic naval duel that now raged across the ocean. The tiny American ships did everything they could to get in the way of the Japanese heavies and keep them away from the carriers, firing with everything they had as planes were diving in and out all over the place blasting away with their guns and bombs. The *Heerman* was trading fire with two heavy cruisers at point-blank range, *Hoel* was fighting for her life against impossible odds as three warships hammered her from different sides, and the little *Samuel B. Roberts* was firing at a rate that would see her expend six hundred rounds from her two guns in the span of just an hour, most of them hammering the heavy cruiser *Chokai* so hard it actually somehow knocked her out of the battle.

For the next hour the fighting was fast and furious, but the situation was getting darker and darker by the minute. The *Heerman* and the destroyer escorts damaged the cruiser *Chikuma*, which turned to escape and was promptly torpedoed into a coral reef by Avenger aircraft, but aside from that, things were slowly starting to turn against the American fleet. *Heerman* then took a round to the bridge, but continued to fight despite being totally on fire and boxed in by a trio of Japanese destroyers.

Swarmed by battleships and cruisers, the *Hoel* was hit by the battleship *Kongo*, a trio of heavy fourteen-inch shells smashing her aft engine and guns and rendering her navigation system inoperable. *Hoel*, virtually dead in the water, still continued on and opened fire with her final torpedoes—aimed manually because the electronics were all toast—the torps striking the cruiser *Haguro*, detonating some of her lower decks, and forcing her to peel out of formation. But *Hoel* was in deep trouble. Unable to evade her attackers and with most of her weapons either depleted of ammunition or broken beyond repair, *Hoel* was struck forty times during the one-hour battle and smashed to bits. The captain finally ordered the crew to abandon ship, but the *Hoel*'s gun crews refused, still firing as the ship sank beneath them, reloading the guns manually because the ammo lifting machines were offline. They were finally silenced only when an enemy round went into the magazine and blew up the ammunition stores. The little *Roberts* was hit as well, a three-round salvo of massive armor-piercing shells forcing her to call to abandon ship, putting an abrupt end to her heroic struggle.

Back in the carrier fleet the American carrier *Gambier Bay* became the only U.S. carrier ever sunk by surface fire after taking a stray round from a Japanese battleship. Though the *Kalinin Bay* was struck fifteen times by enemy shells, she kept floating, which is impressive considering that it only takes five hits to kill a carrier in a game of Battleship, but aside from those two setbacks the rest of the escort carriers continued their desperate sprint to safety, taking full advantage of the brave destroyer escorts now sacrificing themselves to save the day. A second torpedo run by Japanese destroyers was thwarted by quick maneuvering on the part of the escort carriers and by some heroic sharpshooting pilots shooting the torpedoes out of the water with machine gun fire while hauling ass at two hundred miles an hour.

Elsewhere on the battlefield, *Johnston* was valiantly fighting her last stand, firing wildly in every direction, surrounded by four destroyers hammering the superstructure without mercy. Finally, with all of her guns knocked out and her engines flooded, Evans gave the abandon ship order, then subsequently vanished from history, never to be seen again. As the Japanese destroyers sailed off to rejoin the rest of the battle, their men came on deck and saluted the American sailors as they floated in the water.

In a two-and-a-half hour melee off the coast of Samar Island, the Americans lost four ships—the destroyers *Johnston* and *Hoel*, the destroyer escort *Samuel B. Roberts*, and the escort carrier *Gambier Bay*. The Japanese, who had gone into the battle with an unimaginably more powerful force, suffered similar losses—two heavy cruisers were dead (*Chokai* and *Chikuma*) two more were badly damaged (*Kumano* and *Suzuya*), and the battleship *Haruma* sustained severe damage to her superstructure and hull. Deciding that his attack wasn't worth the losses he was taking—and realizing that reinforcements were rapidly approaching in the form of fresh American fighter aircraft and warships—Admiral Kurita called off the attack. Taffy-3 had somehow held off the largest gunship fleet ever assembled, and they'd done it with just six escort carriers and seven destroyers.

Taffy-3 suffered 792 men dead and 768 wounded, and those men who had abandoned ship were stuck spending seventy hours in shark-infested waters before being rescued. But, against all odds, they had accomplished their mission—the carriers and the Leyte landing craft were safe, and the Japanese Center Force had been turned back in one of the most heroic naval battles ever fought. The entire unit received the Presidential Unit Citation, and Captain Ernest E. Evans of the USS *Johnston* was posthumously awarded the Medal of Honor.

Throughout the Battle off Samar, Admiral Kurita had thought he'd been fighting fleet carriers escorted by American heavy cruisers. He had no idea he was actually fighting units half that size.

Yamato would survive the Battle of Leyte Gulf, but would be destroyed a year later during the ill-fated Operation Ten-Go, a last-ditch attempt to defend the home islands of Japan from the American onslaught. With the United States threatening Okinawa (and, by extension, mainland Japan itself), the *Yamato* and nine of its escort ships went on a one-way naval kamikaze suicide attack straight toward the heart of the American fleet, hoping to go out *Samuel B. Roberts* style in a sixty-five-thousand-ton blaze of glory. It never got the chance—*Yamato* and her attack group were intercepted by a mob of over three hundred Helldivers and Avengers, which swarmed in from every direction and sank *Yamato* with fifteen direct hits from bombs, rockets, and torpedoes.

The day before the Battle off Samar, U.S. Navy captain David McCampbell found his seven-plane squadron of F6F Hellcat fighters facing off against a massive Japanese air fleet—forty fighters and twenty bombers on a raid to blow the crap out of American positions in and around Leyte Gulf. McCampbell, the highest scoring U.S. Navy ace of World War II, was unwilling to back down, and he sent five of his seven craft straight in against the bombers while he and his wingman held back in reserve. The five fighters strafed the formation, getting the attention of the Zeroes, but when the Japanese fighters swung in to intercept, McCampbell and his wingman pounced, strafing in from the rear, raking the entire formation with relentless fire and cutting through them like a scythe. McCampbell personally destroyed nine Zeroes in the melee, a single-mission American kill record that stands to this day, as he and his men broke up the attack and sent the Japanese air fleet running for home. When McCampbell made an emergency landing on an aircraft carrier a few hours later, technicians found that he had just two bullets and six gallons of fuel remaining in his aircraft.

⊶⇒ SHIP COMPARISON ⇐⊷

Ship Name:	USS *Johnston*	IJN *Yamato*
Type:	Fletcher-class destroyer	Yamato-class super battleship
Length:	376' 6" (114.76m)	839' 11" (256m)
Displacement:	2,700 tons	64,000 tons
Speed:	35 knots	27 knots
Crew:	273	2,500
Armor:	None	410mm (16") side hull armor
Armament:	Five 5" surface guns	Nine 18" surface guns
	Ten torpedo tubes	Six 6" surface guns
	Six depth charge projectors	Twenty-four 5" surface guns
	Ten 40mm AA guns	160 AA guns of various sizes
	Seven 20mm AA guns	

Ship Name:	USS *Samuel B. Roberts*	IJN *Kumano*
Type:	John C. Butler–class destroyer escort	Mogami-class heavy cruiser
Length:	306' (93m)	661' 5" (201.6m)
Displacement:	1,370 tons	13,660 tons
Speed:	24 knots	35 knots
Crew:	215	850
Armor:	None	39mm (3.9") side hull armor
Armament:	Two 5" surface guns	Ten 8" surface guns
	Three torpedo tubes	Eight 4" surface guns
	Nine depth charge projectors	Twelve torpedo tubes
	Four 40mm AA guns	Fifty 25mm AA guns
	Ten 20mm AA guns	

31

A BRIDGE TOO FAR

Operation Market Garden
September 17–25, 1944
Arnhem, The Netherlands

Only the rawest kind of courage had sustained Frost's men up to now,
but it had been fierce enough and constant enough to hold off the Germans
for three nights and two days. . . . Pride and common purpose had fused them.
Alone they had reached the objective of an entire airborne division—
and held out longer than the division was meant to do.

—CORNELIUS RYAN, *A Bridge Too Far*

IN JUNE AND AUGUST OF 1944, THE ALLIED D-DAY INVASIONS CAUGHT HITLER'S GOOSE-STEPPING MINIONS WITH THEIR SWASTIKA-EMBLAZONED PANTS DOWN, KICKED THEM REPEATEDLY IN THE GRUNDLE WITH AN ENDLESS ONSLAUGHT OF SHERMAN TANKS AND AIR STRIKES, AND SENT THE PROPONENTS OF FASCISM RUNNING ALL THE WAY BACK TOWARD GERMANY. France was swept clear of Nazis, Paris was liberated, and kooky 1940s newsreels were showing cartoons of Mickey Mouse triumphantly chomping on a cigar made from the dried flesh of dead Germans and drop-kicking Heinrich Himmler off the Arc de Triomphe.

By September, however, the situation had changed. Sure, the Nazis had been caught off guard by the sort of surprise one-two throat punch that can only be delivered by the largest amphibious invasion in military history, but now they withdrew across the Rhine River and hunkered down in a hardcore series of impenetrable fortresses known as the Siegfried Line. The Allies' top two soldiers—Generals Montgomery and Patton—had both been stopped in their tracks by a combination of fuel shortages and German eighty-eight-millimeter antitank cannons, and any attempts to bridge the Rhine and drive tanks into Germany resulted in some flaming Nazi jerkwad blowing the bridge up with dynamite like a bad guy in a Hanna-Barbera cartoon.

Faced with a solid wall of German heavy tanks blocking their passage into Germany, the Allies came up with a daring, balls-out-bordering-on-insane idea to outflank the Siegfried Line, blitz across the Rhine, charge their tanks into Germany, and bring World War II to an end before Christmas, finishing Hitler off once and for all while also ensuring that the godless Commie Russkies currently rolling up the German forces in the east didn't conquer and subsequently annex every single country between Moscow and Berlin.

The mission was code named Operation Market Garden. This is a terrible name, considering how awesomely ambitious and over-the-top the mission actually was, but that's how it goes when you're naming missions I guess.

The Allies figured that the only way to follow up the largest amphibious invasion the world had ever seen was to go balls-to-the-wall and attempt the biggest airborne operation in history as well. The mission was bold, daring, and would result in some of the most merciless savagery of the entire war—three full-sized airborne divisions would parachute deep behind enemy lines in Nazi-controlled Holland, haul ass to secure the bridges in their areas of control, and then defend them long enough for the British XXX Corps to drive their tanks straight through

Holland on a one-column suicide blitz toward Arnhem Bridge, a concrete bridge over the Rhine that would drop the Allied tanks straight into the soft, meaty, bacon-flavored industrial heart of Germany. Victory would liberate Holland and bring Hitler's empire to its knees in one badass coup de grâce. All they needed to do was parachute thirty-five thousand airborne soldiers sixty-four miles behind enemy lines in broad daylight, then have them hold out indefinetely against impossible odds while a column of twenty thousand British vehicles sprinted down the only one-lane road in Holland capable of supporting the weight of a Sherman Firefly tank. Sure, it was pretty dangerous, but hey, you only live once, right?

On the afternoon of September 17, 1944, the skies above Holland turned black as forty-seven hundred aircraft roared overhead. The 101st and Eighty-second Airborne Divisions hit the ground and immediately rushed for their objectives in Eindoven and Nijmegen respectively, but the Red Devils—the British First Airborne, the unit with the toughest job and the one farthest behind enemy lines—were stupidly dropped eight long miles from Arnhem Bridge, and they had a hell of a long walk to get where they were going. And, as they'd soon find out, it wouldn't exactly be as easy as they were hoping—thanks to a tragic failure in military intelligence, the Brits had been told their opposition would be composed entirely of Hitler Youth, old men, amputees, street mimes, old ladies, and bicycles with slingshots attached to the handlebars, but in reality they were being dropped right into the middle of the Ninth and Tenth SS Panzer Divisions—ultrahardcore frontline German armored units with multiple years of combat experience in both the Eastern and Western Fronts that had been redeployed to Arnhem for refitting and resupply.

Immediately between the First Airborne and Arnhem Bridge was German SS-Sturmbannführer (Major) Josef "Sepp" Krafft—a resourceful career warrior who'd been stationed in Holland and put in command of the Panzer Grenadier Training Battalion. When Krafft saw the flood of multicolored parachutes landing about a hundred yards away from his recruits, this guy basically lost his mind and went apecrap insane. Outnumbered twenty to one by hardened paratroops, caught completely unprepared, and with little more than raw recruits and untrained scrubs under his command, Krafft still immediately sprang into action. He organized his three training companies along the major roads leading to Arnhem Bridge, threw together a couple of twenty-five-man attack units to launch lightning guerrilla raids aimed at keeping the British off guard, and then opened up with a few hundred salvos from his secret weapon—the überinsane prototype multi-barreled gigantic fully-automatic mortar launchers he'd just been issued a few days earlier. There were only four of these weapons in existence, and, by a terrible stroke of luck, this dude just happened to have all four of them attached to his training battalion, and these video game-style weapons allowed him to fill the skies of Holland with a rain of multi-missile mayhem that immediately pinned down the British First Airborne Division along the road to Arnhem.

But that was just the beginning of the Red Devils' problems. First, their radios stopped working, so nobody knew what the hell was going on. With their comms down, the First's commander, a big Scots general named Roy Urquhart, went to the front lines to figure out what the hold-up was, and was immediately surrounded by Germans, cut off from his headquarters, and forced to hide out in an attic of a house surrounded by Nazi armored cars and infantry. Only one of the three combat battalions in the First Airborne—the Second Battalion, under Lieutenant Colonel John Frost—reached Arnhem Bridge. Frost's five-hundred-man battalion leisurely strolled into downtown Arnhem without encountering any resistance, secured the northern approaches to the bridge, fortified several structures, and prepared to hold out for XXX Corps's arrival. They were immediately cut off and surrounded by the Ninth SS Panzer Division, completely unaware that they were in for the fight of their lives.

Now, the main problem with Operation Market Garden was that it depended on the army doing something quickly, and any time you're banking on the military doing anything in a timely manner you're probably in serious trouble. Sure, the Airborne troops managed to capture their objectives, but XXX Corps was going to have to haul ass to exploit those gains, and moving fifty thousand men and vehicles rapidly down a one-lane road isn't as easy as you might think. So while the American and British paratroopers fought through to the bridges, wasting everything in sight, XXX Corps's artillery, Typhoon fighters, and Guards Armored Divisions smashed turret-first into the German front lines. Of course, the opposition they faced was much tougher than anyone expected, thanks in part to those obnoxious SS panzer divisions that weren't supposed to be there. What was supposed to be a drag race with tanks turned into a drive home during rush hour bumper-to-bumper traffic, as the tank column was hammered every step along the one-lane road by Panzers, antitank guns, and dudes with bazookas.

Back at Arnhem Bridge, Lieutenant Colonel Frost's men were fighting for their lives in a desperate battle against the toughest warriors Germany had to offer, yet somehow holding their own thanks to their capacity for asskicking awesomeness. Frost first attempted to charge the south end of the bridge but was driven back, then fought off a coordinated SS counterattack by barbecuing the Nazis with flamethrowers and poking them with bayonets to make sure they were done. For two days and three nights, Frost battled ferociously, gunning down enemy troops from sniper positions and machine gun nests throughout the city. The Germans, realizing the gravity of the situation, of course threw everything they had at the Brits—guys were rushed in on trains, given satchel charges and World War I–era rifles, and sent straight in to blow up the Brits without even catching their breath first. With battle raging around them, Frost's paratroopers would lay down a field of suppressing machine gun fire, pin down an enemy company, then turn around and find a German dude sneaking up on them with a knife, kill that guy, and turn back around just quickly enough to throw a live satchel charge out the window before it turned the entire house into rubble. Meanwhile, they still had to worry about those annoying heavy German tanks—the Dutch resistance was holding them off by building massive roadblocks on streets throughout Arnhem, but at some point Frost's men were going to have to deal with the fact that they were armed only with frag grenades and bazookas and had to face down a couple hundred dudes riding around in fifty-ton Panzer IVs.

General Urquhart eventually broke out of his attic and regrouped with his division headquarters (they all thought he was dead, like Snake Plisskin), only to learn that apparently it's difficult to run an airborne operation deep behind enemy lines without radio communications or your commanding officer, and that in his absence strange things started going down at the Circle-K. The rest of the division was desperately trying to fight their way to the bridge and support Frost's badly beat-to-hell men, but asking lightly armed paratroops to launch a full-scale frontal attack on a fanatical, heavily armed SS panzer division was basically suicide—the men of the First were being cut down by Tiger and Panther tanks, armored cars, and self-propelled guns, and without communications uplinks they couldn't even call in air strikes to clear a path.

Back at the bridge, cut off with no hope but to wait for XXX Corps, Frost now faced his most dangerous opposition yet—the Reconnaissance Battalion of the Ninth SS Panzer Division, a corpse-melting convoy of twenty-two armored cars, APCs, and troop-carrying trucks driving full speed across Arnhem Bridge, swerving past flaming wreckage, their machine guns blasting ahead. Unfazed, Frost waited for these guys to get almost completely across the bridge, then ordered his men to open up on them with everything they had. Bazookas, rifles, grenades, and machine guns rained down death on the Germans from fortified buildings as the British desperately fought against an assault they had no business facing. Armored cars burst into flaming explosions, snipers capped truck drivers driving full speed from a couple hundred yards away, and steel-plated German death-wagons were bursting into flames or flying off the bridge into the water below in a nonstop frenzy of destruction. When the smoke cleared, the Brits had completely destroyed the entire German attack force.

At this point, XXX Corps was still only at Eindoven, running a good thirty-six hours behind schedule, which was bad news for Frost—his Second Battalion had been ordered to hold the bridge for forty-eight hours, and they'd already been there four days. The bridges at Eindoven had all been expertly captured by the American 101st Airborne with the lone exception of the Son Bridge, which was blown up while paratroopers were a mere fifty yards away from it. Royal engineers worked all night to build a pontoon bridge, and the next morning XXX Corps rolled on toward Nijmegen.

Back at Arnhem Bridge, still cut off, Frost and his gallant heroes fought off repeated attacks from two full-strength SS divisions, but things were starting to look bad. The Dutch homes they'd converted into fortresses were littered with broken glass and splintered wood, ripped up by Nazi bazookas and machine gun fire, and, in some places, still burning. Cellars were piling up with dead and wounded, and the Brits were running low on food, water, ammunition, and medical supplies; since the radios weren't working, the RAF supply aircraft were helpfully dropping Frost's much-needed resupply crates right onto German positions. XXX Corps was still fifteen miles away. The rest of the First Airborne troops were less than a mile from them, but they were being decimated by enemy attacks. German reinforcements were rolling in by the minute.

Knowing his worthy adversaries were now faced with a hopeless situation, the commanding officer of the Tenth SS Panzer Division walked across Arnhem Bridge under a white flag and asked Lieutenant Colonel Frost about the possibilities of surrender. Frost responded by saying that he didn't have enough room to take an entire panzer division prisoner, but that he appreciated the offer.

Back at Nijmegen, the American Eighty-second Airborne now had a few problems of their own. They'd landed seventy-five hundred guys a mere 1.5 miles from the German border and had successfully captured the town with little more than bayonets and trench knives, but Nijmegen Bridge was still under enemy control, flooded with the tanks of the Tenth SS Panzer Division. A direct assault would be impossible, so the men of the Eighty-second came up with an even bolder plan—they were going to launch an amphibious assault across the Waal River and attack the bridge from behind, while the main force of XXX Corps's tanks attacked the panzers head-on.

Knowing that the only way to help their paratrooper brothers in Arnhem was to take Nijmegen quickly, the Americans, under the cover of smoke grenades, launched history's first and only amphibious attack by paratroopers. In a feat of daring that borders on suicide, Major Julian Cook of the Eighty-second Airborne loaded a bunch of guys onto rickety wooden boats and sent them sailing across a four-hundred-yard-wide river in broad daylight, using their rifles as paddles in a balls-out attack against elite SS units that outnumbered them two or three to one.

In the D-Day-style ridiculousness that followed, a bunch of guys who had no idea how to work a boat rowed for their lives, attacking SS panzer units like marines assaulting Iwo Jima as the Germans hammered them with mortars and machine guns. Over half the American boats were smashed into splinters during the excruciatingly slow race across the massive river, but by the time the Eighty-second hit the beaches on the other side, they were super-omega-pissed. Nothing was going to stop these guys from kicking serious ass all over the place—the paratroopers went Vesuvius, charged balls-out across two hundred yards of open ground, climbed a twenty-foot embankment, and dove straight into German machine gun nests with bayonets fixed. In thirty minutes of badass fury the men of the Eighty-second swept the enemy from the beach, slaughtering a force that badly outnumbered them, taking no prisoners as they cleared out heavy-weapon positions and bunkers and secured the bridge for XXX Corps to drive their tanks across.

Back at Arnhem Bridge, Frost was still hanging on by his fingernails. Down to one hundred men, wounded by shrapnel, and not in the mood to put up with any German bullcrap, this daring Brit continued leading his men in a desperate last stand as Tiger tanks rammed into his buildings like bulldozers, leveling the city Killdozer style with battering rams and high-explosive tank rounds. As panzers burst through buildings and German infantry swarmed his positions in desperate hand-to-hand combat, Lieutenant Colonel Frost issued his final radio transmission, which, thanks to the state of the British communications net, was received only by the German radiomen who managed to intercept it. It simply said, "Out of ammunition. God save the king." His position was overrun, and he was taken prisoner.

But, even though the bridgehead at Arnhem had fallen, the battle wasn't completely lost yet. XXX Corps continued its attack, and the remnants of Roy Urquhart's First Division were still holding a small perimeter in the Arnhem suburb of Oosterbeek. Hammered from three sides by panzers, the First was still fighting with every able-bodied man it had—glider pilots, pathfinders, truck drivers, and other folks who had no business on the front line were running around out there attaching satchel charges to Panther tanks and manning antitank cannons. One thermonuclear badass, Major Robert Henry Cain, a battalion commander with an extreme blood-raging fury unparalleled by even the most destructive berserker, personally got out there on the street armed with a PIAT antitank weapon blasting tanks anywhere he could find them. When one rocket launcher blew up in his face, temporarily blinding him, Cain refused medical help, waited until his sight returned, then went right back out and continued fighting. He ended up personally destroying twelve enemy tanks and self-propelled guns, a one-man killing spree that earned him the Victoria Cross.

Two major pushes were made to relieve First Division. First, the Polish Parachute Brigade, long delayed by bad weather in London, dropped in and attempted a daring rescue, but their valiant attempt to reach Urquhart's beleaguered men was driven back by intense fire. XXX Corps then tried a straight-on ride to blitz through the last eleven miles of countryside to Arnhem, but they were met with a steady stream of panzers rolling south across Arnhem Bridge. Finally, after eight days of savage street-to-street fighting, First Division received orders to withdraw. Leaving behind their most badly wounded men to man machine guns and cover their retreat, the Red Devils crossed the Rhine in boats under the cover of darkness, then marched eleven miles to Nijmegen to be evacuated. Of the ten thousand Brits who dropped into Arnhem, only two thousand walked out. They'd seen some of the most brutal fighting of the entire war and proven themselves valiant warriors, but it wouldn't be enough to bring the war to a swift conclusion. The war would go on past Christmas after all.

A platoon leader during Lieutenant Colonel Frost's desperate defense of Arnhem Bridge, Royal Engineer Captain Eric Mackay was embedded in a three-story brick schoolhouse just on the British side of the bridge, where he and a mere thirty men held out against countless attempts to storm the building, unflinching as tank shells knocked the entire structure down on their heads. Mackay only finally abandoned the position once the Tigers started rolling in, and was captured a few miles away, still pointing an empty .45 at the men trying to take him in. He refused to give up any information during his interrogation, then got smashed in the face with the stock of a Mauser when he tried to escape out the back of a POW troop transport. The next morning he tried again, successfully escaped, ran to the water, stole a boat, and rowed down the river to friendly lines at Nijmegen.

Lieutenant Colonel John Frost spent the rest of the war in a POW camp before returning home to England. He later served as a technical advisor for the amazing movie *A Bridge Too Far*, where he provided acting advice to the man portraying him in the film—future Academy Award winner Anthony Hopkins. After one scene where the future Hannibal Lecter sprints from one house to another while Germans fire at him, Colonel Frost casually walked over and informed the eventual four-time Oscar nominee, "You wouldn't run the crossfires that fast. You'd show contempt for danger by crossing the road slowly."

32

THE FASTEST TOMMY GUN ON THE WESTERN FRONT

Edward A. Carter Smokes Some Nazis
March 23, 1945
Speyer, Germany

Men, this stuff that some sources sling around about America wanting out of this war, not wanting to fight, is a crock of bullsh*t. Americans love to fight, traditionally. All real Americans love the sting and clash of battle. You are here today for three reasons. First, because you are here to defend your homes and your loved ones. Second, you are here for your own self respect, because you would not want to be anywhere else. Third, you are here because you are real men and all real men like to fight.

—GEORGE S. PATTON

THE SUN WAS RISING ON THE MORNING OF MARCH 23, 1945, WHEN THE MEN OF THE TWELFTH ARMORED DIVISION MADE THEIR WAY TOWARD THE FORTIFIED GERMAN-CONTROLLED CITY OF SPEYER. The Allies, still looking for that long-lost bridgehead over the Rhine they'd been unable to secure at Arnhem, moved quickly, hoping to get in there, clear the city, and capture the critical bridge before the German sappers could blow it and further frustrate Allied efforts to drive tanks into the heart of the Third Reich.

Staff Sergeant Edward A. Carter was sitting on the side of a Sherman tank, his eyes looking out for enemy strongpoints or ambushes. Even though his outfit, the Fifty-sixth Armored Infantry Battalion, had only been a cohesive unit for about two weeks, Carter was an original gangsta of Fascist-smiting annihilation who'd basically been fighting World War II before anybody knew what the hell World War II even was. The son of African-American missionary parents living in Shanghai, Carter ran away from home in 1931, at the age of fifteen, to enlist in the Chinese National Army, where he fought a two-front war, simultaneously drop-kicking the gonads off of imperial Japanese invader douchebags and battling hardcore Communist revolutionary assholes alike. When the Nationalists eventually dismissed Carter from the army for being ridiculotusly underaged, Carter made his way to Spain and joined the Spanish Republican Army, where he continued the face-tenderizing struggle against the Fascist, Nazi-supported government of Francisco Franco. Carter spent two years with the Abraham Lincoln Brigade—a badass unit of intensely anti-Fascist American volunteers who'd signed up for the sole purpose of putting their combat boots steel-toe-first up the rectums of anyone who didn't think totalitarian dictatorship was the biggest load of crap since the *Star Wars* prequel trilogy boxed set special deluxe edition (with custom plaster cast of George Lucas's balls so you can teabag yourself with them). The "Honest Abes" (I don't know if this was their actual nickname, but it should have been) fought in almost every major engagement of the Spanish Civil War, and even though they failed to prevent Franco from making Spain a Fascist country, Carter did put a whole hell of a lot of hurt on some jerkweeds in the process so it was all good in the end. After the Spanish Civil War Carter came back to the States, and ended up enlisted in the army roughly two minutes after hearing about the Japanese attack on Pearl Harbor in 1941. He had originally been assigned to a supply company, overseeing a bunch of boring truck driver stuff stateside that was about as exciting as a swift kick to the testicles, but Carter eventually agreed to be busted back down to private in order to be transferred to a front-line combat unit and start dropping the hammer on Nazi skulls. He got his wish, and with this guy's ridiculous globe-trotting battlefield expertise it didn't take long to earn those stripes back.

So by the time the battle for Speyer came around, the twenty-eight-year-old sergeant was a fourteen-year combat veteran who had been fighting World War II on three continents for roughly the previous decade and a half. And when the white contrails of a trio of German *panzerschreck* antitank bazooka rockets came streaking through the morning sky, slamming hard into the tank Carter was sitting on, this guy was really the only person in his entire battalion who knew what the hell to do next.

Carter leapt from the tank as it burst into flames beneath him, flying through the air in slow motion, then hit the ground in a commando roll and rallied the three surviving members of his rifle squad. The snap of German heavy machine guns came next, ripping through the American convoy as more antitank fire rained down on the armored column, but Carter didn't even blink.

It didn't take long for the battle-hardened sergeant to assess the situation, and it didn't look good. Most of the heavy flanking fire was coming from hardened positions in a creepy old warehouse on the edge of the town, which was more or less packed balls-deep with German heavy weapons and ammunition. Carter led his team around the warehouse's flank, moving quickly from cover to cover, advancing to within 150 yards of the warehouse undetected. Unfortunately, that last stretch was basically 150 yards of open ground—not much cover from the enemy machine guns. Not like that bothered Carter.

The sergeant gave the order to move move move, and his men immediately got up and started sprinting across the open field toward the warehouse. Within moments their assault was spotted, and the Germans repositioned their guns and ripped open fire with everything they could get their hands on—machine guns, mortars, ninja stars, and grenades. One of Carter's men fell beneath this onslaught of Nazi destruction, dying of a fatal gunshot wound to the head. Carter and the rest of his team hit the deck, pinned down in open ground by the ferocious attack of Fascist misery. Carter immediately ordered his remaining two squad mates back to cover—those green recruits weren't going to do anybody any good getting shot to hell out there, and once they were behind cover they could at least lay down some covering fire for Carter to launch a balls-to-the-wall one-man suicide attack. The riflemen headed back, but unfortunately for our boy Carter they didn't get far—the curtain of steel being thrown out by the warehouse was so intense that both men were Swiss cheesed down before they could get back to friendly lines.

Staff Sergeant Edward A. Carter Jr. was on his own, facing a warehouse full of Germans equipped with rifles, heavy machine guns, and gigantic antitank cannons.

Armed only with his Thompson submachine gun, a couple grenades, and his Colt 1911 .45-caliber service pistol, Carter crawled toward the enemy, trying to keep a low profile. He covered most of the ground in a hurry, staying low to avoid drawing attention to himself, then took up a semiprotected position on a ridge a mere thirty yards from the enemy positions—literally looking into the burned-out ruins of the warehouse, watching the enemy gun crews working. From his secure position, he lobbed a crapload of grenades down into the warehouse, blasting apart an enemy mortar crew and wiping out two enemy heavy machine gun teams. Anyone lucky enough to survive the onslaught of fragmentation grenades was rewarded with an Al Capone-style spray of .45-caliber tommy gun bullets to the face.

Carter's ambush had been exceedingly effective, knocking out three heavy-weapons teams in about twenty seconds and buying the American tank column a slight reprieve to regroup, but now this balls-out sergeant was in deep trouble, completely surrounded and cut off by an ill-tempered force of Germans blasting him from point-blank range with everything they had. Carter, undaunted by single-handedly fighting an entire battalion of blood-raging panzer grenadiers, blind-fired out from his protected position, but a wild burst of MG-42 machine gun fire unpleasantly deposited three decently sized bullet holes in the American's left arm. Carter kept shooting back, capping Nazis with one arm, but a second round from a German rifle ripped into Carter's leg, further accentuating how much this battle was sucking for him.

The hardcore American sergeant dragged himself back behind cover, badly bleeding from four gunshot wounds in various parts of his body, and now he was pinned down by a swarm of furious Germans with nothing better to do than wait for him to stick his head out from behind a rock so they could shoot it into the next area code. Carter, exhausted and sweating, pulled out his canteen and went to take a drink. A German bullet went through his hand and punched a 7.92-millimeter hole in the canteen. That's how bad they had him ranged.

Carter peeked out from cover, presumably to say something witty along the lines of Princess Vespa telling the Spaceballs they shot her hair, but the second he looked out over the rock, all semblance of pithiness immediately died in his throat.

The Germans had lowered an eighty-eight-millimeter antitank cannon at his position.

The Flak 88 is one of the most effective artillery pieces of all time. A large, stationary cannon generally used to take out aircraft and tanks, this thing was devastating against infantry as well, and it fired a high-explosive tank-style artillery shell that detonated into thousands of pieces of white-hot shrapnel. The round exploded closely enough to send shrapnel ripping into Carter's side, the force of the blast knocking him down and rendering him unconscious.

Yet, amazingly, this tough-as-hell American badass still adamantly refused to die under any circumstances. He groggily came to, opening his eyes just in time to see a full squad of German infantry headed his way—presumably to confirm that the American was dead, probably by shooting the body and seeing if it died a second time.

What follows is one of the most epic showdowns of World War II.

So here's Edward A. Carter, lying on his back, bleeding out of eight shrapnel wounds and four bullet holes across his body, arms, and legs, laying motionless in a pool of blood like Jude Law in that one scene from *Enemy at the Gates*. His left arm and hand are utterly useless. Shrapnel and bullets have rendered his leg largely immobile, and his entire body is screaming at him in pain. His pistol is in a holster on his belt. Grenade in his pocket. The only thing that can save him now is his Thompson submachine gun, sitting on the ground, resting just out of reach of his right hand. It was time to decide whether Carter would surrender or fight.

The Nazi rifle squad approached. Eight men—a squad leader armed with an MP40 submachine gun, the rest with bolt-action rifles—cautiously moved forward to inspect the motionless American soldier.

Carter sprung into action.

In a flash, Carter snapped his eyes open, reached out, closed his fingers around the well-worn wooden grip of his trusty weapon, swung it up in front of him, and pressed his finger down hard on the trigger, blasting a sweeping arc of .45-caliber destruction that ripped apart any Kraut bastard stupid enough to be standing in front of him.

Five Germans went down in a cloud of blood and high-velocity lead. One more spontaneously combusted from all the overwhelming awesomeness, bursting into flames on the spot like a meat bomb. The other two men stared down the unflinching barrel of Carter's weapon as his steel eyes silently asked the question that was on all of their minds: "Do you feel lucky? Well, do ya, punks?"

They immediately dropped their rifles. It was one of the single most stone-cold quick-draw episodes ever recorded in human history—a feat of towering badassitude on par with Bruce Willis capping Hans Gruber's tie-wearing East German terrorist henchmen at the end of *Die Hard*.

But Carter wasn't out of the woods yet—he was still only about thirty meters from the enemy lines, a half-mile from his own troops, so badly wounded he could barely walk, and on top of that, now he had to figure out what the hell he was going to do with these two prisoners.

He improvised.

Convinced that the time for stealthiness was over, Sergeant Carter grabbed one of the Krauts as a human shield, and Splinter Celle'd his way out of there making sure to keep his prisoners between himself and the enemy firing line.

When the men of the United States Fifty-sixth Armored Infantry Regiment saw Staff Sergeant Edward A. Carter Marcus Fenix'ing his way backward through the smoke on the battlefield, with a Nazi under one arm and a blazing Colt .45 in the other, they let out a cheer. Carter was guided back to friendly lines and taken back to headquarters with his prisoners. Despite bleeding severely from eight life-threatening wounds across his body, Carter refused to be evacuated to a hospital until he'd had a chance to fully interrogate the prisoners (oh yeah, I forgot to mention that Carter spoke fluent German, as well as Hindi and Mandarin Chinese) and give a report to his commanding officer. After witnessing what they'd just witnessed, the prisoners sang like canaries, giving up critical details on the enemy troop positions that allowed the Allies to capture Speyer intact with minimal casualties.

Black soldiers have received the Medal of Honor in every American conflict since the Civil War, with one exception—World War II. For some obnoxious reason, out of the 433 Medals of Honor awarded for action during the war, the nation's highest award for valor was not issued to any of the 1.2 million black soldiers who fought and risked their lives for their country in the global struggle against totalitarian Fascism. It wasn't until 1996 that the army ran a full investigation into this discrepancy, and after some deliberation the army officially recommended Carter and six other men for the award. In 1997 the Distinguished Service Cross that Edward A. Carter Jr. received for his actions in the battle for Speyer was officially upgraded to the Medal of Honor.

After a tough mission wasting Nazi fools in Normandy, Sergeant Leonard A. Funk of the 101st Airborne Rangers returned to his forward operating base only to discover it had been overrun by the enemy while he was out of town, and now a hundred Germans and a Nazi officer were all standing there pointing weapons at his face. Confronted with this unwinnable situation, this titanium-balled asskicker did the unthinkable. He brought the Funk. In one lightning-quick movement, the paratrooper unslung the tommy gun from his shoulder, swung it around, blew the officer away with a burst of .45 ACP ammunition to the chest and abdomen, then whipped his weapon around and started spraying the Germans behind him with bullets. Over the sound of full-auto SMG fire, Funk screamed for the captured American POWs around him to get off their asses and grab guns off of the dead Nazis. The Germans returned fire on Funk, but the badass sergeant continued firing, blew through his mag, reloaded, and popped off another full magazine of ammunition into the Germans without getting hit. In under a minute of fighting, Funk unleashed sixty bullets, and he and his men killed twenty-one Germans and wounded twenty-four more. Any Germans left standing after this flagrant display of awesomeness wisely dropped their guns and raised their hands.

SECTION V

MODERN WARFARE

Everybody has a plan until they get punched in the face.

—JOE LOUIS

33

THE CHOSIN FEW

The Battle of the Chosin Reservoir
November 27–December 11, 1950
Chosin Reservoir, North Korea

"If it weren't for my marines, we might have been exterminated. But my
goddamned marines, they just kept fighting and fighting, and they never
let up. Here they are, rifle butts and bayonets, and the Chinese had been
running forward, not expecting this, and that turned into a brawl. And it
was an unfair fight, because we kicked the sh*t out of 'em."

—UNCREDITED USMC OFFICER, FROM THE DOCUMENTARY *Chosin*

IT WAS TWENTY-FIVE DEGREES BELOW ZERO ON THE NIGHT OF
NOVEMBER 27, 1950. The winds whipped across North Korea's
Chosin Reservoir at upwards of thirty miles an hour, sweeping in a bitter cold so soul-suckingly miserable that it turned motor oil, canteen
water, medicine, and margarita mix into ice, the arctic blast of misery
freezing the men of the First Marine Division like Han Solo encased in
carbonite or one of those science demonstrations where the dude dips
his balls into liquid nitrogen and then uses them to hammer a railroad
spike through a solid block of steel-plated ferro-concrete.

Suddenly, without warning, the quiet, wind-swept darkness echoed with the piercing shriek of whistles, bells, and bugles screaming down from the mountain ridges on all sides of the reservoir, followed almost immediately by a thunderous stampede of boots so intense that it shook the earth beneath the marines' feet. Red flares rocketed up through the sky, illuminating the landscape in an eerie red glow, and the American troops stared open-mouthed across the hills at a back-lit throng of humanity racing through the darkness toward them from every direction at once. The marines had thought the war was over. Now they were face-to-face with the Chinese People's Liberation Army—an army that wasn't even supposed to be there—and they were outnumbered roughly a hundred to one.

The most intense battle in Marine Corps history had just begun.

The Korean War had started back in June 1950, when some random North Korean dictator named Kim something-or-other got all surly about democracy being total horsecrap, so he blitzed a gigantic murderous rampaging army of fanatical commie nutjobs across the thirty-eighth parallel in an unprovoked invasion of his hated South Korean neighbors. Fueled by an ever-burning hatred for all things capitalist that weren't either iPods, StarCraft, or Courtney Cox, the rapid North Korean assault tore apart two wildly-unprepared American infantry divisions and almost the entire South Korean army, conquered Seoul, and pushed the forces of democracy so far back that all that remained under South Korean control was a tiny perimeter around the port city of Pusan.

The United Nations reacted immediately, sending troops from sixteen countries to help the South Koreans in their struggle for freedom. American general Douglas MacArthur executed a masterful landing at the port city of Inchon, depositing several American divisions deep behind enemy lines inside one of the most difficult-to-navigate harbors in the world, and his rapid strategic double-leg 360-degree flying roundhouse kick to the back of the head cut off the North Korean army, recaptured the South Korean capital, and the constantly-rolling tank treads of the United Nations joint task force drove the Commies all the way back to the Yalu River on the border between Korea and China, sending nearly every fighting man in North Korea fleeing to China to escape the onslaught. The men of General O. P. Smith's First Marine Division, a weird mix of hardened World War II vets and green reservists with no actual combat experience, marched seventy-eight miles to the mountainous Chosin Reservoir on a mission to mop up the last North Korean resistance, secure the south bank of the Yalu River, end the war and destroy North Korea once and for all. They went into the reservoir basin expecting light resistance.What they found were three hundred thousand battle-hardened soldiers of the Chinese People's Liberation Army.

It turns out it kind of upset Chinese premier Mao Zedong's calm that a couple hundred thousand heavily armed capitalist soldiers started hanging out smoking cigarettes and cleaning their machine guns within spitting distance of the Chinese border. He'd already warned the UN to keep its distance. MacArthur ignored the request. He didn't believe the Chinese had the balls to fight him.

They did.

Tracer rounds lit up the sky as the American marines opened fire with every weapon larger than a potato cannon, raking the countryside with fire from small arms, machine guns, mortars, hand grenades, and jack-o-lanterns filled with gasoline. The Chinese infantry barely had clothes, food, or guns (many of them were sent into battle armed only with a club and were ordered to simply take weapons and ammo off their dead comrades or dead marines, which is really not the sort of thing you want to hear from your commanding officer just before running crotch-first full speed into machine guns), but many of these Chinese troops were veterans who had spent the past fifteen years battling the Japanese and winning the Chinese Civil War, and nobody in their right mind can doubt that these soldiers were seriously out-of-control hardcore. The marines watched in awe and terror as these psycho Chinese flung themselves onto barbed wire so their comrades could climb over, charged machine gun nests armed only with bolt-action rifles and clubs, and jumped into American foxholes carrying a primed white phosphorous grenade in each hand. The Fifth and Seventh Marine Regiments blasted anything that moved, but this onslaught was seriously insane—they were just a mere two regiments staring down a massive human wave attack from ten full-strength divisions of Chinese regular army. Aircraft, mortars, and artillery lit up the countryside as the Americans and Chinese battled with everything they had, and when these guys ran out of rifle and machine gun ammo, they pulled their pistols, and when they ran out of pistol mags they resorted to swinging around rifle butts, ammo belts, helmets, knives, boomerangs, nunchucks, screwdrivers, can openers, and anything else they could find in a life-or-death struggle that more closely resembled a full-scale medieval-style melee than a twentieth-century battle.

Against all odds, the marines somehow managed to hold their ground despite suffering heavy losses and having many of their positions completely overrun by swarms of enemy troops, but surviving the night was just the beginning of the frozen hell that they were about to experience—when the sun rose and the smoke began to clear, the marines found that they now held three isolated pockets of resistance: eight thousand men of the Fifth and Seventh Marine Regiments were deep inside the reservoir basin at a place called Yudam-ni, another three thousand Americans held the town of Hagaru-ri (a critical area that controlled the only way in or out of the reservoir to the South), and the First Marine Regiment was ten miles south of them at a place called Koto-ri. Each of these positions was cut off and completely encircled by scores of Chinese, and these guys were going to have a hell of a time trying to fight their way out of this psychotic bear trap of screaming angry commies.

The Chinese attacks kept coming, but heroes emerged. On the night of the November 28, Private Hector Cafferata's entire platoon was wiped out by an enemy attack, but this all-beef USDA-approved marine badass fought on alone, and armed only with his rifle and a shovel he killed fifteen of the enemy, held off the onslaught by himself, and then saved the lives of his wounded comrades by grabbing a live grenade that had fallen into their foxhole and launching it right back at the reds. Farther down the line, Captain William Barber held a three-mile stretch of the road between Yudam-ni and Hagaru-ri with just 220 men, refusing to back down despite constant repeated human wave attacks by a sea of Chinese troops. Even after this dude had been blown the hell up by a Chinese grenade, Barber, a decorated veteran of Iwo Jima, had his men carry him up and down the battle line in a stretcher so he could keep giving out pump-up speeches and encouraging them to fight. Only eighty-two of Barber's men survived the battle, but they kept the only road out of the Reservoir open for five days and six nights of nonstop combat, accounting for almost a thousand enemy dead and refusing to be overrun. Elsewhere on the battlefield a marine lieutenant named Kurt Chew-Een Lee, the first Chinese-American officer in the United States Marine Corps, heard that there was a group of marines who had been cut off from the main lines so he led a company of troops through pitch-black darkness and waist-high snowdrifts with a PLA bullet in his elbow, his arm in a sling, and equipped only with a compass, somehow finding the trapped marines and helping them fight their way back to friendly lines by capping fools with the pistol in his off-hand.

The next morning, the trapped marines in Yudam-ni decided the position was no longer tenable, and they began an excruciating fourteen-mile death march south to Hagaru-ri. Passing through knee-deep snow

78460A

and temperatures of forty below zero, pursued and encircled by nine enemy divisions, and under constant fire from mortars, artillery, and machine guns, the marine battalions leapfrogged one another down the road, fighting a running three-day battle against impossible odds. The Chinese had no food and no winter clothing (many of them were wearing sandals, captured USMC boots, or, even worse, were barefoot), but they were relentless, hammering the Americans and making them pay the iron price for every step of land. The Fifth and Seventh Marines had to pull every able-bodied man into service—they had cooks and truck drivers capturing strategic passes, engineers and radio operators defending against human wave attacks, and guys on K.P. duty fighting off ambushes with potato peelers and pots of boiling water.

The three army battalions unlucky enough to be positioned on the east side of the Chosin Reservoir weren't faring any better than the marines. Cut off and outnumbered eight to one, the soldiers were out of ammo, desperately trying to drive a truck convoy eight miles through to link up with the marines at Hagaru-ri. Their convoy was hammered from all sides at once, and their commander, a daring colonel named Faith, was killed by an enemy grenade while trying to personally bust through an enemy blockade armed only with his .45 pistol. Out of gas and blocked off, the convoy was destroyed by Chinese flamethrower infantry, and the entire army detachment was almost completely annihilated—of the 2,000 soldiers who had entered the reservoir, only 385 men reached Hagaru-ri, most of them by crawling half-dead across a frozen lake in sub-zero temperatures, only to link up with the marines and fall in with the first firing line they could find so they could keep fighting.

The Fifth and Seventh Marines reached Hagaru-ri on December 4, where they linked up with elements of the First Marines, the U.S. Army Thirty-first Infantry Regiment, and a unit of British Royal Marine commandos who happened to be hanging around because apparently for some reason any time some serious hardcore life-or-death fighting is going down anywhere in the world these guys seem to spontaneously materialize right into the middle of it. Together the seventy-five hundred survivors of this beleaguered, weary, exhausted detachment of frozen-solid warriors began their epic fifty-two-mile fighting withdrawal against brain-meltingly lopsided odds. The marines are quick to say this wasn't a retreat—the road was blocked by Chinese soldiers in entrenched defensive positions, so for the purposes of Marine Corps lore this march to the sea was conducted not like a fighting withdrawal, but as a straight-on attack aimed at smashing through enemy lines (a tactic the First Division's commander, the legendary General Lewis "Chesty" Puller, liked to refer to as "attacking in the other direction").

The marines moved during the day, using nonstop bombing and napalm runs from air force, marine, and navy aviators to clear the way, and then they dug in as the sun went down and spent the sixteen hours of darkness fighting off constant charges by Chinese troops doing everything in their power to crush the Americans helmet-first into the soil once and for all. The marines marched day and night, their numbers depleted in some cases to the point where entire companies were being commanded by corporals, but they never gave up, never surrendered, and never backed down from battle. Carrying their dead and their weapons with them, the Americans busted out of there and marched into the harbor like marines on December 11. In two weeks of nonstop battle, they'd suffered horrific casualties—three thousand dead, six thousand wounded, and many more missing in action—but they had clawed their way out of a hellhole that would have spelled the doom of lesser units.

As the marines boarded the ships to leave they worked with the navy to load ninety-eight thousand North Korean refugees onto the boats with them, relocating the villagers to the South, and then blowing the harbor on their way out to prevent the Chinese from being able to use it. Between the freezing cold and the mass proliferation of bullet, napalm, and knife wounds, the Chinese army took somewhere between thirty-five thousand and forty thousand casualties during the campaign—almost four times the number of dead and wounded suffered by the Americans. Two full PLA divisions had been completely annihilated and never appeared on the battlefield again.

The Americans who fought at Chosin would receive seventeen Medals of Honor, seventy-three Navy Crosses, and twenty-three Distinguished Service Crosses. It would be the most decorations ever awarded for a single battle in U.S. Marine Corps history.

After the Battle for Chosin, the Chinese and North Korean forces blitzed south, but the United Nations managed to eventually mount a tough defense along the thirty-eighth parallel, stopping them at places with sweet names like Bloody Ridge, Pork Chop Hill, The Hook, and Heartbreak Ridge. The war ground to a stalemate, and a ceasefire was eventually called in 1953, dividing Korea along the thirty-eighth parallel. An official peace was never brokered, however, meaning that to this day North Korea and South Korea are technically still at war with each other.

The last official bayonet charge in American history took place during the Korean War. Apparently, an army captain named Lewis Millett read a Chinese pamphlet stating that American soldiers were afraid of hand-to-hand combat and cold steel, so he decided to teach those Commie punks that quite the opposite is true. He personally led two platoons on a full-on bayonet charge up a two-hundred-foot-high snow-covered hill, assaulted a full company of Chinese infantry with bayonets and rifle butts, and drove them from their position. Forty-seven of the two hundred defenders were killed, eighteen by bayonet.

A couple years ago a unit of United States Marines traveled to China to do training exercises with the Chinese military. The objective of one mission was to charge up a steep hill and capture a heavily-fortified base lined with machine guns and mortars. The Marines went first: they took two companies (about two hundred and fifty men), and each unit moved quickly from point to point up the hill, staying behind cover and laying down suppressing fire while the other unit advanced, each company leapfrogging the other until they'd reached the top. They took the hill in fifteen minutes, spent several thousand rounds of ammunition, and suffered zero casualties. When it was the Chinese Army's turn, their commander stood in front of his troops and said, "Men, I want that hill in under a minute." He took two regiments (over three thousand men), gave the order to charge, and his men just sprinted to the top of the hill screaming like maniacs. He took the hill in forty-five seconds and lost almost a thousand casualties. After the exercise, the Marine Corps commander said something along the lines of, "What are you doing? The American public would never stand for us taking that many casualties in a single battle." The Chinese commander just looked at him with a confused expression on his face and said, "But we only used thirty bullets."

"God has a hard-on for Marines, because we kill everything we see."

—R. Lee Ermey in *Full Metal Jacket*

Belleau Wood (1918)

Hurled into the meat grinder of World War I, the U.S. Marines were called on to attack through the Belleau Wood during the Second Battle of the Marne. Tasked with rushing straight-on into German machine guns, the marines didn't blink—spurred on by legendary sergeant Dan Daly, who climbed over the top in full view of the enemy and shouted, "Come on, you sons of bitches! Do you want to live forever?" the marines pushed ahead, rushing through the forest, guns blazing despite heavy casualties. The leathernecks engaged the Germans in hand-to-hand fighting, blasting with their Colt 1911s and knife-fighting through enemy trenches over the course of twenty days of constant battle. The Devil Dogs got it done, clearing out the woods of German troops, and while they lost half their men in the battle, they proved themselves as badasses and earned the respect not only of the Allies, but of their German adversaries as well. Nowadays Daly's speech is memorialized forever in the cinematic masterpiece *Starship Troopers.*

Guadalcanal (1942)

Just six months after Pearl Harbor the marines were already taking the battle to the enemy, fighting through pouring rain and untold amounts of suck as they hopped island to island battling the Japanese anywhere they could find them. At Guadalcanal they attacked a ninety-mile-long jungle island in the Solomons, captured a vital airfield, and then, just as the battle started to turn against the empire of Japan, the commander of the imperial forces decided to put together one last-ditch effort to retake the airfield—a tactically sublime, subtle, and intricate battle plan that consisted of "Let's take a heaping crapload of dudes with grenades and bayonets and shove them right up everyone's assholes." A sound plan, but unfortunately for the Japanese, they didn't bank on the fact that Gunnery Sergeant John Basilone was a human force field of bullets who had no intention of sitting back and letting himself get steamrolled by a force two hundred times larger than his own detachment. For three days, Basilone and another marine, Sergeant Mitchell Paige, each lugged their giant-ass one-hundred-pound fifty-caliber Browning heavy machine guns from position to position, constantly readjusting their fields of fire to make sure that everything in front of their positions was coated in a thick hail of tracer fire and crunchy lead death. Basilone alone burned through 125 belts of ammunition, annihilating an entire Japanese regiment almost by himself, while the Serbian-American Paige shook off a bayonet wound to the arm and still held off twenty-five hundred enemy troops by himself for ten hours. When it looked like he might be overrun, Paige (who was born Mihajlo Pejić) ordered his last dozen men to "fix bayonets and follow me," charging straight on into the middle of a banzai charge, bayonet at the ready, and massacred the enemy attack in a brutal hand-to-hand battle that broke their attack for good.

IWO JIMA (1945)

Iwo Jima was a tiny, seven-mile-long strip of island that held two small runways. These runways were launching Japanese fighter aircraft that pissed off Allied bomber pilots on their runs over mainland Japan, so, of course, the marines were sent in to go kill everything they could find. On February 19, 1945, 450 landing craft and 21,000 men hit the beaches in an all-out assault to clear the island and capture the airfields. The Japanese commander, unwilling to fight on the beaches in full view of American aircraft and naval guns, withdrew to the interior of the island, bunkering down in hardened, mined, booby-trapped, fixed positions built deep into the sides of the mountains. Fighting for every square inch of land the marines spent four days fighting up the 556-foot-high Mount Suribachi, opening up with flamethrowers and machine guns on their bitterly stubborn enemies, who were determined to fight to the last and who refused surrender at all costs. The casualty toll was horrific—of the seventy-one thousand marines who landed on Iwo Jima, twenty-three thousand were killed or wounded—but the operation was a success. In the months that followed the assault, 2,251 badly damaged B-29 bombers made emergency landings on the island, making the island one of the most critical air bases in the entire Pacific Ocean.

FALLUJAH (2004)

When the American military blitzed through Iraq in 2003, they went around the fortress city of Fallujah for a good reason. The former home of Saddam's chief party heads and senior army officers, this ornery city quickly became an amped-up fortified stronghold teeming with cranky insurgents actively seeking the death and destruction of all Americans in Iraq, and before long it was serving as the primary stronghold for guerrilla attacks against the new Iraqi government as well as American troops across the country. In 2004, the Iraqi government declared a state of emergency in the city, and the marines were of course ordered to go in and clear out all pockets of resistance with extreme prejudice. Giving up the element of surprise in order to limit civilian casualties, the Marines broadcast warnings for two weeks in November, telling everyone to get the hell out of town unless they wanted a fight, and warning them that after a certain date all hell was going to break loose and anyone left in the city was going to be considered hostile. Then they went in.

In some of the most furious house-to-house fighting since World War II the marines stormed houses and fought street to street against a determined enemy who'd had plenty of time to set up hundreds of ambushes and booby traps. As battle raged on, Captain Doug Zembiec of the Second Battalion, First Marines (the "Lion of Fallujah") was a constant example to his men through his fearless leadership, scrapping for every inch of city, routinely refusing to leave men behind, and resolutely fighting through ambushes to recover the bodies of fallen and wounded marines. Elsewhere, First Sergeant Bradley Kasal, badly wounded in a house attack, blown up with shrapnel in his legs and shot seven times, dove on his friend to shield him from a grenade blast, then continued to fight the enemy with his pistol despite having lost 60 percent of his blood from dozens of white-hot shrapnel and bullets wounds throughout his body. The marines at Fallujah proudly upheld the badass reputation of their beloved Corps and never backed away from combat no matter how ball-shatteringly brutal, killing and capturing over 3,000 enemy fighters in combat while suffering only 95 dead and 560 wounded. Eight Navy Crosses were awarded for bravery in the battle, the most for any single battle since Vietnam.

34

TANGO MIKE-MIKE

Roy Benavidez vs. the North Vietnamese Army
Near Loc Ninh, South Vietnam
May 12, 1968

Sergeant Benavidez' gallant choice to voluntarily join his comrades who were
in critical straits, to expose himself constantly to withering enemy fire, and
his refusal to be stopped despite numerous severe wounds, saved the lives of
at least eight men. His fearless personal leadership, tenacious devotion to
duty, and extremely valorous actions in the face of overwhelming odds were
in keeping with the highest traditions of the military service, and reflect the
utmost credit on him and the United States Army.

—MEDAL OF HONOR CITATION

IT WAS SUPPOSED TO BE A SIMPLE RECON MISSION: A SMALL
TEAM OF ULTRA-ELITE ASSKICKING AMERICAN GREEN BERETS
INFILTRATING DEEP INTO THE THICK JUNGLES SEVERAL MILES
BEYOND THE CAMBODIAN BORDER, ON A SUPERCLASSIFIED
STEALTH MISSION TO GATHER INFORMATION ON NORTH VIET-
NAMESE ARMY TROOP MOVEMENTS. But when the evac choppers
limped back to base looking like they'd just been run through a gigan-

tic, helicopter-sized microwave, it was obvious that things hadn't gone all that smoothly for the men of the First Special Forces.

Thirty-three-year-old master sergeant Roy P. Benavidez was off duty attending church services, drinking his milk, taking his vitamins, and staying off drugs when the fighting began, but he'd spent the last ten minutes anxiously monitoring the radio chatter from the front. The twelve-man squad of Green Berets had stumbled into an intense firefight, and now Benavidez's brochachos suddenly found themselves surrounded and pinned down by a full battalion of hardcore North Vietnamese infantry—somewhere between five hundred and fifteen hundred veteran soldiers who weren't in the mood to sling their rifles and politely ask the Americans why the hell they were traipsing around eastern Cambodia with M16s, cameras, walkie-talkies, and bricks of c4. Nearly every man in the American unit had been wounded or killed in the early moments of fighting, and the three rescue choppers sent in to extract the team were driven off by intense ground fire from heavy machine guns and rocket-propelled grenades.

But if there's one thing you should probably know about the U.S. Army Special Forces, it's that the Green Berets don't screw around when it comes to kicking asses, and they don't leave a man behind for anything. So, when Sergeant Benavidez saw the remains of the crippled evacuation helicopters screeching to a halt on the base runway, he knew what he had to do. There was no way in hell he was leaving his good friends—his brothers—to die alone out there in the middle of the jungle surrounded by their enemies. The off-duty Texan grabbed a knife, a rifle, and as many medical bags as he could carry, and jumped onto the deck of the first chopper headed back to the front lines. Maybe he wasn't going to hold back the entire battalion by himself, but the least he could do was try.

When his helicopter reached the extraction zone, Benavidez got a good look at the situation on the ground, and it wasn't exactly a bunch of unicorns and rainbows frolicking in a lush meadow with a bunch of topless babes. Every man from the Special Forces squad had been wounded, many beyond the ability to fight, and they were completely surrounded and trapped by entrenched enemy troops with mortars and heavy machine guns. Benavidez, who was known by the badass code name Tango Mike-Mike, knew that these men weren't going to be able to get out to the landing zone, and the overabundance of large North Vietnamese death implements meant that the rescue helicopters weren't going to be able to get anywhere near the firefight without exploding into vapor.

So Sergeant Roy P. Benavidez did something that most sane people would never have even considered attempting—he told the pilot to find a nearby clearing and put him on the ground. Sure, maybe he was only one Green Beret surrounded by an assload of enemy soldiers, but so was John Rambo—and while Tango Mike-Mike may never have blown a dude up with an explosive-tipped arrow, the similarities between these two men would soon become painfully obvious to the NVA soldiers unlucky enough to be standing in his way.

Benavidez jumped down from the hovering chopper to the grass below, his rifle slung over his shoulder and his arms loaded with as many medical supplies and first-aid kits as he could carry. This one-man whirlwind of awesome then proceeded to sprint seventy-five meters under heavy enemy fire, hauling ass through fields of tracer bullets and stunned NVA troops looking at him like, "Who the hell is this guy?"

When Benavidez reached the Green Berets' position, he'd already taken a few bullets and some shrapnel in his face, arms, and head, but he was still upright and ready to bite off the enemy's faces and transform those faces into fertilizing manure using the transformative power of digestion. The situation wasn't good—everyone was hurt badly (including one hardass warrior who was somehow still fighting even though one of his eyes had been shot out), and now it was basically down to Sergeant Benavidez to organize this beat-to-hell team and hold off an entire NVA battalion almost entirely by himself.

He immediately sprang into action. Surrounded by a thousand or so NVA troops attacking him with AK-47s, RPGs, mortars, hand grenades, and everything else this side of the Cerebral Bore from Turok: Dinosaur Hunter, Benavidez provided morphine and first aid to the wounded, got the troops to a more defensible position, and directed their fire against enemy weapons teams. Despite being under intense fire Benavidez blazed back with his rifle, and when his M16 ran out of bullets, he picked up an AK off a dead NVA trooper and continued his one-man war against a horde of Commie bastards, holding them off and clearing a path for the team to be extracted to safety. Once the way out was clear, Benavidez threw some smoke canisters, signaling the rescue helicopter, and when a brave pilot landed to get the wounded men out of there, Benavidez yelled "GET TO DA CHOPPA!" Schwarzenegger style, then personally carried the wounded men to the evac point, making six separate trips to assist wounded soldiers and recover classified documents that had accidentally been dropped in the middle of the war zone.

While he was providing covering fire for the last of the Green Berets to board the chopper, however, disaster struck—an NVA frag grenade landed superclose to Benavidez, blowing this insane warrior off his feet and racking his back with shrapnel. As he hit the ground, an AK-47 bullet struck him in the abdomen. He lost consciousness, but only briefly.

When he came to moments later, he looked up to see a flaming, smoking wreck where the rescue helicopter had once been.

Now, Roy Benavidez was a warrior in all aspects of his life. This was a man who had seen adversity, looked it square in the face, then kicked it in the tater tots and did a tap dance on its lifeless, ball-less corpse. A man of Mexican and Yaqui Indian heritage who had battled racism nearly every day of his early adult life, Benavidez had somehow survived despite losing both of his parents by the time he was seven— when times had been hard and food was scarce, he'd dropped out of middle school to work backbreaking labor picking cotton to support himself and his brothers and sisters. In his sixteen years of military service, he had been through a lot of horrible stuff, but he'd always pulled through, no matter what the odds. Just three years earlier, when he was still with the 82nd Airborne, he'd stepped on a land mine during a patrol and the doctors told him he would never walk again. Not only did he walk out of the hospital, but he marched straight to the Green Berets office, volunteered for the Special Forces, and survived some of the toughest training the United States military had to offer. This is a guy who never gave the hell up for anything ever, and this would be no exception. If the North Vietnamese wanted him off their backs, they were going to have to do a hell of a lot better than just shooting him four times, blowing him up with a hand grenade, and shooting down the helicopter he'd just loaded up with wounded soldiers.

Within seconds of coming to, Sergeant Roy P. Benavidez was back on his feet, pulling survivors out of the flaming wreckage of the helicopter and organizing the stunned soldiers to set up a perimeter around the crash site. After checking on the injured guys, giving ammo to the men still capable of holding a rifle, and administering morphine and water to those who needed it, Benavidez immediately got back to the herculean task of holding off a battalion of enemy infantry and heavy weapons basically by himself. Taking yet another bullet in the thigh and bleeding badly, Benavidez got on the radio and started calling down tactical air strikes, attack helicopters, and napalm strafing runs on positions just a few meters away.

By the time the second set of rescue helicopters arrived, Tango Mike-Mike had been fighting nonstop for almost six hours straight. When the chopper hovered over the LZ, Benavidez once again started pulling men to the helicopter, loading the wounded on for extraction. The North Vietnamese, seeing their enemy escaping, decided to mount one final full-on human wave charge to crush these annoying Green Berets once and for all. With a terrifying yell, suddenly enemy troops came running in from every direction, bayonets fixed.

Benavidez was waiting for them. He'd been through too much to lose now.

In intense, no-holds-barred hand-to-hand combat, Roy Benavidez was bayoneted a couple times and had his jaw broken by a rifle butt, but he somehow continued to fight off a horde of swarming enemies with a knife, a bayonet, and a pistol while the remainder of his profusely bleeding Green Beret comrades got onto the rescue helicopter. Suffering from thirty-seven bayonet, bullet, and shrapnel wounds in various parts of his body, Benavidez used the last of his strength to pull himself on board the helicopter, the last man to leave the battlefield. The helicopter was completely riddled with holes, covered in blood, and without any functioning instruments, but the pilot somehow took off and got the team out of there. Benavidez lost consciousness as soon as he knew they were clear.

Sergeant Roy P. Benavidez of the First Special Forces was credited with single-handedly saving the lives of eight men. When a recovery team went through the site a few days later they discovered over thirty empty NVA foxholes with heavy weapons and saw the battlefield littered with more dead than they had time to count.

After the rescue helicopters landed at the base, Roy Benavidez's motionless body was carried off the helicopter, and after a preliminary inspection by the medical personnel on site, the hero was gently laid onto a gurney and wheeled into the coroner's office.

Just as they were zipping up his body bag, Benavidez used the last of his energy to spit in the doctor's face.

The mostly dead Benavidez was rushed into surgery immediately, then transferred to Saigon for many months of intensive rehabilitation. He received the Distinguished Service Cross for his heroic balls-out actions, and once the full details of the battle were declassified the award was upgraded to the Medal of Honor, the highest award for military bravery offered by the United States military. He lived to be sixty-three.

The first Hispanic American to receive the Medal of Honor was Corporal Joseph H. De Castro, the standard bearer of the Nineteenth Massachusetts Infantry in the American Civil War. During Pickett's Charge at the Battle of Gettysburg, De Castro was on the wall when it was stormed by Garnett's Brigade, and he ran forward, battled the standard bearer of the Nineteenth Virginia Infantry armed only with his regimental flag, and captured the enemy's colors. He then rushed back to his commanding general, handed him the captured banner, and immediately turned around and headed back into the fray.

Don't mess with Texas.

But there was one of the Norwegians who withstood the English folk,
so that they could not pass over the bridge, nor complete the victory.

—THE ANGLO-SAXON CHRONICLE

AGIS III (338 BC)

When Agis III succeeded his father as king of Sparta in 338 BC, Alexander the Great was off in Persia fighting Emperor Darius III. Figuring it was a good time to start judo-chopping fools in the throat, A3 rallied anti-Macedonian leaders to his cause, raised a decent army, invaded Crete, and started pushing his way toward Athens. Deciding this guy wasn't messing around, Alexander sent his most ill-mannered general and an army of forty thousand men to open a ten-gallon drum of thermonuclear whoop-ass on the Spartans. On the battlefield outside the city of Megalopolis (they just don't name cities like they used to), the two armies faced off in one of the largest battles ever fought between Greek armies in the Classical Age.

Despite being outnumbered roughly two to one, Agis wasn't going to back down from any opportunity to drench the tip of his spear in a few gallons of human plasma. Screaming the most horrible profanities he could think of, A3 charged out in front and fought like a madman, slashing people with his Spartan blades before receiving a disturbing number of reciprocal wounds across his chest, head, and legs.

Figuring he was dead, A3's guards recovered his severely wounded body, laid him on his shield, and began carrying him from the field. Remembering that he was a codpiece-wrecking Spartan king, A3 decided he wasn't going to let a few pesky mortal wounds keep him on the sideline while his army got destroyed.

So he ordered his army to retreat while he held off the onslaught. By himself.

Unable to stand and bleeding like a poorly wrapped package from the butcher shop, Agis got to his knees, gripped his blades and proceeded to hamstring enough charging enemy troops to buy his army time to withdraw. The Macedonians backed off slowly, presumably because they'd just gotten owned by one dude on his knees. Realizing they didn't want to get anywhere near his swords, someone chucked a javelin through his torso, probably catching at least a bit of his enormous balls in the process.

Sempronius Densus (AD 68)

Sempronius Densus was a grizzled old war veteran who took his job as a Roman imperial guard very seriously. So he wasn't about to run when he saw a few thousand mutinous Roman soldiers marching on the palace preparing to execute the emperor. It's important to keep in mind that Densus had no particular loyalties to Emperor Galba. He just knew that his job description called for him to put his life on the line to save the son of a bitch, and he didn't waste company resources when he was on the job. So Densus walked toward the mob, brandishing his Centurion Whacking Stick—a short cudgel that Roman officers used to administer backbreaking corporal punishment to out-of-line soldiers—and ordered the advancing men to stop.

Seeing that the bloodthirsty, sword-carrying mob of a thousand wasn't listening to the one dude with a stick, Densus pulled his *pugio*, a short dagger roughly half the size of the standard Roman sword. Thinking that should convey just how much business he meant, Densus once again screamed at them to stop. Again, they kept on marching. Certain that they'd been able to hear him that last time, Densus shrugged, probably said, "You asked for it," and lunged on the posse.

Completely surrounded, Densus fought the entire army by himself to defend a man he hardly knew. Hardened by years of combat, he slashed his way through the army, as Plutarch puts it, "for some time." His courageous stand ended when he was brought down by a blow to the back of the knee and enthusiastically murdered by the mob. Unfortunately for the guy he was guarding, the men operating his carriage were so awestruck by Densus's giant balls that they dropped their gear and ran for it, face-planting the emperor in the turf. Galba was killed and decapitated, and his head was paraded around town on a spear. Plutarch fails to mention what the mob did with Sempronius Densus's body, though we have to imagine it involved very little parading and a whole lot of staying the hell away. As slasher films would go on to teach us, you should never assume you've actually killed anyone who can kill that many people with just a knife.

Dian Wei (AD 197)

Dian Wei was a monstrous cruise missile of manslaughter, which is something you'd kind of have to be if you were a guy that had a name that's a homophone for "Diane." His skill as a peerless purveyor of battle-raging carnage helped him rise through the ranks of the military of the kingdom of Wei, until eventually he was hand-selected by the Wei king, a guy named Cao Cao, to serve as his personal bodyguard and the most badass bouncer in imperial China.

Dian's Last Stand took place during the Battle of Wancheng in AD 197, when he essentially curbstomped an entire army into submission by himself. Apparently, some local governor had gotten a little vexed when Cao Cao banged the dude's aunt, so he launched a surprise nighttime sneak attack on the Wei king's camp. When the hordes of oncoming warriors approached the gates, they found his personal bodyguard standing at the entrance brandishing a hulking pair of forty-pound axes.

Failing to appraise just how ready he was to make them look like they'd been on the losing end of a bear attack, the would-be assassins charged, and Dian commenced spraying the countryside with distasteful amounts of high-impact blood spatter. After playing giant-axe Whac-A-Mole with the unfortunate bastards who reached him first, Dian got superpissed and started cracking spines with his bare hands. He killed at least twenty enemies, perhaps more, before another group of assassins that had entered the building from a different direction attacked him from behind, and he was finally brought down by a rain of blows from every direction.

Dian had achieved his goal, however. Cao Cao escaped to fight another day and ended up almost single-handedly conquering all of China and eventually bringing the Three Kingdoms period to a close.

The Viking at Stamford Bridge (AD 1066)

In 1066, the Vikings took a break from ruining the lives of everyone in Europe and got ambushed at a place called Stamford Bridge. The Vikings didn't even have a chance to get their armor on before they noticed a tremendous army of Saxons ready to kick some ass and possibly take names (which they would probably mispronounce).

Only one of the Norsemen was ready for combat—an insane, nameless berserker conjured up from some nightmarish backwater asshole of hell who had positioned himself along the small bridge that separated the two armies. The Saxons, seeing that victory was just one frothing-at-the-mouth berserker away, charged forward to dislodge him. This proved to be a mistake.

In the horrific carnage that ensued, countless Saxon soldiers were transformed into a continuous volcanic eruption of gore as the Viking's mighty axe blows cleaved shields and helmets like they were made out of deliciously melty butter. Arrows, spears, and swords were useless against him. He seemed incapable of feeling pain, or really any sensation other than an unstoppable zest for killing every single person on Earth.

Eventually, one enterprising Saxon warrior figured out that, like any good video game boss, the Viking hero had a weak point. The Saxon went upstream, floated a barrel into the river, jumped in, and drifted down toward the bridge. As soon as he was below the scene of the battle, this cowardly douche canoe thrust his spear up between the planks, striking the Viking juggernaut in his lone weak point: the ballsack.

The Viking champion dropped down to his knees, as is to be expected from a guy who just took a piercing blow to the nads, and was subsequently cut down and probably used as firewood.

Frank Luke (AD 1918)

Lieutenant Frank Luke of the United States Army Air Service had earned a reputation as a lights-out "balloon buster," which sounds kind of like a lame-ass Atari game but was actually quite hardcore. Back before the days before UAVs, satellite imaging, and Imperial Psykers, artillery spotting and intelligence gathering were usually involved some dude standing around in a hot-air balloon with a pair of binocs and a radio. Popping one of these things usually meant you were saving trenchloads of infantrymen from a direct hit from a canister of mustard gas and human feces. Since the tethered balloons were also relatively stationary, high-priority targets, they were usually escorted by fighter squadrons and surrounded by ground-based antiaircraft batteries, making them pretty tough to get to. So, as lame as the name might be, the guy's job was basically the Death Star trench run at the end of Episode IV with the added bonus that you got to turn an enemy target into the *Hindenburg*.

He was good at it, too—in just seventeen days of combat he took out eighteen enemy aircraft, including one battle where he shot down two balloons and three fighter planes in the span of ten minutes. Another time he was on one of his trademark "lone-wolf" missions and his gun jammed, so he climbed out, fixed it in midflight, turned BACK AROUND, hunted his target down, and killed him.

Being such a balls-out deathmeister eventually caught up with Luke, however, and his last stand began in the skies above Murvaux, France, in 1918. He was alone, deep behind enemy lines and intent on taking out a large cluster of enemy aircraft and balloons. He started with a low run that barely cleared the treetops, but handily turned two German observation balloons into raging airborne infernos. However, while he was dodging ground fire from antiaircraft batteries and machine gun towers, a squadron of eight German fighters dove down from above and began pursuing him as well. It was beginning to seem like Frank Luke had gotten in over his head here.

Well, Luke wasn't going to piss his pants just because a couple hundred German soldiers were filling the air with more bullets than a Gradius boss battle. Luke continued to press the attack, surrounded on all sides by gunfire, and managed to take out the third and final balloon stationed at this aerodrome.

By this point Luke had been hit by enough gunfire that his plane and his body were both beginning to fail. Deciding there was time for one final run, and realizing there was nothing left in the sky for him to kill, he strafed six enemy infantrymen before crash-landing in an open field. Luke, never one to show any mercy or ask for it, now found himself surrounded on all sides by heavily armed German soldiers closing in on his position. Badly wounded and in hostile territory, Luke defied authority to the end. When the assembled enemy troops called for his surrender, he responded by un-holstering his .45 and capping a few more Germans. After he died from a chest wound, he became the first member of the USAS to ever receive the Medal of Honor.

THOMAS A. BAKER (AD 1944)

Sergeant Baker was part of a combined army and marine corps expedition to capture the Mariana Island of Saipan from the Japanese. In the days prior to his final stand, when his squad was pinned down by heavy machine gun fire, Baker grabbed a rocket launcher, ran within a hundred yards of a Japanese bunker, and turned it into cinder-block dust with one shot.

On the day he died, Baker found himself facing down a tricked-out banzai charge of roughly five thousand Japanese infantrymen flying bayonet-first out of the jungles and screaming "Long live the emperor!" Imperial Space Marine style. Seeing the enemy closing in on three sides, Baker simply cracked his knuckles, swore under his breath, and loaded a new clip into his weapon.

The initial wave left Baker seriously wounded by enemy rifle fire, but he refused to run, back down, or show any emotion other than anger. He stood his ground, firing like crazy with any weapons he could get his hands on, sometimes from as close as point-blank range. When he ran out of bullets, he Hulked up (Banner or Hogan, your choice) and beat off the attack with his fists, an admittedly ballsy move that left him even more messed up.

His weapon was smashed beyond recognition and he was bleeding profusely from a number of gaping wounds when some of his men came up and started carrying him from the battlefield. By this time the perimeter was buckling, the fight was lost, and the Americans were falling back to regroup, but Baker didn't give a damn. He knew that dragging his half-dead ass along the ground was only slowing down the withdrawal, so he told his men to prop him up against a tree facing the enemy. He borrowed a Colt 1911, made sure that it had a full eight-round magazine, and told his men to get the hell out of there while he bought them some time.

When the final American advance pushed forward and captured Saipan later that same month, they found Sergeant Baker's body propped up against the tree, facing his enemies right where they'd left him. The eight rounds the Americans had left him with, meanwhile, were now in the eight dead Japanese soldiers scattered before him.

35

ZVIKA FORCE

Lieutenant Zvika Greengold in the Yom Kippur War
Golan Heights, Israel
October 6, 1973

I was alone, and surrounded from the front and to the right.
I fired in both directions, destroying a number, moving backwards
all the time. They began a search with lights. I destroyed a few more.
The brigadier asked over the radio how many tanks I had. I told him:
"My situation isn't good and I can't tell you how many."

—ZVIKA GREENGOLD

ZVIKA GREENGOLD WAS SITTING AT HOME ON HIS KIBBUTZ ON
OCTOBER 6, 1973, SPENDING A QUIET, PEACEFUL DAY OBSERV-
ING YOM KIPPUR, THE HOLIEST DAY IN THE JEWISH CALENDAR,
WHEN SUDDENLY HE HEARD THE FAMILIAR BUT UNEXPECTED
SOUND OF ISRAELI FIGHTER JETS STREAKING THROUGH THE
SKY OVER HIS HOME. Zvika knew that no Israel Defense Forces ex-
ercises would ever be held on the most solemn of the Jewish high holy
days, and immediately knew that something was awry. He rushed to
his military radio, scanned through the frequencies, and frantically
searched for some indication as to what the mother hell was going on.

What he heard confirmed his darkest fears: war. Egyptian military forces had launched a sneak attack on Israeli positions in the Suez Canal, catching the IDF at the worst possible time. Even more alarming than this were the reports of Syrian armored troops launching an all-out assault on the Golan Heights to the north.

The Golan Heights had been captured by Israel in 1967, in the royal ass-stomping that was the Six-Day War. The Heights were of critical strategic importance to the survival of the fledgling Jewish state, for any Arab artillery batteries placed on their slopes would be easily capable of striking strategic targets deep within the heart of Israel. Greengold understood the gravity of the situation. He also knew that the IDF, having been caught unprepared, would be severely outnumbered and outgunned by the powerful Syrian armored tank divisions that were now pouring into the Heights. It was a time that would separate heroes from cowards, and Lieutenant Zvika Greengold of the Israel Defense Forces knew that it was time for him to be a total badass.

Lieutenant Greengold rushed to his room, threw on his military uniform, and ran out to the street, where he hitchhiked a ride to a nearby army base. When he arrived, Zvika was told that there wasn't much that could be done. But badasses like Zvika don't ever take that as an answer. They get things done. Lieutenant Greengold radioed in to brigade HQ and requested to be put in charge of his old tank company. His request was granted, and Greengold hopped in a half-track and hauled ass to the Israeli forward base at the Nafah crossroads—a critical choke point on the Israeli side of the Golan Heights, and a position that absolutely could not fall into Syrian hands.

When Zvika arrived at the Nafah base, he was dismayed to see that it was populated almost entirely by wounded IDF soldiers and that it had next to no operational military equipment. However, Greengold was intent on kicking some asses, and he was going to do it any way that he possibly could. He noticed two severely damaged IDF Centurion tanks sitting unmanned at the corner of the base, and immediately knew what he had to do. Zvika grabbed a hose, washed the dried blood out from the insides of the wasted tanks, fixed them up as best he could, grabbed the first seven or eight dudes he could find, and radioed brigade HQ, telling them that he had "a tank force" and was requesting permission to go into battle against the invading Syrians. HQ of course accepted, not having any clue that this newly commissioned "Zvika Force" consisted of two half-destroyed tanks led by one totally balls-out IDF Lieutenant.

By this point, night had settled in and the battle on the slopes of the Golan Heights was not going well for Israel. The IDF generally undergoes a large-scale demobilization for the Yom Kippur holiday, and as a result the Israelis had a force of two tank brigades (about 188 tanks) trying to defend a critical gateway to Israel against five full divisions of Syrian armor, consisting of over two thousand Russian-made T-62 main battle tanks. The beleaguered, demoralized, and outnumbered IDF troops on the front reported a great surge of confidence when they heard that their position was going to be reinforced by Zvika Force, only to be slightly confused and probably a little pissed off when two dudes rolled up in half-broken tanks claiming to be ready for action.

Zvika Force didn't even give a crap. The two tanks sped to the front lines at top speed and ran turrets-first into a huge mass of Syrian armor, blasting and firing at anything that moved.

After a particularly intense fight, Greengold suddenly realized that the other tank with him had disappeared into the darkness, and now the Syrians were closing in on his position with searchlights. At a time when most people would have spazzed out, panicked, and run away like schmucks, Greengold continued to roll backward, continually firing at the seemingly endless stream of Syrian tanks. He eventually relinked up with his other tank and the two of them executed hit-and-run night raids on Syrian positions. At one point, Greengold's tank was hit by enemy fire, severely burning the right side of his body and wounding him with shrapnel. Greengold wasn't about to be slowed down by this, so he simply got out of his flaming inferno of a tank and transferred over to the other Centurion in his command. The one-tank Zvika Force then spent the entire rest of the evening zipping around the Heights in a lone tank helping out Israeli forces wherever it could, frequently swooping in at critical moments from an unexpected direction to turn the tide of a skirmish in favor of the IDF.

At dawn on October 7, brigade HQ sent a company of IDF tanks to reinforce Lieutenant Greengold's command. Greengold deployed his Force in a defensive position along the Tapline Road, a critical crossroads that was crucial to the defense of the Heights. The Syrians had had enough of Zvika Force's bad attitude and sent an entire division of T-62s out to bombard this guy with enough tank shells to nuke Earth. In the grueling battle that ensued, the sixteen tanks of Zvika Force were able to hold their own at close range against seemingly impossible odds. In the heat of the battle, however, Greengold heard radio chatter that the IDF forward base at Nafah had fallen under attack by the Syrians. Realizing that the battle he was now embroiled in was merely a feint to pull Zvika Force out of position, Zvika and one other tank broke off from the battle and rushed back to defend Nafah.

Zvika Force rolled into Nafah base only to find IDF troops falling back in disarray in the face of overwhelming Syrian numbers. Zvika's tank driver saw this, exclaimed, "I'm too old for this s#@$," popped the hatch, and ran away—his nerves at this point were too fried to continue. (Also, that's kind of an obligatory line in any balls-out action movie.) Once again, Zvika was forced to change tanks in order to continue fighting.

The next several hours consisted of the one-man Zvika Force driving around to various strategic positions throughout the Nafah base, firing on the approaching Syrian hordes with determination and deadly precision in a desperate last stand. During the intense fight, an Israeli brigade commander drove up on the ridge behind Nafah base and radioed back to HQ, "There's no one in the camp except a single tank fighting like mad along the fences."

Despite being alone in a damaged tank, dangerously low on ammunition, and impossibly outgunned, Lieutenant Zvika Greengold battled furiously in the defense of his homeland. He was not going to let himself buckle in the face of the enemy, and he had no intention of allowing the Syrian forces to capture this critical foothold into Israel. He would die before he would let Nafah base be overrun.

Finally, IDF tank units reached Zvika's position to reinforce him. According to one source, "During a lull [in the battle] Zvika Greengold painfully lowered himself from his tank, covered with burns, wounds and soot. 'I can't go on anymore,' he said to the staff officer who had sent him into battle 30 hours before. The officer embraced him and found a vehicle to carry Greengold to the hospital." Greengold collapsed from exhaustion, having fought for his life in numerous high-intensity conflicts for over thirty hours straight and facing countless hair-raising battles. The Yom Kippur War would have to continue without him.

Lieutenant Zvika Greengold's actions on the Golan Heights in the opening days of the Yom Kippur War were critical to Israel's victory. His small force consisting of anywhere between one and sixteen tanks managed to halt the Syrian advance on the Tapline Road and stall the invasion long enough for substantial IDF reinforcements to reach the front and join the battle. His guerrilla-style tactics and high kill rate had the Syrian commanders convinced that they were fighting a much larger tank corps than they actually were—effectively allowing Zvika Force to hold off five full Syrian armored divisions with only two Centurion tanks (it helped that they were monitoring IDF radio frequencies, so that whole "Zvika Force" thing had thrown them into confusion as well). Thanks to his gallant actions, Nafah base never fell into enemy hands. Rather, in the days and weeks that followed, the IDF was able to push the Syrians completely out of the Golan Heights and reestablish a defensive line on the Syrian side of the pass—a line that marks the border between the two nations to this day. For his heroic actions in defense of his people, Zvika Greengold was awarded the Medal of Valor, the highest military honor offered by Israel. During his thirty-hour battle, Zvika was personally credited with over sixty tank kills, making him probably one of the most prolific and badassed tank aces of all time.

In 1967, Syria, Iraq, Lebanon, Egypt, and Jordan all banded together, equipped themselves with the most badass modern weapons the USSR had to offer, and mobilized three hundred thousand troops on Israel's borders. Before they could attack, however, Israel launched a preemptive strike, initiating the Six-Day War by sending a full wing of fighter-bombers screaming in under the radar and utterly destroying 416 enemy aircraft and dozens of air-defense stations in Egypt and Syria. With uncontested air superiority, Israel broke out its armored divisions, taking about five days to shellac seven full divisions of Arab armor and capture territory stretching from the Suez Canal to the Golan Heights. Israel lost about eight hundred killed in action and forty-six aircraft.

Originally designed by the British, the Centurion tank was nicknamed "Sho't" by the IDF, meaning "Scourge." Equipped with a 105-millimeter main gun, two 7.62-millimeter machine guns, and one .50-caliber machine gun, this thing is almost universally acknowledged as Israel's most badass tank.

Elsewhere in the Golan Heights, the men of Israel's Seventh Armored Brigade were involved in a similarly ultimate firefight with Syrian armor, battling for their lives in a tiny, fifteen-kilometer-long region known as the Valley of Tears. During fifty hours of nonstop fighting, pounded by both artillery and tank fire, the 80 tanks of the Seventh miraculously held off the brunt of a hardcore full-scale Syrian armored assault, knocking out 260 enemy tanks and over 500 other vehicles and preventing a full-scale breakout of Syrian armor into Israeli lands. Only seven IDF tanks survived the firefight.

36

THE LION OF PANJSHIR

Ahmad Shah Massoud Takes on the Soviets
Panjshir Valley, Afghanistan
December 24, 1979–February 15, 1989

We consider this our duty—
to defend humanity against the scourge of
intolerance, violence, and fanaticism.

—AHMAD SHAH MASSOUD, MUJAHIDEEN COMMANDER

THE STORY OF THE FALL OF AFGHANISTAN IS LIKE A HARDCORE
TOM CLANCY NOVEL, FILLED WITH POLITICAL INTRIGUE, BAD-
ASS COVERT SPY AWESOMENESS, AND OVERLY COMPLICATED
DESCRIPTIONS OF OPERATIONAL DETAILS NOBODY OUTSIDE OF
THE SOVIET GENERAL STAFF WOULD EVER REALLY CARE ABOUT.
It starts in 1979 with a dude named Hafizullah Amin. President
Amin (and the term "president" here is used more like *presidente-
por-vida* rather than "democratically represented official") was the
Communist dictator of Afghanistan, and a total bastard who enjoyed
carbonated beverages, atheism, blond women, and binge-purging po-
litical opponents by having them double-tapped in the dome execu-

tion style by his omnipresent army of secret police jackasses without so much as a sham trial. Needless to say, the whole "agree with me, renounce your religion, overthrow the bourgeoise, and bow before your new totalitarian overlord or prepare to taste your own brains" stuff didn't sit super well with his constituents—the uneducated, fanatically religious country folk in the mountains weren't exactly about to ditch fundamentalist Islam just because some asshole in a suit told them that going to mosque is for chumps, and the educated students and intellectuals from Afghanistan's urban areas saw through Amin's baloney and knew that he was a puppet of the Soviet Union trying to impress his Russian overlords by busting out his best impression of Josef Stalin having a bad hair day.

Amin knew that everybody totally hated his stinking guts, so in order to maintain his iron grip on Afghanistan he kept going to Russia and asking the Soviets for money, soldiers, advisers, and God knows whatever the hell else. Eventually the Russians got sick of having to hold this guy's dick every time he had to take a leak, so they had Amin's personal cook (who was secretly a KGB agent, by the way) pour some poison into Amin's Coke one day. Luckily for Amin, the plan failed—the carbonation in the soda negated the chemicals, rendering the poison inert through some scientific process I won't pretend to try to understand. When Chef Cyanide failed his mission, the Russians had to do it the old-fashioned way—on the evening of December 27, 1979, a team of Spetsnaz operatives stormed Amin's palace, annihilated the presidential bodyguards in a brief but unbelievably bloody firefight, and killed the dictator, his son, and anyone else unlucky enough to be standing in the building at the time. Shortly thereafter, teams of paratroopers combat-dropped into critical locations throughout the country, APCs and tanks rolled across the border from the Tajik SSR, and before anybody knew what the sweet Jesus cinnamon titties was going on, the men of the Soviet Fortieth Army controlled every road, airfield, communication building, government building, and armory in Afghanistan. Anyone who had a problem with that was executed Spetznaz style by being thrown into a spinning helicopter rotor.

Now, as you might have heard, Afghanistan is a tough place, and these folks don't really like it when world superpowers try to screw with them. This is a country that has fought off invasion attempts by Cyrus the Great, Alexander the Great, Victorian England, and Tsarist Russia, and these hardcore killmongers weren't about to start memorizing Marx just because they were outnumbered, outgunned, and completely overmatched by a modernized world superpower that technically should have dominated them in every possible tactical and strategic level. Within months, nearly two-thirds of the Afghan army defected against their Soviet masters. Urban populations rioted in the streets. Muslim clerics around the world declared a global jihad.

Of course, the USSR was no stranger to whiny citizens, and these guys knew how to handle uppity whippersnappers—with violence. They'd rolled into Afghanistan with artillery, antiaircraft guns, and T-72 tanks, but they weren't exactly ready for it when platoon-sized units of local tribesmen launched midnight raids on horseback carrying World War I–era bolt-action rifles and homemade Molotov cocktails, overwhelmed lightly defended garrisons, and left behind the skinned bodies of dead soldiers. This wasn't exactly the European land war against NATO that the Soviets had been training for.

Among the mujahideen ("soldiers of God") who fought the Russians, the most famous and well respected was a man named Ahmad Shah Massoud. Massoud was a twenty-seven-year-old warrior who had studied engineering at an Afghan military academy as a teenager, spoke fluent French, and was basically the Islamic version of Patrick Swayze's character from *Red Dawn*. From his base of operations in the mountainous Panjshir Valley, a ninety-mile canyon in the Hindu Kush mountain range, Massoud led three thousand untrained fighters against the entire Red Army for almost a decade, proving himself to be such an epic pain in the lunchbox that the Soviets tried to assassinate him four times and launched nearly a dozen full-scale military operations solely centered around messing him up on a molecular level.

Massoud started causing trouble for the Russkies almost immediately. The Panjshir Valley was only forty-five miles from Kabul, where nearly eighty-five thousand Red Army soldiers were stationed, but that didn't stop this guy from blasting the Marxism out of Soviet aircraft at Bagram Air Base and ambushing supply convoys heading along the Salang Highway (the only road in or out of Afghanistan), blasting everything that moved, and then running back to the Panjshir with armloads of explosives and AK-47s.

Massoud and his mujahideen Wolverines eventually caused so much trouble that the Reds decided they were going to go out there and kick every puppy and goat in the Panjshir Valley until Massoud started bleeding Leninism out of his eyes. The Reds launched two separate raids against him in 1981, and suddenly Massoud's civilian soldiers found themselves in intense firefights with Spetznaz commandos trained in everything from mine laying and AK-47 marksmanship to killing a dude by throwing scissors at him (and yes, they seriously train the Spetznaz in this). Both times the Soviets were sent back home to their manifestos, and Massoud's men helped themselves to all the bullets and artillery shells the Russians left behind.

Massoud's plan for defending a ninety-mile canyon against a motorized rifle division with only three thousnd men was pretty ingenious. He divided his force into ten-to-thirty-man squads, with each squad trained either in fixed defense or mobile response. When the Russians would roll through Panjshir, the fixed defense units would ambush the invaders, pinning them down with machine gun fire, while mobile response teams would move through a network of caves and flank the enemy from the high ground. If things got too bad and it looked like the defenders of that position were totally boned, everyone would retreat back to the next set of preprepared fortifications.

The raids on Soviet transportation continued, but Massoud really cramped the Soviets' style in April 1982 when he brought a bunch of mortars and RPGs to Bagram in the middle of the night and turned a decent number of Russian aircraft into giant jet-fuel-enhanced explosions. The USSR responded by craterizing the Panjshir Valley with air-to-ground bombs for a week straight, dropping paratroopers in the mountains, and then charging a column of fifteen thousand infantrymen in APCs right into the mountain pass that led into the valley. Massoud calmly evacuated civilians to the caves while the bombs rained down, fought off the Spetznaz, and then nonchalantly got into position so he could watch the column enter the valley. As soon as the first section of troops were safely in the Panjshir, Massoud detonated TNT on either side of the pass, cutting off a large portion of the vanguard, who, surrounded by dudes with antitank rockets pointed at them, immediately surrendered to avoid being popped like eggs in the microwave. Not only had Massoud survived a full-scale attack by a Westernized superpower without losing any meaningful number of fighters, but he'd also just acquired nine top-of-the-line Soviet T-72 main battle tanks, a couple of 155-millimeter howitzers, and a half-dozen trucks with antiaircraft guns mounted on the back.

The war continued like this for three more years—Massoud would avoid combat with the main Russian army, then run out and kick them in the taint when they weren't looking. The Russians attempted to get to him by depopulating the villages in the Panjshir, dropping napalm on entire cities, hammering the valley with artillery, and allegedly developing antipersonnel mines shaped like baby dolls for the sole purpose of blowing up children (this detail is still fiercely debated), but instead of weakening Massoud's support it only made him more psyched up to wipe out the invaders. The attacks continued—Massoud ambushed fuel convoys, blew up bridges, hit the garrisons at Kabul and Bagram, and tore up parts of the highway.

Finally, the Russians wised up to what the pickles was going on here. In 1985 they launched yet another assault—Panjshir VI—and this time they had a plan.

First came the Tu-24 Badger bombers, strafing the entire valley with napalm and conventional warheads. Then came the artillery barrage— heavy fire from giant cannons and MLRS rocket systems. Then Mi-24 Hind attack helicopters swooped in low over the valley, firing their air-to-ground rockets and heavy chain guns at anything that moved, while minesweeping trucks cleared Massoud's booby traps away from the entrance of the pass. Then the tanks, APCs, and infantry rolled in, supported, as usual, by elite paratroopers. Massoud reacted as he had reacted before—kick their asses, then slink into the caves when things get too hot—but this time the Spetznaz were in the caves waiting for them. They knew his tricks, and they hit him hard where he least expected it. It was a bloodbath. In April 1985, Russian television announced the complete and utter destruction of "Ahmad Shah Massoud and his criminal gang of dirty terrorist counterrevolutionaries" (or something like that) and showed glorified images of a fortified Soviet garrison sitting proudly at the base of the Panjshir Valley.

Two months later, in the middle of the night, the presumed-dead Ahmad Shah Massoud took a team of soldiers, cleared the minefield surrounding the garrison (in total darkness, no less), defeated a battalion of Soviet infantry with just a few thousand men, and captured 130 Red Army officers, including a general and several colonels. Simultaneous attacks were launched at two heavily guarded bases well outside Panjshir. When the Spetznaz commando team came to respond to the garrison's distress signal, Massoud's men shot down their transport and wiped them out at the landing zone.

Massoud had done a hell of a job holding out against Ivan for nearly six years. He caused nothing but trouble for the Russian government, which was stuck in an increasingly domestically unpopular war, and before long Massoud was appearing on French TV and getting golf tips from CIA operatives and Green Beret advisors attached to his camp. The final decisive blow, however, came in 1986, when the United States started shipping Stinger missiles to the Afghan people. This heat-seeking ground-to-air weapon blasted the ass out of Russia's attack and transport helicopters, and before long made it impossible for them to carry on the war. By February 1989, the Soviets had pulled out of Afghanistan entirely. Ahmad Shah Massoud had done his service to his people, and the Lion of Panjshir had done his duty to drive the invaders out of his beloved homeland.

The world's first air-to-ground attack helicopter, the Soviet Mi-24 Hind is one of the most hardcore gunships ever fielded and the bane of the mujahideen's existence. Equipped with twin-linked thirty-millimeter cannons in the nose and six wing-mounted hard points for rocket pods and missiles (not to mention enough room to transport eight fully equipped Spetsnaz commandos), this thing could travel 208 miles an hour, was utterly impervious to RPG and small arms fire, and had an armor-plated cockpit and rotors that could withstand direct hits from a twenty-millimeter antiaircraft shell. After seeing this thing in action, the Americans would crib the Soviets' idea and develop their own helicopter gunship, the AH-64 Apache.

American involvement in Afghanistan was increased exponentially thanks in particular to twelve-term congressman Charlie Wilson—a hard-partying, skirt-chasing Texan who staffed his entire office with hot babes (affectionally known as "Charlie's Angels") and spent his nights and weekends drinking whiskey and getting investigated by the House Ethics Committee for various drug, booze, or hooker-related transgressions. Wilson, who despite all these moral outrages still managed to be played by Tom Hanks in the movie about his life, was the man largely responsible for increasing the CIA's Afghanistan covert ops budget from $500,000 to $600 million, bringing an influx of weapons and aid to the mujahideen, and providing the Soviet Union with their own private Vietnam.

After the withdrawal of the Soviet Union, Massoud faced a new threat—the Taliban. Massoud and his forces, known as the Northern Alliance, hated the Taliban and fought militantly against them for control of the government. When the Taliban won, he continued to fight a guerrilla war against the brutal regime, arguing that a democratic, free government be installed. He was assassinated by al-Qaeda operatives on September 9, 2001, two days before the terrorist attacks on the World Trade Center.

37

WHO DARES WINS

The Iranian Embassy Siege
London, England
May 5, 1980

"Look, these guys have killed people. They've threatened to kill others.
They're baddies. And they're on our home turf."

—SERGEANT JOHN MACALEESE, BRITISH SPECIAL AIR SERVICE

AT 6:30 P.M. ON THE EVENING OF MAY 5, 1980, THE BODY OF TWENTY-FOUR-YEAR-OLD IRANIAN PRESS SECRETARY ABBAS LAVASANI WAS ROLLED OUT ONTO THE FRONT STEPS OF THE IRANIAN EMBASSY IN LONDON. He had been shot in the head after having bravely volunteered to be the first hostage executed by a highly trained team of ruthless gunmen. Now the terrorists inside the building issued a warning—they would execute one hostage every half hour until their ridiculous demands were met.

But the United Kingdom doesn't negotiate with terrorists. It sends the Special Air Service to shoot them in the face.

Everyone knew the operation was going to be risky. Situated in the heart of London, the Iranian Embassy building consisted of fifty rooms along four floors, many of which were covered with booby traps. Inside were six jumpy terrorists armed with submachine guns, pistols, and hand grenades. The exact positions of the terrorists were unknown, and each gunman had been given strict orders to start wasting the nineteen British and Iranian hostages at the first sign of trouble. The SAS would need to get in, clear the house, and kill every baddie inside before even one of those assholes had enough time to pull the pin on a hand grenade. Conservative estimates predicted 40 percent civilian casualties in the operation. Not great, but better than the 100 percent casualties if they did nothing.

Dressed in all black, and equipped with MP5 submachine guns, nine-millimeter Browning automatic pistols, fireproof Kevlar body armor, flashbangs, CS gas grenades, and scary-as-hell-looking A6 respirator gas masks, five teams of badass counterterrorist SAS assault troopers would simultaneously enter the structure through four entry points. First, a team on the roof would lower a charge and blow out the skylight in the ceiling to create a diversion. Then, two teams would enter through the back door on the ground floor and clear the reception area and the basement. Another team would climb onto the second-floor balcony and breach the windows, and the final team would rappel down the back of the building, smash in through the third-floor windows, and make a mad dash to the two rooms where the hostages were probably being held. Oh, and the entire thing was going to happen in broad daylight on national television with news crews from around the world set up in a perimeter around the embassy. The mission was code-named Operation: Nimrod, as in, "You'd have to be a nimrod to screw with the SAS."

It took the SAS less than an hour to get in position for the attack. While police negotiators kept the terrorist leader busy humoring his douchebag requests and pretending he gave a crap, assault teams moved into position. At 7:25 p.m., they received the order to kick ass. The skylight charge detonated with a crazy-loud bang that shook the building, pasted the entire reception area with a shotgun blast of broken glass, and filled much of the structure with black smoke. Almost simultaneously, the other teams sprang into action.

Four SAS operatives rappelled down the back of the building on ropes, moving fast to get to the hostages before the terrorists opened fire on them. The first dude down breached the third-floor window like Bruce Willis on the side of the Nakatomi building in *Die Hard*, but the guy right behind him wasn't so lucky—the dude got tangled up in his ropes on the way down. While the other two team members tried to help untangle their buddy, the lone soldier on the second floor looked through the windows and saw a terrorist inside desperately trying to set fire to the carpet with a pack of matches—he'd already soaked the entire room in gasoline, and within seconds the entire place would be in flames.

The lone trooper busted through the glass, lined up the terrorist in his sights, and pulled the trigger. He got the "dead man's click"—his MP5 had misfired. The terrorist stared open-mouthed at him for a second, but when the SAS man quick-drew his pistol and opened fire, that guy got the hell out of there and started running for the hostage room. The SAS trooper rushed after him.

On the ground floor, teams crashed through the front and back windows with sledgehammers and breaching charges and entered the structure. In the main ground-floor corridor the terrorist leader, a cold-blooded murderer named Selim, dropped the phone, pulled his pistol, and prepared to move into action. He turned to run to the hostage room and was immediately confronted by one hostage he really didn't want to screw with—Trevor Lock, a British police constable who worked as the security guard for the embassy. Lock, finally seeing an opportunity for the first time during the six-day siege to stuff this guy's gob with a knuckle sandwich, charged the terrorist leader like a rampaging rhino, smashing into him with his body, flattening the dude with a nasty tackle that sent him to the ground and knocked the pistol from his hand. Lock, who outweighed the lanky terrorist by about fifty pounds, immediately overpowered Selim, powerbombed him to the mat, and started ruthlessly pummeling him repeatedly in the face. Seconds later, he looked over to see two small green "lemon-looking things" skitter across the carpet toward him.

The flashbang grenades went off in a tremendous explosion of deafening sound and blinding light. When Lock finally regained his senses, he was staring at four gigantic, heavily armed dudes in gas masks and Selim was laying on the ground with fifteen bullets in him. The SAS team continued clearing the ground floor. They rushed into the next room, found another Tango firing his pistol, and drilled him as he dove for cover behind a couch.

Upstairs, the lone SAS soldier was racing down the third-floor hallway, desperately trying to catch the terrorist before he started offing hostages. The shell-shocked terrorist screamed to his buddy, who opened the door to the hostage room to see what in the name of John T. Crapper was going on, and when that guy saw his fleeing buddy get capped in the back of the head with one round from a Browning pistol, he immediately spun and sprayed a burst of automatic weapons fire from his Scorpion SMG into the crowd of hostages. He was capped by an SAS sniper from across the street almost immediately, but not before he'd killed one hostage and wounded another.

The hostages were now free, and the SAS teams on the first and second floors immediately started passing them down the steps and out the door. As the terrified embassy staff ran down the structure's main stairwell, however, one woman grabbed an SAS man and pointed out that one of the "hostages" was actually a terrorist—the SAS trooper couldn't open fire on him in the middle of a crowd of hostages, so the dude cracked the terrorist douchebag in the skull with the butt of his

MP5, kicked him down the steps, and sprayed him with bullets. The dead man's hand opened to reveal a grenade—luckily he'd been shot just before he'd had the chance to pull the pin.

The rest of the hostages were brought outside, handcuffed, and searched for weapons. It was here that the sixth terrorist was found when one of the hostages pointed him out. The SAS grabbed him, took him out behind the building, prepared to unceremoniously shoot him, but then realized that it probably wasn't a good idea to cap an unarmed dude on national television. The terrorist was arrested and sentenced to life imprisonment.

The entire battle took seventeen minutes. Five terrorists lay dead, one was in police custody, and eighteen of the nineteen hostages had been rescued in one of the most high-profile (and badass) counterterrorist raids ever attempted. The only SAS casualty was the one man who was slightly crispy after being burned while entering the second floor.

The terrorists had demanded two main things—first, they wanted freedom for the Iranian region known as Arabistan, and second, they demanded the release of ninety-one Arab prisoners who were being held in Iran. This didn't really work out great for them—Iran had already executed all those prisoners, and since the Arabistan region accounts for roughly one-tenth of the planet's oil production, Iran wasn't really in the mood to give it up.

———

The SAS was formed during World War II, originally as a special operations unit aimed at taking down German airfields and bases in North Africa. Commanded by hard-as-hell guys like Ulsterman Paddy Mayne (a dude so tough he had to be bailed out of prison Marcus Fenix style before he could be recruited to the service), these dudes would haul ass across the desert in jeeps armed with giant machine guns on the back, race onto airstrips deep behind enemy lines, shoot the entire place up, plant explosive charges on the Nazi aircraft, and then peel out of there before anybody had any clue what the heck just happened.

———

Germany developed the world's first dedicated counterterrorism force in the wake of the 1972 Munich Olympics disaster: the Grenzschutzgruppe 9, better known as GSG-9. These German Jack Bauers got a chance to show their stuff in 1977, when a group of asshole Palestinian terrorists hijacked a Lufthansa civilian airliner, capped the pilot, and forced the Boeing 737 down in Mogadishu. That night, while Somali police created an explosion on the runway to distract the terrorists, GSG-9 (and a few SAS) operatives sprinted down the tarmac with black ladders, climbed up onto the wings on either side, and kicked in both emergency doors at the same time. The passengers reported seeing a bunch of black-masked Germans screaming for them to hit the deck, hearing the deafening bang of a few flash grenades, and watching the GSG-9 troops rush in, MP5s blazing. The entire battle was over in less than five minutes—three terrorists were killed, one was critically wounded, and all of the hostages were rescued.

38

DESERT STORM

The First Iraq War
February 24–27, 1991
Kuwait, Iraq, and Saudi Arabia

"Our strategy in going after this army is very simple.
First we're going to cut it off, and then we're going to kill it."

—GENERAL COLIN POWELL

IN JANUARY 1991, IRAQ HAD THE THIRD-LARGEST ARMY IN
THE WORLD. Half a million tough-as-hell veterans hardened by over a
decade of constant warfare, supported by tens of thousands of modern
battle tanks, artillery pieces, fighter aircraft, antiaircraft missile batteries, and infantry fighting vehicles produced and supplied by world
superpowers. Arrayed in heavily fortified bunkers along the coast of
the Persian Gulf, supported by the heavy muscle of elite Republican
Guard armored divisions, this was one of the most formidable armies
in the history of modern warfare.

By March 1, it had almost completely ceased to exist.

Saddam Hussein had managed to amass this seemingly unstoppable force of land-based asskicking thanks to his ability to foster good relationships with both the United States and the Soviet Union. The Sunni Muslim nation of Iraq had spent the previous decade or so locked in a never-ending death feud with her Shi'ite neighbor Iran, and since neither America nor the USSR could stand Iran they both decided to be chill and pitch in as many MiGs, T-72 battle tanks, and shoulder-mounted antitank rockets as the Iraqis could carry in the hope that they'd blast the crapballs out of Iran and put an end to this whole ayatollah nonsense once and for all. Saddam Hussein paid for his epic collection of badass military hardware by borrowing a ridiculous amount of cash from his monstrously oil-rich neighbor, Kuwait, and then, once the Iran War was over, he decided that the best way to repay the massive debt he'd accumulated was simply by marching his now-gigantor army across the border, conquering Kuwait, declaring it a province of Iraq, and then zeroing out all the money he owed them.

While this is colossally diabolical and/or quite possibly "the bomb" (I guess this is what you get for helping your tyrannical dictator neighbor buy a garage-full of artillery pieces) on the part of Saddam Hussein, when the autocratic mustachioed madman moved his tank divisions into Kuwait City the response from the rest of the world was pretty much the same: this aggression will not stand, man.

So now, despite the fact that almost all of Saddam's forces were entrenched along the coast of the gulf in a bunker network that roughly resembled German defenses at Normandy wigged out on steroids, and even though the military geniuses in the Pentagon were predicting massive, "oh-God-the-humanity"-style casualties resulting from the head-to-head collision of world superpowers, the United States assembled a coalition of dozens of countries from across the world and prepared to go in there and kick Saddam so hard in the nutsac that his eyeballs popped out and were replaced with testicles.

What resulted was one of the most one-sided asswhompings in the long, bloody, storied history of warfare.

The U.S.-led coalition only outnumbered the Iraqis by a count of 600,000 to 545,000, but the Iraqis had quite a few force multipliers working in their favor—they were hunkered down in readily defensible positions, bulletproof bunkers, and they had the ability to drop an ass-load of chemical and biological weapons all over everyone in the world without feeling even the slightest bit bad about it. But the Americans had a plan. Devised by hardass generals like "Stormin'" Norman Schwarz-kopf, a Vietnam vet who had once received a medal for running into a minefield to pull a wounded, legless man to safety, and Colin "KaPow" Powell, a man who once ripped a burning helicopter apart with his bare hands to pull wounded crew members out of the fiery inferno, the U.S. plan basically amounted to this: you jerks have fun sitting in your cute little concrete bunkers along the coast, we're going to haul ass through the middle of the Saudi Arabian desert Khalid ibn al-Walid style, sneak-attack you from the direction you least expect it, and then sucker-punch you in the spine with Apache helicopters until you're barfing out kidney stones.

After every ground-attack aircraft in the known universe spent forty days relentlessly teabagging every single MiG, radar station, communications structure, bridge, and road between Baghdad and Kuwait City with their gigantic bombs, and a diabolically badass counterintelligence operation that involved stuff like cracking the enemy communications ciphers and faxing fake orders to Iraqi command posts, the coalition finally launched its initial attack on enemy positions at 4:00 a.m. on February 24, 1991.

The first wave came right where Saddam Hussein expected it. U.S. marines and Saudi Arabian forces hit the beaches of the Persian Gulf, marching right into the teeth of the enemy in what was strategically planned to be a feint to draw the attention of the enemy. While the marines were cutting through the Iraqi defenses with a degree of success neither side had expected (this is what you get for underestimating the marines, I suppose—it also helped that they simultaneously pushed in from the flank, crossing over thirty miles of a seemingly impenetrable minefield in a single day), the main body of the coalition force advanced along a ridiculously huge five-hundred-mile-wide front on the Saudi Arabian border. Despite oil field fires blackening the sky and making visibility incredibly difficult, American airborne, air cavalry, and special operations divisions dropped into the middle of the desert, blew through the lightly defended Iraqi installations, and set up forward bases while the armored units rolled forward like an unstoppable juggernaut of mechanized awesome.

February 25 opened the way the 24th ended—with severe gluten-free organic free-range asskickings. Airborne troops jumped from their newly established forward operating bases, this time dropping smack in the middle of Highway 8, the only road from Baghdad to Kuwait City. Now, you'd think the purpose of this would be to prevent Saddam's reinforcements from advancing to the battle zone, but in reality the objective here was much more sinister—it was to lock them IN to Kuwait City and cut off any possible avenue of retreat. Within forty-eight hours of combat, the coalition was already behind enemy lines.

Elsewhere on the 25th, the allied armored divisions made their first contact with the Iraqi tank units, moking the F out of them like a hyperactive samurai cleaving through the canned food section at the grocery store. The Iraqi frontline units were crumpled up into tiny aluminum foil balls and thrown in the garbage can, and down in Kuwait City the marines dug in and fought off dozens of coordinated counterattacks by division-sized forces.

Things were already looking rough for our Iraqi friends, but on February 26 the allies delivered the terminal coup de grâce that sundered the enemy's morale and turned the third-most-formidable army on Earth into a disorganized assortment of dudes ready to surrender to any military unit more organized than a CNN camera crew. It was on this day that the U.S. and Saudi armored divisions—which, by the way, were formed up in the middle of the desert with only their handy-dandy new out-of-the-box GPS systems to guide them—made a coordinated ninety-degree turn, crashed turrets-first into the flank of the Republican Guard forces, and TomTomm'ed their way to victory.

Nowadays the Iraqi Republican Guard gets an unfairly bad rap. These guys weren't always a laughable joke in the footnotes of history— they were a grizzled cadre of veterans who were fanatically loyal to Saddam, trained by Soviet tank commanders, and hardened by dozens of desert land battles against Iranian armored units. They all piloted relatively new Soviet-built T-72 battle tanks—nothing to laugh at in 1991— and were the best troops Saddam Hussein could field, staring through their laser range finders against American, British, Canadian, Saudi, Syrian, and Egyptian tank crews who had never seen live-fire combat before in their careers.

Unfortunately for the Guard, however, the American M1A1 Abrams' battle tank had a range of fire a thousand meters longer than the T-72's, was kitted out with thermal and night-vision imaging scopes, boasted almost-unhittable sloped frontal plate armor that deflected enemy tank shells pretty damn effectively, and shot 120-millimeter depleted-uranium shells at such a velocity that it wasn't uncommon for an American shell to hit a T-72, blow it to crap, punch through the other side of the tank, and then hit and kill a SECOND tank behind it. It was like that scene from *Indiana Jones and the Last Crusade* where Indy shoots through three guys with a Luger, only real life and with a mildly radioactive explosive shell that was about five inches in diameter.

They were boned. Like, seriously boned. As in, when the first wave of M1A1s started rolling in, the Iraqi commanders thought their buddies were getting blown up by aircraft, because they were getting hit by tanks parked outside range of their RADARS.

Probably the best example of this is the battle for 73 Easting, when twelve tanks and a few Bradley IFVs of the Second Armored Cavalry Regiment got mixed up in a terrible sandstorm and ended up stumbling dead into the center of two Iraqi Republican Guard armored divisions—two hundred T-72 tanks entrenched in a reverse-slope defense behind a minefield, with a reserve force held back for a counterattack and an infantry screen equipped with antitank rockets and RPGs. The Second ACR, commanded by the awesomely named Hugh McMaster, plowed ahead, surrounded on all sides by enemies spitting lead at them from point-blank range, but they didn't even slow down— the M1A1s, seventy-ton armored sledgehammers, ripped up the desert at thirty miles an hour, accurately throwing out four forty-five-pound armor-piercing shells every minute. The American tanks raced ahead, surrounded by gigantic fireballs of death, causing an uncontrollable tsunami of McDisaster as T-72 rounds bounced off them from every direction. The Americans used an old Erwin Rommel strategy, using their speed to strike hard and throw the enemy off balance, and since the only way to move the turret of a T-72 is for a crew member to turn it with a hand crank, the Iraqi gunners had a tough time keeping up. In ninety minutes, the twelve American tanks had destroyed 180 Iraqi T-72s and killed or captured thousands of enemy soldiers. The Second ACR suffered one KIA and twelve wounded, and had to change a flat on one of their Bradleys.

Back in Kuwait City, the marines seized the airport and the outskirts of the city, and continued kicking so much ass that the Iraqis decided to bail out and run for their lives. The Iraqis loaded up commandeered Kuwaiti civilian cars with pilfered loot and hauled ass down the main road out of Kuwait City as fast as they could, putting the entire Iraqi military in a nice little four-lane strip that was like a shooting gallery for ground-attack aircraft. In one day of bombing, a three-mile stretch of the newly dubbed "Highway of Death" became so clogged with burned-out overturned vehicles that it looked like a scene from the *Walking Dead.*

At this point the fat lady was belting out "Camptown Races," and as American Apaches and tanks aerated the last of Iraq's land troops, columns of Syrian and Egyptian forces entered Kuwait City, officially liberating it from Saddam's clutches. All it took was a hundred hours of near-constant kidney-punching awesomeness to completely obliterate thirty-eight of the forty-three divisions in the Iraqi military. Casualty estimates range from 1,500 to 150,000 depending on who you ask, but most folks can agree that about 8,500 Iraqi vehicles were Hindenburged in the onslaught and around 83,000 soldiers surrendered to coalition forces. The allies lost 390 dead and had 21 prisoners of war taken, all of whom were returned immediately after the cease-fire.

The man who finally captured Saddam Hussein was an Arab-American Special Forces operator from St. Louis known only as Samir—an Iraqi-born badass who was forced to flee his homeland after participating in a failed attempt to overthrow Saddam immediately following Desert Storm. When this hardcore SpecOps soldier triumphantly pulled the deposed Iraqi dictator from his spider hole after the 2003 Iraq War, his first instinct was, naturally, to emasculate him in his native language, telling Saddam (in perfect Arabic, no less), "If you were a man you would have killed yourself!" Saddam responded by calling Samir a traitor. Samir objected, so he punched Saddam Hussein in his face a couple times and then spit on him. It was probably the only time in his life that Saddam was ever treated like that by an Iraqi. You know, until they hanged him.

———

One of the most lopsided armored asskickings of all time took place in June 1944, when the highest-scoring tank ace of all time—Captain Michael Wittman of the First SS Panzer Division—looked out the window of his command post and saw an entire brigade of British armor rolling right past him. Instead of kicking back and radioing in for backup, Wittman did the last thing most people would expect—he jumped into his Tiger tank, drove right into the middle of their formation, and laid waste to a trio of tanks. With tanks firing at him point-blank from every direction, Wittman continued down the line, knocking the enemy tanks out with deadly precision, never missing once. He destroyed between fifteen and thirty enemy tanks and APCs in under an hour before an AT gun finally knocked his drive gear out of action, at which point he bailed out of the tank, fled fifteen kilometers on foot out of town, and regrouped with his unit. He finished the war with 138 enemy tank kills and 132 antitank-gun kills.

———

While seizing the high ground above Kuwait City, one large-balled M1A1 commander named Jim Warner, concerned that a close-range shot from a nearby enemy tank would possibly shoot through his target and inflict friendly fire casualties on an American tank just beyond it, actually got out of his own vehicle, ran over to an Iraqi T-55, pulled the cover off the engine with his bare hands, dropped a thermite grenade in there, and ran back to the cover of his M1A1 before the thing blew the hell up.

Say what you want about the air force being a bunch of pussies or whatever, but for my money it doesn't get a whole lot more badass than the A-10 Warthog ground-attack aircraft. The thing is a damned flying tank from hell equipped with a badass thirty-millimeter Avenger Gatling gun the likes of which would make the Terminator soil his extratight leather pants. The Avenger (even the name is badass) fires armor-piercing rounds capable of tearing gigantic sucking wounds in even the most formidable Soviet-built battle tanks, and can be switched over on the fly to dispense forty-two hundred high-explosive rounds per minute when it needs to grind less heavily armored crap like trucks, artillery, APCs, SUVs, hang gliders, and renegade hot dog stands into a white-hot pile of scrap metal shavings.

If that doesn't float your boat, the thing's also equipped with enough explosives to blast the moon into about eight billion tiny inedible cheese wheels. It's got a few superaccurate laser-guided air-to-ground missiles and various other high-yield bombs for taking out bunkers, SAM emplacements, radar sites, and grounded fighters, and also has air-to-air missiles in case it needs to show some enemy jets what it's like to be on the receiving end of some good old-fashioned red, white, and blue American Grade-A top-choice beef sirloin whoop-ass. It's also so heavily armored that it can withstand direct hits from armor-piercing and high-explosive projectiles up to thirty-seven millimeters in size, can survive having a 2002 VW Beetle launched at it at extremely high velocity by a Russian-made Volkswagen cannon, and has heat-shielded engines (and sundry other countermeasures) so no Commie Nazi Terrorist Unitarian bastards can jam a heat-seeking missile up its ass. Seriously, on one occasion, an American combat pilot named Kim Campbell (whose call sign, awesomely enough, is "Killer Chick") got the hell blown out of her aircraft by a few million antiaircraft rounds that blew out her stabilizers, destroyed the hydraulic systems, nearly blew off a wing, and riddled the fuselage with over two hundred shrapnel holes, but Captain Campbell was still able to fly the thing a hundred miles back to base and land it safely.

The A-10 is like the grizzled old-school linebacker of the United States Air Force. It's not flashy, it's not superfast, it's not going to do like twenty barrel rolls just to try and prove to you how huge it's junk is—it just shows up, ruins everyone's life, and goes home. Even its name is a good indicator of the fact that this plane doesn't screw around. Think of it this way: while all those other hotshot fancy-pants jets are out there flying around doing loop-de-loops, feathering their hair and listening to "Danger Zone" with nicknames like "Eagle," "Falcon," "Tomcat," and "Raptor," the A-10 is the Warthog. Have you ever seen a warthog before? It ain't pretty. It's not a graceful or elegant creature. It's an angry pig that roots around in crap all day and gores lesser creatures to death with its giant awkward tusks. That's like the A-10. It's not designed to get out there like a purebred poodle and perform air shows at the Eukanuba Nationals, it's designed to fly out, support the infantry, go toe-to-toe with a company of badass tanks and jack their front ends up like a AAA tow truck driver on an emergency service call. In terms of getting down and dirty, it's like a women's competitive mud-wrestling champion among beauty queens.

Probably the most telling indicator of the Warthog's ultimate badassitude comes from its numbers against the Iraqis in 1991. During Desert Storm, A-10s flew eighty-one hundred sorties and were credited with killing 987 tanks, 926 artillery pieces, 1,106 trucks, 51 SCUD missile launchers, and a buttload of support vehicles and bunkers. I mean, holy cow, fighter pilots get a medal after *five* kills . . . these Desert Storm A-10 pilots were racking up those kinds of numbers on their bathroom breaks.

39

SHOOTOUT AT A MEXICAN HACIENDA

Don Alejo Garza Tamez
Victoria, Mexico
November 14, 2010

Say hello to my little friend!

—Tony "Scarface" Montana

THE CRIME SITUATION IN RURAL MEXICO THESE DAYS IS SORT OF MESSED UP. Sure, this may be an overly harsh characterization of what's actually going on out there, but with all the killing, maiming, and general anarchy being perpetuated by a seemingly endless horde of frothing-at-the-mouth, completely unscrupulous drug cartels, assassins, and other *Walker, Texas Ranger*–grade villainy, I really don't think it would be out of line to characterize the conditions south of the border as being "problematic" or perhaps even "whack"—much in the same way a person might define the warlord-infested mountains of southeast Afghanistan as "marginally unruly" or "slightly dangerous."

It seems like every day there are new reports of bandits and drug cartels massacring innocent people, fear and intimidation have become a way of life for some particularly oppressed regions, and the police and military are having a tough time containing these modern-day warlords simply because they're completely outnumbered, outmatched, outgunned, and undermined by corrupt and/or newly dead government officials. I don't have a criminal justice degree or anything, but it's a bad sign for your country's stability when the cops are outmatched by the superior firepower of a bunch of guys who are basically a cross between fedora-deficient 1920s Chicago bootleggers with face tattoos and the bad guys in *Mad Max Beyond Thunderdome*.

The worst tragedy of this gigantic crap-vortex of a situation is that there's not a whole hell of a lot that average Mexican citizens can do to improve their situation in life. Any noncorrupt, nondead police or politicians they elect to office immediately become either corrupt or dead, and it's usually not a great idea for your everyday average Joe (average Jose?) to go out there and start talking trash to an irritable roided-up horde of conscienceless gangsters with unfettered access to high-powered assault weapons and no compunction about beheading nuns using shanks they fashioned from the bones of murdered orphan kittens. Of course, if everyone in the world backed down and sucked on oppression every time they faced off against overwhelming odds and ultimate evil, there wouldn't be guys like Don Alejo Garza Tamez: guys who look the archenemies of humanity in the face and instinctively rip off a no-look rabbit punch uppercut to the sac.

Don Alejo Garza Tamez was a man who had worked his entire life. Starting with a manual labor job in his father's sawmill as a child, eventually working his way up to becoming the owner of a successful farm and ranch in Victoria, Mexico, the seventy-seven-year-old Don Alejo was an old-school badass from back in the days when any time anybody wanted to go somewhere they had to walk uphill both ways in the snow while Cyclopes lobbed boulders at them.

Don Alejo had owned his quiet ranch for a few decades (give or take), having bought it with money he earned himself through hard work, dedication, ambition, and a strict policy of not killing every single person who disagreed with him, so you can probably imagine what was going through this dude's head on the morning of Saturday, November 13, 2010, when a truckload of cartel gangsters rolled up to his front door and told him he had twenty-four hours to get the hell out of town and hand his property over to them. I'll spell it out for you—he wasn't happy. When he expressed his unwillingness to fork over his life's work just because some *ese* was waving a Beretta in his face in a semithreatening manner, the gangsters told him they were coming back that night, and that if he was still hanging around, he was a dead man.

But they had failed epically in their efforts to intimidate a seventy-seven-year-old man with balls of granite.

He told them he'd be waiting for them.

No sooner had the unmarked pick-up trucks sped out of sight down the dusty road than Don Alejo went into action. He quietly called over his employees and told them to leave early and take the weekend off. Then, without saying a word, he opened his cellar door and went down to his secret what-the-hell-is-going-on-down-here *Terminator 2* subterranean weapons bunker loaded with enough weaponry and ammo to make the Vault system from Fallout look like the frozen food aisle at the grocery store, grabbed as many weapons and bullets as he could carry, and started turning his home into an impenetrable fortress of destruction. Every window and door in the hacienda was stocked with a hunting rifle and a stack of ammunition. When the trucks and cars of the cartel showed up at his ranch at 4:00 a.m. the next morning, Don Alejo was there waiting for them, just like he said he'd be.

Unfortunately for the douchebag thugs of this particular jerkburger cartel, Don Alejo was big into MMA—which, as Danny Trejo will tell you, of course stands for "Massive Mexican Asskicking"—and he wasn't shy about dishing out a little vigilante justice to these dirtbags who were trying to confiscate his hard-earned property. When the guys in the trucks started honking their horns, flashing their bright headlights on the house, shouting profanity into their megaphones, and shooting their guns wildly in the air, Don Alejo simply started shooting his guns directly at them, and in a manner significantly more controlled, busting caps in their punk asses and reminding these tough-guy cartel thugs that they really aren't as invincible as they think they are.

It didn't take long for the cartel to return fire on the ranch, but Don Alejo had taken great pains in the hours before to make his home an irrationally ridiculous hardened battle station. In order to avoid drawing too much fire from something on the order of thirty or forty full-auto assault rifles, he would run to a window, take aim, shoot a guy, then run to another window or door when the bad guys started firing in the direction of his most recent shot. This old man was running from station to station like the Assault event in *American Gladiators*, busting one well-aimed shot and then quickly moving out of sight, single-handedly defending his home against these wifebeater-clad bozos. I imagine that it was like the end of *The Outlaw Josey Wales*, only if Clint Eastwood were the age then that he was in *Gran Torino*, and if the Kansas Redlegs carried AK-47s.

Four thugs were killed in Don Alejo's initial rampage, but they quickly regrouped and started moving toward the house, running from cover to cover to avoid his deadly accurate fire. Two overambitious gangsters actually succeeded in reaching the house, only to find that Don Alejo wasn't even a little bit surprised by them—the second they stepped into the doorway he greeted them *Scarface* style, only instead of an M16 with a grenade launcher he was firing a hunting rifle in each hand, which is even more inescapably badass somehow. Don Alejo capped both men, sending them spinning to the ground, alive but unconscious. However, much like the brave yet doomed defense of the Alamo, Don Alejo's last stand also had a tragic end. Completely unable to bust through the force field of lead spewing forth from the general vicinity of the Don of Destruction's raging adamantium nutsac, the horde of bandito douchebags perhaps unsurprisingly opted for a significantly more cowardly tactic than an unrelenting face-to-face steel-cage deathmatch—they ran back to their trucks, got some damn *grenade launchers* (did I already mention that the police have a tough time matching the firepower of these cartel leaders?), and peppered Don Alejo's ranch with a flurry of high-explosive hail until everything within fifty yards was blown into crushed-out cinders. The entire battle lasted little more than five minutes. When a response team of Mexican marines showed up a few hours later, they found Don Alejo's body amid the rubble, still clutching a hunting rifle in each hand. They also found four dead drug dealers, two other thugs lying unconscious in pools of their own blood, and bloody patches outside indicating that there were other wounded gangsters who had left with the posse.

Don Alejo's brave-bordering-on-insane actions defending his home probably won't do much to dry down the acid bath of sulfuric suckass that seems to be encompassing much of rural Mexico these days, but it's a hell of a thing to see a guy like that take a stand against hopeless odds to fight for what he believes in. He was given a hero's burial in Monterrey at the end of November 2010.

40

BISHNU SHRESTHA AND THE FORTY THIEVES

Knife Fight on the Maurya Express
West Bengal, India
September 2, 2010

It is better to die than be a coward.

—GURKHA MOTTO

BISHNU SHRESTHA WASN'T LOOKING FOR A FIGHT ON THE EVE-
NING OF SEPTEMBER 2, 2010. As his express train roared through
the darkness, this Nepalese ex-soldier sat quietly, looking out the window into the calm stillness of the night sky above. The thirty-five-year-
old veteran was finally on his way back home, having just retired from
his position as a naik (corporal) in the Seventh Battalion of the Eighth
Gurkha Infantry—a famously hardcore regiment of epic asswhompers
that had produced catastrophically awesome military heroes dating
back to before World War II, and a unit in which Shrestha's own father had served during Vietnam. One in a long line of warriors, Bishnu
himself had seen plenty of combat in Iraq, Afghanistan, and probably

a half-dozen other locations that may never be declassified, and now, after having spent a good part of his adult life busting faces with the stock of his assault rifle and charging enemy positions armed with a bayonet and his ultrabadass kukri knife, he was looking forward to finally seeing an end to the constant fighting, settling down, and building a family in the quiet mountains of his homeland. On this evening he rode the Maurya Express, a passenger train appropriately sharing its name with historical badass Chandragupta Maurya, enjoying the serenity of the Indian night.

But there would be no rest for the weary. Around midnight, in the jungles of West Bengal, the mighty locomotive ground to a halt unexpectedly, sending passengers lurching forward in their seats. Without warning, while everyone was still trying to figure out what the hell was going on, from seemingly every direction passengers stood up and began to whip out all manner of frighteningly gruesome-looking weaponry—guns, knives, clubs, and old-school giant swords (seriously, who robs a train with a sword?)—shouting for everyone to sit still, get out their valuables, and prepare to get ripped the hell off.

As if that wasn't bad enough, from a side door more armed thugs leapt into action, pouring into the train from the jungle beyond. Dozens of unscrupulous goons began making their way down the aisles, shaking down everyone for their pocket change, stealing wallets, stripping jewelry from the necks of old women, snatching laptops and cell phones, and waving knives in the faces of terrified hostages.

Despite the chaos around him, Naik Bishnu Shrestha just sat there quietly. Not saying anything. Not betraying his emotions. Even when the thugs took his own wallet, he remained silent. Like a true badass, he knew that this wasn't his fight. Just be quiet, give them what they want, and survive. It's just a few hundred bucks. It's not worth dying over.

But then things got out of hand. You see, it just so happened that Shrestha was sitting near a cute eighteen-year-old girl, and when this gang of baby-kicking terrorists came by her seat they decided it would be awesome to be the complete slime of the earth and gang-rape her in front of her own terrified parents just for the hell of it. The terrorist leader cut open her shirt while she cried for help.

That was it. Bishnu Shrestha couldn't just sit by any longer.

Unfortunately for the douchebags of West Bengal, when the thugs had robbed Bishnu they'd made one fatal mistake: they didn't take his kukri. This ultrahardass Gurkha warrior, one in a long line of head-cleaving soldiers tempered by centuries of hand-to-hand combat (and a steady diet of steel tacks and the corpses of their slain enemies), had willingly given up his money without a word, but he knew better than to ever relinquish his weapon. Slowly, effortlessly, he eased the hilt from its hiding place under his seat. Now these crapbaskets were going to see what it felt like to get a taste of their own steel-tipped medicine, and it was going to taste like dental-grade pain and a roll of nasty old pennies.

Corporal Shrestha leapt to his feet, drawing the ultimate symbol of Gurkha badassitude with one fluid motion. He flew across the train car, grabbed the would-be rapist from behind in a sleeper hold, and used him as a human shield while he lunged out and slashed one of the sword-swinging thugs, sending the hapless dude spinning off in a vicious tornado of blood. One of the other jackwagons, unwilling to stab in the direction of his own boss, instead took the manly man's route and tried to cut the girl, slashing his knife wildly at her neck, but the girl only took a minor wound before Shrestha dropped him with a lightning-quick strike. With the terrorists in the immediate vicinity disposed of, he sliced the throat of his human shield and went looking for more thugs to get his blood-rage off on.

Even the firsthand news reports are unfortunately vague about what happened during this epic battle (even the above paragraph is merely my interpretation of the phrase "he took control of the attacker and killed everyone around him"), but what happened next is pretty obvious—one lone balls-out Gurkha innards-wrecker from one of the world's most over-the-top insane military organizations suddenly found himself in the middle of a hostage-filled train crawling with forty well-armed, highly organized terrorists. This was *Die Hard* without the cowboy references. *Delta Force* without Lee Marvin. *Under Siege* without the Dramamine. *Passenger 57* without the always betting on black thing. And, worse yet, it was happening in real life.

Over the next twenty minutes, Corporal Bishnu Shrestha raced through the aisles giving those wannabe punk-ass thugs a first-class ride on the Pain Train to Severed Arteryville, cutting, dodging, and back-alley knife-fighting anyone carrying a weapon larger than a ball-point pen. He took on the entire train by himself—forty men—at once, killing three and wounding eight more with a ferocious series of neck stabs and whirling slashes. Even after he took a nasty sword blow that severed every major artery and vein in his left hand, this guy continued carving up douchebags with his kukri, all the while spraying what I like to imagine to be a pseudocomical amount of blood from his nonkilling hand.

The sight of a real man was too much for those weak-willed thugs, and once they realized that they weren't just beating up schoolchildren and robbing crippled old ladies of their wedding rings and were instead facing a psychotic Gurkha with balls so gigantic they barely fit through the doorway of the train car, the surviving bad guys dropped all their loot and ran for it like pussies. When the train pulled into the next station, police and emergency personnel were there to treat the wounded and rush Shrestha to the hospital, where he spent two months recovering from the injury to his hand. When the police searched the dead and dying thugs, they recovered forty gold necklaces, two hundred cell phones, forty laptops, and nearly ten thousand dollars in stolen cash. Those idiots lucky enough to be left alive were hauled to jail.

Bishnu Shrestha was temporarily unretired from the Gurkhas for the purposes of being promoted and subsequently awarded two medals for bravery and awesomeness. His former unit awarded him with a presumably righteous-looking silver-plated kukri (kind of like how when you beat GoldenEye you unlock the Silver PP7) and a cash bonus of fifty thousand rupees, which I assume is a decent amount of money. The Indian government also awarded him the bounty that was on the heads of this vicious gang, and granted him discounted airfare and train tickets for the rest of his life. I guess after hearing this guy's story they just decided to say, "Screw those backscatter X-ray machines, the best antiterror homeland security measure our country can take is to make sure this guy is on as many flights and trains as possible."

Ultimately, like a true badass, Bishnu Shrestha didn't need any thanks for doing what he needed to do. The family of the girl he saved offered him a reward of sixty-five hundred dollars, but the dude never stopped by to collect it. That wasn't the point. The man himself said it best, responding to reporters by saying, "Fighting the enemy in battle is my duty as a soldier. Taking on the thugs on the train was my duty as a human being."

Another badass Gurkha in recent memory was Sergeant Dipprasad Pun of the Royal Gurkha Rifles. In 2010, while serving as the lone on-duty guard patrolling a small one-room outpost on the edge of the Afghan province of Helmand, Pun was suddenly ambushed by somewhere between fifteen and thirty Taliban warriors armed with RPGs and assault rifles. During his Ultimate Mega Gurkha Freakout Limit Break Mode, the five-foot-seven-inch sergeant fired off four hundred rounds of machine gun ammunition (every bullet he had), chucked seventeen grenades, detonated a remote mine, and then took an enemy soldier down by chucking a twenty-pound machine gun tripod into the dude's face.

⇥⊸ BRINGING A KNIFE TO A GUNFIGHT ⊸⇤

When I fight someone, I want to break his will. I want to take his manhood.
I want to rip out his heart and show it to him.

—Mike Tyson

Saint Moses the Black (c. AD 335)

On a warm desert night in the fourth century, four heavily armed bandit thugs broke into the Coptic monastery in Scetes, Egypt, looking to plunder the money from the offering plate, kick some puppies, and do a bunch of other horrible unsavory things that are only done by total assholes with no conscience. What they found was Saint Moses the Black—a gigantic, hulking Ethiopian badass who had only recently joined the monastery as a way to escape persecution for his life as a toxic bandit leader and who was so jacked you could grill a burger on his abs. The men rushed this ridiculously ripped man of the cloth, but Moses struck down upon them with great vengeance and furious anger, breaking their faces with his fists while badass Halo music played in the background. Knowing it wasn't Christian-like to kill the men, Moses tied them up, carried them to the head monk's office, and asked what the goat cheese they were supposed to do now. The bandits, impressed by Moses's holy strength and his mercy, all ended up joining the monastery themselves. Nowadays Saint Moses the Black is the patron saint of nonviolence, but I like to think of him as the Orthodox Church's equivalent of Samuel L. Jackson from *Pulp Fiction*.

Shaolin Monks vs. Ninja Pirates (1553)

While the Shaolin monks are famous for being totally chill and all one-with-the-universe and everything, these Buddhist martial artists can actually flip out with the best of them. At one particularly bloody battle in 1553, a hundred Shaolin monks were called into action when a raiding party of a hundred Japanese pirates armed with katana and spears landed near the monks' monastery and started trashing everything like total jerks. The Shaolin got psyched up into whatever the Shaolin version of being pissed off is called, ran out there, beat down the ninja pirates, and then spent the next ten days chasing the surviving pirates twenty miles down the coast, killing every last scurvy bastard they could find by either pummeling the poor suckers with roundhouse kicks or smashing their skulls with iron rods.

THE PETTICOAT DUEL (1792)

One of the weirdest duels of all time took place at teatime in a wealthy London neighborhood during the height of the Victorian era. It started when the uncouth dolt Mrs. Elphinstone politely remarked that her hostess, Lady Almeria Braddock, must have been a very beautiful woman in her youth—to which Lady Braddock responded that she was not even thirty years old yet. Elphinstone didn't drop it, guessing Braddock's age at closer to sixty, and things blew so out of proportion that the two women decided to take it outside and have a "ten paces, turn and fire" pistols-at-dawn duel in the middle of Hyde Park. Braddock's shot missed, but Elphinstone's bullet ripped a hole in Lady Braddock's hat, pissing her off even further and prompting Braddock to whip out a hefty cavalry saber and charge her boorish party guest. Elphinstone, who had also procured a sword from somewhere, was happy to oblige. The two exceptionally foppy Victorian women with ridiculous posh British accents started wailing on each other with blades, engaging in a lace-filled battle that presumably resembled the swordfighting in *The Secret of Monkey Island* ("How appropriate, you fight like a cow!"). Braddock eventually wounded Mrs. Elphinstone in the sword arm, she yielded, and both women "quitted the field with honor."

CAPTAIN JONATHAN R. DAVIS (1854)

Captain Davis was strolling through the California mountains with three of his good friends, looking for a decent place to start a gold-panning operation, when all of a sudden a gang of eleven six-gun-toting bandits leapt out of the bushes and opened fire with a hail of bullets. The hardened killers, who had been terrorizing the region for weeks, killed or wounded all of Davis's companions, but the South Carolina native didn't flinch. Davis quick-drew his revolvers, the barrels barely leaving the leather of his awesome-looking Han Solo thigh holsters before he'd already snapped off two unbelievable shots and sent a pair of bandit douchebags straight to hell without passing Go or collecting two hundred dollars. Davis instinctively flipped his internal badass-o-meter into Freak Mode as bullets ripped through his clothes and hat, and all the gang managed to do was mutter, "Oh, crap," under their breaths as Captain Jonathan R. Davis prepared to tear them all a collective new asshole and then bury their corpses inside of it. Davis emptied both revolvers into the bandits, killing seven men with just twelve shots. Reloading was a real bitch back in the days when revolvers and rifles were still cap-and-ball affairs, so with Davis and the remaining four bandits all out of ammunition, there was only one way to settle the score—a badass knife fight. Three of the bandits drew a set of knives of various sizes. Their leader pulled out a four-foot cavalry saber. Davis calmly reholstered his revolvers (probably twirling them on his fingers first), slowly unsheathed a twelve-inch bowie knife from his belt, and killed everyone with it.

Fazal Din (1945)

After charging a Japanese position in Burma and overwhelming a couple of machine gun crews, Indian soldier Fazal Din turned just in time to see a crazed Japanese infantry officer come running at him with a friggin' samurai sword. The officer stabbed Fazal Din through the abdomen, impaling him on the katana's blade, but through sheer force of will, Fazal Din snapped his eyes open, reached out with his bloody hands, grabbed the hilt of the sword, and, with one powerful stroke fueled by adrenaline and anger alone, wrenched the weapon from the hands of its startled owner and pulled it out of his own body. The Indian berserker then lifted the sword above his head and struck his nemesis down with one earth-shattering blow. Horrifically wounded and bleeding profusely from a vicious gut wound, Fazal Din flipped the hell out, hacked his way through a couple other dudes, held the captured sword above his head, and screamed for his soldiers to press the attack. His squad got totally pumped up, charged out, and won the battle. Fazal Din stumbled back to Allied lines, dutifully filed an after-action report with his superior officer, and then promptly collapsed and died.

Samuel Toloza (2009)

Corporal Samuel Toloza was outside Najaf, Iraq, with his sixteen-man unit when suddenly a ton of heavily armed Iraqi rebels showed up and started blasting at them with machine guns, rifles, and rocket-propelled grenades. After a brief but fierce firefight, the El Salvadoran NCO was one of just four men left standing from his unit. His ammunition was running dry, but this didn't stop him from dropping the hammer on those insurgent sucktards—when a team of enemy fighters rushed in, grabbed one of Toloza's friends, and started dragging him off as a prisoner, Toloza went into blood-rage mode, whipped out a three-inch pocketknife, and surprise prison-shanked the crap out of every single one of them. The startled, wounded men, largely unprepared for some Spanish-speaking ninja lunatic to start shivving them in the neck, dropped the prisoner and retreated, leaving the blood-soaked Toloza in sole command of the battlefield.

RUKHSANA KAUSER (2009)

In September 2009, a superevil al-Qaeda terrorist commander named Abu Osama was wandering around the Jammu region of India just looking to have some fun by creating a bunch of murder-carnage, for no reason other than to satisfy his raging death boner, when he heard about a cute girl that lived there and decided to pay her a visit. He thought he'd ingratiate himself to her relatives by beating the holy living bejeezus out of them with a large stick and dragging her off by her hair Neanderthal style. He got together five of his closest terrorist buddies and went over to the humble farmhouse where eighteen-year-old Rukhsana Kauser lived. Abu politely knocked on her door and greeted Rukhsana's parents, a couple of defenseless farmers, by jamming a gun barrel in their faces and then thumping the snot out of them. Rukhsana and her teenage brother were hiding under a bed, where they had a front-row seat to the severe beating of their parents at the hands of Rukhsana's soon-to-be rapist and five of his best assault-rifle-toting friends. Needless to say, this was kind of a problem. So, rebelling against every instinct of self-preservation, she got super-mecha-enraged, grabbed the first thing she could find—which just so happened to be a giant hatchet—climbed out from under the bed, grabbed the notorious terrorist Abu Osama by his head, and slammed the back of his skull up against the wall of her living room with enough force to crack a cue ball. Then, as he was backed up against the wall, she smashed him with the axe just for good measure. As he slowly started to slump down, badly jacked up by this brutally insane ball-crushing sneak attack, Rukhsana reached down, grabbed his AK-47, and forcefully wrenched it out of his hands in one motion. Clutching the captured assault rifle in both hands, she belted Abu in the face with the stock of the rifle, flipped it around, and unleashed a burst of automatic weapons fire that pumped twelve rounds into the criminal mastermind's head and torso at point-blank range, killing him instantly in a thick spray of crimson. Then Rukhsana went off like Princess Vespa ouside the penal colony on the Planet Spaceball, spraying hot lead at anything moving in front of her and blasting the fail out of those jacknut terrorist dickfaces who foolishly thought they could come into her small farming village and treat her family like whatever the Indian version of a piñata might be called. In the few seconds that followed, she wounded two more terrorists and sent the rest running for their lives.

JOSEPH LOZITO (2011)

One ordinary weekday morning in February 2011, Joseph Lozito was taking the New York subway to his job when all of a sudden some maniac on the train car whipped out an eight-inch kitchen knife and started walking toward him muttering the phrase, "You are going to die." It turned out the dude was a bona-fide spree killer in the middle of a twenty-eight-hour stabbing rampage that had already left four people dead and five more wounded across the boroughs of New York City, but Joseph Lozito wasn't impressed. This six-foot-two-inch, 260-pound lifelong MMA fan unflinchingly leapt up from his seat and used his leg to swipe the spree killer's feet out from under him, knocking them both to the deck. In the ensuing struggle Lozito received a tremendously gnarly series of slashes on his hands, face, neck, and chest, but he kept fighting back, telling his attacker, "You've messed with the wrong guy. You'd better hope I die, because I'm gonna kill you." The doctors who stitched Lozito back together again couldn't understand how this guy was even still conscious—let alone how he'd single-handedly beat the hell out of a knife-wielding mass murderer in a fight for his life that resulted in the capture of one of NYC's most wanted men.

ACKNOWLEDGMENTS

Youth and skill will always be overcome by age and treachery.

—My father, by way of Waylon Jennings

This book is dedicated to everyone who has ever put their lives on the line to defend their beliefs—particularly those who go out there every day and risk everything in the service of their country. It's fun to read stories about battles from days past, but we will never forget that it's your sacrifices that give the rest of us the luxury of sitting back and cracking dick jokes about World War II. Thank you.

Writing this book was an incredibly tough process, which I could not have completed without the support and help of my amazing family and friends. I would like to thank all of you for always putting up with me, even when I'm a huge pain in the ass because I've spent all day stressing out about Soviet attack helicopters when I should have been paying my rent or calling my mother.

Huge thanks are due to all the readers who helped me proof the first draft—Clay Thompson, Brian Lum, J. Matt Hoch, and Badass Intern Alyssa Isaacks—as well as to my family, my parents, my brother John (who shepherds the weak through the valley of darkness), and to Simone Radinovic, Matt Kipnis, John Coffey, Andrew John, and Quynh-An Phan for their endless support.

Thank you to Michael Signorelli, my editor at William Morrow, for giving me valuable feedback and edits on those rare occasions in which he wasn't soaring majestically through the Martian atmosphere on an eight-breasted dragon that looks like it was ripped out of a Boris Vallejo painting.

Thank you to my amazing agents, Farley Chase of the Chase Literary Agency and Sean Daily of Hotchkiss, for continuing to believe in me, and for at least pretending that I'm not a total dumbass every time I go to them with some ridiculous idea for a book or a screenplay or something.

To Greg Villepique for copyediting the final draft of this manuscript and reminding me that the *m* is capitalized in WrestleMania.

And last, but never least, I want to thank all of the amazing people out there reading my site, sending me pump-up e-mails, giving me favorable Amazon reviews (nudge nudge), and getting way too excited when they see me at conventions. I know I suck at responding to my e-mails sometimes, but all of you guys are incredible and without your support I could never have done any of this. Thanks for sticking with me.

BIBLIOGRAPHY

I put my heart and my soul into my work,
and have lost my mind in the process.

—VINCENT VAN GOGH

Abbot, Jacob. *Cyrus the Great*. Harper, 1903.

Abiva, Huseyin, and Noura Durkee. *History of Muslim Civilization*. IQRA, 2003.

Adelman, Bob. "Don Alejo Garza Tamez." *The New American*. November 30, 2010.

Adhikari, Manoj, and Santosh Pokharel. "Lone Nepali Gorkha Who Subdued 40 Train Robbers." *The Republica*. January 13, 2011.

Adkin, Mark. *The Waterloo Companion*. Stackpole, 2002.

Aeschylus. *The Persians*. Trans. Alan H. Sommerstein. Loeb Classical Library, 2009.

Agrawal, Lion M. *Freedom Fighters of India*. Gyan, 2008.

Agte, Patrick. *Michael Wittman and the Waffen SS Tiger Commanders of the Liebstandarte in World War II*. Stackpole, 2006.

Al-Makkaki, Ahmed ibn Mohammad. *Mohammadan Dynasties in Spain*. Trans. Pascual de Gayangos. W. H. Allen, 1843.

Alexander, Bevin. *How Great Generals Win*. W. W. Norton, 2002.

———. *How Wars Are Won*. Crown, 2002.

Alexander, George. *The Influence of the Sea on the Political History of Japan.* General Books, 2010.

America at War. Dir. Michael Maclear. History Channel, 2004.

American Valor. Dir. Norman S. Powell. PBS, 2003.

Andrews, Lewis M. *Tempest, Fire and Foe.* Trafford Publishing, 2004.

Anglo-Saxon Chronicle. Trans. Rev. James Ingram. Everyman Press, 1912.

Aristophanes. *Lysistrata.* Trans. Sarah Ruden. Hackett, 2003.

Armstrong, Pete. *Bannockburn 1314.* Osprey, 2002.

———. *Stirling Bridge and Falkirk.* Osprey, 2003.

Arostegui, Martin C. *Twilight Warriors.* Macmillan, 1997.

Asher, Jerrold S., and Eric Hammel. *Duel for the Golan.* Pacifica, 1987.

"Attack on Kenya Orphanage Yields $80k in Donations." Associated Press. February 2, 2012.

"Australian Grandmother Beats Off Attacking Shark." BBC News. February 14, 2010.

Axelrod, Alan. *Profiles in Audacity.* Sterling, 2006.

Balfour, Amy C. *Lonely Planet Arizona.* Lonely Planet, 2011.

Barnes, Ian, and Charles Royster. *The Historical Atlas of the American Revolution.* Psychology Press, 2000.

Barra, Allen. *Inventing Wyatt Earp.* University of Nebraska Press, 2009.

Barrett, Andrew, and Christopher Harrison. *Crime and Punishment in England.* Psychology Press, 1999.

"The Battle of 73 Easting." *Greatest Tank Battles.* Dir. Paul Kilback. History Channel, 2010.

Bauer, S. Wise. *The History of the Medieval World.* W. W. Norton, 2010.

Baxter, Stephen David. *Early Medieval Studies.* Ashgate, 2009.

Beasley, William Gerald. *The Perry Mission to Japan.* Psychology Press, 2002.

Belanger, Jeff, and Rick Powell. *Who's Haunting the White House?* Sterling, 2008.

Bell, Bob Bose. "The Gang Slayer." *True West Magazine.* February 1, 2008.

Bellamy, Chris. *Absolute War.* Random House, 2008.

Benavidez, Roy, and John R. Craig. *Medal of Honor.* Brasseys, 1995.

Benavidez, Roy, and Oscar Griffin. *The Three Wars of Roy Benavidez*. Corona, 1986.

Benjamin of Tudela. *The Itinerary of Benjamin of Tudela*. Trans. Marcus Nathan Adler. P. Feldheim, 1964.

Bennett, Martyn. *Historical Dictionary of the British and Irish Civil Wars*. Scarecrow, 2000.

Bennett, Matthew. *The Hutchinson Dictionary of Ancient & Medieval Warfare*. Taylor & Francis, 1998.

Bernstein, Adam. "Daring Soldier Was Awarded Medal of Honor." *Washington Post*. November 18, 2009.

Bhullar, Pritam. *The Sikh Mutiny*. Siddharth, 1987.

Bhusal, Bhibhu. "India to Honour Pokhara Youth for Chivalry." *The Himalayan Times*. January 11, 2011.

Bishop, Chris. *The Encyclopedia of Weapons of World War II*. Sterling, 2002.

Bizzarro, Salvatore. *Historical Dictionary of Chile*. Scarecrow, 2005.

Blind Harry. *The Wallace*. Canongate, 2010.

Boardman, John. *The Cambridge Ancient History*. Cambridge University Press, 1982.

Boertlein, John. *Presidential Confidential*. Clerisy, 2010.

Botting, Douglas. *The Pirates*. Time-Life Books, 1978.

Bowra, C. M. *Classical Greece*. Time-Life, 1965.

Bradford, Alfred S. *With Arrow, Sword and Spear*. Praeger, 2000.

Braithwaite, Sir Roderick. *Afghantsy*. Profile, 2011.

Breuker, Remco E. *Establishing a Pluralist Society in Medieval Korea*. Brill, 2010.

Brighton, Terry. *Hell's Riders*. Macmillan, 2004.

Brown, Max. *Australian Son: The Story of Ned Kelly*. Network Creative, 2005.

Brzezinski, Richard. *Polish Armies 1569–1696*. Osprey, 1987.

———. *Polish Winged Hussar 1576–1775*. Osprey, 2006.

Brockman, Norbert C. *Encyclopedia of Sacred Places*. ABC-CLIO, 2011.

Brownell, Henry Howard. *The Eastern, or Old World*. American Subscription House, 1856.

Bryant, Anthony J. *Sekigahara 1600*. Osprey, 1995.

Buchholz, Chris. *Mustang Aces of the 357th Fighter Group*. Osprey, 2010.

Bucy, Carole Stanford. *Tennessee Through Time*. Gibbs Smith, 2007.

Bufalo, Andrew Anthony. *Hard Corps*. S&B Publishing, 2004.

Bunson, Matthew. *Encyclopedia of the Roman Empire*. Infobase, 2002.

Bury, John Bagnell. *A History of Greece to the Death of Alexander the Great*. Macmillan, 1900.

Bury, John Bagnell, et al. *The Cambridge Medieval History*. Macmillan, 1913.

Butler, Alban, and Paul Burns. *Butler's Lives of the Saints*. Continuum, 1995.

Callo, Joseph. *John Paul Jones*. Naval Institute Press, 2011.

Camp, Dick. *Operation Phantom Fury*. Zenith, 2009.

Canuti, Felidio F. *The Siege and Fall of Constantinople*. Volz, 1887.

Carr, James Revell. *Seeds of Discontent*. Bloomsbury, 2009.

Cassius Dio. *Roman History*. Trans. E. Cary. Harvard University Press, 1961.

Castillo-Feliu, Guellermo I. *Culture and Customs of Chile*. Greenwood, 2000.

Catholic Encyclopedia. Robert Appleton, 1908.

Catton, Bruce. *Gettysburg*. Doubleday, 1990.

Cawthorne, Nigel. *The Immortals*. MBI Publishing Company, 2009.

——. *Military Commanders*. Enchanted Lion, 2004.

——. *Warrior Elite*. Ulysses, 2011.

Chacon, Richard J., and Ruben G. Mendoza. *The Ethics of Anthropology and Amerindian Research*. Springer, 2011.

Chamberlain, Joshua L. *The Passing of the Armies*. University of Nebraska Press, 1998.

Chambers, Robert. *The Book of Days*. W&R Chambers, 1888.

Chambers, John W. *The Oxford Companion to American Military History*. Oxford University Press, 1999.

Chant, Chris. *Tanks*. Zenith, 2004.

Chapman, Steven. "Meet Omari. Reddit Raised $50k for Him and His Orphanage in Under 14 Hours." *ZDNet*. January 27, 2012.

Chen Shou. *Three Kingdoms*. Trans. Giao Chau. Zhonghua Book Company, 2009.

Chosin. Dir. Brian Iglesias. Post Factory Films, 2010.

City University of Hong Kong. *China*. City University of HK Press, 2007.

The Civil War. Dir. Ken Burns. PBS, 1990.

Clements, Jonathan. *A Brief History of the Samurai*. Running Press, 2010.

Clephan, R. Coltman. *The Medieval Tournament*. Courier Dover, 1995.

Cochran, Hamilton. *Noted American Duels and Hostile Encounters*. Chilton Books, 1963.

Cockburn, John. *The History of Duels*. General, 1888.

Coleman, Charles Winston. *Famous Kentucky Duels*. Henry Clay Press, 1969.

Colenso, Frances Ellen. *History of the Zulu War and Its Origin*. Chapman and Hall, 1880.

Collier, Peter. *Medal of Honor*. Artisan, 2006.

Collingwood, R. G. *Roman Britain and English Settlements*. Biblo & Tannen, 1998.

Cook, Bernard A. *Women and War*. ABC-CLIO, 2006.

Cooke, James G. *United States Air Service in the Great War*. Greenwood, 1996.

Cornell, David. *Bannockburn*. Yale University Press, 2009.

Cowley, Robert, and Geoffrey Parker. *Reader's Companion to Military History*. Houghton Mifflin, 2001.

Craig, William. *Enemy at the Gates*. Penguin, 1973.

Craughwell, Thomas J. *How the Barbarian Invasions Shaped the Modern World*. Rockport, 2008.

Crider, Lawrence W. *In Search of the Light Brigade*. Crider, 2004.

Crile, George. *Charlie Wilson's War*. Atlantic, 2008.

Crompton, Samuel Willard. *The Third Crusade*. Infobase, 2003.

Cross, Robin, and Rosalind Miles. *Warrior Women*. Metro, 2011.

Crow, John Armstrong. *The Epic of Latin America*. University of California Press, 1992.

Crutchfield, James A. *It Happened in Arizona*. Globe Pequot, 2009.

Daftary, Farhad. *The Assassin Legends*. I.B. Tauris, 1995.

Davies, Norman. *Europe: A History*. HarperCollins, 1998.

Davis, Paul K. *100 Decisive Battles*. Oxford University Press, 2001.

De Benneville, James. *Tales of the Wars of the Gempei*. Bibliobazaar, 2001.

de Crespigny, Rafe. *Generals of the South.* Australian National University, 2004.

De Pauw, Linda Grant. *Battle Cries and Lullabies.* University of Oklahoma Press, 2000.

De Quincey, Thomas. *Joan of Arc.* Sibley, 1892.

"Death of the Japanese Navy." *Dogfights.* Dir. Robert Kirk. History Channel, 2006.

Diodorus. *Library of History.* Trans. C. B. Wells. Harvard University Press, 1967.

"Divergent Portraits of War." *The Ottawa Citizen.* May 7, 2005.

Dodge, Theodore Ayrault. *Alexander.* Houghton Mifflin, 1890.

Dorell, Oren, and Gregg Zoroya. "Battle for Fallujah Forged Many Heroes." *USA Today.* November 9, 2006.

Dull, Paul S. A Battle History of the Imperial Japanese Navy, 1941–1945. Naval Institute Press, 2007.

Dunstan, Simon. *The Yom Kippur War.* Osprey, 2007.

Dunstan, Simon, and Peter Dennis. *The Six Day War 1967.* Osprey, 2009.

Durschmied, Erik. *The Hinge Factor.* Arcade, 2000.

Duruy, Victor, et al. *The History of the Middle Ages.* H. Holt, 1891.

Dvorchak, Robert J. *Battle for Korea.* Da Capo, 2003.

Encomium Emmae. Trans. Alistair Campbell. Cambridge University Press, 1998.

Evans, Michael. "Plain Medal Still Honours Rare Mettle, 150 Years On." *The Sunday Times.* June 27, 2006.

Farrokh, Kaveh. *Shadows in the Desert.* Osprey, 2007.

Farwell, Byron. *The Encyclopedia of Nineteenth-Century Land Warfare.* W. W. Norton, 2001.

Feifer, Gregory. *The Great Gamble.* HarperCollins, 2010.

Feldman, Ruth Tenzer. *The Fall of Constantinople.* Twenty-First Century, 2007.

Ferguson, Robert. *The Vikings.* Penguin, 2009.

Fey, Will, and Henri Henschler. *Armor Battles of the Waffen SS, 1943–45.* Stackpole, 2003.

Fielder, Arkady. *303 Squadron*. Trans. Jarek Garlinski. Aquila Polonica, 2010.

Fines, John. *Who's Who in the Middle Ages*. Barnes & Noble Publishing, 1995.

Finkelman, Paul. *Encyclopedia of African American History*. Oxford University Press, 2006.

Ford, Daniel. *Flying Tigers*. HarperCollins, 2007.

Forrest, Sir George. *The Indian Mutiny 1857–1858*. Indian Military Department, 1902.

Forte, Angelo, et al. *Viking Empires*. Cambridge University Press, 2005.

Franks, Norman. *Albatros Aces of World War I*. Osprey, 2000.

Fraser, Antonia. *The Warrior Queens*. Anchor Books, 1988.

Frederic, Louis. *Japan Encyclopedia*. Harvard University Press, 2005.

Fremont-Barnes, Gregory. *Rescue at the Iranian Embassy*. Rosen, 2011.

Fricker, John. *Battle for Pakistan*. I. Allan, 1979.

Froissart, Jean. *Chronicles*. Trans. Geoffrey Brereton. Penguin, 1978.

Fortescue, Sir John William. *A History of the British Army*. Macmillan, 1920.

Frederiksen, John C. *American Military Leaders*. ABC-CLIO, 1999.

Furneaux, Rupert. *Invasion: 1066*. London: Prentice-Hall, 1966.

Gammell, Caroline. "Mr. Asbo the Swan Attacks Unsuspecting Rowers." *The Telegraph*. April 7, 2009.

Garrison, Chad. "I Punched Saddam in the Mouth." *Riverfront Times*. April 13, 2005.

Genovese, Michael A. *Encyclopedia of the American Presidency*. Infobase, 2010.

Gerli, Michael E. *Medieval Iberia*. Taylor and Francis, 2003.

Gershevitch, Ilya, and William Bayne Fisher. *The Cambridge History of Iran*. Cambridge University Press, 1985.

Gibbon, Edward. *The History of the Decline and Fall of the Roman Empire*. Penguin, 2001.

Goldberg, Harold J. *D-Day in the Pacific*. Indiana University Press, 2007.

Graham-Campbell, James. *The Viking World*. Frances Lincoln, 2003.

Grant, James. *British Battles on Land and Sea*. Oxford University Press, 1873.

Grant, R. G. *Battle at Sea*. Penguin, 2011.

———. *Commanders*. Penguin, 2010.

Green, John Richard. *The Conquest of England*. Macmillan, 1883.

Green, Thomas A. *Martial Arts of the World*. ABC-CLIO, 2001.

Green, William. *The Great Book of Fighters*. Zenith, 2001.

Guanzhong, Luo. *Three Kingdoms*. Trans. Moss Roberts. Univ. of California Press, 2004.

Guinn, Jeff. *The Last Gunfight*. Simon & Schuster, 2011.

Guinot, Laura. *Conspiracy in Mendoza*. Trafford, 2009.

Gullace, Nicoletta. *The Blood of Our Sons*. Macmillan, 2002.

Gunton, Michael. *Submarines at War*. Carroll & Graf, 2005.

Gupta, Om. *Encyclopaedia of India, Pakistan, and Bangladesh*. Gyan, 2006.

"Gurkha Gets UK's Second Highest Medal for Bravery." *The Himalayan Times*. March 25, 2011.

"Gurkha Soldier Who Fought 40 Train Robbers to Be Felicitated in the Republic Day of India." *Nepali Times*. January 16, 2011.

"Gurkha Who Repelled Taliban Attack Gets Bravery Medal." *BBC News*. March 24, 2011.

Guttman, Jon. *USAS 1st Pursuit Group*. Osprey, 2008.

Halarnkar, Samar. "Legacies of Kargil." *India Today*. August 30, 1999.

Hallet, Jean-Pierre. *Animal Kitabu*. Random House, 1967.

Hamm, Diane L., and James L. Gilbert. *Military Intelligence*. Minerva Group, 2001.

Hammel, Eric. *Chosin*. Pacifica, 1981.

Hamilton, Bernard. *The Leper King and His Heirs*. Cambridge University Press, 2005.

Hancock, Anson Uriel. *A History of Chile*. C. H. Sergel and Co., 1893.

Harbron, John D. *Trafalgar and the Spanish Navy*. Naval Institute Press, 1988.

Harmon, R. Barry. *5,000 Years of Korean Martial Arts*. Dog Ear, 2008.

Harris, Benjamin. "Fallujah—Looking Back at the Fury." *Marines Magazine*. June 29, 2010.

Hassig, Ross. *Aztec Warfare*. University of Oklahoma Press, 1995.

Hastings, Max. *The Korean War*. Simon & Schuster, 1988.

Hawley, Samuel Jay. *The Imjin War*. University of California, 2005.

Hawthorne, Julian. *Spanish America*. P. F. Collier & Son, 1899.

Hazen, Walter A. *World War I*. Good Year, 2006.

Heather, Peter. *The Fall of the Roman Empire*. Macmillan, 2010.

Helgaeson, Agnar, et al. "mtDNA and the Islands of the North Atlantic." *American Society of Human Genetics* 68(3): 723–37. March 2001.

Helgaeson, Agnar, et al. "Sequences from First Settlers Reveal Rapid Evolution in Icelandic mtDNA Pool." *PLoS Genetics* 5(1). January 2009.

Herodotus. *Histories*. Trans. George Campbell Macaulay. Macmillan, 1904.

Herskowitz, Mickey. "Farewell to Nolan Ryan." *Baseball Digest*, February 1994.

Hillsborough, Romulus. *Shinsengumi*. Tuttle, 2005.

Hitti, Philip K. *Makers of Arab History*. Harper, 1971.

Hogsdon-Marshall, G. S. *The Secret Order of Assassins*. Mouton, 1955.

Hodgson, Natasha R. *Women, Crusading, and the Holy Land in Historical Narrative*. Boydell Press, 2007.

Holman, Katherine. *The Northern Conquest*. Signal Books, 2007.

Holmes, Tony. *Spitfire vs. Bf-109*. Osprey, 2007.

Holt, H. P. *The Mounted Police of Natal*. J. Murray, 1913.

Hornfischer, James D. *Last Stand of the Tin Can Sailors*. Bantam, 2005.

Howard, Michael Eliot. *The Franco-Prussian War*. Psychology Press, 2001.

Howarth, Steven. *The Knights Templar*. Barnes & Noble Publishing, 1991.

Howitt, Mary Botham. *Biographical Sketches of the Queens of Great Britain*. Bohn, 1862.

Hubbard, Jeremy, and Jessica Hopper. "Joseph Lozito Used Martial Arts Tactic He Saw on TV to End Alleged Stabber's Spree." *ABC News*. February 14, 2011.

Hudson, Fallon. "Two-Metre Shark Attacked Woman." *Brisbane Times*. February 15, 2010.

Hudson, James J. *Hostile Skies*. Syracuse University Press, 1997.

Hughes, Matthew. *Allenby and British Strategy in the Middle East*. Taylor & Francis, 1999.

"Iranian Embassy Siege." *Special Forces Heroes*. Dir. Mark Hedgecoe. Dangerous Films, 2008.

Jager, Eric. *The Last Duel*. Broadway Books, 2004.

Jain, Simmi. *Encyclopaedia of Indian Women through the Ages*. Gyan, 2003.

Janin, Hunt. *Medieval Justice*. McFarland, 2009.

Jarymowycz, Roman Johan. *Cavalry from Hoof to Track*. Greenwood, 2008.

John, Eric. *Reassessing Anglo-Saxon England*. Manchester University Press, 1996.

Johnson, Charles. *A General History of the Robberies and Murders of the Most Notorious Pirates*. Lyons, 1998.

Jones, Gwyn. *A History of the Vikings*. Oxford University Press, 1968.

Jones, Michael. *The Cambridge Medieval History*. Cambridge University Press, 2005.

Josephus. *Complete Works*. Trans. William Whiston. Thomas Nelson, 2003.

Joshi, Binoo. "Kashmir Girl Fights Off Militants." *BBC News*. September 29, 2009.

Kagan, Neil. *National Geographic Concise History of the World*. National Geographic, 2005.

Katz, Samuel M. *Against All Odds*. Twenty-First Century, 2004.

Katz, Yossi. *A Voice Called*. Gefen, 2010.

Khazanov, Dmitriy. *La-5/7 vs. Fw-190*. Osprey, 2011.

Kim, Myung Oak, and Sam Jaffe. *The New Korea*. AMACOM, 2010.

Knight, Ian. *Rorke's Drift 1879*. Osprey, 1996.

———. *The Zulu War*. Osprey, 2003.

Kohn, George C. *The New Encyclopedia of American Scandal*. Infobase, 2001.

Konstam, Angus. *Historical Atlas of the Napoleonic Era*. Globe Pequot, 2003.

Korda, Michael. *With Wings Like Eagles*. Harper, 2002.

Kulczyk, David. *California Justice*. Word Dancer Press, 2007.

Kurowski, Franz. *Luftwaffe Aces*. Stackpole, 2004.

Laffin, John, and Mike Chappell. *The Australian Army at War*. Osprey, 1982.

Lake, Stuart Nathaniel. *Wyatt Earp, Frontier Marshal*. Bantam, 1959.

Landale, James. *The Last Duel*. Canongate, 2006.

Lane-Poole, Stanley. *Saladin*. Putnam, 1906.

Lanning, Michael Lee. *The Battle 100*. Sourcebooks, 2005.

Lanning, Michael Lee, and James F. Dunnigan. *The Military 100*. Citadel, 2002.

Larned, Josephus Nelson. *History for Ready Reference*. C. A. Nichols, 1895.

Lewis, Bernard. *The Assassins: A Radical Sect in Islam*. Basic Books, 2003.

Lewis, Charles Lee. *Famous Old-World Sea Fighters*. Ayer, 1929.

Lewis, David Levering. *God's Crucible*. Norton, 2008.

"Lewis Millet: American Valor." http://www.pbs.org/weta/americanvalor/ stories/millett.html. Retrieved April 23, 2011.

Little, Benerson. *How History's Greatest Pirates Pillaged, Plundered and Got Away with It*. Fair Winds, 2010.

Lockard, Craig A. *Societies, Networks, and Transitions*. Cengage Learning, 2010.

Logan, William Stewart. *Hanoi*. UNSW Press, 2000.

MacDonald, John. *Great Battlefields of the World*. MacMillan, 1984.

Madden, Thomas F. *The New Concise History of the Crusades*. Rowman & Littlefield, 2005.

"Man Bites Snake in Epic Struggle." BBC News. April 15, 2009.

Mayled, Jon. *Sikhism*. Heinemann, 2002.

McLoughlin, Denis. *The Encyclopedia of the Old West*. Taylor and Francis, 1977.

"Meet Omari." http://www.reddit.com/r/pics/comments/oye34/meet_omari_ two_days_ago_he_returned_from_the/?limit=500. Retrieved February 2012.

Menendez, Robert. *Growing American Roots*. Penguin, 2009.

Metz, Leon Claire. *The Encyclopedia of Lawmen, Outlaws and Gunfighters*. Infobase, 2003.

Meyers, John. *Doc Holliday*. University of Nebraska Press, 1955.

Miles, Rosalind, and Robin Cross. *Hell Hath No Fury*. Three Rivers, 2008.

"Miracle Resistance Remembered in Chechnya." *Russian Times*. February 22, 2008.

Mishra, Patit Paban. *The History of Thailand*. ABC-CLIO, 2010.

Missal, John, and Mary Lou Missal. *The Seminole Wars*. University Press of Florida, 2004.

"Modest Gurkhas Relive Heroic Deeds Done on Behalf of Britain." *The Independent*. October 4, 2008.

Moore, Christopher Paul. *Fighting for America*. Random House, 2005.

Morelock, J. D. *The Army Times Book of Great Land Battles from the Civil War to the Gulf War*. Berkley, 1994.

Morison, Samuel Eliot. *The Two-Ocean War*. Naval Institute Press, 2007.

Morozov, Boris. *Documents on Jewish Soviet Emigration*. Psychology Press, 1999.

Murasaki, Shikibu. *Tale of the Heike*. Trans. Helen Craig McCullough. Stanford University Press, 1994.

Mortimer, Ian. *The Greatest Traitor*. Macmillan, 2006.

Murphy, Edward F. *Vietnam Medal of Honor Heroes*. Random House, 2005.

Nelson, Dean. "Farmer's Daughter Disarms Terrorist and Shoots Him Dead with AK-47." *The Telegraph*. September 29, 2009.

Newton, Paula. *Columbia*. Viva Publishing Network, 2009.

Nicolle, David. *The Third Crusade 1191*. Osprey, 2005

Nicolle, David, John F. Haldon, and Steven R. Turnbull. *The Fall of Constantinople*. Osprey, 2007.

Nyassy, Daniel. "Man Bites Snake in Hour-Long Battle to Survive." *Sunday Nation*. April 14, 2009.

O'Leary, De Lacy. *The Saints of Egypt*. Kessinger, 2005.

O'Malley, Vincent J. *Saints of Africa*. Our Sunday Visitor, 2001.

O'Neal, Bill. *Encyclopedia of Western Gunfighters*. University of Oklahoma Press, 1991.

O'Shea, Stephen. *Sea of Faith*. Walker, 2007.

"Operational Unit Diagrams." http://www.army.mil/info/organization/unitsandcommands/oud/. Retrieved March 22, 2012.

Osborne, Eric W. *Cruisers and Battle Cruisers*. ABC-CLIO, 2004.

Otis, Ginger Adams. "High Noon at Not-OK Corral." *New York Post*. December 5, 2010.

Padden, Robert Charles. "Cultural Change and Military Resistance in Araucanian Chile, 1550–1730." *Southwestern Journal of Anthropology* 13(1): 103–121, Spring 1957.

Paddock, Richard C. "Russians Confirm Troop Deaths." *Chicago Sun-Times*. March 12, 2000.

Pagden, Anthony. *Worlds at War*. Random House, 2008.

Page, Raymond Ian. *Chronicles of the Vikings*. University of Toronto Press, 1995.

Paige, Mitchell. *A Marine Named Mitch*. Vantage, 1975.

Paton, George, et al. *Historical Records from the 24th Regiment*. Simpkin, Marshall, Hamilton, Kent, 1892.

Patterson, Richard M. *Historical Atlas of the Outlaw West*. Big Earth, 1984.

Pausinas. *Description of Greece*. Trans. W. H. S. Jones. Loeb Classical Library, 1918.

Pendle, George. *The Remarkable Millard Fillmore*. Random House, 2007.

Peterson, Barbara Bennett. *Notable Women of China*. Sharpe, 2000.

Philip, George. *Middle England from the Accession of Henry II*. Boston School Supply, 1884.

Pigott, Peter. *Flying Canucks*. Dundurn, 1996.

Perrett, Bryan. *At All Costs!* Arms and Armour, 1993.

Pliny the Elder. *Natural History*. Trans. H. Rackham. Loeb Classical Library, 1952.

Plutarch. *Life of Themistocles*. Trans. Bernadotte Perrin. Loeb Classical Library, 1914.

———. *Lives*. Trans. W. Heincman. Loeb Classical Library, 1988.

Pohl, John D. *Aztec Warrior, AD 1325–1521*. Osprey, 2001.

Polmar, Norman, and Dana Bell. *One Hundred Years of World Military Aircraft*. Naval Institute Press, 2004.

Polo, Marco. *The Travels of Marco Polo*. Cosimo, 2007.

Potholm, Christian P. *Winning at War*. Rowman & Littlefield, 2009.

Poulos, Terrence. *Extreme War*. Citadel, 2007.

Preble, George Henry. *Origin and History of the American Flag*. N. L. Brown, 1917.

Preston, R. M. P. *The Desert Mounted Corps*. Kessinger, 2007.

Procopius. *History of the Wars*. Trans. H. B. Dewing. Loeb Classical Library, 1914.

Price, Alfred. *Battle of Britain Day*. Greenhill, 1990.

Proffatt, John. *A Treatise on Trial by Jury*. S. Whitney & Co., 1876.

Putney, Martha S. *Blacks in the United States Army*. McFarland, 2003.

Rabinovich, Abraham. "Shattered Heights." *The Jerusalem Post*, September 25, 1998.

Rabinovitch, Abraham. *The Yom Kippur War*. Random House, 2005.

Rainwater, Bert. *American Wars*. Xlibris, 2010.

Raugh, Harold E. *The Victorians at War, 1815–1914*. ABC-CLIO, 2004.

Rayner, Michael. *Battlefields*. Struik, 2006.

"Reddit Donates $80,000 to Orphanage After Man Trying to Save Kids Attacked with Machete." http://www.huffingtonpost.com/2012/01/27/reddit-donates-kenya-orphanage_n_1237016.html, February 6, 2012.

Reed, Sir Edward James. *Japan*. J. Murray, 1880.

Reef, Catherine. *African Americans in the Military*. Infobase, 2010.

Reese, Peter. *Wallace*. Canongate, 1996.

Regan, Geoffrey. *The Book of Military Blunders*. ABC-CLIO, 1991.

Reid, Struan. *Inventions and Trade*. James Lorimer & Co., 1994.

Rendall, Ivan. *Rolling Thunder*. Simon & Schuster, 1999.

Reston, James. *Warriors of God*. Anchor Books, 2001.

Riley-Smith, Jonathan. *The Crusades*. Continuum, 2005.

Roberts, Andrew. *The Storm of War*. HarperCollins, 2011.

Roberts, Craig, and Charles W. Sasser. *Crosshairs on the Kill Zone*. Simon & Schuster, 2004.

Roberts, Priscilla Mary. *Encyclopedia of World War I*. ABC-CLIO, 2005

Robinson, Francis. *The Cambridge Illustrated History of the Islamic World*. Cambridge University Press, 1996.

Roscoe, Theodore. *United States Destroyer Operations in World War II*. Naval Institute Press, 1953.

Roosevelt, Theodore. "The Battle of New Orleans." In *A New Nation*. Ed. Charles Lester Barstow. Century Co., 1912.

Rothrock, James. *Live by the Sword*. WestBow, 2011.

Rottman, Gordon L. *Soviet Field Fortifications 1941–45*. Osprey, 2007.

Rudel, Hans-Ulrich. *Stuka Pilot*. Ballantine, 1958.

Runciman, Steven. *The Fall of Constantinople*. Cambridge University Press, 1990.

Ruiz, Ana. *Vibrant Andalusia*. Algora, 2007.

Russian General Staff. *The Soviet-Afghan War*. University of Kansas Press, 2002.

"Russians Admit Rout in Chechnya Killed 84." *Los Angeles Times*. March 11, 2000.

Ryan, Cornelius. *A Bridge Too Far*. Simon & Schuster, 1995.

Sabine, Lorenzo. *Notes on Duels and Dueling*. Crosby, Nichols & Co., 1859.

The Saga of Ragnar Lodbrok. Trans. Ben Waggoner. The Troth, 2009.

Salisbury, Joyce E. *Women in the Ancient World*. ABC-CLIO, 2001.

Sakaida, Henry. *Heroines of the Soviet Union*. Osprey, 2003.

———. *Imperial Japanese Navy Aces, 1937–45*. Osprey, 1998.

Sandler, Stanley. *Ground Warfare*. ABC-CLIO, 2002.

Sankey, Charles. *The Spartan and Theban Supremacies*. Longmans, Green, and Co., 1888.

Saxo Grammaticus. *The History of the Danes*. DS Brewer, 1999.

Scarre, Chris. *The Penguin Historical Atlas of Ancient Rome*. Penguin, 1995.

Scott, Ronald McNair. *Robert the Bruce*. Basic Books, 1996.

Schadle, Robert. *Historical Dictionary of the British Empire*. Greenwood, 1996.

Scholey, Pete, and Frederick Forsyth. *Who Dares Wins*. Osprey, 2008.

Scriptores Historiae Augustae. Trans. David Magie. Loeb Classical Library, 1932.

Seal, Graham. *Encyclopedia of Folk Heroes*. ABC-CLIO, 2001.

———. *The Outlaw Legend*. Cambridge University Press, 1996.

Sears, Stephen W. *Gettysburg*. Houghton Mifflin, 2004.

Sekunda, Nicholas. *Marathon 490 BC*. Osprey, 2002.

Seth, Michael J. *A Concise History of Korea*. Rowman & Littlefield, 2006.

Seward, Desmond. *The Hundred Years War*. Penguin, 1978.

Shahar, Meir. *The Shaolin Monastery*. University of Hawaii, 2008.

Shannon, Mike. *Tales from the Dugout*. McGraw-Hill, 1998.

Sharma, Gautam. *Valour and Sacrifice*. Allied, 1990.

Shaw, Stanford J. *History of the Ottoman Empire and Modern Turkey.* Cambridge University Press, 1977.

Shinnie, Margaret. *Ancient African Kingdoms.* Mentor, 1965.

Shores, Christopher. *British and Empire Aces of World War I.* Osprey, 2001.

Sima Qian. *Records of the Grand Historian.* Trans. Burton Watson. Columbia University Press, 1993.

Sinton, Starr, and Robert Hargis. *World War II Medal of Honor Recipients.* Osprey, 2003.

Sismondi, Jean-Charles-Leonard. *Historical View of the Literature of the South of Europe.* H. G. Bohn, 1853.

Smith, Bonnie G. *The Oxford Encyclopedia of Women in World History.* Oxford University Press, 2008.

Smith, Gene. *Mounted Warriors.* John Wiley & Sons, 2009.

Smith, Melvin Charles. *Awarded for Valour.* Macmillan, 2008.

Snow, Edward Rowe, and Jeremy D'Entremont. *Women of the Sea.* Applewood, 2008.

Spielvogel, Jackson J. *Western Civilization Since 1500.* Cengage, 2008.

St. John, Philip A. *Battle for Leyte Gulf.* Turner Publishing Company, 1996.

Staff, Wellesley K. *Year of Four Emperors.* Routledge, 2003.

Stanhope, Philip Henry. *The Life of Belisarius.* J. Murray, 1829.

Stefansson, Jon. *Denmark and Sweden.* G. P. Putnam, 1917.

Stenman, Kari. *Finnish Aces of World War 2.* Osprey, 1998.

Steward, William. *Admirals of the World.* McFarland, 2009.

Stoneman, Richard. *Palmyra and Its Empire.* University of Michigan Press, 1995.

Sturluson, Snorri. *Egil's Saga.* Trans. Bernard Scudder. Penguin, 2005.

Sun Zi. *The Art of War.* Columbia University Press, 2009.

Sutcliffe, Thomas. *Sixteen Years in Chile and Peru.* Fisher, Son, and Co., 1841.

Tacitus. *Histories.* Kessinger, 2004.

Tanner, Stephen. *Afghanistan.* Da Capo, 2002.

They Call Me Killer Chick." http://www.nasm.si.edu/events/eventDetail .cfm?eventID=133. Retrieved March 27, 2012.

Thimm, Carl Albert. *A Complete Bibliography of Fencing and Duelling.* John Lane, 1896.

Thomas, Lowell. *Raiders of the Deep.* Naval Institute Press, 2004.

Thomas, Paul. *Outlaws.* Black Rabbit Books, 2002.

Thompson, Ben. *Badass.* HarperCollins, 2009.

Thompson, Frank. *The Alamo.* Hyperion, 2004.

Thucydides. *History of the Peloponnesian War.* Trans. Richard Crawley. Longmans, 1875.

Toland, John. *In Mortal Combat.* HarperCollins, 1993.

Tucker, Spencer. *Battles that Changed History.* ABC-CLIO, 2010.

———. *A Global Chronology of Conflict.* ABC-CLIO, 2009.

———. *Encyclopedia of World War I.* ABC-CLIO, 2005.

Tufail, M. Kaiser. "Alam's Speed Shooting Classic." *Defense Journal.* September, 2001.

Turnbull, Stephen R. *Fighting Ships of the Far East.* Osprey, 2002.

———. *Katana.* Osprey, 2010.

———. *Samurai—The World of the Warrior.* Osprey, 2011.

———. *The Samurai.* Routledge, 1996.

———. *The Samurai Invasion of 1592–98.* Osprey, 2008.

———. *The Samurai Swordsman.* Tuttle, 2008.

———. *Warriors of Medieval Japan.* Osprey, 2007.

Tyagi, Vidya Prakash. *Martial Races of Undivided India.* Gyan, 2009.

Tyerman, Christopher. *God's War.* Harvard University Press, 2006.

Tyson, Ann Scott. "Soldier Wins Silver Star for Her Role in Defeating Ambush." *The Washington Post.* June 17, 2005.

Urquhart, R. E. *Arnhem.* Pen and Sword, 2008.

"Victoria Cross." http://www.mod.uk/DefenceInternet/DefenceFor/Veterans/Medals/VictoriaCross.htm. Retrieved March 15, 2012.

Villalobos, Sergio R. *A Short History of Chile.* Editorial Univeritaria, 1996.

Walsh, William Shepherd. *Heroes and Heroines of Fiction.* J. B. Lippincott, 1914.

Walton, William. *Paris from the Earliest Period to the Present Day.* G. Barrie & Son, 1899.

Wang, Ke-wen. *Modern China*. Taylor & Francis, 1998.

Warry, John. *Alexander, 324–323 BC*. Osprey, 1991.

———. *Warfare in the Classical World*. Salamander, 1980.

Watson, Robert Grant. *Spanish and Portuguese South America During the Colonial Period*. Trubner & Co., 1884.

Wawro, Geoffrey. *The Franco-Prussian War*. Cambridge University Press, 2005.

Weal, John. *Jagdgeschwader 54 'Grünherz.'* Osprey, 2001.

Weichselbaum, Simone. "Joseph Lozito Fought for His Life in Subway Face-Off with Knife-Wielding Madman Maksim Gelman." New York *Daily News*. February 13, 2011.

Weir, William. *50 Military Leaders Who Changed the World*. New Page, 2007.

———. *History's Greatest Lies*. Fair Winds, 2009.

Welsh, Charles. *Famous Battles of the Nineteenth Century*. A. Wessels, 1907.

West, Willis Mason. *The Ancient World from the Earliest Times to 800 AD*. Allyn and Bacon, 1904.

Whitaker, Julie. *The Horse*. Macmillan, 2007.

White, Charles. *History of Australian Bushranging*. Angus and Robertson, 1903.

Wilkinson, Paul. *Terrorism Versus Democracy*. Taylor & Francis, 2006.

Willbanks, James H. *America's Heroes*. ABC-CLIO, 2011.

Wills, John Everett. *Mountain of Fame*. Princeton University Press, 1996.

Wilson, Joe. *The 761st "Black Panther" Tank Battalion in World War II*. McFarland, 1999.

Wilson, Wayne. "Museum Exhibit Honors WWII Hero." *The Sacramento Bee*. February 17, 2000.

Wilson, William Scott, and Gregory Lee. *Ideals of the Samurai*. Black Belt Communications, 1982.

Wolfram, Herwig. *The Roman Empire and Its Germanic Peoples*. University of California Press, 1997.

Woodward, David. *Hell in the Holy Land*. University of Kentucky Press, 2006.

Wyatt, David K. *Thailand*. Yale University Press, 2003.

"Wyatt Earp." *The American Experience*. Dir. Rob Rapley. PBS, 2010.

Wynbrandt, James, and Fawaz A. Geges. *A Brief History of Saudi Arabia*. Infobase, 2010.

Xenophon. *A History of My Times*. Trans. Rex Warner. Penguin, 1979.

Xenophon. *Cyropaedia*. Trans. Walter Miller. Loeb Classical Library, 1914.

Yamada, Nakaba. *Ghenko: The Mongol Invasion of Japan*. E. P. Dutton, 1916.

Yamamura, Kozo. *The Cambridge History of Japan*. Cambridge University Press, 1998.

Yate, Arthur Campbell. *Lieutenant-Colonel John Haughton, Commandant of the 36th Sikhs*. J. Murray, 1900.

Yenne, Bill. *Alexander the Great*. Macmillan, 2010.

Yi Sun-sin. *Nanjung Ilgi*. Trans. Ha Tae-hung. Yonsei University Press, 1980.

York, Alvin C. *The Diary of Alvin York*. Alvin C. York Institute, 2006.

Young, Edward M. *Meiktila 1945*. Osprey, 2004

Zabecki, David T. *World War II in Europe*. Taylor and Francis, 1999.

ILLUSTRATION CREDITS

Steven Belledin (stevenbelledin.com): Second Punic War, Teutoburg Forest, Third Crusade, Kono Michiari, Hundred Years' War, Fall of Constantinople, Araucanian War, James Macrae, Roy Benavidez, Bishnu Shrestha

Miguel Coimbra (miguelcoimbra.com): Sacred Band, Richard the Lionheart, Alba Gu Brath, Imjin War, Aussie Light Horse

Thomas Denmark (thomasdenmarkportfolio.blogspot.com): Boudicca, Cao Cao at Red Cliff, Last Caliph, Great Heathen Army, Edward A. Carter, Don Alejo

Ben Dewey (deweydraws.blogspot.com): Cyrus War Chariots, Death Ride Battle, A-10 Warthogs

Helene Adeline Guerber (1859–1929): Vikings in boat

Matt Haley (matthaley.com): Wallace Leaping, Warrior Women, Saint Moses the Black

Rhonda Libbey (rhondalibbey.com): Ad Decimum, Bridge Too Far, Chosin Reservoir

John Opie (1761–1807): Boudicca giving a speech

Brian Snoddy (snellsoftware.com/briansnoddyart): Salamis, Trial by Combat, Rani of Jhansi, Gettysburg, Von Bredow's Death Ride, Samurai Showdown, Rorke's Drift, OK Corral, Twenty-one Sikhs, Battle of Britain, Pavlov's House, Tin Can Sailors, Zvika Force, Lion of Panjshir, Who Dares Wins, Desert Storm

Manny Vega (badassconcarne.com): Hot Air Balloon Duel

Thom Zahler (thomz.com): Attack at Red Cliff, Chamberlain at Gettysburg

About the Author

Ben Thompson is the writer and creator of badassoftheweek.com and author of the books *Badass, Badass: Birth of a Legend,* and *Badass: Ultimate Deathmatch*. He has written articles for *Cracked, Fangoria, Penthouse, Soldier of Fortune,* and The American Mustache Institute, was once selected "Seattle's Sexiest Dungeon Master" by a local newspaper, and can occasionally beat the *Star Wars Trilogy* arcade game with one quarter.

BOOKS BY BEN THOMPSON

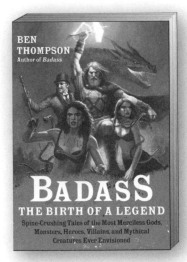
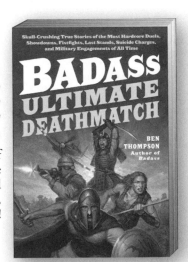